"Read Geralyn Dawson and fall in love!"

—*New York Times* **Bestselling Author**
Christina Dodd

Praise for the novels of Geralyn Dawson

Give Him the Slip

"Dynamic characters, folksy writing leavened with tension and suspense, and a steady dose of steamy romantic interludes . . . create a truly enjoyable romance." —*Booklist*

"Dawson pens a complex, intricately plotted novel, and creates a community full of offbeat characters and circumstances." —*Romantic Times*

The Bad Luck Wedding Dress

"The feel-good book of the month. The wonderfully funny, poignant romance has just the right balance of humor, sensuality, and engaging characters to make it a treasure. Ms. Dawson has written a book that gives you that warm glow." —*Romantic Times*

continued . . .

The Bad Luck Wedding Cake

"Warm and delicious enough to satisfy the sweet tooth of any reader. Geralyn Dawson leaves me hungry for more." —Teresa Medeiros, author of *After Midnight*

My Long Tall Texas Heartthrob

"Take a wonderful romance, add some intriguing mystery and a tad of dangerous suspense, sprinkle it liberally with humor, and you have *My Long Tall Texas Heartthrob*." —*Romantic Times*

"A terrific fairy-tale romance." —The Best Reviews

"With her trademark emotional storytelling and many touches of humor, Ms. Dawson has penned another winner." —A Romance Review

Also by Geralyn Dawson
Available from Signet Eclipse

Give Him the Slip

GERALYN DAWSON

NEVER SAY NEVER

A SIGNET ECLIPSE BOOK

SIGNET ECLIPSE
Published by New American Library, a division of
Penguin Group (USA) Inc., 375 Hudson Street,
New York, New York 10014, USA
Penguin Group (Canada), 90 Eglinton Avenue East, Suite 700, Toronto,
Ontario M4P 2Y3, Canada (a division of Pearson Penguin Canada Inc.)
Penguin Books Ltd., 80 Strand, London WC2R 0RL, England
Penguin Ireland, 25 St. Stephen's Green, Dublin 2,
Ireland (a division of Penguin Books Ltd.)
Penguin Group (Australia), 250 Camberwell Road, Camberwell, Victoria 3124,
Australia (a division of Pearson Australia Group Pty. Ltd.)
Penguin Books India Pvt. Ltd., 11 Community Centre, Panchsheel Park,
New Delhi - 110 017, India
Penguin Group (NZ), 67 Apollo Drive, Rosedale, North Shore 0745,
Auckland, New Zealand (a division of Pearson New Zealand Ltd.)
Penguin Books (South Africa) (Pty.) Ltd., 24 Sturdee Avenue,
Rosebank, Johannesburg 2196, South Africa

Penguin Books Ltd., Registered Offices:
80 Strand, London WC2R 0RL, England

First published by Signet Eclipse, an imprint of New American Library,
a division of Penguin Group (USA) Inc.

First Printing, October 2007
10 9 8 7 6 5 4 3 2 1

For Christina and Mary—
Friends like you make this writing gig a joy.

Chapter One

If they caught her, she'd die.

Torie Bradshaw's pulse pounded with fear as she crashed through the island's dense tropical foliage. In the dim, dappled sunlight, she pretended she didn't see the snake coiled around a low-hanging branch on her right or the huge ball of termites hanging from a high branch on her left. Razor-sharp palm fronds sliced at her exposed skin, and thorns pierced the negligible protection of beach shoes on her feet. *If I'd known fleeing for my life was on the afternoon's agenda, I'd have worn something more than a bikini and flip-flops.*

Torie fought to keep panic at bay. So she was in a spot of trouble. She'd been in trouble before, hadn't she? What about the time she got arrested by the French gendarmes for taking photographs in the Louvre? Or that time when the Federales nabbed her because of a shot that included a government official frolicking on the Mexican Riviera with a woman who wasn't his wife? It hadn't been pleasant, but she'd found her way out of those scrapes, hadn't she? She could make her way out of this one.

Maybe. Possibly.

If they caught her, they'd kill her.

Oh, God.

Ironically, for once the trouble was not of her doing. Her work had nothing to do with her being on the wrong beach at the wrong time. She'd come to this godforsaken island off the coast of South America as a favor to her sister. Helen had wanted her to see firsthand that Collin Marlow wasn't the snake Torie suspected him of being.

Torie had seen, all right. She'd seen the bastard in action and had taken pictures to prove it.

If only she'd been satisfied with the kissing shots. If only she hadn't decided her sister might need stronger evidence to break off her engagement. Then Torie wouldn't have put herself in plain view on the beach, angling for what was basically a porn shot with her zoom lens, when the other boat approached. She wouldn't have the photos of a man shooting Collin Marlow and dumping him over the side of his yacht. If she'd settled for the kissing shots, she'd be back at the compound instead of running through the jungle for her life, the digital camera's memory stick tucked snugly between her swimsuit top and her breast.

From Torie's left came the haunting cry of a howler monkey. At least, she hoped that was what it was, and not the cry of some other poor sap who'd gone out for a swim and stumbled across a murder.

Torie swallowed a fearful whimper and forged ahead, breathing hard in the heavy, humid air. Every few minutes, she paused a moment to catch her breath and listen beyond the cacophony of birdsong for the sounds of human pursuit. On her third such rest break, she heard it. Sure enough, something or someone—multiple someones—thrashed through the forest behind her.

She shuddered in fear, praying they weren't as close behind as they sounded. Weird things happened to sound in the rain forest, right? The canopy above messed with acoustics. The killers could be a long way away instead of right on her tail.

Oh, God. I don't want to die.

She still had dozens of items to accomplish on her To Do list. She hadn't gone white-water rafting yet. She hadn't seen the Great Wall of China. She hadn't had sex with a man she loved in broad daylight on a secluded tropical beach.

Torie startled when a bird let out a shrill shriek right above her. Her heart no sooner calmed from that bit of excitement than the tiny hairs on the back of her neck rose.

She wasn't alone.

She lifted a foot to take off running just as a hand shot out of the shadows and clapped hard over her mouth, muffling her scream. Simultaneously, an arm gripped her waist and yanked her back against a hard body. Startled, scared to death, Torie froze stiff as a rough voice whispered in her ear, "Quiet. I'm here to help. You need to follow me."

Not believing him, she struggled, trying desperately to get away. His grip on her tightened. She felt the warm heat of a gun barrel against her bare stomach.

"Stop it. Your father sent me."

Dad? Hope rose within her, and she trembled as her thoughts came in a flurry. Was the general here on the island? Had the cavalry arrived? Was the island surrounded by a small army of soldiers, sailors, and marines waiting for the signal to attack? Would they sweep onto shore and arrest the bad guys and free the damsel in distress?

Except nobody would consider her a damsel. Most people—her father included—lumped her in with the wolves of the world, predators who preyed on the innocents. They didn't understand that eighty percent of the time, the innocents weren't innocent at all. But then, they'd come to rescue Helen, hadn't they? Not her. She wasn't supposed to be here.

Maybe this wasn't a rescue at all. Maybe he'd lead her back toward the house, where he'd turn her over to the killers for interrogation, torture, and execution. Maybe by going with him, she'd be acting as naive as her sister.

The gun in his hand was no toy. This man was a *real* predator. By throwing in her lot with him, she might be condemning herself to the very fate she tried to escape.

Yet, what choice did she have? She *knew* the other guys were bad guys. They'd shot at her, chased her. They'd kill her if they found her. Mystery Man, here, might just be the answer to her prayers.

Behind her, the sounds of pursuit grew closer. The stranger's arm tightened around her waist as Torie nodded her agreement. The hand over her mouth moved away, but he tapped her lips with his finger twice, signaling the continued need for silence.

She nodded and swallowed her need to grill him for information. Despite the surge of patriotic gratitude she felt at the idea that the army had come to her rescue, now was not the time to break out into "The Star-Spangled Banner."

The arm around her waist fell away. She turned and got her first good look at him. Holy Moses. He wasn't dressed in fatigues, but in the dark slacks and white shirts the scientists on the island tended to wear to work. And dress shoes! All he was missing was a lab coat. He was no more suited for jungle running than she.

Nor did he have the rough-and-ready drill-sergeant look she expected in one of her father's minions. He looked like . . . hmm . . . James Bond. The man was a gorgeous combination of Sean Connery and Pierce Brosnan salted with a hint of Daniel Craig's earthiness.

Could he be army intelligence? A soldier spy? That worked for her. As long as he was a good guy, she didn't care what uniform he wore.

He clasped her hand in his and stepped forward at

an angle to the direction she'd been traveling in. He moved like a jungle cat, Torie thought. Silent and graceful. Deadly. She really really really really hoped he was truly on her side.

Plants scratched and sliced at Torie's skin, but she hardly noticed the discomfort. It took all her concentration to keep up with him while making only minimal noise. He must have considered her efforts inadequate, because he stopped abruptly, shoved the gun into the holster at his hip, scooped her up, and tossed her over his shoulder in a fireman's carry. With his hand on her nearly bare butt, holding her.

Well. This was . . . interesting. Her instinct was to struggle, but she forced herself to remain still.

His big hand felt like a branding iron on her cheek.

With him carrying her, they moved much faster than they had when he'd dragged her along behind him. For the first time in a long time, Torie was happy that she didn't have the tall, statuesque build she'd always coveted in other women. Petite was a positive thing today.

She startled at the sound of a torrent of angry Spanish coming from off to their left a short distance away, and she burrowed her head against her rescuer's back. He smelled of salt and sea and healthy sweat. She figured she must reek of fear.

With her head down, her eyes closed, and her heart pounding, flung over the broad shoulders of a stranger, Torie tried not to feel like a wuss. Ordinarily, she wasn't a coward. A coward wouldn't dangle from a helicopter to get the primo shot at a celebrity wedding. A coward wouldn't sneak a miniature camera into a courtroom to capture the moment a Hollywood star learned his sentence after his conviction for a drunk-driving homicide. A coward certainly wouldn't have crept into the locker room at the Super Bowl to get the money shot of the quarterback lip-locked with the team owner's wife.

Yet, here in the inky darkness of a rain-forest jungle on a tropical island, as she bounced on the shoulder of a stranger, armed with nothing more than her own besieged wits, the only thing keeping Torie from peeing her pants was the fact that her legs were draped over a government agent. Death was preferable to the humiliation of peeing on James Bond.

"We're here," he murmured. He eased her effortlessly forward, but rather than setting her on the ground, he stopped when they were chest to chest. Instinctively, her arms encircled his neck and her legs wrapped around his torso. "Get ready. It's cold."

"What's cold?"

"The cenote."

The cenote? He'd brought her to one of the caves that dotted the island and gave access to the underground river?

"We're going in."

"What!" she said with a yelp.

Rather than respond, he stepped forward. Torie loosened her death grip around his neck long enough to yank the memory stick from her bikini top and toss it onto dry ground even as she sank into the icy water.

The cold sucked her breath from her lungs and she inadvertently squealed until her rescuer shut her up.

By kissing her.

Matt Callahan didn't want to be on a South American island. He wanted . . . needed . . . to be in the Balkans, tracking down the latest rumor about his personal Enemy Number One, Ivars Ćurković, the soulless asshole of a warlord who'd tortured and murdered Matt's little brother, John. Matt's main goal in life was to find Ćurković and kill him, and he resented every minute away from his main pursuit. But he owed a debt, so here he was freezing his balls off in an underground river half a world away from where he needed to be.

At least the job had its perks. Matt had all but

swallowed his tongue yesterday when he arrived on Soledad Island and got his first glimpse of Helen Bradshaw, Ph.D.

The sexy scientist was just a little bitty thing, but man, what a package. Full breasts, tiny waist, and legs that stretched surprisingly long for someone who barely topped five feet. He'd always been a sucker for blondes, and he wanted badly to see what her hair looked like out of its tidy long braid. Her face . . . well . . . Helen was an apt name. Helen of Troy couldn't have been more beautiful than Helen of Applied Genetics Research Inc.

And he'd formed that opinion before seeing her in her bikini. That incredible sight would be burned into his memory forever—unless he did something totally stupid like lose himself in the heat of her kiss and forget they had gunmen on their asses. But dammit, what red-blooded man wouldn't take advantage of the opportunity to take advantage of such a fine example of womanhood?

So Matt indulged a second or two longer than necessary in the kiss. She tasted as sweet as she looked.

He wondered what had happened to make the shit hit the fan this morning. After searching the lab overnight, he'd caught a few hours' sleep in the jungle. His plan had been to publicly arrive on the island midmorning and approach Dr. Bradshaw with her father's concerns about her fiancé, leaving himself plenty of time to snatch her before Marlow's scheduled afternoon arrival if she chose not to cooperate. Then gunshots woke him and his plans had changed.

Reluctantly, Matt attended to business by kicking hard with his legs and propelling them to the surface, where he ended the kiss and allowed her a breath. She gulped in air, then muttered, "I don't think my father sent you to do that."

Matt murmured in her ear, "Quiet now. Can you swim?"

"Yes, but—"

"Shush. Listen to me. I've a place for us to hide until dark. It's a short swim, but—" Now it was Matt's turn to break off midsentence as his senses warned him of approaching danger. Two, maybe three men approached from their right. He squeezed her waist in warning, then felt her shudder and nod. "Breathe," he said. Then he pulled her beneath the water.

Matt always prepared at least one bolt-hole when he went on the job. When he'd stumbled across the cenote yesterday, and having utilized a similar spot in the Yucatán years ago, he'd recognized the advantages it had to offer. Dr. Delicious's pursuers would need incredible luck to find her here. He'd hide in the cave with her until night fell. Then he'd see about getting them both safely off the island.

He led her into a narrow tunnel that was black as night. He kept hold of her, which made swimming awkward, but he dared not let her go. He wished he'd had time to prepare her for this swim. Cave diving was dangerous even when a person knew what he was doing, but for a novice . . . well . . . he hoped the good doctor wasn't claustrophobic. If she panicked, she could put them both in a world of hurt.

He spied the glimmer of light that identified their objective, and swam toward it. Unfamiliar with Helen Bradshaw's lung capacity—well, except in relation to that lengthy kiss—he determined it best to send her up first. He yanked her past him and in water turned blue with light, he pointed out, then up. Hoping she got the idea, he shoved her into the short tunnel that opened off the main one ·they'd entered. That-a-girl, he thought as she swam toward the light.

As Matt followed her out of the tunnel and into the lit cavern, he realized he looked forward to the next few hours. He kicked hard, shooting for the surface, knowing they had lots of time to kill before dark. He was curious to hear her story. After that, who knew?

Maybe Dr. Delicious would need some comforting.

Torie gulped air when her head broke the surface. She swam toward a rocky ledge and held on, resting, breathing, trying to calm her wildly beating heart. That swim through total darkness, not knowing where she was going and following the lead of a man she didn't know from Adam, had been the most frightening experience of her life. Worse than being shot at.

Of course, she'd been shot at before. Tunnel swimming had been a first for her.

Now that she had oxygen in her lungs again, she took a look around her. She was inside a large cavern complete with stalactites hanging from the ceiling. Or was that stalagmites? Whichever they were, they were gorgeous. This whole place was gorgeous.

Utterly captivated by the scene, Torie only vaguely noted when the man's head broke the surface behind her. Sunlight beamed through a hole the size of a dinner plate in the ceiling, the single source of light in the entire cavern. It turned the crystal-clear water blue and illuminated the cavern in such a way that made it seem almost magical. Her gaze tracing the path of sunlight down into the water, Torie gasped. From the bottom of the cave rose a perfect pyramid of white sand. It must have been falling through the hole above for eons, undisturbed by man or beast.

"My God," she breathed, then turned to stare at her rescuer, who was treading water in the middle of the cave. Her voice echoed as she asked, "How did you know about this place?"

"I've dived the underwater cave system in the Yucatán. The topography of this island is similar, so when I found the cenote, I thought it worth exploring. It's always handy to have a place to hide if you need it. Are you okay?"

Torie took stock. She had a few scrapes that stung, a few bruises, but nothing serious. Though the water was cold, she'd grown accustomed to the chill. "I'm fine."

"There's a place we can get out of the water over here," he said, jerking his head toward the right. "Behind that stalagmite."

"Okay."

He swam away from her and Torie took another look around. Such a beautiful place. Clean and peaceful. Relaxing. Torie took a minute and floated on her back, the tension that had held her in its grip since that awful moment on the beach flowing out of her, leaving calmness in its wake.

Color abounded in the rock formations. Reds and pinks and purples. The places where sunlight reached sparkled like jewels. Torie sighed inwardly at the sheer beauty of the moment.

Then calmness descended into fatigue and she knew she'd best get out of the water before she drowned. Rolling over, she swam in the direction he'd indicated. Rounding the curve of the cave, she was treated to yet another sight of natural beauty—her rescuer's naked backside.

Glory be. How many years had she been waiting for James Bond to drop that towel?

He was tanned and toned from head to toe with broad shoulders and corded muscles that flexed and stretched as he used one of AGR Inc.'s green-striped beach towels to wipe the wetness from his skin. Torie revised her mental description of the man. He was James Bond with a bit of Adonis mixed in. Or maybe James Bond combined with a broader version of Michelangelo's *David*.

How about James Bond with the best set of buns she'd ever been privileged to see?

He glanced over his shoulder and caught her gawking, but didn't react beyond a slight lifting of his brow.

He stepped casually into a pair of khaki shorts, then turned. She tried not to stare at his firm pecs, dark chest hair in just the right amount—not too thick or too thin—and mouthwatering six-pack abs. But Torie couldn't help herself. She stared. She goggled. *God bless the U.S. military.*

He smirked a little as he extended his arm to help her from the water. When his hand clasped hers and he yanked her effortlessly out of the pool, sudden awareness of her own lack of clothing washed over her. She wished she'd worn Helen's one-piece rather than her own suit.

Her feet hit dry land, and he handed her the towel. She tangibly felt his gaze as she made a few quick swipes, then wrapped the towel around herself, tucking one end at her chest. Then, summoning her confidence, she offered him a smile. "So, to whom do I owe my thanks? Captain Galahad? Lieutenant Knight-in-Shining-Armor?"

"I'm Callahan. Matt Callahan." He flashed a grin in return. "No title. I'm not in the military, Dr. Bradshaw."

She folded her arms, not certain she bought his claim. Did military-intelligence people routinely deny their position? "But you know my father, Mr. Callahan?"

"Yeah."

"How? Don't tell me you're a simple civilian. I won't believe it."

After a moment's pause, he replied, "General Bradshaw assisted me during a visit to the Balkans."

The Balkans? Events in Eastern Europe might not be making headlines these days, but Torie knew that struggle and strife continued in that area of the world. "That's not exactly a tourist spot. Why were you there? How did my father help you?"

"It's complicated. However, I'm glad to have the opportunity to help him in return."

She puzzled over that for a moment. "Help him how? Not even my omniscient father could have anticipated what happened this morning."

"Just what did happen?" Those gorgeous blue eyes narrowed. "Did Marlow arrive early? Did you stumble onto something you're better off not knowing? Something to do with Gleaming Way, perhaps?"

Gleaming Way! Torie's eyes went wide. She'd learned about the Peruvian terrorist organization when they'd kidnapped a Bolivian starlet a couple of years ago. Had Helen's boyfriend been involved with them? Maybe his status as a pharmaceutical mogul somehow tied them together. A drug manufacturer and drug runners did seem to go together.

"You answer my questions first. What brings you to the island?"

He studied her a moment, then nodded. "Your father is protective of you. When you confided your fear that a by-product of your cancer-drug research had the potential of being used as a biological weapon, he decided to take a look at everyone in your life. He didn't like what he discovered about Collin Marlow. Three days ago, the general learned that Collin Marlow's name is on a terrorist watch list. Two days ago, he contacted me and asked me to . . . escort you back to Washington, where he can oversee your safety while you complete your work."

That sounded just like the general. For once, Torie wouldn't quibble over his methods.

Torie waited for Matt Callahan to elaborate, but when it became obvious he didn't intend to say more, she tried to fit together what pieces she knew. Why send Callahan? Why not come himself? Unlike Torie, Helen listened to their father. She'd have done as he asked.

"I'm surprised he didn't come himself."

Something flickered across Callahan's face. He agreed with her? That was interesting.

"Something he said . . . well . . . it occurs to me that sending me might have been an attempt to, uh, well, play matchmaker."

"Whoa. Really? Who are you, Callahan?"

Grimly, he said, "I'm someone who can keep General Lincoln Bradshaw's daughter safe."

God, she hoped so. Even if she was the wrong daughter.

"Are you a mercenary?"

His lips twisted. "Do you honestly believe your father would want you involved with a mercenary?"

No. He wouldn't. For Helen, the general would want only the best. He'd want someone who could fit into the elite social circles in which he moved. He'd want someone strong and smart and sneaky. He'd want . . .

The answer hit her like a fist. Torie's jaw dropped. Her brows flew up. "Oh, my God. You're CIA, aren't you? You really *are* James Bond!"

Chapter Two

Matt Callahan blinked twice, then drawled, "I understand that a person has to be bright to become a biochemist and molecular geneticist. Nevertheless, I'm curious to know how you connected those particular dots."

"I know my father." Torie yanked the scrunchie from her braid, then finger combed her dripping hair. "I'm right, aren't I? You're a spy. My father sent a spy to save He—me."

Callahan's gaze remained locked on her hands and hair. "General Bradshaw is worried about you."

"Why?"

"You told him you were in love. He didn't think you'd listen."

"Rather than call and at least try to explain, he sends in a spy?" Sarcasm dripped from her words as she added, "How typical of the general."

Her rescuer arched a brow at that. "I understood that you and your father are close."

The general and *Helen* were close. Torie gnawed her bottom lip. Here was her opportunity to explain that the woman Matt Callahan had come to the island to rescue was on a shopping trip in Rio.

Yet, Torie hesitated. What did Callahan know about

her family? What if her father had told him about her? What if he shared her father's opinion that she was an embarrassment, the Bradshaw family shame?

Damn. If General Lincoln Bradshaw had been the one hiding in the rain forest, he might well have let her run past. If Matt Callahan knew who she was . . . well . . . he might not leave her to the killers, but he certainly wouldn't look at her with the respect and admiration she saw in his expression right now.

Frankly, she wasn't up for the usual disgust about her work and lifestyle. She didn't need the snide remarks and nasty comments bound to emerge from her rescuer's talented lips once he learned just who she really was. For the moment, then, she'd play along. People liked Helen; they respected her. It'd be easier to be Helen for now, so she'd continue the charade.

So, then, what would Helen say about the general? The words stuck in Torie's throat. "Daddy can be overprotective at times. He loves me dearly, and sometimes he goes a bit overboard."

"Not in this case, apparently."

"No," she solemnly agreed. "Not in this case."

"Tell me what happened this morning."

Hmm. Well. How to do this? This part of the charade would be even more difficult than speaking of her father without puckering up with bitterness. Torie didn't have a naive bone in her body. She'd never have fallen for a slick bit of slime like Collin Marlow, God rest his soul. Pretending that she'd acted so foolishly to a man the likes of Matt James Bond Callahan would be hard on her pride. She'd need all her acting skills to pull it off.

Torie glanced toward his stash of supplies. "I don't suppose you have anything to drink in there? Vodka? Vermouth?"

"That bad, huh?" He gestured toward a flat spot where she could sit and rest her back against the cavern wall. "I've got a granola bar."

"No chocolate?"

He frowned and scratched the hard line of his jaw. "That's a problem, Dr. Bradshaw. I prize my chocolate. Don't know as I want to share."

Torie eyed the supply stack with renewed interest. She *really* wanted that chocolate. "How about I make you a trade?"

His eyes widened imperceptibly; then he gave her a slow once-over. "Something tells me we're probably not thinking of the same type of barter."

Whoa. She wouldn't be surprised to find burn marks on her skin along the path of his stare.

"Probably not," Torie agreed, rather reluctantly. A part of her—okay, more than one part of her—wouldn't mind taking him up on his blatant invitation. She'd always dreamed of being a Bond girl. Honey Ryder. Mary Goodnight. Not Pussy Galore, though. That name had always struck her as way too crass.

In order to withstand temptation, she turned to business. "What I have to offer are photographs of Collin Marlow going at it with another woman as another boat pulls up and a man shoots him and dumps him into the lagoon."

"Marlow is dead?"

She closed her eyes. The image of Marlow's bloody body going over the side of the boat was burned into her brain. "I don't know how he could have survived."

"And you have photos of the murder."

"Yes."

"Who was the shooter?"

"I haven't a clue. All I know is that one minute I'm watching Collin Marlow make love to another woman and the next minute there are bullets spitting the sand at my feet."

Matt took a Hershey's bar from a backpack and handed it over. "Maybe you'd best start at the beginning. How did you get tangled up with Marlow in the first place?"

"Does it really matter? Do we have to talk about it?"

"It could help me save your life."

Okay, that was a good reason. Torie took a seat and tore into the candy bar. She needed chocolate. "You probably know that Marlow Pharmaceuticals has been trying to purchase Applied Genetics Research."

He nodded. "Your father said that AGR is your baby and that you don't want to sell."

"It'd be a stupid move," Torie said, a touch of bitterness in her voice as she recalled the argument she'd had with Helen. "AGR is doing fine financially and the scientists have total autonomy. When we turned down their offers, Collin came to negotiate personally and that's when . . . well . . ."

"He turned on the charm."

Poor naive Helen hadn't stood a chance. "I was a sucker. He romanced me and I fell for it."

"Did you tell him about the mutation thing?"

Mutation thing? What mutation thing? The biological-weapon thing he'd mentioned?

Judging by the look on Matt Callahan's face, whatever it was wasn't good. *Oh, Helen. What have you gotten messed up in?*

Knowing her sister, Torie made an educated guess. "I might have mentioned it."

"We need to see what else or who else shows up in those pictures." Callahan stretched out beside her, angling his long legs away so that they didn't dangle over the ledge.

"Why would Gleaming Way kill Collin?"

"Terrorists never need an excuse to kill, but the photos might give us a clue."

Torie nodded, grateful she'd taken some close-up shots of the faces on board that boat. She'd been right about Marlow. He'd left her unsettled the one time she'd met him. When Helen had called with news of her engagement, Torie's instincts had gone on high alert. She'd accepted Helen's invitation to visit for the weekend, to get to know Collin better and see for herself that he was the Mr. Wonderful Helen believed him to be. Wanting time to talk to her twin before Lover Boy's scheduled visit, she'd shown up two days early only to find that Helen had done the unimaginable and taken a few days away from her research to go to Rio to buy a wedding gown.

"Go through it again," Callahan instructed. "Tell me everything that happened. Your father understood that Marlow intended to visit you this weekend, arriving this afternoon."

Torie let out a long, heavy sigh. "That was the plan. Collin said he'd be here shortly before suppertime. So I decided to take an R & R day. I hiked over to the lagoon and swam a bit, and I was lying on the beach reading when I heard the boat enter the lagoon. I was alone and I thought I should be cautious, so I gathered up my stuff and stepped into the trees. When I recognized Collin's yacht, *Windseeker*, I was surprised."

"You didn't show yourself? And you hung around and watched?"

"I was surprised to see the boat so early and on the wrong side of the island."

"Then what happened?"

"A man and woman walked out on deck. I thought they intended to swim, but then they got distracted with each other. When I realized just who was burying his face in that woman's breasts, I got angry. I was careless. I didn't pay any attention to the other boat when it approached, not until I saw Collin get shot."

"Did he kill the woman, too?"

"I don't know. I remember her screaming, but then the shooting started at me. . . ."

"So the gunmen came from the second boat?"

"I think so, yes. But honestly, I can't be certain."

"And you didn't recognize the man who shot your fiancé?"

"Please don't call him that." Torie winced. "No, I've never seen that man before in my life. That much I do know."

"Well, the pictures will tell the tale." Matt stared up at the hole in the rocks. "Here's the problem, Helen. With evidence of murder on your film—"

"Memory stick. It's digital."

"Whatever. Look, Marlow's suspected of having dealings with a terrorist organization based in Peru."

"Gleaming Way. I know about them."

He nodded. "If the photos can in any way betray information about that group, they won't stop looking for you. They'll call in reinforcements from the mainland, and they'll have this island covered by dark."

"That's not good."

"No, it's not." He frowned and rubbed the back of his neck. "You know, I could be home working in my vineyard right now. We'll have our first harvest in August. It's gonna piss me off if I die before I get to pick my grapes. We need the camera. Tell me where it is and I'll—"

"We don't need the camera," she interrupted. "I have the memory stick. I tossed it into the brush just before we jumped into the water."

He flashed a quick grin at that. "It's out of sight?"

"I think so. I barely had time to toss it before you had us in the water. I aimed for that bush with red flowers and lots of foliage on it, so unless someone saw me throw it, it should be safe enough. But if someone saw me, well, then we wouldn't be safe." She paused a moment, then said, "We are safe, right?"

"Yeah. I think so. For now, anyway." Agent Callahan grabbed a handful of pebbles from the ledge and began tossing them one by one into the pool.

Torie watched circles of ripples expand across the

water and reflected on the events of the day and her companion's observation. She feared he was right. Even if the gunman had to send to the mainland for reinforcements, a fast boat could get them here in two hours. Or they could helicopter in like most visitors. "Maybe we shouldn't wait for dark."

"It's a risk either way."

"Can't you send for reinforcements?"

"This was a favor for your father, not an operation. I'm flying solo here."

She eyed his stash in the corner. "No goodies from Q to help us out of this bind?"

He stared at her for a long moment, then replied in a dry tone, "I'm afraid I didn't have time to run by Q Branch before I left."

So, touchy about JB, was he? She gave a little smile and said, "Too bad. What's the plan to get us off the island?"

"That's a really good question, Dr. Bradshaw. I have a Zodiac stashed on the other side of the island. The problem with that is if they spot us, we'll be sitting ducks on the water. You have some high-powered craft in your little marina. We couldn't outrun them in the Zodiac."

"So the trick would be to escape without being noticed. Definitely better chances for that after dark."

They both took a moment to think the process through; then Matt Callahan shook his head. "I don't like it. It gives them too much time to prepare. If I'm right about who and what these men are, they'll have a lot of resources within easy reach. This is a small island. They can turn it into a fortress in hours." He turned his head and pinned her with a laser gaze. "How many of your people are on the island today? I saw a crowd leave yesterday."

She nodded. "There's a symposium in San Francisco that all of the scientists are attending." Helen had been scheduled to speak, but she canceled when Collin said he was coming to visit. "The housekeeper and her husband live in a cottage at the compound. The rest of the help is day help who come over from the mainland."

"That's what . . . three miles away?"

"About."

"Think you could swim that distance?"

Torie shuddered. "Not in those waters. Sharks. Lots and lots of sharks. I'll take my chances with the Zodiac."

Callahan bent one leg and clasped his arms around his knee, drawing Torie's gaze to his muscular legs. Being little herself, she'd never cared for big, muscular men. They intimidated her. Made her feel less than safe.

Callahan was different. Once she'd gotten past those first terrifying moments when he'd grabbed her, she'd felt safe in his arms. Felt safe even when he carried her with his hand on her butt. Even when he'd kissed her. And Callahan was a big man. Six two at least, maybe taller. Lean, but not lanky, he moved with strength and grace, and he was gorgeous to look at. Candy for the eyes. Maybe when they left the cenote he'd want to carry her again. She wouldn't mind his putting his hands on her . . . putting his mouth on her . . . putting his—

Whoa. What was the matter with her? This was not the time to be thinking about sex.

Yeah, well. The way things are shaping up, you might not have another chance to think about it, much less do it.

It was the thought of sharks that turned her mind in this direction. She really, really hated sharks, so she'd shied away from thinking about them, but that took her naturally to other predators, which made her think of men, which led to thinking about one man. Looking at this man. And looking at this man, she naturally thought of sex. Any woman would.

"I think we'd better go for it," he declared.

"What?" Torie choked. Had she said it out loud?

"The numbers are on our side now. If we wait much longer, it could be us against an army. I don't think we can wait for dark."

"To escape."

"Yeah."

Okay. All right. Not sex. Possible suicide. Oh, God. She didn't want to die. "So, what, we're going to take one of the boats? The Donzi is the fastest."

"They'll surely have a guard on the boats."

"So we'll hike across the island to your Zodiac?"

"That'll take too much time."

No boat. No inflatable craft. What, then? "I'm not swimming!"

"No." He flashed a daredevil's smile and said, "I think we should fly."

She blinked twice. "The helicopter? You're gonna steal the helicopter?"

"That depends. Can you fly it?"

"Me? No!"

"Good. Then they won't be expecting you to head for the copter. I think it's our best bet." He rolled to his feet, then extended a hand down to her. "You game?"

"Now? You want to go right now?"

"Sooner the better. I imagine they're still pushing inland looking for you. Better make our move before they double back."

Torie's stomach took a nervous roll. She put her hand in his and allowed him to pull her to her feet. But when she looked at the placid pool before her, the idea of getting wet again, of swimming through the tunnel and surfacing out in the open, weighted her feet like cement boots. "Maybe we could just stay here," she babbled. "It's a great hiding place. I don't have a problem waiting them out. You won't believe the patience I have when I need it. When they don't find me, maybe they'll think I tried to swim out and sharks got me."

"If they were run-of-the-mill drug runners, I'd agree with you, Doc. But with these men . . . the stakes here are too high. They'll keep looking until they find you—unless you bring them down first."

Torie closed her eyes. "You know, all I wanted to do today was to relax. Work on my tan. Read about Lizzy and Mr. Darcy again."

Again, he flashed that sizzling smile. "Jane Austen and James Bond. I have to admit, Ms. Bradshaw, you're not at all what I expected to find in a molecular geneticist and biochemist."

She gave her head a toss. "I'll take that as a compliment."

"It's meant as one." He gave her a slow once-over, and the light in his eyes warmed. "Intelligent women appeal to me. Beautiful intelligent women are difficult to resist. Beautiful intelligent women who are also down-to-earth truly float my boat. If we get out of this situation alive, maybe we could make your daddy happy and have a drink, go to dinner."

"You mean, like a date?"

"Yeah. Like a date. Unless you need time to mourn your—"

"Don't! The fact that he's dead doesn't mean I can't despise him."

"True."

Torie's pulse sped up. "What do you think our chances are of getting off this island alive?"

"Oh, fifty-fifty. That's if we leave this cenote in the next few minutes."

Fifty-fifty. She'd have preferred better odds, she decided as she watched Matt Callahan begin gathering up his kit, but she guessed she could live with these. Guessed she'd have to.

A date. She wouldn't mind going out to dinner with a spy. This spy. In a way, their jobs had something in common. They'd have something to talk about. Except he thought she was Helen. He was an acquaintance of her father's. No way would he keep a date with her if the odds fell in their favor.

"About this date," she said as he separated weapons from the pile of supplies. "Are you talking something traditional? You pick me up, take me to a restaurant, then take me home and give me a good-night kiss?"

He glanced over his shoulder. "At least."

She considered that as she watched him retrieve a clear piece of line she'd not previously noticed that ran up to the plate-sized hole in the cavern's roof. To the line he tied a rope; then to the rope he affixed a bag, to which he added those items he obviously didn't want to get wet—two more guns, ammunition, boots, a pair of pants, and two T-shirts.

When he turned to her and raised a questioning brow, she said, "Okay, then. Yes, I'd love to go to dinner with you. But in light of those odds, seeing that fifty-fifty isn't all that great, do you think I could get an advance on that good-night kiss?"

His lips twitched. "Is this a rebound thing?"

"Oh, no. If anything, it's a James Bond thing."

"Now, *that's* annoying." He rolled his tongue around his mouth. "Dr. Bradshaw, I don't know whether to be flattered or offended. You don't think I'll get you out of this alive?"

"Better be safe than sorry," she said, with a shrug.

He advanced on her slowly, a predator's gleam in his eyes. "I must be better than I thought if you'd be sorry to die without another one of my kisses."

"It wasn't great or anything," she said, shrugging. Lying. "It just showed promise."

"Now you're lyin'. Despite the fact I kissed you to shut you up rather than to seduce you, it was a great kiss." He reached out and yanked the towel wrapped around her. As it slipped to the ground, he added, "I always give great kisses."

Yes, please. "Maybe you should prove it. . . . "

He stepped close, backing her up against the cool cavern wall. His body heat enveloped her.

"Double . . . oh . . ."

He put his hands on her waist, then slid them down until they cupped the cheeks of her butt and like last time, he lifted her. Only this time, rather than taking her all the way to his waist, he held her at his hips, where the prominent ridge of his arousal hit her sweet spot just right.

". . . yeah!"

Talk about being between a rock and a hard place.

His mouth settled against hers and as his tongue prodded and pillaged, Torie wondered if perhaps she hadn't been paying attention. Maybe she'd already died.

Because she was pretty sure she'd just gone to heaven.

Chapter Three

Matt wondered if he'd lost his fucking mind. Hiding on a tropical island from badasses ready to put metal on his meat, he was acting more like a horny high schooler than an efficient, no-nonsense United States government operative. With the daughter of a man he respected, at that.

But dammit, he'd had a lust buzz on since he'd first laid eyes on Helen Bradshaw yesterday. She'd walked onto the veranda of her oceanfront home in bare feet and a flirty little sundress. Matt had watched from the trees while she lunched with one of the scientists, her ready smile and gentle laughter as appealing as the generous curves her slip of a dress revealed.

There was nothing gentle about the woman in his arms right now, though. She was a tigress, vibrating with energy, using her tongue and her hands and her hips to drive him to the brink of crazy.

He was moments . . . seconds . . . from lowering her to the ledge and stripping off that tiny excuse for a swimsuit when sanity prevailed. One time wouldn't satisfy him with this woman. He'd need a whole night—hell, a whole week—and they simply didn't have time. Not now. Once they made it off the island . . . well . . . maybe he would take a couple days' R & R. Perhaps if he recharged his batteries, he'd work more efficiently and have better luck in his search for Ćurković.

Though it just about killed him, Matt stepped back and gently lowered her feet to the floor. "You mentioned promise. . . . Let me promise you this, Dr. Bradshaw. We *will* finish this, but it won't be on the floor of a tropical cenote with a clock ticking. We'll be in a big, soft bed with all the time in the world and maybe a can of whipped cream at our disposal. So." He gave her ass cheek one more squeeze, then released her. "You ready to go steal a chopper?"

"I . . . uh . . . oh, wow. Whipped cream." She shoved her fingers through her damp hair. "Just give me a minute. My knees are a little weak."

Matt gave her a wink, and if he strutted a bit as he moved to strap on his knives, no one could have blamed him. "I'll lead the way back through the tunnel, but when we reach the outer cavern, I want you to stay hidden until I give you the signal that it's safe."

"All right."

"Let's go, then." He gestured for her to enter the pool, then watched her graceful dive with a deep twinge of regret. He couldn't recall the last time he'd wanted a woman this bad. They'd damn well better survive this.

Matt positioned himself slightly in front of her as he led her into the inky cavern, his senses attuned to her location at every second. It was awfully easy to get turned around in these tunnels. They'd swum submerged a little over a minute when the welcome presence of sunlight pierced the darkness ahead. Three hard strokes carried him to the light source. He rose to the surface at a spot still well inside the cave and waited for Helen to join him seconds later. He heard her fill her lungs with air; then he placed a finger over her lips. Their gazes met and held. *You okay?* he silently inquired.

She nodded. *Yes.*

He held up one hand, palm out, signaling for her to stay where she was. Again, she nodded.

Matt turned his attention to their surroundings. Slowly, cautiously, he eased out into the open, listening hard. His vision was blocked by the rise of earth surrounding the cenote on three sides, so when he determined he heard no sounds other than those natural to the rain forest, he drew his knife, climbed quietly from the water, and snaked up the slope to survey the scene.

Nobody around but the iguanas. Good. He sheathed his weapon.

Moving quickly now, he descended to where Helen Bradshaw could see him, and waved her from the water. When he saw her safely aground, he went to retrieve his kit. The heavy-duty fishing line that supported the rope lay invisible against the rocky ground, and even knowing where to look, Matt had trouble finding it. By the time he'd pulled the bag through the hole, Helen had joined him, holding the memory stick triumphantly in her right hand.

"Good job," he murmured, swiftly removing the items from the rope. He handed Helen one of the dry T-shirts, then stripped off his sodden shorts and stepped into the dry fatigues, ignoring his companion's strangled gurgle. After pulling on his boots, he holstered his nine-millimeter at his waist, then looked at her. "Can you handle a gun?"

After the slightest hesitation, she said, "Yes."

"You sure? If you don't know how to use it, then it's better for me to carry both of them."

"I've shot a gun before. I just don't like to."

"Fair enough." He handed her the Glock. "If things go our way, neither one of us will have to use it."

Matt stored his ammunition and other small necessities in the pockets of his fatigues, then held out his hand for the memory stick. When she hesitated, he scowled at her. "You need your hands free, woman, and it's not like you have any pockets. Look. We can't lose those pictures."

"I managed to keep up with the stick during the run through the jungle," she grumbled, handing it over.

"This time you'll be busy keeping up with the gun."

Matt checked the compass on his watch, then leaned down and gave her a quick, hard kiss on the mouth. "Let's do it."

In the interest of speed, he traveled an animal path through the rain forest, pausing every few minutes to listen to their surroundings. Helen stayed close on his heels. They didn't speak and when he stopped to listen, she spent her time looking around her and above her, shying away from snakes and shuddering at spiderwebs. For a research scientist whose work revolved around the rain forest, she appeared surprisingly ill at ease with the flora and fauna. Bordering on phobic. Curious, he decided. Maybe she spent her time in the lab, sending others to gather the rain forest's bounty for her to study.

They'd traveled twenty minutes when Matt noted voices approaching. He grabbed Helen's hand and pulled her off the path, heading for the deepest, densest foliage around. Thorns pricked and tore at his skin, but he pressed on until thick green foliage surrounded them. When Helen let out one barely audible squeak, Matt turned quickly. He brushed a spider the size of a small bird from her hair, then wrapped his arms around her and gathered her close against him. He could feel the thunder of her pulse.

The hunters spoke in Spanish and carried automatic rifles. As they passed, Matt picked up a valuable piece of information. Reinforcements were due within the hour, but for now, the searchers numbered six men only. Six men to evade on an island approximately twenty acres in size. Decent odds. He raised his estimation of the chances of their success to sixty-forty.

After the voices faded, he waited five minutes before whispering into Helen's ear. "You okay?"

"Get me out of here."

"I will. It's safe enough now. If I've figured correctly, we'll reach the compound in about five minutes or so. At that point, everything needs to happen fast."

"Get. Me. Out. Of. Here."

Whoa. I think she means it. Matt guided them out of the concealment, and only then noted both the wild look in the scientist's eyes and the deep red scratches on her skin. "Poor thing," he murmured.

"I hate spiders," she snapped, her voice rising on every word. "And snakes. Did you see the snake on the tree beside me?"

Uh, no. "Missed that."

"Next time I'll take my chances with the gunmen. Got it?"

"Calm down, honey. We don't have time for hysterics. You're all right. So far you've escaped all the snakes in this forest. I'm doing my best to keep it that way—we've gotta go."

Grabbing her hand, he pulled her down the path, ignoring her murmured, "Hysterics? That wasn't hysterics. That was pure, unadulterated fear, and I think I held up pretty good under the circumstances. Did I scream? Did I shout? No. I let out one little tiny whimper is all. One itty-bitty tiny little squeak."

"Shush," he cautioned. "Listen."

Matt didn't hear anything, but then if there *had* been something to hear, he couldn't have heard it over her yammering.

The brilliant research scientist responded by poking him on the shoulder and sticking out her tongue. Matt's grin stayed with him until the research compound came into sight.

He signaled for her to stay put; then he worked his way closer to the heliport. He removed a small pair of binoculars from a pants pocket, went down on one knee, and surveyed the clearing.

As he'd figured, the bad guys had a guard stationed at the boat dock, an M249 assault rifle at the ready. Matt swung his glasses north until movement between the laboratory and the main house caught his attention. A brunette sobbed against a man's shoulder while he held a cell phone to his ear. Was she the woman who'd been with Marlow? Was the man the shooter? Both faces were turned away, so Matt couldn't identify either of them.

Matt moved his glasses over toward the heliport. The good news was that no one was guarding the bird. The bad news was that there was absolutely no cover to hide their approach. He and Dr. Delicious would be sitting ducks during the sprint from the forest to the copter.

Of course, that lack of cover could help them during those dangerous thirty seconds to a minute between engine ignition and liftoff. Matt decided to focus on the positive. He reminded himself that he'd been in much worse spots than this over the years, and he'd always made it out just fine. Today would be no different—except for the fact he'd be bringing a drop-dead gorgeous woman out with him.

Now, that was a James Bond moment. He thought of how the 007 movies so often ended—Bond getting laid by a beautiful woman. He'd always despised the quips and comparisons his brothers and others made about the fictitious agent, but maybe in this case, he wouldn't complain about Dr. Bradshaw's little movie fantasies.

He worked his way back to Helen and said, "It's as clear as it's going to get. You ready?"

"I guess. Tell me exactly what I need to do."

"When I give the word, run like hell for the helicopter. If somebody shoots at you, shoot back. Otherwise, keep down and send up some prayers."

"Prayers." Her full lip trembled. "I can do prayers."

She still had that wild look to her eyes, so Matt took a moment to calm her down. Smiling, he placed his hand on her cheek. "We'll get through this, Helen, and once we do, remember, we have a date."

He gave her another quick kiss, then turned, preparing to run.

"Torie," she said.

Concentrating on the mission at hand, he almost didn't hear her. "What?"

"My name is Torie. I thought you should know just in case you make it and I don't."

Matt forgot all about the mission. "What did you say? You're not Helen Bradshaw? Dr. Helen Bradshaw?"

"No. I'm Torie."

"But you look—"

"Just like her. I know. We're sisters. Helen and I are sisters. I'm—"

"Victoria Bradshaw," he breathed. "Holy crap. You're the Evil Twin!"

Torie was too busy feeling afraid to let the old resentment linger for long, but she definitely felt a flash of it. Her father had tagged her with that nickname when she and Helen were in grade school. Her mother used to scold the general for it, but after she died, when the twins were twelve, he used it all the time. Torie admitted she was the more adventuresome of the girls and as such, she got into trouble more often. But evil? She'd never done a truly evil thing in her life!

"Where's your sister?" Callahan demanded. "She's in just as much danger as you are. We can't leave the island without her."

Now Torie was pissed. "You think I'd go off and abandon my twin to killers? Well, screw you, buster. Helen isn't on the island. She's gone shopping."

He blinked. "And you just forgot to mention that little detail?"

She gave him a bitter smile. "Yeah. That's right. Look, aren't we in a hurry here? Or are you going to leave me to save myself now that you know I'm not the Bradshaw you came looking for? The general wouldn't care, so it's up to you. You have the memory stick, so I'm expendable."

She couldn't quite read the emotion in his glare. Disgust? Fury? Insult? A little of all three, most likely. Shoot, it probably matched the look in her own eyes.

He snapped out instructions in a cold, hard tone. "When I say go, run for the bird. Try not to make noise, but if it's a choice between loud and fast, pick fast."

Torie's pulse pounded as she bounced on the balls of her feet getting ready to run. She briefly considered removing her flip-flops in favor of bare feet, but knowing her luck, she'd step on something that would cripple her with pain and she'd stumble and fall and miss her ride.

"Now!" Matt said. "Go. Go. Go."

Torie sucked in a deep breath and took off.

Three years ago at age twenty-nine, Torie had completed a marathon, 26.2 miles, in just under five hours. Nevertheless, this thirty-yard run was the longest of her life.

She ran as hard and fast as she could manage, holding the automatic in a death grip, aware all the while that with his long-legged gait, Callahan could leave her in the dust. Instead, he stayed with her stride for stride. Every second, she expected to hear a shot or to see the spit of dirt where a round hit the ground, or, even worse, to feel one bite into her body. Instinct made her want to close her eyes, but she kept her focus on the goal—the open doorway of the red and white private helicopter.

Then, she was there. Alive and unharmed. Panting

hard. She dived through the door and scrambled into the passenger seat while Matt started flipping switches before he'd even settled in the driver's seat. The rumble of the turbine engines as they engaged sounded like rockets to Torie's ears. Really loud, really slow rockets.

"They'll be on us now," he shouted. "Look sharp. We need at least thirty seconds."

"Will bullets bounce off the helicopter?"

"Not the kind being shot from those guns."

Damn.

Ten seconds passed before she spotted the first gun-wielding man, too far away, thankfully, for his bullets to damage. Another five seconds ticked by before she spied another one. He rounded the corner of the storage shed, and she recognized that he was close enough to kill even as she spied his ugly smile. Torie shuddered as he reached for his gun and brought it up. Her gun was pointed his way, her finger on the trigger, but she couldn't quite manage to make her finger move. Callahan muttered a curse, his hand flew up, and his gun fired.

A bullet hit the side of the helicopter at the same time a splatter of red appeared on the thug's chest.

Oh, Jesus. "Let's go, Callahan. Hurry up. Take off."

He fiddled with some switches. "Almost."

Then Torie spied the man who'd killed Marlow running from the direction of the house. He had an automatic pistol in his hands and he approached them from her side of the helicopter, out of Callahan's line of sight. Beyond his firing line.

Jesus, Mary, and Joseph. The whine of the engine was high-pitched now. Surely they'd lift off any second. Be safe any second.

The terror chilling Torie's blood intensified when she got a good look at the gunman's expression. Evil. Pure evil. *Dear Lord.*

Running forward, the killer lifted his gun. Beside

her, Callahan did something and the aircraft began to lift.

A fusillade of bullets struck the copter. One punctured the passenger door and lodged in the seat, missing Torie by a fraction. Torie squealed and Callahan cursed. "Shoot the sonofabitch before he brings us down! Give us some cover."

She tried. She truly did. She pointed the gun, pulled the trigger, but couldn't quite manage to keep her eyes open. More bullets hit the helicopter and Matt Callahan let out a string of vulgarly inventive curses. Torie clenched her teeth, pointed the gun, and pulled the trigger over and over and over. With the helicopter moving, her arm shaking, and her eyes closing each time, the chances of her aim being true ranged somewhere between slim and none. Then they were airborne, up and away, thank God. She sighed heavily. "We made it. I think we made it!"

"You all right?" Callahan asked.

Torie took stock. Except for her heart being lodged up against her back teeth, she believed she was okay. "Yes, I think so. I think so. Oh, God. And you? Are you okay?"

"Got nicked, but it's nothing."

She glanced at him and saw the streak of red that sliced across his temple. "That's your head. You got shot in the head! Oh, my God."

"It's just a graze. I'm fine."

"But you're bleeding!"

"Yeah, hurts like a sonofabitch, too. However, bleeding like this under these circumstances is a good thing because it means I'm still alive." Grinning, an adrenaline high glittering in his eyes, he spared her a glance. "We made it, Ms. Bradshaw."

She dropped her head back, closed her eyes, and took two deep, calming breaths. *Thank you, God. And thank you, Double-Oh-Yeah.*

As she took a third deep breath in an attempt to

slow her pounding pulse, something landed in her lap. A headset. Callahan had already put his on, blood dribbling down the side of his face. She donned her headset; then spying a box of tissues in the console between them, she grabbed one and dabbed at his wound. "Wouldn't want liquid to short out your headphones," she murmured.

He accepted her ministrations without comment, his gaze on the gauges and dials in front of him. Torie settled back into her seat and steeped in the sensation of safety. What a day. What an awful, horrible day.

She wondered how much longer it would last. "Where are we going?"

"Aruba. The U.S. military has an FOL—Forward Operating Location—there and I figure that's the safest place to stash you while I collect your sister."

"You're still going after Helen?"

"Of course. I gave your father my word. I need to get to her pretty fast, too, because we can't have her or any other members of her team returning to that island before we've dealt with this. Where is she?"

"Rio." Torie's teeth nibbled at her bottom lip. "She's shopping for a wedding gown. She should be safe enough for now, shouldn't she? In fact, the bad guys will think it was Helen on the island, not me. No one but Helen knew I was coming, and when Marlow called yesterday, I pretended I was her."

Matt Callahan's mouth settled into a grim smile. "That twins-switching-identities childishness really chaps my butt. I have twin brothers who used to pull that trick, but they grew out of it by the time they were ten years old."

Torie's chin came up. "We didn't switch identities. Not this time. I just thought it was easier at the time to pretend I was her rather than explain that I'd come to the island to determine whether or not he really was the slime bucket I suspected him of being."

"How far were you going to go to prove it?" he

asked, his tone scathing. "Would you have slept with him as Helen like you were about to do with me?"

Torie sucked in a quick breath. "Where did that come from? That's an awful thing to say." She crossed her arms and tried to ignore the hurt. "You don't know me. Why would you say something like that?"

He stared straight ahead, a muscle working in his jaw. Silence stretched for almost a minute before he said, "You're right. Sorry."

Torie wasn't one to let things go. She liked answers. She wanted to understand. "What exactly has my father told you about me?"

Though she wouldn't have thought it possible, his jaw went even harder. "It doesn't matter."

"No, I want to know!"

"I don't want to talk."

She wanted to challenge him, berate him, hit him, even, but he *was* wounded *and* piloting the helicopter, so she refrained. She settled for drumming her fingers against her thigh and tapping her foot and grousing beneath her breath.

After not quite five minutes of that, he spit a curse. "I don't like what you do."

"Look, sometimes it's simpler not to explain who's who."

"It's not the twin thing. I don't care about . . . well . . . yeah, I don't like it, but that's because of the stuff my brothers used to pull on me. I'm talking about what you do. For a living. Your father told me that. The paparazzi thing."

"Oh." Torie couldn't say she was surprised. It was a reaction she'd grown accustomed to over the years. Sighing heavily, she answered the question everyone eventually asked. "I wasn't anywhere near Paris the night the princess died."

"I didn't think you—"

"What right do you have to judge me, anyway? It occurs to me that our jobs share some similarities. We both eavesdrop, snoop, invade people's privacy. At least when I shoot I do it with a camera instead of a gun."

"A camera can be just as devastating a weapon as a gun," he snapped back, his voice all but vibrating with anger.

Whoa. Touched a nerve there.

"It's a stupid way to make a living," he continued. "Does the world really need to know when a celebrity couple buys a can of tuna?"

"The world may not need to know it, but it wants to know it. Half the time—shoot, seventy-five percent of the time—celebrities want the world to know whether they prefer StarKist or Chicken of the Sea. You wouldn't believe the number of calls I get from publicity agents to 'tip' me on the fact that one of their clients will be vacationing on Nevis or visiting a topless beach on the Mediterranean. It's gossip and glamour. It's entertainment. Paparazzi are a spoke in the wheel of a multibillion-dollar industry. I do a good job that serves a purpose and pays me well. I won't apologize for it."

"Well, I think it's bullshit that with all the troubles in the world, newspapers waste their space on drivel."

"Oh?" Sweetness dripped from her tone. "Like the sports page?"

He shot her a scowl. "Sports is different."

"Uh-huh."

"It is. Athletic competition is a noble endeavor. However, athletes themselves are no more deserving of adulation than the man who recites dialogue and looks pretty on a movie screen. All the bowing and scraping the public does to celebrities shows how screwed up most people's priorities are. Actors aren't heroes. They're not working to cure cancer or develop alternative fuels or to protect and defend our country. They do what they do to get people to drop nine bucks a pop for a movie ticket."

"And just what do you do for entertainment, Mr. Callahan?"

Ignoring the question, he continued his rant. "And don't even get me started about celebrities and politics. Why should anyone give a rat's ass about who Andy Actor thinks we should vote for? Celebrity worship is shallow, stupid nonsense, and you pander to it with your pictures. It's disgusting."

Torie clenched her teeth. She was willing to cut the man some slack because he had, after all, just saved her life, but she'd never been a doormat for any man.

He fired off a few questions about Helen and her exact whereabouts. The respect in his voice when he spoke of her sister grated on Torie's nerves, and despite her best intentions, the old childish jealousy rose up inside her.

Torie loved Helen more than anyone on earth. She truly did. Sometime during their teenage years, she'd come to the conclusion that the reason the egg had split in their mother's womb was because someone special like Helen was going to need someone to watch over her. That's why Torie existed.

For the most part, she was happy with her role. She honestly didn't begrudge Helen her brilliance. It wasn't as if cell division had given her twin *all* the brains. Torie wasn't stupid. She'd seen up close and personal what a burden superior intelligence could sometimes be, and most of the time, she thought she'd been given the better end of the deal. Pretty much the only time she'd gone green-eyed over the subject was when her father was involved. His favoritism had been a big old bitter drink to swallow for as long as she could remember. Their mother had recognized it, too, and she'd always made sure to counter the effect with a little extra attention for Torie.

The worst time came following their mother's death when General Bradshaw turned to Helen to share the grieving and left Torie out in the cold. Her life had teetered on the edge of real trouble for a few years after that. She'd dabbled in drugs, lost her virginity way too soon, and flirted with a life of crime—all the while making sure Helen never came near any of it. She had a few minor brushes with the law, but it wasn't until she landed in some serious trouble that she finally caught her father's attention.

Joyriding in a stolen car hadn't seemed all that big of a deal at the time to a sixteen-year-old Torie. Truth be told, she'd committed a few worse crimes without being caught. Yet, it was that fateful theft that brought about her first separation from Helen and enrollment in the reform school that gave direction to her life.

At seventeen, Torie found photography. The rest was history—as printed in *Star*, *National Enquirer*, *People*, and dozens of other tabloids and gossip magazines.

Now history was repeating itself, so to speak, in that a man frighteningly similar to her father was offering Helen his respect while dissing her. That, Torie thought, chapped *her* butt.

"Why do you care, anyway?" she demanded after a long stretch of silence between them.

He shot her a "You're crazy" look. "I guess because after all we went through today, I'd just as soon not get shot down for trying to land at a U.S. military facility without clearance."

Oh. That must have been what all the radio talk was about. She hadn't been paying attention while she was brooding. "Not that. My job. What possible difference does it make to you what I do for a living? Our worlds are a million miles apart."

"Not always," he grumbled.

Torie pounced on that like paparazzi on a scandal. "What do you mean? What happened? Have you and I met before?"

His jaw went hard and his gaze glittered with hostility. At first, Torie didn't think he'd answer, but finally, he said, "No. It wasn't you. It was one of your cohorts."

She leaned away, studied him. He had a white-knuckle grip on the wheel. Ooh. This looked serious. Trepidation swelled inside her as she asked, "Did a photographer interrupt a mission? Maybe compromise an asset? Blow somebody's cover?"

"Read a lot of spy thrillers, do you?"

"What happened, Callahan? I have a right to know."

He snorted.

"I do. You asked me on a date if we survived and we survived." The alarm in his gaze caused her stomach to take a bitter roll as she pressed on. "Now it's obvious that date will never happen despite the fact the heat between us all but melted rock, and it's because you'd rather keep a hard-on for my job than for me."

"Damn, woman."

"You owe me an explanation, Callahan."

"I saved your life. I don't owe you squat."

She lifted her chin. "You'll damage my self-esteem if you walk away and leave me in the dark. I'm fragile."

He snorted. "Fragile as granite. What you are, Victoria, is a piece of work."

She folded her arms and stared at him. "What happened, Matt? Did paparazzi cause you grief sometime?"

"Grief? Hell. A camera-toting stalker sued me for attempted murder and damned near cost me my career. That's not causing me grief. That's assault."

She put the clues together. "You beat up a photographer?"

"The sonofabitch intruded on a private moment between me and a lady and bared my ass to the world. He's damned lucky he's still breathing!"

Suspicion niggled at her brain. "Who was the lady?"

"It doesn't matter. That's all the explanation you're going to get. Now be quiet. I need to concentrate. We'll be landing in just a few minutes."

Torie shut her mouth, but her mind kept running. She ran through the list of altercations she could recall between photographers and their subjects in the past few years. She had lots to choose from until she narrowed them down to a photographer, an American man who wasn't on the paparazzi's radar, and a female celebrity. Of those, she could recall only four.

And only one that involved a man's naked butt.

The image was one she easily recalled. It'd been splashed all over the European tabloids two, maybe three years ago. It'd been a beach shot taken with a zoom lens. He'd lain atop the woman, nude, his body blocking everything but her face. The Italian movie star's face was easily recognizable in the photograph, as was the ecstasy in her expression.

Three months after the photos were published, the photographer who'd taken them was dumped at the emergency room door of a Paris hospital with both index fingers broken. He blamed the actress's lover, whose identity remained a mystery.

Torie had drooled over that picture for . . . well . . . ever since. It's a wonder she hadn't recognized his rear in the cenote. "You dated Sophia Martinelli?"

His hands jerked. The helicopter dipped. "How the hell—?" He broke off abruptly, set his jaw, and said through clenched teeth, "Not another word."

She complied because the landing field was in sight and radio traffic between Callahan and the base intensified. As the giggles—of relief, amusement, she wasn't sure which—rose within her, she tried to hold them back. She did.

But when the helicopter landed and he reached up to flip off switches, she could contain it no longer. Laughter burst from her mouth like water from a fountain jet.

Matt Callahan glared at her. She attempted to swallow her mirth. "I'm sorry. I just . . . that picture . . . I know it. It's karma. I think today was meant to happen."

"Get hold of yourself, Ms. Bradshaw."

"It's the sexiest piece of photography since the beach scene in *From Here to Eternity*. Helen bought a print and had it blown up into a poster for my birthday gift. I have it hanging in my workroom. Right next to the *Man with the Golden Gun* poster. You know the one. The one where Bond holds his gun like this?"

She lifted the gun from the console and held it up beside her face like in the movie advertisement. "It's Double-Oh-Seven and Double-Oh-Yeah right beside each other on my wall. Karma, I tell you. Kismet."

He let out a growl and reached for the gun at the same time Torie went to set it down.

She wasn't certain how it happened. Bad luck. Bad karma. Truly awful kismet.

The gun fired. Blood splattered. Torie's heart all but stopped.

Matt Callahan, savior and spy, stared down at the wound on his leg, his mouth gaping in shock. "Holy fuck, you shot me!"

They were the last words he spoke to her before the medics arrived and carted him off.

Six months later, Torie returned to her California studio after an extended trip following the latest Hollywood couple on a do-gooders' trip through India. She unlocked her front door, stepped inside, and immediately knew something was wrong. Someone had been in her studio. Within seconds, she discovered that she'd been robbed.

The thief left behind all of her valuable cameras and equipment. All that was missing was a poster from her wall.

Chapter Four

Eighteen months later

Ivars Ćurković was dead. One week ago today, the goddamned motherfucker sonofabitch died in his goddamned motherfucking sleep in a five-fucking-star hotel in goddamned fucking Paris.

Matt had learned the news two days ago upon returning to Langley following a weeklong trip to Pakistan on a mission he almost couldn't complete because his fucking leg gave out halfway up a goddamned mountain.

People liked to say that life wasn't fair, but that simply didn't go far enough. Sometimes, life was a Chuck Norris kick in the balls.

Hearing that John's killer had died such an easy death—one that Matt had absolutely no part in making happen—had been just that kick. Ever since the agency had pinned his brother's death on Ćurković, he'd lived to take revenge on the warlord. He spent at least part of every day trying to track the sonofabitch down. He'd made more trips into the rugged mountains of Eastern Europe and the hellholes of the subcontinent looking for his enemy than he could bear to remember. Most of the time, his efforts had proved fruitless, but on a handful of occasions, the trail had turned warm. Once he'd come within half an hour of catching the slippery sonofabitch. Still, he'd stayed hot on his trail with high expectations of finally running him to ground. Then, he'd done a man a favor and run afoul of That Damned Woman. He never came close to Ćurković after that. Now he'd run out of chances.

Ivars Ćurković was dead.

And Matt's opportunity to assuage his guilt for his own part in his brother's death had died with him.

So what did he do now? What purpose did he have in life? How the hell was he going to live with himself from here on out?

They were questions he desperately needed answers for, and he'd come home hoping to find them. As he spied the carved wood sign that marked the turnoff to his land, his mouth lifted in a weary smile. Everything else in his life might have gone to hell, but at least this was good. He had a place to come to now. For the first time in a very long time, he had a home, a place where someone he cared about waited for him.

Even if that someone was a crusty old barnacle, a former sailor with a porcupine attitude and a priceless nose.

Matt slowed his F-150 pickup and took a right onto the gravel road, seeking the peace that descended upon him whenever he made this particular turn. Sure enough, his muscles relaxed, and the invisible band around his chest loosened. This was one of the few places in the world where he could let down his guard. He appreciated that. A man would be a fool to do otherwise.

Rolling down the driver's-side window, he breathed deeply of the fresh country air. He smelled wild onions and home, and a smile flirted with his lips.

It was springtime in Texas, and this northwest section of the Hill Country was alive with color. Green grass proved that the March showers had indeed arrived as needed. Yellow dandelions, purple asters, and pink prairie phlox dotted the rocky landscape and hugged the thick ankles of the grazing cattle on Scooter Harwell's Rocking H ranch on the left side of the road. Matt's land stretched off to the right.

Rolling, rocky hills protected the prettiest valley in Texas. The creek winding through his land had been named Black Eagle Creek by local Indians and fed into the Brazos River a short distance below the dam that formed Possum Kingdom Lake. Matt owned twenty-five hundred acres, but he leased the majority of it to area ranchers. His interest and that of his partner, Les Warfield, lay in the hundred acres he drove toward now—Four Brothers Vineyard and Winery.

He spied the trellises on the hillside first. When he'd left the vineyard back in January, the grapevines had been barren wood. Now he saw sprigs of color against the gray vines. "April," he murmured, thinking back to Les's viticulture lessons. They'd had bud break in March and April. Buds would mature in June, and harvest in this part of Texas happened in August.

Matt didn't know if he'd be here for harvest this year or not. Basically, that's what he'd come home to figure out. Since he'd spent the last decade making life-and-death decisions in an instant, surely he could get a handle on his current problem in three friggin' weeks. He just needed some downtime to gather his thoughts and make up his mind.

Knowing he'd find Les in the lab at this time of day, Matt drove past the old ranch house where Les had taken up residence to the new building. There, he switched off the engine and climbed down from the truck's cab, pausing to stretch the stiff muscles of his left leg before shutting the door behind him. For a long moment, Matt stood beside his truck, taking stock of the scene around him. Above, puffy white clouds drifted in a brilliant blue sky. Yellow sheets drying on the clothesline behind the house flapped in the gentle breeze. Les's tuxedo cat, Queenie, strolled nimbly along the wooden fence rail that stretched between the house and the Four Brothers tasting room, currently open only on weekends. If he looked just right, he could see the chimney of the lake house a half mile away where he stayed when he came to Texas. This was a good place, he thought. A dream of a place.

But in all honesty, it was Les's dream, not his.

Twenty years Matt's senior, the old sailor had taken Matt under his wing on his first tour of duty and the two men had bonded. In subsequent years in ports of call all over the world, they'd solidified their friendship over a common interest in fine wine. When Les retired five years ago, he'd approached Matt with the idea of founding a vineyard, and they'd formed a partnership utilizing Les's talent and Matt's treasure.

Matt had wavered about what he wanted from this hunk of land ever since he'd bought it. Originally, he'd purchased the Double R ranch as a way to stick it to his father. The owner of the Double R, Randolph Rawlings, had been Branch Callahan's bitter rival, and Branch had coveted the ranch land for years. Rawlings sold his property to Matt with the proviso that Branch never set foot on it. Of course, now that Rawlings was cooling his heels in prison on a variety of charges, including the attempted murder of Matt's sister-in-law, Maddie, Matt felt no need to honor that agreement.

Nevertheless, Matt wasn't ready to let bygones be bygones and invite Branch to Four Brothers. His loyalty to Les was the most convenient reason for that decision. Les and Branch got along about as well as a couple of tomcats living in the same barn, and because of that, Matt didn't need to analyze his own confused emotions where his father was concerned. He wouldn't run across Branch Callahan at Four Brothers Vineyard and Winery. He could spend his mental energy on other concerns—like whether or not he wanted to leave his job and make this place his full-time home.

Sometimes he thought that was exactly what he wanted. Other times the notion made him feel trapped. Matt not only had to figure out *what* he'd do next in life; he had to figure out *where* he wanted to do it.

"Three weeks, Callahan," he muttered as he walked into the yeasty-scented winery. He'd taken three weeks' leave and given himself that deadline to make a decision. Surely by then he'd know whether he wanted to be part of this endeavor or if he should turn it all over to Les—lock, stock, and French oak barrels.

Les Warfield sat at his workbench in the lab, bent over a notebook, his long white hair pulled back in its customary ponytail, his lips pursed in a frown that accentuated the lines crisscrossing his leathery complexion. Looking up, he let out a disdainful sniff. "So, you're back. I trust the world is safe from the forces of evil once again?"

"One hostage is free of the assholes who snatched her. Though with little help from me, I'm afraid." Matt took a seat across from Les and eyed the half-dozen jars sitting on the table between them. He picked up one that was half-filled with a red liquid. A small chip of wood sat in the bottom. "What's this?"

"I'm testing different barrel woods. Put it down. Tell me about the operation."

Aware that his partner had no patience for interference with his experiments, Matt returned the jar to its place. "She was a schoolteacher from Alabama doing mission work through her church. Nice lady. Scared to death. Cried big old silent tears from the moment we left the mountain camp where she'd been held until we delivered her to the embassy."

"Unharmed?"

"No." His tone was flat, his look hard. "A couple of them liked her red hair."

Les waited a moment, then asked, "Are they dead?"

"No." Matt expelled a long sigh. He grabbed a new cork from a bowl full of them and tossed it from one hand to the other. "Went against my grain to leave 'em alive, but our timeline was tight and we had trouble with the extraction."

"What happened?"

"Me. I had no business being on the team, Les. I couldn't keep up."

"The leg."

Matt nodded. "That and the fact I was damn near a decade older than everyone else on the team. Hell, even the schoolteacher scaled the cliff faster than me." He dropped the cork back into the bowl and added, "I've been offered a desk job at Langley."

Les winced. "Ouch."

"Yeah." Matt pushed to his feet and paced the path between the stainless steel fermentation tanks. "I thought I could come back from the gunshot. I thought I had. I thought my leg was stronger than ever. But I was a hindrance out there in the field, Les."

"Bitter pill to swallow, I imagine."

"It was humiliating. The bitter pill waited on my desk when I returned." Matt then told Les the news about Ćurković.

Les laid down his pencil and leaned back in his chair. "Thank God."

Matt's jaw tightened. It wasn't the reaction he'd been looking for.

"That obsession of yours wasn't doing you a bit of good."

"Now, look," Matt began.

"No, you look." Les shoved to his feet and punctuated his words by banging on the table in front of him. "Killing Ćurković wasn't going to bring your brother back, but it easily could have sent you to the grave along with him. You didn't think straight in situations that involved him, Matthew. You let your emotions override your good sense and put yourself in danger. So I'm glad the asshole is dead. I'm glad you had nothing to do with it. Maybe now you can put that whole mess behind you and move forward with your life."

"Doing what?" Matt exploded, guilt churning inside him. Les didn't know his part in John's death. Nobody did. Nobody would understand. "Riding a desk at Langley?"

"Why not? You're closer to forty than thirty. Field ops is a young man's game. It was bound to happen sooner or later."

"Yeah. Well." Matt curled his lip. "It'd be later rather than sooner if not for That Damned Woman."

Torie Bradshaw. Anger churned through Matt. The woman had wreaked havoc on his life. He'd endured three operations on his leg because of her. Spent months in grueling rehabilitation that failed to return him to one hundred percent despite his and his doctors' best efforts. The injury had cost him two informers he'd spent more than a year cultivating and effectively set back Uncle Sam's infiltration of a particularly nasty human-smuggling ring out of Turkey for months.

Worst of all, Torie Bradshaw cost him Ćurković. Matt had missed a golden opportunity when the motherfucker showed himself in Vienna. At the time, Matt had been laid up with an infection following his second surgery.

And as if all that weren't bad enough, to add insult to injury, That Damned Woman haunted his sleep. At least once a month he'd wake up hard as a railroad spike after dreaming about the witch. It was as if the picture of Torie Bradshaw and her string bikini was imprinted on his mind, and he could do nothing to erase it.

"Speaking of women," Les said, interrupting Matt's black thoughts, "another one of 'em called here yesterday looking for you. I told her you'd be back today."

"What! Why'd you do that?"

" 'Cause I'm not your social secretary, that's why. You've got to do something about this harem of yours, Matthew. They won't leave me the hell alone. One of 'em drops by nearly every day hoping to catch you here. And the phone calls! For God's sake. The message machine filled up the first week after you left, so now they call and call and call until I give in and answer. I tried leaving it off the hook, but that just gives 'em more of an excuse to come out here."

Matt dropped back into his chair. "Remind me to kick Luke's ass next time I see him. This is my brother's fault."

"How's that?"

"He got married. Made the women in town think it's open season on Callahan brothers."

"But you're the only Callahan within a hundred miles of Brazos Bend."

"That's the problem." Matt's expression went glum.

"It's been *my* problem and I'm tired of it," Les fired back. "I expect you to deal with it while you're here. Understand? Tell them you're attached, celibate—hell, tell 'em you're gay. I don't care. I just want them to leave me the hell alone."

"I'll take care of it," Matt replied, grimacing. At least that would be one good thing about choosing a desk job over retirement to grow grapes. He wouldn't have to worry about the Brazos Bend babe parade.

Wanting to get his mind off troublemaking women, he asked Les how the season was progressing in the vineyard. The two men spent the next twenty minutes discussing pump troubles, the flea beetles that showed up on the yellow sticky square at the end of an experimental row of Sangiovese, and the weather forecast for the rest of the week. Matt did more listening than discussing. He knew the wine market exceptionally well, but when it came to actually growing grapes and making magic in the winery, he had a lot to learn.

"What does a flea beetle look like?" he asked his partner.

Les shook his head in disgust. "I swear. How is it that you grew up in West Texas and you don't know a leafhopper from a nematode?" Standing, he strolled for the door, saying, "Come with me, grasshopper, and I'll teach you a bit about bugs."

Outside the winery, Les motioned for Matt to climb into the driver's seat of Les's modified golf cart. Then he pointed toward the section of grapevines planted on the hillside. "Take us up there."

The warning alarm on the golf cart beeped as Matt backed it in a half circle, turning around. He shifted into forward and headed for the vineyard. The golf cart traveled less than ten yards before a red and white MINI Cooper came speeding into the parking lot.

"Sonofabitch!" Matt exclaimed, slamming on the brake, the cart sliding on the loose gravel.

The car's driver braked, and gravel crunched as the MINI Cooper skidded. Matt tried to see through the tinted windows into the car to identify the driver.

"One of the harem, I suppose?" Les asked, his voice laced with disgust as the car door opened.

"I don't . . ." A blonde climbed out of the car. "No!"

"You don't know her?"

Matt couldn't answer because he'd gone into shock. His mouth went dry. His pulse began to pound. Adrenaline surged through him. He couldn't believe his eyes.

"Matt?" Les's eyes widened as he spied the nine-millimeter in the female's right hand. The *pink* nine-millimeter. She held a dog, one of those fluffy little designer-dog purse pets, in her left.

"I know her," he replied flatly. "She's That Damned Woman."

"Which . . . oh, you're kidding." Les gaped in amazement. "She's the Evil Twin?"

"Yeah." He met Torie Bradshaw's gaze and added, "The fluff-headed, picture-taking bimbo who put me in the hospital for months and cost me Ćurković. That's her."

Well within hearing distance, she sucked in a breath. "Fluff-headed bimbo?" she repeated. "Bimbo!"

Matt climbed out of the golf cart and turned toward the house. "Get rid of her, Les. There's a rerun of a ball game on ESPN Classic I want to watch."

"That's it," she snapped. "I'm done. I'm finished with being ignored. I'm through with being treated like—"

He looked back over his shoulder. "You deserve?"

"You jerk!" she shouted. "How dare you . . . ? I can't believe . . . *aargh!*" She kicked a stone and sent it skidding across the ground. "Tell you what, Callahan. Instead of Evil Twin, you can call me the Killer Twin, because that's what I'll be if you take one more step without listening to what I have to say."

"Go away, Ms. Bradshaw." He took two steps away.

Les called out a warning. "Matt!"

He turned in time to see her gun come up; then both he and Les dived for cover. Matt heard the shot, followed immediately by the sound of breaking glass. He looked up. "She shot my truck. Goddammit, she shot out the headlight on my truck!"

"That's right. I hit what I aim at now; I've been taking lessons. Turn your back on me again, Callahan, and I'll take aim right at your hard ass."

* * *

Stress, frustration, and bone-deep, mind-numbing fear had led Torie to the edge of sanity. Matt Callahan pushed her right on over.

She shook with fury. Bimbo. Ooh. To think she'd wasted even a handful of brain cells in the past by fantasizing about this . . . this . . . Double-Oh-Jerkface. Her finger twitched on the trigger as she considered blowing his windshield to smithereens.

"Put the gun down, Victoria," Callahan demanded with more arrogance in his voice than what a man pinned by gunfire behind a golf cart should risk.

"When I'm ready. I'm not ready yet."

The older man with Matt piped up. "And what is it you need to get there, miss?"

"I need—" She broke off with a scornful laugh. "I need what apparently is the impossible. I need the police to listen to me. I need my father to pay attention to what I'm saying. It would have been nice if Mr. Superspy, here, could have found just a scintilla of compassion in that cold, arrogant heart of his and spared me a moment of his precious time. What I need, sir, is for every man on God's green earth to disappear. Disintegrate. Vaporize. Maybe then poor Gigi finally would be safe!"

"Who's Gigi?"

"This is Gigi." She cuddled her dog closer. "He put her in the oven! She could have died. What if she'd fallen asleep in there? She sleeps deeply. I brought home chocolate-chip cookie dough. I could have pre-heated the oven!"

"What the hell are you talking about?" Matt snapped.

"*Now* you want to know, hmm?" Blood coursed through Torie's veins wild and hot. "Now you're ready to listen? Because I shot your pretty truck? Well, let's make sure you listen good." She shot out his other headlight.

"Goddammit!" Matt shouted. "What's the matter with you?"

"I'll tell you what's the matter. It's nasty e-mails, hang-up calls, and ugly letters. It's the sense of being followed every time I step out my front door. It's finding pictures of me sleeping hanging on the drying line in my own darkroom. It's finding Gigi in the oven!"

The sentence hung in the air for a long moment until the gray-haired man with Callahan said, "Now, that's just wrong."

Matt scowled and concluded, "You're being stalked."

"Yes!"

"So now you know what it feels like," he said with a sneer.

Torie let out a screech of frustration and eyed the truck again. The older man said, "Uh, Matt? You might want to motor back on the attitude." Then he offered Torie a hesitant smile. "Ms., um . . ."

Torie and Matt shouted simultaneously, "Bradshaw!"

"Ms. Bradshaw." The man moved cautiously from behind the golf cart, his gaze flicking from her face to the gun, which remained aimed at the pickup. "My name is Les Warfield, and I own a stake of Four Brothers Vineyard. Obviously we have a problem here, and I'm happy to help solve it. It'd be helpful if you'd lower the firearm and give me a little more information."

Torie kept the gun trained on the truck. "The problem, Mr. Warfield, is that I'm frightened and frustrated and at the end of my rope. No one believes me. Not the police, not my father. But I'm in trouble and I need help, and silly me, I thought your partner might provide it."

A storm of tears welled up inside Torie, but she battled them back. She wouldn't cry in front of him, the bastard. She wouldn't give him that pleasure.

Matt cleared his throat and stepped out from behind the golf cart, his palms up. "Please put the gun down, Victoria. Les here has a weak heart. Gunshots tend to screw up his pacemaker."

Les patted the left side of his chest with his right hand and offered her an apologetic grin. "He's telling the truth about that. The ol' ticker doesn't do well with a lot of excitement."

Matt took a step closer. "I'll listen to you. I give you my word."

Torie nibbled at her bottom lip. She was tired. She was scared. The last thing she needed was for Les Warfield to drop dead because of her. Was he looking a bit gray? Oh, God. She slowly lowered the gun.

Fast as a striking snake, Matt covered the distance between them and stripped the weapon from her hand. Gigi, bless her heart, lunged and bit the fingers clutching Torie's arm.

"Hey!" He yanked his hand away.

"Good dog," Torie praised.

Man and dog glared at each other, the lips of both curling.

"Oh, for God's sake," Les grumbled. "I could use a glass of sweet tea. You want to come inside, Ms. Bradshaw?"

"Thank you."

"Hold on just one minute," Matt protested as he released the magazine and dropped it in his pocket. He scowled at the gun and clicked on the safety. "Pink. Jesus."

After tucking the firearm in his waistband at the small of his back, he continued. "She shows up here uninvited, takes potshots at my truck, and you want to treat her like a guest?"

"That about sums it up," Les agreed.

Torie gave Les a warm smile before turning a smug one toward Matt. He looked frustrated, disgusted . . . and older than he had back on the island. New lines were etched into his brow and weariness clung to his features.

Major medical trauma would do that to a person.

Torie sighed heavily and forgot about being smug as guilt settled on her shoulders. She'd put those lines there. Silently, she followed Les up the front porch steps and into the restored two-story Victorian complete with gingerbread and a wraparound porch.

"Come on into the kitchen," the older man directed. The austere furnishings in the living room reflected a bachelor household. Other than the two recliners with a lamp table between them, the only items in the room were a huge plasma television, a bookshelf filled with a mix of hardbacks and paperbacks, and a card table with plastic pieces and the skeleton of a model battleship spread across its surface.

Not exactly James Bond luxury, she decided. Gigi squirmed in her arms, and Torie tucked her away into her shoulder bag as they entered the kitchen. There, she stopped in surprise. Behind her, Matt Callahan said, "Looks like a frosting bomb went off in here."

Baked goods filled every inch of counter space and the entire surface of the kitchen table. Pies, cakes, cookies—the selection was vast and highly caloric.

"It's your harem," Les grumbled. "That's less than a week's worth of stuff. Some women have absolutely no pride. I'm telling you, Matt, you have to do something to stop it. My arteries clog up just from looking at all this."

Harem? That figured. Guilt forgotten, Torie shot Matt a scathing glance. Women with no pride adored men with no shame.

Les gestured for Torie to take a seat while he cleared a spot at the table. "Tea's in the fridge, Matt. Why don't you pour us all a glass?"

Matt bristled with offense. "Oh, so now I have to serve her?"

"Don't be rude," the older man responded.

"Yeah," Torie agreed.

Callahan's cold stare could have frosted the chocolate cake in front of her. Torie battled back with a glare hot enough to melt the ice cubes he added to the glasses he removed from the cupboard, muttering and grumbling all the while. When he opened the refrigerator door, two plastic bags filled with what appeared to be meatballs fell out onto the floor.

"Angie Rametti dropped those off. With sauce and a spinach lasagna. Her stuff, we're keeping."

"Angie? She's closer to your age than mine." When Les simply shrugged, Matt's brows winged up. "Oh. I see. I'm not the only bull in the pasture, now, am I? How much of this stuff was brought by women over forty?"

"Not much."

"Whose fried chicken is this?"

Les repeated his shrug. "Alice Moncrief's."

Matt smirked, his point apparently proved. "The meat loaf?"

"That's one of the young uns'. She can't cook worth a damn. You need to pitch that."

Torie glanced past Matt to see that the appliance was literally stuffed to overflowing. A plastic tub filled with pasta salad slid out onto the floor. "This is ridiculous," Matt muttered, and tossed the meatballs back into the fridge. The other stuff he pitched into the trash before grabbing the jar of sun tea from the refrigerator shelf. "I swear, women are the bane of my existence. Damned women. That Damned Woman."

Torie stifled the childish urge to stick out her tongue at him. "I can't believe how wrong I was about you. You are *so* not James Bond."

He glanced over his shoulder at her. "Honey, in your case, you're better off thinking of me as the Terminator."

"I do." That's why she was here.

Matt sighed heavily as he poured three glasses of tea. Setting them on the table, he took a seat across from Torie, then perused the sugared offerings, choosing what appeared to be a banana muffin. Les Warfield said, "Would you tell us your story now, Ms. Bradshaw? From the beginning? I'd like to know why I almost got shot in my own driveway."

Torie ducked her head, embarrassed. Seldom did she allow a man to put her in her place, but this aging hippie did it with a chastising look. "I'm sorry if I frightened you, sir. Believe me that you never were in danger. I'm careful with guns."

"Yeah," Matt drawled. "Right."

Keeping her gaze on the older man, she continued. "It's basically what I mentioned earlier. For the past six weeks, I've been stalked and terrorized. At first, it was little things. I noticed items in my apartment had been moved in my absence. I had the sense of being watched. It occurred to me that Callahan might be behind it."

"Me!" Matt exclaimed. "Why me?"

Torie continued to address Les. "He despises me. He's hated me from the moment he found out he'd rescued me—the Evil Twin—rather than my sister. That was well before the gun accident, I might add."

"True." Matt nodded and took a bite of muffin. "I may despise you, but that doesn't mean I'd do anything to you."

Torie's mouth flattened. Even though she knew he hated her, nobody liked to hear someone admit it. "Will you deny that you broke into my home and stole from me?"

"No, that I won't deny." He awarded the point to her with a nod.

Les's eyes widened. "Callahan! What did you—"

"The poster, Les."

"Oh." The older man nodded and picked a

chocolate-chip cookie off a plate. He chuckled softly as he added, "It makes me laugh every time I think about—"

"Les, please. Will you let her tell her story so this doesn't drag out past lunchtime?" Frowning at Torie, Matt demanded, "Continue."

This time she did let her tongue dart out in his direction. While he gaped, she said, "I pretty much mentioned everything before. The letters and phone calls. Finding the pictures in my darkroom totally creeped me out. That's when I went to the police. They thought it was a publicity stunt."

"Can you blame them?" Matt muttered into his iced tea.

Torie folded her arms. "Then I came home from work three days ago and discovered poor Gigi trapped in the oven. I went back to the police and they made a cursory investigation, but their hearts weren't in it. They decided I'd probably made a celebrity angry and they were playing with me out of revenge. Without proof of who, they couldn't—they wouldn't—do anything."

"Did they find any physical evidence? Any finger-prints on the oven door handle, for instance?"

"The only fingerprints they found were mine. That made me think of you again. You're a spy. You'd know not to leave fingerprints."

"Any idiot who watches television would know not to leave fingerprints," he drawled. "You know, woman, it pisses me off that you'd think I'd do something so sick. I like dogs. Hurting them in any way goes against my grain. If I'd wanted to trap any living being in the oven of your apartment, it would have been you, not your sharp-teethed vicious little purse pet."

"Gigi isn't vicious. She's protective of me and maybe just a little high-strung upon occasion." Hearing her name, Gigi stuck her head out of the bag. The pink glitter bow at her cream-colored crown sparkled in the sunshine beaming through the kitchen window.

"I'm not the only person in the world who has reason to hold a grudge toward you, you know," Callahan continued. "Your enemies are undoubtedly legion. And you decided I was the guilty one all because I reconned that poster?"

"I didn't say I decided you were my stalker. I said I considered you."

Callahan snorted and Les suggested, "Go back to the pictures you mentioned before. Tell us about those."

Torie's stomach went a little sour thinking about the eerie photos she'd found in her darkroom, so she broke a homemade gingersnap in half and nibbled on it to give her digestion something to use all its excess acid on. "I was chosen as the photographer for JJ's new baby," she said, referring to Hollywood's latest darling couple, Jack Brunier and Julie Kelley.

"Didn't I read that you were paid a cool million for those shots?" Callahan's voice was laced with disgust. "What did you do? Hide under the bassinet, then blackmail them?"

"They asked me to take pictures of the baby. The Jays then sold them for charity, to fight juvenile diabetes. Julie's little brother died of that disease, not that it's any of your business."

"I do think I read that somewhere," Les offered.

Matt gave his friend an incredulous look. "Since when do you read the tabloids?"

"I was in the dentist's office." Les shrugged. "Go on with your story, Victoria."

She drew a deep, calming breath, then said, "I went to New York for the weekend. When I came home, I found a set of photographs of me hanging in my darkroom. They'd been taken at different spots around town during a three-day period the week before my trip."

Les drummed his fingers on the tabletop. "I'll bet you were spooked."

"Scared to death." She licked her dry lips and added, "A couple of them . . . well . . . he got close to me. Too close."

"Do you have them with you?" Matt asked.

She opened her mouth to deny it, but something in Matt's expression halted her. "Why?"

"Sometimes it's possible to pick up clues from the backgrounds of photographs," he said.

"I know that. I'm a photographer."

"So did you analyze the pictures?"

No, she couldn't bear to look at them. Whenever she tried, her knees turned to water and started banging together. She reached into her bag, gave Gigi a little pat, and dug around for the envelope containing the photos. She handed them to Matt, then stood up and walked over to the kitchen window and stared out at the vineyard. "I bet it's pretty here when the grapes ripen," she observed, turning her mind to something—anything—other than the photographs.

She didn't want to look at the pictures. She didn't want to think about someone stalking her. Peeping at her. Watching her.

Because it's a taste of your own medicine? Isn't that what you've done to countless folks? Only this time you're not the stalker; you're the prey. It's not a nice place to be.

Behind her, paper crinkled as he opened the envelope. She heard the photos slide out and she started babbling. "I photographed a party at a winery once on a Saturday during harvest. Traffic was stop-and-go from one end of Napa Valley to the other from daylight to dusk. Beautiful place, though. The house was Spanish architecture and the rooms were huge. The party planner is a friend of mine and she told me—"

"Hush."

"She didn't tell me to hush."

"I'm telling you to hush." Matt looked up from the photographs. "Could these have been made from a remote position?"

Despite the gingersnap, her stomach continued to roll. She knew why he'd asked that particular question. "No. I checked, and the police checked, but there are no cameras hidden in my bedroom."

There were three pictures of her asleep in her bed.

Callahan frowned down at the photographs. "Cold. Very cold."

"I changed the locks after that. I put in good locks and an alarm and I thought I was safe. Obviously I was wrong because Gigi ended up in the oven."

Matt slipped all but one photograph back into the envelope. That he handed over to her. "This one catches the photographer's shadow. I'm surprised you didn't see it."

Wary, she took a look. It was a shot of her coming out of the dry cleaner's, and sure enough, the shadow was unmistakable. "I didn't look closely before. This is a man and . . . hmm." She studied the picture with a photographer's eye rather than that of a victim. "Look at the proportions. Whoever took this picture is quite a bit shorter than you."

"The defense rests," Matt said, then took a long sip of his tea. "Although if you're still not satisfied, I can get my passport out of my truck and prove that I've been out of the country for the last nine weeks."

"I knew it wasn't you, Callahan."

"Then why the gun? Why did you shoot up my truck?"

"Since this started I carry my gun with me all the time. As far as your truck goes . . . I lost my temper. You really shouldn't call a woman with a gun a fluff-headed bimbo. Nevertheless, I'll pay for the repairs."

"Damn right you will."

Gigi poked her head up out of Torie's bag and let out the little yip that meant she needed to go outside.

Torie was grateful for the distraction; his attitude had her temper at a slow boil once again. "May I take her . . . ?" She gestured toward the back door.

"Of course." Les Warfield smiled magnanimously. Matt Callahan folded his arms and leaned back against the counter. "If she craps on the patio, you'll clean it up. And don't try to run off without making good on your debt."

"Oh, bite me."

"No thanks. All that foaming at the mouth . . . rabies is a turnoff."

She snarled at him and flounced outdoors. There, Gigi took care of business, then decided to explore a bit. Torie let her wander. She was in no hurry to face the men in the kitchen again.

The soft breeze carried the scent of rain, and Torie looked up and noted the thunderclouds building in the west. She stood there, soaking in the peace of the place, and slowly her mood eased. She'd always enjoyed the country. She loved taking long weekends at a bed-and-breakfast somewhere in rural America. It grounded her. Kept the craziness that was Hollywood in perspective.

When she heard the screen door squeak open behind her, she didn't need to turn and look to know that Matt Callahan had come out to join her. Determined not to let him get her goat this time, she summoned up her nerve to say something long overdue. "I am truly sorry that I shot you when we were in the helicopter. It was an accident, but my foolishness caused it. While I'm at it, I apologize for coming here with my gun blazing, too. It was a stupid thing to do."

"Finally we agree on something." He stood beside her and stuck his hands in the pockets of his jeans. "Where did you find a pink Glock, anyway?"

"I had it Durocoated." She chewed her lower lip a moment, debating the intelligence of bringing the next subject up, but since she was apologizing . . . "I understand that the rehabilitation on your leg was . . . difficult."

He gave her a droll look. "Difficult? That's not the word I'd use."

"I'm very sorry you had to go through that because of me."

He shrugged, then, after a moment, gave her a sidelong look. "You talk to your sister about me?"

"Your name came up a time or two." Actually, it had been daily.

After surgery on his leg, Matt rehabbed at Walter Reed in DC. Helen, who'd been spirited out of Rio and recruited to study her potentially dangerous discovery for Uncle Sam, worked in a lab nearby. She'd been thankful for his help in rescuing Torie and regretful of his injury, so Helen took to spending her lunch hour visiting Matt.

She'd been devastated by Collin's betrayal. Study of the pictures Torie had taken on the island had revealed that the woman with Collin wasn't just any Latina beauty, but the sister-in-law of Esteban Romo, who was the brother of Gleaming Way's number one man in Rio, Alejandro Romo. Apparently, Marlow's popping up on the terrorist watch list wasn't due to dealings with terrorists, but with a terrorist's relative. Helen had told Torie that visiting Matt helped her come to terms with everything that had happened.

Torie's response to her sister's action was complicated. She felt horrible about the accident. Matt's reaction when Helen walked into his hospital room and he thought she was Torie didn't help. At least the bedpan he threw at her twin had been empty. While she was glad her sister could help him, she . . . well . . . it was the first time in a very long time that she'd been jealous of Helen. Plus, she'd never been able to forget the fact that Helen admitted she and Matt Callahan shared a kiss.

That might have had something to do with her itchy trigger finger today.

"Helen said she thought you'd forgiven me for the accident. Otherwise, I never would have come here."

His only reaction to that was a "humph."

Gigi trotted out from behind the pecan tree where she'd been rooting around, and spying Matt, she bared her teeth and growled. He shook his head in disgust. "What kind of dog do you call that?"

"Peke-a-tese. She's a Pekingese and Maltese cross."

"In other words, a minimutt. Considering your circumstances, you should have a real dog. A German shepherd, a Rottweiler. Something that could protect you."

Torie sighed. "When I started getting the phone calls and threatening letters, I tried bringing home a retriever. Having another dog around upset Gigi's aura, so I gave the retriever to a friend."

"You gave away the wrong dog."

"Gigi was a gift from the Jays. Once the baby came, Jack thought Julie was giving Gigi too much attention, so they gave her to me." Torie lowered her voice and added, "I knew if I gave her away, I'd never work in Hollywood again. That's beside the point, though, because I fell in love with her."

Gigi offered unconditional love—something Torie always found to be in short supply. Gigi didn't care if Torie was paparazzi. She didn't mind that the prospect of studying biology, chemistry, and genetics made Torie's eyes cross. Gigi truly wasn't concerned whether Torie ever bought a house.

"No accounting for taste." He curled his lip at Gigi, who'd continued to growl; then he pinned Torie with a stare. "How did you know to look for me here? I'm not around all that often."

"I made a few phone calls. Remember who my father is? I'm connected."

He thought about that a few moments, then asked,

"So what's the deal with the general? Why isn't he helping you?"

"He's overseas." Now it was Torie's turn to shrug. "Besides, he doesn't believe me. He thinks I'm making everything up to get his attention."

"General Bradshaw is a sharp hombre."

"This time he's wrong." She looked at him, her gaze imploring. "He's absolutely wrong, Matt. I'm not making this up. It isn't in my mind and I'm not crazy. Someone is out to get me. Surely you could see that in those pictures. He broke into my house, terrorized my dog, and took pictures of me while I slept. The police say that can't prove a crime has been committed and frankly, they don't care. They have no intention of helping me." Torie drew a deep breath, then looked him straight in the eyes. "I'm hoping you'll be different."

Matt let the moment drag out before he chuckled softly. "If you're not a piece of work. I curse your name every morning when I get out of bed and have to work the soreness out of my knee. You cost me my career. You cost me a goal I've pursued for years. You have a job I don't respect, a dog I pity, and you shot up my truck. Why in the world would you think I'd help you?"

Okay, so that didn't sound so good. "Because you have a thing for Helen and helping me would keep you on her good side?"

"You think I have a thing for your sister?" he asked, his tone incredulous.

"Don't you?"

"No, I don't. I wish I did. Don't think I haven't tried to talk myself down that road. Helen is a wonderful woman. She's smart, honest—a paragon. I'd feel a helluva lot better if it were Helen starring in my dreams at night, but no. Oh, no."

He pinned her with a look of half anger, half self-disgust. "I have to dream about you."

Torie blinked twice. "Me? You have dreams about me?"

"Hot ones. Sheet scorchers."

Wow. Oh, wow. Now, that was a surprise. "How do you know it's me and not my sister?"

"Oh, I know."

Hmm . . . should she tell him she'd had some hot erotic dreams about him, too? "Why are you telling me this?"

"Because it pisses me off, Victoria. I want to forget you. More than just about anything, I want you out of my life and out of my mind and far, far away from my truck. Today."

She exhaled in a rush. "What about the stalker?"

"He's your problem, not mine."

She didn't let him see how much his callous declaration hurt. Instead, she folded her arms and set her foot to tapping. "So you're just abandoning me? You're not gonna help me at all?"

"Tell you what. I'll forgive the debt you owe me on the truck. Just take your designer dog and get your sexy little ass on down the road."

My sexy little ass? Torie couldn't help but preen a bit. And here she'd been thinking she had some spread and slippage action going on. Then she gave her head a shake. The state of her buns was of secondary importance here.

Torie started pacing, fiddling with her earring, playing with her hair. She recognized the agitation in her movements, identified the anxiousness that had her stomach rolling, but she couldn't do anything to stop it. She couldn't deny that she was deathly afraid.

She couldn't let Callahan send her away. That was all there was to it. It was the bottom line.

So. How to change his mind? She spied no sign of wavering in those bright blue eyes of his. She could try seduction, but with a harem at his beck and call, that option didn't appear too promising. Bribery? With what? Helen said Matt Callahan was filthy rich. The only thing she could think of was to attempt to appeal to the hero hidden deep in his soul.

Good Lord, I'm doomed.

Nevertheless, Torie decided to give it a try. She spoke from her heart, hoping he'd hear the truth, praying he'd see it. "I'm a basket case, Callahan. I haven't been thinking, only reacting. And my reaction was to flee to the one person I knew who could keep me safe."

She put her hand on his arm and did something she very rarely—if ever—did. Torie begged. "Please help me, Matt. I don't know anyone else who can. You're my last resort."

She saw him waver. Indecision drifted across his face like a cloud, raising her hopes. Maybe he would look past his righteousness to the gallantry Texas boys were raised to display toward women.

Then his gaze fastened on the logo of the sign beside the tasting room door. "Four brothers," he murmured, then, "Damn. Look what happened last time I tried to help you. I may be slow, but I'm not stupid."

He grabbed a snarling Gigi by the scruff of the neck and handed her to Torie. "You can be in Fort Worth by lunchtime. The police department is downtown by the courthouse. Walk in there and twitch your tail and you'll have guys falling over themselves to help you."

Torie gasped. "That's just mean."

He turned and headed for the house, giving her a wave over his shoulder. "There's an office-supply store on the way into town. Why don't you stop and buy a notebook—one with lots of pages—so you can make a list of your legions of enemies? They'll need that. Good-bye, Victoria."

He was almost to the back porch when she found her voice again. "So you're throwing me to the wolves? You're gonna let the bad guys win? What kind of white-knight hero are you? You're supposed to be my guardian angel!"

This time his laugh was genuine. "White knight? Guardian angel? Honey, you truly live in a fantasy world, don't you? You have it all wrong. Just ask someone in Brazos Bend what folks around town like to call me."

Thirty minutes later, she pulled into the parking lot of a Dairy Princess and did precisely that. The woman behind the counter who'd introduced herself as Kathy Hudson clucked her tongue and shook her head, which sent her dangling star earrings swinging. "So he's back, is he? There's been rumors around town about it for a week, but those rumors have been wrong before. I'd best make a quick trip to the market. They're liable to sell out of eggs by closing time tonight because every single woman in town will start to baking for Demon Callahan."

"Demon Callahan?" Torie repeated. "They call him Demon Callahan?"

"Yep. Even before his brothers were born his father was calling him a little demon. The name stuck, especially after the others came along and their poor mother, God rest her soul, named them after saints. The Callahan boys were troublemakers from the git-go. Didn't take long at all for townspeople to start calling them the Holy Terrors, led by the eldest, the Demon himself."

At that, Torie started to laugh. You had to like a town so brutally honest as to label the children of a leading citizen as the mischief-makers they apparently had been. Throwing logic out the window and relying on instinct alone, she made a decision. She needed to hide somewhere. Why not Brazos Bend? "Can you recommend a hotel or maybe a B and B in town?" she asked. "I'll be staying awhile."

Kathy Hudson's brows arched. "You plan to compete for Demon's attention?"

"You know what? Maybe I do." Not in the same way his harem competed, and certainly not with the same goals. But after the events of the day, she liked the idea of being a thorn in the Demon's side. What more appropriate skin could an Evil Twin prick?

She winked at Kathy and added, "I'll tell you a secret, Ms. Hudson. Demon and I? We're a match made in hell."

Chapter Five

Los Angeles

The lock snicked open. The intruder slipped inside the apartment. Ah, lovely. The signs of panic were unmistakable.

Torie Bradshaw had left a mess behind in her apartment.

Earlier visits had shown her to be tidy, if not excessively neat. Today, the television played to an empty room, a rain jacket lay on the carpet, and in the kitchen . . . ah . . . a gallon of milk sat spoiling on the countertop. A tube of raw cookie dough lay on the kitchen floor and the oven door stood open. The aroma of fear still clung to the air. Or was that baked puppy?

How delicious.

But time was wasting. While topping the last effort might prove difficult, the game must continue. Terror level stood at yellow. Torie still had orange and red to reach.

Orange. A lovely color. Orange required something a bit more . . . intrusive . . . than trapping a pet in an oven.

Time to go to work on Torie Bradshaw's next surprise.

*   *   *

Inside the air-conditioned office of Brazos Bend Automotive, Matt thumbed the off button on his cell phone and blindly watched as the mechanic drove his F-150 onto a lift in the shop. His mind wasn't on the pesky engine whine he'd decided to have checked while his truck was in the shop for repairs. Instead, his brain churned with the information he'd gathered in the hours since Torie Bradshaw spun her tires leaving Four Brothers Vineyard.

He'd tried to ignore the entire incident, but between the chastising looks Les gave him and the nagging of his own conscience, he'd finally given in and made a few calls.

It looked like she'd been telling the truth. According to a detective named Vance, she'd filed a report with the Hollywood police last week and the pictures did exist. But stalkers were a dime a dozen out there in La-La Land, and she was way down the list of sympathetic victims for the authorities.

She hadn't told Vance about the mutt-in-the-oven incident, and his apparent lack of interest when Matt relayed the facts convinced him she'd read the detective right. Torie Bradshaw would get no help from that quarter.

The muffled croon of Patsy Cline played over the shop's stereo system and Matt absently hummed along. Though he watched the mechanic wipe his greasy hands on a red rag as he inspected the truck's shocks, Matt's mind's eye remained focused on the vision of a pistol-toting paparazzo.

After speaking with Detective Vance, Matt made a few more phone calls to contacts in both Washington and Europe and discovered that during the months he'd been recovering from a gunshot wound, she'd been busy making more enemies.

Surprise, surprise.

She'd dumped a boyfriend not long after her return

from Soledad Island. Some "journalist" who wrote stories for the rags that published her pictures. Old boyfriends made good stalker suspects. Of course, so did offended zealots. Somehow Torie Bradshaw had managed to be involved in the brouhaha that had erupted last winter with that invent-a-religion band of corporate weirdos on a private island off the Carolina coast. What was it with that woman and islands?

Then there was the incident at the Oscar party. Matt didn't blame Torie for showing off her jujitsu moves on that free-handed actor, but she'd cost a lot of people a lot of money by breaking his million-dollar nose.

And those were just three of the seemingly endless possibilities.

Matt wondered why she didn't go to her father for help. When the general visited Matt in the hospital after his second operation, he'd declared his intention to disown Torie. Knowing firsthand what a blow such an action could be, Matt couldn't wish it on even the likes of the Evil Twin. He'd argued against it and felt downright righteous doing so. Bradshaw had backed off on his vow then, but Matt wondered if the old soldier had followed through on his threat after all. Otherwise, why wouldn't Torie have turned to the general for help rather than drive halfway across the country seeking assistance from a man she damn well knew held a grudge against her? It didn't make sense.

But then, with Torie Bradshaw, what did?

His phone rang and he checked the number. His brother Mark was finally returning his call.

They exchanged the usual insults as greetings; then Matt got down to business. "I need you to do some electronic tracking for me."

"Me?" After a moment's pause, Mark said, "Excuse me, but aren't *you* the spy?"

"This isn't spying. This is personal, a private investigation. That's what you do, isn't it, now that you've left the military and hung out your own shingle?"

"Yeah, but I work for paying clients," Mark grumbled. "You still owe me for that Nolan Ryan card you bought from me in 1986. So, what's this about? Where are you, anyway?"

"Right now I'm watching Al Ayer take a wrench to the shocks on my truck."

"You're in Brazos Bend? I thought you were overseas."

"Makes me worry about your investigative skills, then, bro. I got back last week." With that, Matt decided they'd spent enough time on brotherly bonding. "I need to find someone who left here about four hours ago. You can probably track down her credit card to a gas station despite the fact that she was driving a MINI Cooper."

"A Cooper? Makes my legs cramp just to think about it. So, who is this woman? Does this have something to do with Branch? If so, I'm going to charge you double."

"I know better than to ask you to have anything to do with the old man." Of the three surviving Callahan brothers, Mark nursed the hardest feelings where their father was concerned. Luke had mellowed somewhat in his hatred of Branch Callahan since his marriage to Maddie Kincaid, and while Matt remained pissed as hell at the old bastard about his handling of the ransom demand for John, a part of him did understand his father's point of view. As a result, he wasn't quite ready to lay every bad thing that happened in the universe at Branch Callahan's feet.

Now, Torie Bradshaw was another matter altogether. He wouldn't be surprised if she were responsible for global warming, the eruption of Mount Saint Helens, and the Christmas tsunami.

Matt grimaced and, knowing he'd catch hell, bit the bullet. "It's Torie Bradshaw. Victoria Lynn Bradshaw."

There was a long silence. Out in the shop, the mechanic stepped from beneath his truck and flipped the switch to lower the lift. Finally, Mark said, "That Damned Woman?"

"Yeah."

"She came to Brazos Bend?"

"I'm afraid so."

Another moment of silence, then, "Are you bleeding anywhere?"

Matt couldn't help but laugh. "It's your intuitive nature that makes you such a good investigator."

"What happened?"

Matt began a rundown of the events of the morning. "Damn," Mark interrupted. "She killed your ride?"

"Maimed it."

As Matt continued his explanation, his brother made no further comment. When he'd finished, Mark asked, "So, you sent her off and what . . . you want to make sure she's gone?"

"Well, uh . . ."

"Sonofabitch. You're having second thoughts, aren't you? You want to help her."

"No. I don't. I just . . . hell."

"It's that damned conscience of yours. It doesn't keep you out of trouble, but it makes you suffer afterward. I wish you'd explain to me how a man with your background can let a piece of ass play mind games like—"

"Knock it off, Mark," Matt interjected. "I'm not getting involved in this. I'm just gonna help her find someone else who will. I believe That Damned Woman truly is in danger and it won't hurt me to refer her to someone who can help. When I find out where she's going, I'll figure out who's available and have them contact her. You'd do the same damned thing. Don't try to tell me otherwise."

"Yeah, well."

"So, will you let me know where she goes to

ground? My guess is that she'll drive to DFW and get on a plane sometime tomorrow."

After Mark agreed to provide the information Matt sought, the brothers traded a few more insults to end the conversation. Matt disconnected the call and noticed the mechanic waiting for him holding a clipboard and a handwritten estimate. Ten minutes later, Matt was on the road again in a rented truck, with no real place to go.

Which was probably why he found himself driving past his father's Country Club estate.

He pulled over to the curb in front of the house and sat idling, allowing the memories to flow. He could all but hear the laughter floating from the windows, smell the aroma of hamburgers on the grill, see the ghosts of a summer evening playing tag in the front yard.

Once upon a time, the walls of the place overflowed with happiness. Margaret Mary Callahan had ruled the family roost with love, laughter, and the ability to keep her boys—all five of them, including Branch—in line with little more than a stern look. When she died, the light went out in all their lives and the Callahans descended into a darkness that had yet to lift. With John gone, it probably never would.

The front door to the house opened and something small and furry exploded from inside, raced down the front walk, planted its four paws—at least, Matt thought there must be paws under all that hair—and started yipping. No way that noise was deep enough to be termed a bark.

Another purse pet. Two in one day. He found something about that to be kind of scary.

Even scarier was the figure who followed the dog out the front door. Branch Callahan was dressed in a nylon running suit sporting the Dallas Cowboys logo. He had white running shoes on his feet and carried his own grandfather's hickory cane in his hand. He leaned heavily upon it as he walked.

Well, that was something new. The last time Matt had seen Branch, he'd used a walker exclusively. Maybe the new physical therapy program his sister-in-law, Maddie, had arranged was doing some good.

"Matthew!" Branch's voice boomed, and a smile blossomed across his craggy, deeply lined face. "You're home, safe and sound. Thank God. I heard you were back in the States, but I didn't know if I'd see you. I'm so glad you're here."

Well, you drove over here, fool. Bowing to the inevitable, Matt turned off the engine and climbed down out of the cab. He met his father beside the mailbox. The yappy dog stood at his feet and continued his squeaking. Because it looked as if his father intended to reach out and hug him, Matt seized on the obvious distraction. "What the hell is that?"

Branch grinned down at the dog. "Matthew, meet Paco. He's the newest resident of Callahan House."

"Paco?"

"Maria named him," Branch replied, referring to one of the Garza sisters, who'd worked for Branch for years. "He's a Pomeranian who's due for a trip to the groomer's."

"So he's Maria's dog," Matt clarified.

"No. He's mine. Having Luke and Maddie's Knucklehead around made me realize how much I missed having a dog. I mentioned it to Maddie, and the last time she talked Luke into visiting, she helped me find Paco. He's good company."

Matt couldn't believe Branch had brought home a dog, especially not a lapdog like this one. The family had always owned golden retrievers, but when the last one, Ralph, died when Matt was seventeen, Branch swore he was done with dogs.

"Why not another golden?"

"Considered it." Branch glanced back toward the

house as if looking for Ralph's ghost. Sighing, he explained, "I wanted a puppy, and I knew I couldn't keep up with a golden. You know how rowdy they are. This one, I can manage." He nudged Paco with the toe of his shoe and made stupid cooing noises. "You won't knock me over, will you, boy?"

The dog wiggled and jumped in circles, gazing up at Branch with total devotion as Branch made more unfortunate gushy sounds. Matt shook his head in disgust. Didn't anyone get *real* dogs anymore? Yet, Branch was obviously besotted with the yappy thing and Matt realized that having a pet probably made the old man feel a little less lonely.

Guilt tried to snake its way into Matt's mind, but he slammed the door against it. Or at least, he tried to. And failed. Dammit, this was why he didn't like to come around the old man's house.

Matt's relationship with his father made his job with the CIA look simple. The trouble started when his mother died and Branch lost himself in grief. Without adult guidance or supervision, but with plenty of money to spend and lots of misery to drown, the Callahan brothers went wild. They lived up to their "Holy Terrors" nickname with wild parties, dangerous drag races, and other general stupidity. What finally did them in was a drunken prank that accidentally set the town's boot factory on fire and cost dozens of people their jobs.

That got Branch's attention. He sent the brothers away, splitting them up geographically and cutting their purse strings. At the time, they thought he'd abandoned them entirely, but in fact, he'd kept a distant eye on them. They'd learned to sink or swim on their own, and the experience, tough as it was, had made a man of each of them.

They all hated their father for what at the time seemed like cruelty, but as they matured, the Callahan men began to mellow. Matt thought they probably would have reconciled if not for the fuckup that cost their youngest brother, John, his life.

With that memory on his mind, Matt's tone was sharp as he snapped, "Can't you shut him up?"

"He's a friendly dog. Hunker down and let him get to know you. That'll calm him down."

Matt stayed where he was. "He doesn't need to get to know me. I won't be here long."

Rather than respond to that, Branch managed to bend down and scoop the dog into his arm. Addressing the animal, he spoke in a calm voice. "This is Matthew, Paco. I've told you all about him. He's the only one of my boys who's moved home to Brazos Bend. We don't get to see him much because he travels a lot protecting our country."

The dog quieted as Matt smothered a sigh. He hadn't moved to Brazos Bend. He kept an apartment in Virginia. Though he could count on both hands the nights he'd spent there in the past three years, it remained his permanent address. If he took the desk job he'd been offered, he'd probably buy a house.

"Come on in, son. It's afternoon snack time. I think the Garzas baked Snickerdoodles."

"It's after five. You're having Snickerdoodles instead of scotch?"

Branch patted the left side of his chest. "It's the ticker. Doc limits me to one drink a day."

So he substituted fat- and calorie-laden cookies for booze? Matt doubted that's what Branch's doctor had in mind.

But that was none of his business, was it?

"I'm not staying. I was in town on an errand—I thought I'd drive by and say hello. I have to get back to the vineyard. Les has a list of chores for me a mile long."

At mention of his partner, Branch's expression went mulish. "I can't believe you let that damned grape farmer run roughshod over you. He wouldn't have anything if not for you."

The anger that bubbled up inside Matt had been aged like fine Bordeaux. "I wouldn't be alive if not for him," he lashed out. "I guess that gives Les one up in my book. Always will. He was there for me when you weren't and don't you forget it because I never will."

His father took it like a fist to the chin. He closed his eyes and cuddled his pet closer, his expression stricken. The tension in the air caused the dog to whimper.

Matt's mouth settled in a grim line. He felt like a heel. "Goddammit. I don't know why I even try to do this. Every time I come here, it's the same shit. I shouldn't come."

"No, you're right." Branch set the dog on the ground, then drew himself up and squared his shoulders. "I fucked up with you boys after your mother died and we all know it. I'm trying to make amends, son, if only you and your brothers will let me."

Amends? That was easier said than done. Way easier. "It isn't as simple as amends, Dad. What you did to us as kids—maybe we needed that. But what happened afterward . . . with Johnny . . ." Matt raked his fingers through his hair. "There's a lot of anger."

Branch Callahan's voice broke as he said with wonder in his tone, "You called me Dad."

Well, crap. Matt was fumbling for something to say when his phone rang. Checking the screen, he recognized Mark's number. Good. "Excuse me, Branch. I have to take this. I'll . . . uh . . . see you later."

He stepped around to the driver's side of his truck and brought the cell phone to his ear. "Whatcha got?"

"More than you probably want to know. Are you somewhere you can talk?"

Matt's gaze flickered toward his father, who had

turned and was shuffling his way up the walk. He looked old, Matt realized. Old and sad with nothing but a purse pet and the Garza sisters to keep him company. Matt swallowed the lump of guilt and regret in his throat and muttered, "You don't want to know where I am."

After a beat, Mark snapped, "Shit. You're at his house, aren't you? You're just a cliché, a glutton for punishment. Don't get caught up in his schemes, bro. He's playing on your sympathies, isn't he? Trying to make you feel sorry for him. Trying to worm his way back into your life. He's been halfway successful with Luke. Don't you dare let him do the same thing to you."

"He's bought a lapdog, Mark. A lapdog! He's an old man with a bad hip, a cane, and a purse pet. I can't help but think that one of these days he's going to drop dead and . . ."

"And what? None of us will be there to cry over his corpse? Serves him right, the old bastard."

Matt shut his eyes. Frustration made his voice tight. "Let's not talk about Branch. Do you have information for me?"

Mark Callahan paused a moment before laughing softly. Hearing it, Matt knew he wasn't going to like what he heard.

"Your bird hasn't used her credit card since leaving California. However, she did buy a milk shake at the Dairy Princess and she asked Kathy to recommend a good place to stay."

Matt closed his eyes. "A place to stay?"

"She's checked into Cottonwood Cottage Bed and Breakfast. She's rented a room for a week."

"You lie."

"I called Kathy Hudson to get an accurate view of what was happening in Brazos Bend."

Kathy Hudson, the owner of the Dairy Princess, was

the pulse of Brazos Bend. If Kathy said it, it was true. Torie Bradshaw was still in town.

Matt dropped his chin and banged his head on the steering wheel. Maybe he should have defected to the Russians when they asked.

Chapter Six

Torie stood at the second-floor bedroom window and gazed with delight at the scene taking place along the roadside across from Cottonwood Cottage B and B. On this beautiful spring evening with the sky painted with streaks of vermilion and gold, three couples had plunked their young children and toddlers into the ocean of blooming bluebonnets to pose for photographs. Her artist's eye framed the shots she'd take, and driven by an urge to escape into innocence, she grabbed both her camera bag and her dog and headed downstairs.

"Ms. Bradshaw?" the B and B's manager called out. "I'm sorry, but I forgot to return your driver's license when you checked in." Giving a little laugh, she added, "All that cash distracted me. I can't recall the last time a guest paid their bill in cash."

"No problem." Torie pocketed the license, then explained with a smile, "I'm weaning myself off credit cards. I learned they can be evil things."

It was the same excuse she'd used as she traveled across the country. She'd made it a point to stay at independently owned bed-and-breakfasts. They all asked to see identification at check-in, but she'd decided the risk of using her own name was minimal, since it wouldn't go in any database. Besides, she'd signed everything "Vicky Bradshaw"—a name she'd never used in her life.

It was a decent compromise, she decided, and since she'd had no false identity documents lying around, she hadn't exactly had a choice.

Outside, she captured some great candid shots of Mom and Dad trying to pose their squiggling kids. After deflecting some suspicious stares by focusing on Gigi as a model—the sweet pea was such a ham—she got the shots she wanted when a towheaded toddler decided playing with a puppy was more fun than sitting still.

The boy's parents introduced themselves as Janice and David Williams. Torie responded, naming herself Vicky Bradshaw. "Ryan is our first," the young mother told Torie. "My plan is to take a bluebonnet picture every year until he graduates high school. I want a collage that's a little different from the usual school pictures."

"That's a great idea." Torie grinned at the playful boy and tail-wagging dog, grateful that Gigi was tolerant of children. When the boy dropped down on his diapered behind and Gigi climbed into his lap and laved his giggling face with her own brand of kisses, Torie shifted into professional mode, excited by what she was seeing in her camera lens.

"You look like you know your way around that fancy camera," David Williams observed.

Torie lowered her Hasselblad. "I'm a professional photographer."

"Oh? Jim Barker has added help at his studio?"

From that, Torie gathered that Jim Barker had the only studio in town. "No, I'm just visiting in the area. I work freelance."

"That's interesting." Janice's eyes lit with curiosity. "How does it work? Are you hired to take certain sorts of pictures or is it the other way around? You take pictures and then you sell them?"

"It's usually a combination of both," Torie explained. "Even when I'm on assignment, I'll take photos that interest me. I have a list of regulars who often buy my stuff. In fact, I know of a travel magazine that would probably take one of these of your Ryan. Would you be willing to sign a release?"

"You mean, to get Ryan's picture in a magazine?" his mother asked.

"What would it cost us?" his father added with a frown.

"Nothing." Torie smiled her reassurance. "I'll give you copies of the photos, of course."

Janice Williams's eyes sparkled with excitement. "Our Ryan in a magazine? How exciting! We'll be happy to sign a release."

While Torie pulled the form from her bag, Janice peppered her with more questions. Torie basked in the woman's admiration. It felt good to be appreciated for a change. Only when the woman asked what brought her to Brazos Bend did Torie hesitate.

She certainly couldn't announce that she was hiding from a stalker. This was a small town. She'd already been asked the question twice. She'd faded it with the Dairy Princess woman and the manager at the B and B, but now she obviously needed some kind of cover for her time in Brazos Bend.

"It's the bluebonnets," she said, seizing on the first possibility that popped into her mind. "I'm putting together a coffee-table book of springtime in the Texas Hill Country."

That's all it took. The Williamses suggested so many places for her to shoot that Torie actually began warming to the idea of a book.

David Williams read over the release and while he asked her a few questions about it, Janice shared her good news about Ryan's magazine debut with one of the other couples. That mother made a beeline to Torie, saying, "Would you take my Amy's picture, too, please? Not for a magazine or anything. Just for me? I'll be happy to pay you. I need a photo to include in our Christmas cards next year, and I want one that shows just how beautiful Texas can be."

She gestured toward the glorious sunset above the wildflower-blanketed field and added, "How people who are still buried in snowfall this time of year can climb on their snotty high horse about Texas being an ugly place is beyond me."

When Torie agreed, the third mother repeated the request and before Torie quite knew what was happening, Janice Williams got on her cell phone, and Torie found herself booked for half a dozen sittings the following morning and another five that afternoon. Three of the eleven requested Gigi's participation, also. Torie wondered if she'd have any trouble finding a darkroom in town to use.

It was dusk when she waved good-bye to her new friends. Torie decided the best thing about the blue-bonnet interlude was that she spent a good forty-five minutes not thinking about either her stalker or Matt Callahan. She'd met six very nice people and played with four delightful little kids. The respite was welcome and relaxing and exactly what she needed.

Unfortunately, it ended when a dark blue pickup came tearing down the road. Brakes squealed; the truck shuddered to a stop. Matt Callahan climbed from the cab with frustration simmering in his eyes.

"At least this enemy I can see," she told Gigi, who, having concluded her exploration of the bluebonnet field, trotted up to Torie and let out a demanding whimper. Torie scooped her baby up into her arms.

Gigi growled at Matt when he approached. He bared his teeth right back.

"You are a pain in the ass, lady," he said by way of greeting.

He looked tense and bedeviled with his temper on a slow boil, but in his presence, Torie felt that last lingering bit of tension roll off of her. She wanted to smile. She wanted to melt against him, to be held tightly in the strong, safe haven of his arms.

How foolish was that?

"What the hell do you think you are doing?" he demanded.

She glanced around and shrugged. "Walking my dog."

"You can't do this."

"Leash laws, huh?"

He smiled coldly. "You can't stay here. This is *my* town."

"Hmm. So we've, what, shifted from *Goldfinger* to *High Noon*?"

"Whatever it takes, sweetheart." He braced his hands on his hips. "I could make this place unsafe for you with a phone call."

"What do you mean?"

When he smiled, Torie shivered with apprehension. "This story of yours is quite compelling. The tabloids write about what Jack and Julie had for lunch. A story about their former dog's life being endangered would make the front page of *The National Enquirer*. Hell, I'll bet it'd even make *People*."

His nerve took her breath away. "You'd use a poor defenseless puppy that way?"

"There is nothing defenseless about that dog."

Torie set Gigi on the ground and muttered, "Bite him, girl."

"Christ," he muttered, taking a step away and keeping a wary eye on Torie's pet.

"This is ridiculous. Listen, Callahan, Brazos Bend is big enough for both of us. I promise I won't get anywhere near you with or without a gun. You have no reason to feel threatened by me."

"I'm not threatened by you," he scoffed.

She quirked a doubtful brow. "Uh-huh."

"You complicate things, and the last thing I need right now are more complications."

"Now, that's not fair. You're the one complicating matters here. All I did was check quietly into a B and B. You're the one who came racing over here all but frothing at the mouth. I have to say, Callahan, you're acting more like a rabid Lassie than 007."

"Would you stop with the stupid Bond business? God, I hate that." He raked his fingers through his hair. "I need an aspirin. Hell, I need a shot of whiskey."

"You need something, that's for sure." Like a good lay. That'd get rid of some tension. Torie sniffed and lifted her chin. "You're not acting rationally."

He gaped at her. "This from the woman who shot up my truck?"

Ignoring that, she continued. "I thought secret agents were supposed to be calm, cool, and collected. Smart. Blackmail isn't smart, Callahan."

A muscle ticked in his jaw. *Whoa. Struck a nerve there.* Almost a minute dragged by before he let out a long sigh and spoke again. "What are you doing here, Victoria?"

"I really don't have to explain myself to you, but out of courtesy, I will. It's rather simple. Someone is after me. I don't want them to find me. Brazos Bend is a good place to hide until I can figure out what to do next."

Matt lifted his stare from Gigi and met her gaze. "Look, Victoria, after you left, I made some calls."

"So?"

"I confirmed that you told me the truth."

"I see." He wouldn't take her word. He'd had to confirm it independently. Typical.

After a moment's hesitation, he nodded. "I don't blame you for wanting protection."

Hope flickered. "So you'll—"

"No. But I know someone in Dallas who might be interested in the job."

"Why won't you help me?"

"I don't want to."

So much for him being one of the good guys. He really didn't like her, did he? Disappointment washed through her. Because he'd gone to the trouble to track her down at Cottonwood Cottage, she'd thought he'd changed his mind and would help her. Instead all he really wanted was to get rid of her.

No wonder he and her father were friends. They thought just alike.

Matt reached into a pocket and pulled out a small notebook. He jotted down a phone number. "He's a bodyguard for a financier who regularly travels to Mexico. He has free time now because his boss is on vacation and—"

Sure, pawn me off on someone else.

"No, thank you," Torie interrupted. "I'm sure he's probably a very nice guy, but I once dated a body-guard and I swore I'd never get involved with a man like that again."

He rolled his eyes. "I'm suggesting you hire him, not sleep with him."

"I don't like bodyguards. Between Bruno and the ones I've run into on my job, I've had nothing but bad experiences with them."

Matt stared at her as if she were an unknown bug under a microscope. "You dated a bodyguard named Bruno?"

"He was Swiss. The accent did it for me." Torie shrugged off the memory. "Having a bodyguard around all the time would make me as nervous as having a stalker on my tail."

"That's a stupid reason for putting yourself in danger."

He did have a point. By refusing the guard, she was

letting her stubborn get in the way of her smart. *Dumb, Bradshaw. Dumb.*

All right, she'd give his friend a call and ask him to meet her here in Brazos Bend. Torie opened her mouth to tell him, but Matt Callahan was on a roll and she couldn't get a word in edgewise.

"Look, Victoria," he said. "You need to rethink your entire plan. Small towns are notoriously bad places to hide. Everyone knows everyone here, so newcomers invariably create a stir. The gossips love nothing more than fresh meat and you'll be fresher than most. You'll be the talk of Brazos Bend by morning."

Okay, fine. Maybe he had *another* point. Maybe she would be safer in the anonymity of a big city. But she wasn't ready to throw in the towel. Not yet. "So they talk. Who will they talk to? Are there other members of the paparazzi in town? No one here knows me. Besides, who's going to connect Vicky Bradshaw, which is the name I've used here, with Torie Bradshaw?"

"Maybe nobody, but can you afford to take the chance?"

She thought it through another minute, then sighed and whined just a little. "I like it here."

"Come back and visit another time. For now, you need to hide yourself in a big city, preferably with a bodyguard to watch your back, while a professional investigates these incidents. I can give you names of good investigators, too."

She folded her arms and sighed heavily. "All right. You win, Callahan. You can have your town back. I'll leave first thing in the . . . no, wait. I can't go tomorrow. I'm booked the entire day."

"Booked?" His blue eyes narrowed. "What do you mean, booked?"

"Photo shoots. Bluebonnets and babies." She told him about meeting the Williamses and the snowball effect of agreeing to that first sitting.

"You've got some nutcase stalking you and you booked an entire day with little kids? Are you insane?" His lip curled in a sneer. "That's great. Just great. Dammit, Torie, don't you ever think about the consequences of your actions?"

Oh, jeez. She fell back a step, taking it as a blow. She hadn't connected the children and her stalker. She'd felt safe in Brazos Bend. Dammit, Callahan was right, one more time. This was getting really old. "I wasn't thinking about the stalker."

"Obviously."

His scathing tone raised both defensiveness and temper. "You know what? I'm tired of being the bad guy here." She advanced on him now, her back straight, her chin up. "I'm sorry that I shot you, okay? I'm sorry that I shot your truck. Good God, I'm sorry I freaking exist! But I'm not sorry about wanting to enjoy a few hours out in the sun with smiling babies and their parents. I don't get that kind of gig very often, Callahan. I just wanted to forget about my troubles for a few hours. I didn't think about endangering the kids. You're right. I'll call and cancel the sittings, and then I'll leave town. So you can just get happy. Your mission is accomplished."

She turned to storm away, but he reached out and grabbed her. "Wait a minute. Just who are you supposed to take pictures of?"

"I told you. Children."

"Which children?"

Torie glared down at his hand holding her arm just above the elbow. When he released her, she slipped her notebook from her camera bag and read the first name.

Matt immediately groaned. "Janice teaches kindergarten and Sunday school and she's a blabbermouth. You'll have every rug rat in town lined up here tomorrow. Way to keep a low profile, Shutterbug."

Torie scratched Gigi behind the ears and frowned at

Matt. "I already said I'd cancel. It's too bad because everyone was so excited and besides, I keep my word."

"Yeah, right."

Jerk. "Tell me the truth, Callahan. How much a risk would it be for me to hang around another day?"

After a moment's hesitation, he asked, "Who else are you supposed to photograph?"

She continued her list. After the second one, he groaned again. After the fifth one he muttered a curse. After the eighth name he threw out his hands. "That's it. Martine Rodriguez is Juanita Garza's godchild. She'd never make me Snickerdoodles again if I chased you out of town. Stay and take the pictures, Victoria. You'll be safe here that long."

"Are you sure? I don't want to be stupid about this."

"I'll guard the kids while you do your thing."

She studied him. She didn't see any sign of hesitation or misgiving on his part. Matt Callahan wouldn't put children at risk, so it would be okay for her to stay. "All right, then. I'll leave here the day after tomorrow."

"Good." He nodded decisively, then shoved his hands in his pockets. "Where will you go?"

"I don't know. I haven't exactly had time to figure everything out, but I don't need to be anywhere in particular until the Cannes Film Festival in a few weeks."

"Will you consider the bodyguard? If my guy in Dallas doesn't do it for you, I know a woman who worked for the governor. . . ."

"I'll think about it."

"And the private investigator?"

"That, too."

"Good." Matt rocked back on his heels. "That's good."

"Well, then." She extended her arm for a handshake. "Good-bye."

He stared at her coral-colored nail polish a long minute. "I'll check on you tomorrow."

"Thank you." Finally, she reached for his hand and shook it. "Good night."

He didn't let her go. He kept his gaze fixed on their joined hands and the air between them swelled and sizzled with tension. What was he thinking? Was he going to kiss her? She could live with that. One for the road, so to speak.

She swayed toward him. Licked her lips.

"Damn me for a fool," Matt Callahan muttered as he swooped in and took possession of her mouth.

It was the kind of kiss that women fantasize about. Hard and hungry. Devouring. There was nothing of the suave, sophisticated spy in the pressure of his lips, the thrust of his tongue. This was a man at his most basic, a strong man compelled by desire too powerful to resist. Desire for her. *Her!*

It was the headiest moment of her life.

His arms dragged her to him and she melted against his hard, muscular length. He tasted of spearmint and smelled of Polo aftershave and a hint of motor oil. When his hands started to move, his fingers stroking up and down her back, drifting down to cup her buttocks and clutch her against him, she thought she might dissolve to a puddle at his feet. The hardness pressing against her belly made her deliciously wet and achy.

He made a growling sound low in his throat that cut off abruptly when a horn honked and a carload of teenage boys blew by, calling out, "Get a room!"

Matt tore his mouth away from hers. "Good idea. Yours is closest."

He released her, taking a step back, and they stared at each other, both of them breathing heavily. Her knees weak, Torie grabbed for something . . . anything . . . to hold on to. She came within a hair-breadth of snapping the antenna off his truck.

"Come on." He grabbed her hand and started pulling her toward the B and B. Her wits scattered, and aroused to the point of pain, Torie went along blindly until she banged her sandal-clad toes on a rock hidden by the ankle-high grass. The pain shocked her from her sexual stupor and she planted her feet. "Wait a minute. Just wait one minute."

"Let's not." He gave her hand a tug. "Let's hurry."

She tugged back. "I'm not sure that's a good idea."

"Sure it is."

"I need to think about this."

"No, you don't. Thinking is a bad idea. I've been trying to do that all day, but I'm ready to give it up. Let's both just go with feeling, and in twenty minutes we'll feel a whole lot better."

"Twenty minutes? That's all?" Good God, they might as well be married.

"Judging by that kiss, I doubt we'll last that long."

Torie yanked her arm hard, pulling her hand from his grasp. "Well, if I'm going to do this, I want longer than twenty minutes."

"Fine. Do you have condoms?"

Torie blinked. "Uh . . ."

"I only have one with me. If you want more than twenty minutes, we'll need more than one."

"I don't carry them with me." What kind of woman did he take her for?

"Well, that's stupid. Having unprotected sex in this day and age is—"

"I don't have unprotected sex! I don't have sex at all. I haven't had sex since the island!"

Matt Callahan froze. "What did you say?"

"You heard me."

Obviously stunned, he gaped at her. "We didn't have sex on the island."

"Tell me about it."

"Did you have sex with someone else on the island?"

"No. I had sex with someone else before I went to the island, but not since I came back."

"Why?"

"Because I'm picky, that's why! Which makes what I'm doing right now completely beyond belief. You might be sexy as sin, but you hate me. I don't make a habit of lusting after men who despise the ground I walk on."

"Look, I don't hate you."

"But you don't respect me."

"Maybe not, but I dream about you, Victoria. Why do you think I tried so hard to get you to leave? You threaten me. I dream of you at least once a month. All right, twice. Then I think about those dreams during the daytime. I'm haunted by you. I want you, okay? Bad. That should make you feel good."

Well, yes. That *was* a boost for her feminine ego. But still . . . "It makes me feel cheap."

"Cheap! Lady, you're the most expensive piece of"—he checked his words when she shot him a glare—"work I've ever run across. Do you want to know how much my hospital bill was?"

She sniffed. "I offered to pay."

"I don't want your money." His voice dropped and he trailed a finger down her arm, both his words and touch bringing a shudder to her skin as he softly declared, "God help me, I want *you.* Beneath me. On top of me. Every way I can have you. Now."

Oh my God.

Heat rushed through Torie and it took every ounce of strength she could muster not to throw herself into his arms in wild, wanton abandon. But dammit, he might not respect her, but she respected herself. She wasn't going to fall into bed with a man just because kissing him curled her toes. "We haven't even had a date."

"I'll take you to dinner." He stepped forward, bent, and kissed her neck. "Afterwards."

It was tempting—he was tempting—but she did have her pride. "I don't sleep with men on our first date."

"Then consider this our second. The first was on the island." He nibbled her earlobe, then said, "Let's go upstairs, Victoria."

She wavered. It had been an awfully long time. She licked her lips, swallowed hard, then startled when she felt the stroke of a canine tongue against her ankle. Gigi. She'd forgotten all about her. And the promise she'd made to Janice Williams.

"I can't go upstairs. I have to go to the groomer."

"I don't care if your legs are shaved or not."

Gee, thanks. "Janice Williams made an appointment for Gigi at her pet groomer for me, since so many of the parents wanted shots with her with their children tomorrow. The shop is staying open late to accommodate Gigi, so I have to go."

Matt grimaced and released her, letting out a long sigh. "Right now, dogs have taken a big fall on my list of favorite animals. All right, Victoria. You have a safe trip to . . . wherever."

He turned around and walked away.

Torie's heart sank as she cuddled Gigi close and watched him leave. He was leaving, just like that? They'd been minutes away from naked and he turned off his turn-on like a light switch?

Jeez, he really was James Bond.

She sighed and whined at Gigi. "Sweetie, couldn't you have found a rabbit to chase instead of my ankle to lick?"

As Matt Callahan opened the door to his truck and climbed into the cab, Torie tried to tell herself that this was for the best. It wasn't in her character to fall into bed with a man because of a kiss—even a world-class kiss like Matt Callahan's. If they'd gone to bed, she'd probably have regretted it in the morning.

But at least you'd have had an orgasm. Maybe even multiples.

Their gazes met and held for a long moment. Then he smiled crookedly and she sighed with real regret.

He started the truck, put the engine into gear, and made a U-turn on the road in front of Cottonwood Cottage. "Good-bye, Double-Oh-Yeah."

She tried to pretend that the whimper came from Gigi rather than herself.

Then, to her shock and surprise, the brake lights on the pickup lit up. He stopped in the middle of the road and left his truck running when he flung open the door and marched in her direction. Torie's heart climbed to her throat and everything feminine within her clutched tight.

"We can drop the dog at the groomer, then make a quick stop by the drugstore. Just so we're clear on this, Victoria, this compromise of mine only goes so far. One time will not be enough for me."

"Really?"

"Yeah. I intend to buy the big box of rubbers. I want the whole freakin' night."

Her smile bloomed like the bluebonnets. Multiples! Thank God.

Chapter Seven

Over the years, in places all over the world, Matt had learned to trust his instincts. Whenever he faced a decision with no clear-cut answer, he invariably went with his gut. Usually, it worked out well, but then, seldom were his instincts at war with themselves like they were right now. His gut was telling him to run like hell.

A more primitive urge pulsed louder.

As he climbed back behind the wheel, he admitted that some instincts were simply stronger than others. He, apparently, had surrendered to it.

As Torie buckled her seat belt, he reached for the CD case he'd rescued from his own truck. Moments later, pulsating hard-rock mood music filled the cab. "So, where we taking the mutt?"

As the Stones rolled off a drum riff, Torie reached over and turned down the stereo. "A place called Kountry Klippers. Do you know it?"

"Yeah. We'll be there in five."

They dropped the dog off at the groomer, and while Torie cooed and cuddled her good-byes, Matt made arrangements for the groomer to board Gigi overnight. Now that he'd decided which body part to listen to, damned if he'd let the four-legged puff ball interfere.

Next Matt made a quick call to Les to check the readiness of the lake house adjoining his property, making sure he'd have the privacy and other necessities he'd need for tonight. Les confirmed that the babe parade still didn't know he owned the house, thank goodness. There were steaks in the fridge and wine in the cellar and locks on the doors. Now all they had to do was get there. When Torie finally tore herself away from her dog and joined him, Matt was pacing the parking lot.

"I'm sorry, Matt. This is the first time I've allowed Gigi out of my sight since the oven incident and it's difficult to leave her. Maybe it'd be better if we went and had dinner while she's being groomed. Then we could pick her back up on our way to . . . well, wherever you're taking me."

"No." It was all Matt could do not to scoop her up and throw her over his shoulder, then into the truck.

"But—"

"Gigi will be fine. I want to take you to bed, Victoria. Immediately."

"You want a one-night stand, which is—"

"Standing. Lying. Sitting."

"Oh, wow. Listen, Matt, that's irresponsible enough as it is, but to leave my dog—"

"Swimming. Have you ever made love in a lake, Victoria?"

She reached for the truck to steady herself. "Water sex? Oh, talk about fantasy."

"You can talk. I prefer to act."

"Oh wow oh wow." As his grin slowly dawned, she insisted, "I'm not easy, Callahan."

"You're telling me." His tone was dry as he backed her toward his truck.

"I have my pride. But thinking about you naked and wet . . ."

He growled low in his throat.

"Pride?" she muttered, then grumbled almost to

herself, "Pride? Who am I kidding? At this point, I'm about ready to lay down in the parking lot for you." She gave her head a disbelieving shake and added, "You might not believe it, but the fact that I even considered this . . . this . . . interlude . . . is out of character for me."

"Interlude is a nice word." His gaze focused on the creamy length of her neck. He wanted to bite it.

He took another step forward and backed her against his truck. Heat from its sunbaked metal wafted from its surface. He pressed his hot body against her front. He wondered which she thought was hotter.

"I figure it's the stress," she babbled as he leaned his head down and nibbled at that swanlike neck. "I wanted a time-out. An escape. A fantasy."

"We'll check my father's attic." Holding on to his control by a thread, Matt opened the passenger-side door. "I think one of my brothers stole a French maid's costume and stashed it—"

"Not that kind of fantasy. It's like I said before. Candlelight and soft music—not a quickie in an F-150, Callahan. I want to wake up in your arms, not on your console."

His hands grasped her waist and lifted her. "You want seduction."

"I want romance."

"I can do romance." He set her in her seat, then grabbed a handful of her shirt at her breasts and pulled her toward him. This kiss was a slow, wet exploration designed to so distract her senses that she didn't notice him loosening her shirt buttons until his hand slipped inside her bra and cupped her bare breast.

His rough palm spread over her soft, silky skin, cupping her, measuring her weight. He teased her nipple with his thumb and when she gasped against his mouth, he almost lost it.

A few minutes—or maybe hours—later, he ended

the kiss, removed his hand, and shut the door. As he walked around to the driver's-side door, he saw her looking into her visor mirror, fanning her rosy cheeks. Climbing into the cab, he heard her mutter, "Face it, Bradshaw. You are, too, easy."

"Thank God."

They left the town of Brazos Bend on the main highway headed south. Matt concentrated on his driving for a time, effectively banking the heat between them. When he turned off the highway onto a two-lane farm-to-market road just about ten minutes from his lake place, he started in again. "What about fine red wine and dark chocolate?"

"What?"

"Do you find red wine and dark chocolate romantic?"

"Yes." She drew in a shuddering breath. "Definitely."

"Jazz or classical guitar?"

"I'm a John Coltrane fan."

He tuned his satellite radio and the sultry sounds of a saxophone soon floated through the cab. "How about a starry sky and a full moon? Are those romantic?"

She glanced out the window to the star-studded sky above.

"Definitely."

In a whiskey-smooth voice, he asked, "What about a man who wants you beyond reason?"

"Oh, God."

"Ah, now, Victoria." He winked at her. "You can call me Matt."

Demon. Devil. Temptation driving a truck.

Torie's thoughts spun as she watched his fingers beat a steady tempo on the steering wheel. Danger . . . danger . . . danger, it seemed to warn. Yet, he made her feel safe. And hot. And wet.

Man oh man. I'm losing it.

Hell, she'd lost it back in the parking lot.

What was she doing? Thirty minutes ago, she wouldn't have let him touch her on a bet. Now she thought if he didn't touch her soon, she might explode.

She needed this. The escape from the fear of the past few weeks. The fantasy that had haunted her since the island. She wanted to explode. She wanted to erupt in the so-long-ago-she'd-almost-forgotten-it pleasure of an orgasm, and to have this man for one night with no regrets.

Torie sat back in her seat, closed her eyes, and asked herself if she was emotionally prepared to give herself under these circumstances. If she could pull it off without suffering regrets. "You don't even like me. I'm the Evil Twin."

"I've always been pulled toward the dark side."

"But—"

"Listen, Shutterbug, I don't know why it is, but you and I have enough chemistry between us to stock a research lab. I'm done fighting it. I suggest you do the same. I'll give you the romance you want. I'll make your body sing. Let that be enough."

Torie drummed her fingers against her thigh. "Sing?"

"Like Kate Smith."

"Kate Smith?" Torie frowned. "Does that visual really work for you?"

A faint smile played across his mouth. "The only visual I have room for in my mind is the one of you in that scrap of a swimsuit on Soledad Island. You're so damned beautiful. A fantasy. My fantasy."

Okay. That, she liked. The girl in her couldn't help but be flattered.

The woman in her recalled her own vision—the one of Matt Callahan naked in the cave. Agent Yummy Buns.

All right. You win. "So, you mentioned something about a date?"

"I was thinking of a moonlight cruise. I keep a couple of runabouts at my lake cabin and the weather tonight is perfect. We'll need to wait an hour or so before the moon comes up, but I figure we can find a way to pass the time."

A moonlight cruise with Matt Callahan. Yeah, that could be romantic. "We could eat supper."

He chuckled. "I have steaks in the fridge. I'll cook for you if you'd like. After."

"After?"

"Sex. We're almost to the house, Victoria. I can't wait any longer to have you."

Whoa. She didn't know what to say after that, so she sat back and shut up and tried to remember how to breathe.

The truck's headlights cut through the darkness and illuminated an armadillo swaggering across the pavement. Torie cleared her throat. "Beefsteak, right? No weird meats?"

He chuckled. "Honey, you're welcome to sample any meat I have."

"I was talking about armadillo."

"I wasn't."

No, she hadn't figured he was.

He turned off onto a narrow dirt road and stopped in front of an aluminum gate. She focused on his steady breathing, trying to calm her own. After fishing a key from the console, he said, "We're here."

As Matt climbed out of the truck to unlock the gate, Torie's gaze lingered on the seat of his pants. He bent over to fit the key in the lock of the chain securing the gate shut, and she decided he was right about the chemistry. Pheromones must be as plentiful as oxygen molecules in the truck cab.

He pushed the gate open, then turned. Their gazes met and held, his blue eyes glowing like a cat's eyes in the night, the heat in them setting her aflame.

With long-legged strides, he marched back to the truck and climbed in, never breaking eye contact. He reached across the console and hauled her against him, his mouth swooping down to kiss her hard.

Torie sighed into his mouth as his fingers delved into her hair. His tongue plunged and plundered. He tasted of spearmint and need and when Torie closed her mouth around his tongue and sucked it, he growled low in his throat.

His hands slipped to her shoulders. His fingers gripped her tight. He broke off the kiss roughly. "Jesus."

Amen.

His jaw was set, the angles on his face as sharp as she'd ever seen them. The heat and intensity of his gaze held her spellbound.

He set her back into her seat, put the truck in gear, and spun his tires in the dry dirt. The pickup flew down the road, bouncing on potholes and ruts. She hoped he didn't damage his truck. She'd hate to be responsible for two such incidents in one day.

Wow. Was it only this morning that she'd pegged his truck? This had been an exceptionally long day.

She wondered how long her night would last.

The pickup's headlights illuminated a two-story house made of Austin stone dead ahead of them. She saw a fully equipped outdoor kitchen on the right and a three-car garage on the left. "Is *that* your place?"

"Yeah," he said with a distinct sigh of relief.

"That's no cabin."

"Sure it is. In this part of the world if a house is on the lake, it's a cabin. It's like I told you before, Brazos Bend isn't like other places."

He pulled into the driveway and shut off the engine. By the time Torie got her purse gathered up and her door open, he was waiting. Before she could breathe, his mouth was on hers, his hand threading through the hair at the base of her neck. Holy macaroni, this man knew how to kiss. Did they teach this art in spy school or something?

He put his hands around her waist and lifted her, sliding her down against his hard body until her feet touched the ground. He backed her against the truck, his body trapping hers in place as once again, he kissed her thoroughly, his mouth hot and borderline vicious. Primal, and shockingly intense.

It was thrilling. He was thrilling. Her arms circled him, her fingers diving into his hair. His urgency was a total turn-on, filling her with a sense of power and potency. Considering she'd spent the last few days feeling afraid and helpless, it was a welcome change.

Releasing her long enough to reach into the cab for the plastic sack from the drugstore, Matt slammed the passenger door and grabbed her hand, tugging her toward the house. Torie's heart pounded. Her blood hummed. She recognized that she'd probably regret this in the morning, but for now, she'd simply enjoy it. Enjoy him.

Motion-detector lights flickered on as they approached the oak front door. Matt had his key out and ready, and within seconds, they were inside. He didn't bother to turn on the lights, but led her straight to the staircase.

Torie, feeling rather wicked, had the notion to tease. Dragging her feet, she said, "I don't know, Callahan. Maybe we shouldn't rush into anything."

He whirled on her, his mouth gaping. "Rush, hell! We've been working our way here since the island."

"But don't you think—"

"No. Thinking's not allowed. Tonight is all about feeling." He scooped her up into his arms and carried her up the stairs. James Bond as Rhett Butler. It was, Torie thought, the most romantic moment of her life.

Inside the master bedroom, light from the rising full moon beamed through the wall of windows overlooking the lake. Torie caught only a glimpse of her surroundings—huge room, stone fireplace, heavy furniture—before Matt Callahan tumbled her onto a huge bed. She smelled sunshine in the bedding and felt the feather bed beneath cradle her softly. He knelt on one knee beside her, reached over her, and switched on a bedside lamp. Soft, golden light filled the room, and Torie's attention was captured by the glitter of desire glowing in Matt Callahan's eyes. "I want to see you," he murmured, his impatient hands tugging her shirt from her shorts.

Torie's innate modesty compelled her to say, "You, I don't mind, but the neighbors . . . I'm not into that sort of thing."

"There are no neighbors." His fingers found her bare skin and stroked across her belly. "This is an isolated part of the lake. We're the only two people around for miles."

Yeah. That's what James said in *Goldeneye* just before all the marines popped up from the grass.

Before she could form a protest, he straddled her and ripped at her shirt and she forgot the argument. She was alone in the middle of nowhere with a dangerous man riding the edge of violence. If she had any sense, she'd feel at least a little bit frightened.

She didn't. She reveled in the fierceness of his reaction to her, and she arched her back when he released the center clasp of her demi-cup bra and closed his hands over her naked breasts. His hands kneaded her; his thumbs flicked across her hardened nipples. "So beautiful, silky," he murmured as he lowered his head and took her into his mouth.

Oh, God, she'd missed this. Pleasure flared to her very core as she writhed against him, the suction steady and strong and driving her up. His rough tongue stroked across her sensitive nipple. His teeth gently nipped. Torie bit back a whimper and decided she'd had enough. That he'd had control long enough.

She pushed up and rolled on top of him. She strad-dled him, kissed him, tore at his clothes with wild, reckless craving until they both lay naked, Matt be-neath her, tension visible in the sculpted length of his muscles, his arousal jutting temptingly before her.

Torie shuddered with delight. It had been so long since she'd felt this heat. So long since she'd enjoyed a man's body. And she'd never enjoyed a body like Matt Callahan's.

The man was gorgeous. A god. A scarred god with marks on his chest and stomach, and that unfortunate set of lines on his knee, none of which detracted from his sheer physical male beauty. "You are so hot."

"Tell me about it. I think my blood is about to boil."

She gave a half laugh and reached to touch the vel-vety steel of his penis. Matt sucked his breath past his teeth. "You do much of that and this will be over before it starts."

"I thought you were in a hurry."

"To get you naked. To get my hands on you." He flipped her over. "Now that we're to the good part, I like to go slow."

"Oh."

He trailed his index finger along her collarbone. "Tell me where you like to be touched, Victoria."

"I'm not picky."

Amusement curved his lips. "Then let's try this, shall we?"

He dipped his head and trailed open-mouth kisses from the base of her throat to the swell of her breasts. His breath was hot against her skin and she shivered in response. As his hands began a slow, sensual explo-ration of her body, the elemental need for release had her moving, flexing her hips, tossing her head from side to side. Torie wanted . . . wanted. . . .

He licked the underside of her breast, stroked the sensitive skin at the backs of her knees, then, ever so slowly, slid his hand upward toward her heat. Torie trembled and quaked and hissed out a sigh when he finally pressed his palm against her mound and rubbed her. When he slid a finger over her, then into her, her eyes drifted shut.

"None of that," he told her. "Look at me. I want you with me. You're so tight, so hot, so wet. You turn me on, Torie. I want to see your eyes glaze over and hear you scream when I make you come."

She opened her eyes, saw the smug satisfaction in his, and a twinge of annoyance intruded on her enjoyment of the moment. What made him think he got to call all the shots? Matt Callahan was a little too full of himself. This might just be a one-night stand, but her pride demanded it be one he'd remember.

She needed to take back control again.

Later, her inner hussy begged as his hand worked wonders between her thighs, and his mouth made magic at her throat.

Pleasure sizzled along her nerves. *If I don't do it now, there won't be a later.*

Torie sucked in a deep, steadying breath, then reached for his hot, heavy erection.

"Damn, that's good," he said as she ran a finger over his tip, traced his length, teased him with her touch. "Ahh . . . Torie."

Not "Victoria." Power intoxicated like wine. There was something truly enthralling about making a strong man weak. "I want to hear you beg."

He drew back and his fingers momentarily stilled. "That sounds like a challenge, Ms. Bradshaw."

Smiling, she slowly licked her lips. "You up to it, Callahan?"

His gaze locked on her mouth. He flexed his hips, instinctively pushing himself against her hand. "You'll have to show me your best stuff if you want a chance at winning."

"Darlin', my best stuff might kill you."

He laughed, then lowered his head to kiss her, and Matt and Torie went to war. They rolled and grappled and grabbed. She loved running her hands over the firm cords of muscle across his back. She gloried in his earthy male scent and the salty-sweet taste of his skin. When he used his strength against her by shackling her wrists above her head with one hand and torturing her sweetly with the other, she retaliated by whispering into his ear what she wanted to do to him with her mouth. When she sucked on his earlobe, he shuddered.

When she won the opportunity to show him, his groan melded with hers.

He was big and thick and delicious, and Torie's excitement escalated. She had Double-Oh-Yeah at her mercy and she'd never felt more powerful. Or more turned on.

She glanced up. He was tense, trembling, his hands fisting the bedcovers to hang on. He was obviously on the edge, but fighting it, unwilling to give up his control. Which of course made Torie determined to make him lose it, and she devoted herself to her task with extra zeal.

But Matt Callahan wasn't one to surrender easily. When he let out a growl and shoved her away, shoved her back on the bed, and set about returning the sexual favor, she knew she wouldn't last. Wouldn't win.

So lose already, cried her inner hussy.

Need clawed at her. The room began to spin. She clenched her teeth against a scream and rotated her hips in silent encouragement. Her fingers dug into his shoulders, which were slick with sweat.

"Fuck this," he growled, wrenching away, reaching for the drugstore sack.

"No, me!" she all but wailed.

He laughed. "Oh, honey, I will."

He ripped through the package, yanked on the condom. "We both win," he declared as he levered her hips high and plunged into her, driving home with a single hard thrust.

For just a second, he didn't move. He filled her, stretched her. Completed her. "Yes," she breathed in relief, in supplication, as his hips began to piston.

Her nails dug into his back. The vicious tension stretched and strengthened and . . . burst.

Pleasure flowed through her like a warm, hot river and she went limp and motionless until Matt Callahan collapsed on top of her and gasped, "God help me."

At that, Torie Bradshaw smiled.

Chapter Eight

Matt didn't try to speak until he caught his breath. Then, he didn't know what to say.

It was an unusual circumstance, to say the least. Ordinarily, he had après-sex banter down to a suave and sophisticated science. Just like he knew how to charm women into his bed, he knew how to finesse them out of it and send them on down the road.

Tonight, his mind had gone blank. Sex with Victoria Bradshaw had wiped all signs of intelligence from his brain. The one thought he managed to put together was the fact that he wasn't finished with her yet.

Of course, that bit of thinking was being done by his little brain, which appeared to be the only one functioning.

"I have to go," she said, breaking the uncomfortable silence.

"Why?" Lying beside her, he propped himself up on his elbow.

"I . . . well . . . I don't know. It seemed like the thing to say."

The wrong thing. He was certain of that. "You can't go. I owe you a cruise."

"Actually, you owe me supper, too."

Matt arched a brow. "Are you trying to claim you didn't get enough meat?"

"That was cake." Her lips twitched. "Beefcake."

He snorted and rolled from the bed. "Let me see what I can stir up in the kitchen."

Matt took a pair of blue swim trunks from the bureau and pulled them on, then padded downstairs barefoot, flipping on light switches along the way because he expected Torie to dress and follow him. Instead, as he yanked open the refrigerator door, he heard the shower come on in the master bathroom.

"Waste of time, that," he murmured. He had every intention of taking her skinny-dipping at some point during their cruise.

Glad that Les had asked the caretaker to stock the pantry and fridge, Matt set about filling a small cooler with essentials: cheese, fruit, some cold roast beef—the steak would have to wait—a loaf of French bread, that wine he'd promised, and, of course, the chocolate. By the time Torie made her way to the kitchen, he had the cooler and a couple of beach towels in one hand and the keys to his Fountain in the other.

While some men had a thing for cars, for Matt, it was all about boats. He currently owned four of them—a Grady-White he kept on the Texas coast for fishing trips, a Crownline he berthed in DC, and the Formula and Fountain he kept here. Matt had fallen in love with the water as a child and he'd carried that love with him all over the world. He'd dreaded assignments in landlocked countries and reveled in those where he could incorporate boating into his mission. One time he'd even been involved in a boat chase through Venice à la 007. Imagine what Torie would say about that.

He led the way to the boathouse and a short time later, the Fountain slowly cruised from his cove toward the main body of the lake. Torie lay on her back across the aft sundeck staring up at the sky. "It's beautiful here."

"Yeah, it is." Matt smiled, pleased that she could see it. Not everyone did. "It's not slap-you-in-the-face gorgeous like the Swiss Alps or the Amalfi coast. It's a subtle beauty that can sometimes take your breath away. The sunsets here can rival any I've ever seen."

"You love it."

Matt considered that for a moment. "At times, there's not another place on earth I'd rather be."

Yet, at other times—usually those that somehow involved his father—Brazos Bend was the last place on earth he could bear to be.

"Because it's home," Torie said. "Your childhood home. Being a military brat, that's something I've always envied. We never lived any one place long enough for Helen and me to put down roots. For a long time whenever someone asked me where I was from, I stumbled over the answer."

"What answer do you give now?"

She hesitated before murmuring, "Oh, what the heck. I tell people I'm from Clearwater, Iowa."

"Where's that?"

"In my dreams. I made it up. It's the hometown I wish I'd had."

It was another reminder that Matt couldn't trust a word the woman said. Nevertheless, he asked, "Tell me about Clearwater, Iowa."

"It's relatively small, though there are two high schools in town. My parents owned a home in a middle-class neighborhood next to a city park, and Helen and I walked to elementary school. We were in Girl Scouts and played softball and sang in the Christmas pageant. And, of course, we had a dog."

"A little rat dog?"

The white glow from the stern light illuminated her

disdainful scowl. "You leave Gigi out of this. Actually, Prince was a golden retriever."

"Aha. So you *do* prefer real dogs over those little purse pets."

"We had a big yard in Clearwater that could accommodate a larger dog like Prince," she protested.

"Give it up, Bradshaw. You could have had any dog you wanted in your fantasy, and you chose Prince. You wanted a good dog."

She came up on her elbows. "Hey, we had a Pekingese, too, in Clearwater."

"Oh, now, that's just pitiful. You're lying about your fantasy."

"Yeah, well . . ." She plopped back down, lacing her fingers behind her head, a smile playing on her lips. "It's not lying. It's editing. I'm the author of the fantasy. I can rewrite it however I wish. You just like to argue with me."

"That's not true."

"Now who's the liar?"

He grinned and bumped up the speed of the boat.

They cruised for a few minutes without conversation while Matt steered away from shore. Upon reaching the middle of the lake, he cut the engine and joined Torie at the stern. "Tell me something, Victoria. If small-town living is your ideal, why do you live in Hollywood?"

"It's difficult to photograph celebrities in Clearwater, Iowa."

"So why don't you do something else?"

A note of defensiveness entered her voice. "I'm good at what I do. I enjoy it. It pays well. I like the freedom of being my own boss. Few jobs out there are perfect, but this one suits me."

"I wonder." He set out supper on the small round cockpit table, glad that he'd loaded up the cooler. He was hungry. Good sex did that to him.

Come to think of it, he was starving.

He popped a piece of beef into his mouth before pouring the wine. Handing her a glass, he asked, "So how does an army brat get to be a paparazzo?"

"My college roommate was Jenna Wilson and—"

"The country singer? Where did you go to school?"

"Vanderbilt."

"Nashville. Makes sense. Jenna is one hot woman. I'll bet the frat boys wouldn't leave you two alone."

"Do you want to hear my story or not?"

He grinned and popped a grape into his mouth, then tended their position. They'd drifted too close to the rocks.

Torie continued. "Jenna sang for tips in a bar on Music Row on the weekends and I was there taking pictures of her the night Clint Holcomb decided to join her for a duet. At the end of the song, he kissed Jenna. It was all very innocent, but I got a shot of it—for her—and there was a record producer in the audience who saw me take the picture. He's the one who suggested I sell it to the *Enquirer.*"

"I'll bet he's the one who signed Jenna to her first record contract, too."

"The publicity gave her a big boost. It gave us both careers."

"Hmm." Matt tapped the throttle just a bit and the boat picked up speed.

Torie held her hand out to catch the cold spray. "What about you? How did a Brazos Bend boy end up a double-naught spy?"

Glancing back over his shoulder, he drawled, "Watched a lot of *The Beverly Hillbillies* growing up, did you?"

She laughed. "Jethro wasn't very smart, but he sure was pretty to look at. How about you? Was it Jethro envy that brought you to the CIA?"

"I was recruited. I'm good with languages and I was living overseas."

"When did you leave Texas?"

Matt wasn't about to go into that whole ugly story. Torie Bradshaw didn't need to know what a screwup he'd been, so he gave her a partial truth. "College. I never came home after that."

"Until you bought the vineyard."

"I bought a ranch that we're partially converting into a vineyard."

"You must have wanted to come home, though, to buy it."

"No," he denied automatically. "That's not . . ." His voice trailed off when he realized that she might have a point. "I like having a connection to this place."

"It's roots. You have roots here. Brazos Bend is your place, and your roots are real rather than imagined. I envy you that."

Uncomfortable with the turn of the conversation, Matt sipped his wine and attempted to change the subject. "Have you ever considered working in front of the camera rather than behind it?"

"What?" Now she sat up. "You mean act? Me?"

"You certainly have the looks for it, and you do have some acting experience, what with pretending to be your sister." He dodged the cracker she threw at him and added, "Or a reporter. You have that nosy quality that comes in handy for reporters."

"Don't you need to steer the boat or something?"

Since they were back in the center of the lake, he cut the engine. "We're drifting."

"This conversation is drifting into areas I don't like."

"Then how about we stop talking?" He set aside his wine and approached her, brushing his mouth over hers once, twice, before laying claim to her lips in a soft, slow, intoxicating kiss.

He laid her back against the cushioned sundeck. Her hair spilled like a waterfall over the red towel she'd spread there earlier, the golden waves appearing silver white in the moonlight. He saw starlight reflected in her eyes.

"I need to have you again," he told her as he traced the full swell of her breast with his finger. "Let me have you again, Victoria."

His hand slipped beneath her shirt and skimmed across the silk of her bra, teasing her sensitive point. She gasped. "You mentioned something earlier about water sex?"

"You like the idea of that, hmm?"

She shrugged. "I admit to a certain curiosity."

"I was thinking hot-tub sex beneath the stars."

"*A View to a Kill*. Nice, but what about beach sex? Like in—"

"There's no beach around here."

"Bummer," she said on a sigh. "What about here? *Thunderball*, except in the lake rather than the ocean."

"Would you stop with the stupid Bond business? We could have water sex here if you want. It's not impossible. Just more difficult. Besides, it's only April. The water is still cold."

"Oh. I see." She paused, made a show of dropping her gaze, and said, "You're afraid of . . . shrinkage."

It was a clear challenge by a wicked-tongued tease.

Matt couldn't in clear conscience let her get away with it. "No, darlin'. That was just a warning. I didn't want you to be . . ." He swooped in and picked her up. Taking two steps to the edge of the boat, he finished, ". . . surprised."

He tossed her over the side.

She surfaced, squealing. "It's cold!"

He tossed a pair of boat cushions into the water and dived overboard. The cold hit him like a fist. Shrinkage, hell. His balls had drawn up into his belly.

But when his head broke the surface, she was within arm's reach and laughing. The sight and sound chased the chill right out of his body.

He pulled her into his arms and kissed her. As they sank into the water and lust heated his blood, he was reminded of their first kiss in the cenote. He should never have let her out of that cave without having her first.

He was getting in over his head with this woman. Literally and figuratively. And he couldn't seem to find it inside himself to care.

Torie pumped her legs, signaling her need for air, and Matt kicked hard, propelling them to the surface. She drew in a deep breath, then grabbed the cushion floating nearby. She smiled at him and said, "If I'd known then what I know now, I would have had my way with you in that cenote."

"It's frightening how alike we think at times." Treading water, he unbuttoned her shirt and slipped it off her shoulders.

"Don't lose that," she cautioned.

"You don't need it." He tossed it into the boat.

"I will tomorrow."

"Let's forget about tomorrow for now." As one hand worked the button on her shorts, the other slid inside to cup her. His finger slipped into her tight heat. "Hold me, Torie. I'm cold."

"Holy Moses."

They played for a time, teasing and taking it slow, making good use of the wraparound swim platform on the boat. Finally, the mood turned serious and Matt wanted out of the water and into her. He lifted her onto the swim platform, then up onto the sundeck, where she lay shivering from cold. Grabbing a towel, he dried the water from her skin and soon her shivers came from something other than cold.

When she tried to cover herself with the towel, he moved it aside. "Don't. You are the most beautiful woman I've ever seen."

"We're in public."

"We're alone, Torie. All alone." He cupped her

breasts, her skin soft and milky in the moonlight. Unable to resist, he bent his head to taste her.

She moaned softly, shifting instinctively, the natural eroticism in her movements challenging his desire to continue a slow seduction. He sucked and licked and tugged her, murmuring flattering observations interspersed with earthy words. Craving the feel of her skin against his, he lowered himself to her once more.

"Mmm . . . ," he growled low in his throat when her hot skin quivered against him. What was it about this particular woman that gave rise to such tearing, desperate need within him? Why did Torie Bradshaw, of all women, make him burn?

Then, as she wrapped her arms around him, dug her nails into his back, neither questions nor answers mattered any longer. His lips roamed over her silky skin. His hands caressed the spots where he'd learned she liked to be touched. He smelled the arousal on her skin and groaned with pleasure.

He kissed his way across her flat stomach toward his glorious goal. Anticipation clawed at him and he battled back the need to hurry, to rush. He had tonight with her. Just tonight. He'd by God make it last.

"I feel so wicked," she breathed. "Out here like this, naked beneath the stars with the devil himself."

"Demon," he murmured, slipping off the sundeck to kneel on the cushioned bench below. Lifting her legs over his shoulders, he repeated, "I'm Demon."

He tasted her, drank of her hot, sweet nectar, and the demon in him stirred. His blood pounded as her body writhed. His fingers dug into her hips as her hands dragged through his hair. He greedily feasted as she wept out his name, and when he plunged his tongue into her, she softly screamed.

She came, trembling like a tree in a gale.

"Again," Matt demanded. He was frantic now, wild and hungry with lust scorching his blood. He wanted her bucking, shouting, out of control, so he drove her up again with relentless concentration.

"Matt . . . please," she sobbed, hovering on the peak.

"Fall, Torie. Fall."

Instead, contrary woman that she was, Torie fought back. Rearing up, she scooted away, just out of his reach, the challenge in her eyes daring him to come after her. When he did, she launched herself at him, knocking him to his back, and they thrashed and rolled and rocked the boat. Her frenzied mouth streaked over him, her greedy hands tearing off his swim trunks. She reached for him, cupped him, stroked him until he groaned.

When she wrapped her hot lips around him, Matt couldn't stop himself. His head buzzing, he pumped his hips, once, twice, drowning in the wet pleasure of her merciless, most intimate kiss. "You win," he conceded, his breath coming in vicious pants.

He yanked himself away from that heavenly suction and kneed her legs apart. His hands gripped her hips and he lifted her into position. "Wait," she cried, coming up on her elbows. "Safe sex!"

He'd forgotten. He never forgot!

"Don't tell me you forgot them!"

"In the basket." He scrambled off the sundeck.

"Then get one. Hurry!"

He tore into the basket, tossing aside napkins and plastic bags, muttering beneath his breath as he groped for that blessed square of foil. When finally he found it, he let out a cheer of triumph.

Back on the sundeck, Torie Bradshaw laughed. The sound rippled across the water and called to Matt like a siren's song.

"Are you laughing at me, lady?"

"At us, Callahan." She beamed at him. "At us. You know, sex doesn't always have to be a war."

"Ya think?"

"I think you're magnificent and I'm the luckiest lady in Texas right now."

And I'm the luckiest man.

In that moment, he wanted her more than he'd ever wanted another woman. His hand shook as he tore open the packet and smoothed the condom on. He went to her, rose above her, and said, "How about we do this together?"

"Oh, oh, yeah."

As he drove into her she rose to meet him, fitting him like a hot, wet glove. Their gazes met and held as he stroked, slowly, steadily, taking them both up again. Tension built; his pace picked up. The need for release pressed at the base of his spine.

This beautiful woman. This beautiful moonlit night.

Torie cried out, her body contracting around him. Helpless, Matt fell with her into the warm, rushing whirlpool of pleasure.

When he could breathe again, one thought alone existed in his mind. *Good Lord, I'll never forget her.*

Chapter Nine

Torie focused her camera lens and snapped off a half-dozen shots of the towheaded toddler as he played with an indulgent Gigi. She was getting some great shots. The little boy's parents would be thrilled.

This was her next-to-last appointment, and the morning had gone fast. The kids had arrived on time and for the most part performed their job of sitting in the bluebonnets looking adorable without complaint. The weather was gorgeous—the sky blue, the bluebonnets bluer. Torie's heart, however, was the bluest of them all.

She didn't want to leave—not these kind, welcoming people of Brazos Bend, and not their favorite bad boy, Matthew "Demon" Callahan.

She was seriously infatuated with the man. At some point during her mostly sleepless night, she'd declared him aptly named. Demons were supernatural beings with special powers, after all. How else could she explain the things he'd done to her last night? She ached in places that hadn't ached in years, was sore in places that had never been sore before.

How delicious was that?

She glanced across the road to where the man stood guard. He looked every inch the G-man today, she thought, though more Secret Service than CIA. Dressed in dark slacks and a sport jacket—to hide the bulge of a gun—and wearing dark glasses and a fierce expression, he kept close watch on the surroundings, making sure no one posed a threat to Torie or the families who'd arrived for their bluebonnet shots.

Out at his lake house, the morning had gotten off to a shaky start. Tired, cranky—the man didn't own a coffeepot—and a little embarrassed by the way she'd woken up screaming in orgasm during what he called his breakfast surprise, she'd not known how to act around him. Unaccustomed to such awkwardness, she'd covered it with senseless, shallow prattle, which only made her feel even more stupid. Torie wasn't a prattler.

Matt hadn't helped. Mr. Smooth had disappeared at dawn, leaving Mr. Silent-and-Sort-of-Snotty in his wake. He'd refused her request to join him on his morning run, then returned in a short, snippy mood. It had been obvious she'd overstayed her welcome, but what was a girl supposed to do? Hitchhike back to Cottonwood Cottage?

He'd barely spoken to her on the ride into town, the jerk. She didn't know why. She'd made him a happy camper last night, too, by God. He needed to work on his morning-after routine, and that surprised her. Someone with his experience should have that down by now.

Of course, she needed to work on her own morning-after response. She had no more business being blue than he had being snarky. Somehow, though, she'd let him past her defenses. She'd learned better than that years ago. How dumb could she be?

Torie had brooded about it on the drive into town, keeping her own mouth shut. After retrieving Gigi from the groomer, she'd briefly considered just getting in her car and making tracks, but by the time she'd gone up to her room at Cottonwood Cottage and changed her clothes, her first customer had arrived. No way could she resist the two-year-old's big brown eyes.

Once she'd gone to work, she'd been able to forget about Matt. Well, for the most part, anyway. Time spent behind the camera was a pleasure, and the novelty of doing something different and creative a joy. While scoring the money shot of a badly behaving celebrity produced an adrenaline rush that was hard to beat, capturing a toddler's delight when a yellow butterfly landed on his fingertip provided its own high.

She glanced up from her viewfinder to see a black SUV with tinted windows approach the bed-and-breakfast. Matt went on alert, hanging up his cell phone and waving for the driver to stop. Nerves danced in Torie's stomach. Her stalker wouldn't just drive up and say hello, would he?

The driver's-side window slid down, but Matt blocked her view of the person inside. She breathed a little sigh of relief when he stepped back and motioned for the driver to park in front of Cottonwood Cottage.

Maybe it was her next appointment. She checked her notebook. Must be the Hardeman family.

Instead, a man the size of a mountain climbed out of the vehicle. Oh. Her bodyguard. Matt's replacement.

He'd probably leave now.

Her one-night stupendous stand was over, and now she had to start worrying about her stalker again.

Torie's stomach sank. Her mood plummeted. For the first time since yesterday, she felt scared.

Don't be stupid, she told herself. *Look at this man. He's huge. He's probably twice the bodyguard that Matt would be.*

Yeah, but he wouldn't be guarding her body in quite such an intimate way.

Sighing, Torie repositioned herself and sneaked in

a backside shot of Matt as he spoke with the man from Dallas. It couldn't replace the poster he'd stolen, but a clothed butt shot of Matt Callahan was better than no butt shot at all.

Determined to act both professionally and with pride, she dismissed the events in the road and focused her attention on those in the field. Gigi and darling little Travis Nelson were playing tug-of-war over a blue baby blanket. In the next few minutes, she got what she anticipated would be the best photos of the day as Travis achieved victory in battle, and she focused tight on his rosy cheeks and toothy grin.

When she finished up with Travis, she scooped Gigi into her arms and crossed to where the two men stood. Gigi growled at Matt, who frowned back before introducing Torie to Bill Reynolds. "I'm pleased to meet you, ma'am."

He could have been any of the dozens of soldiers under her father's command whom she'd met over the years. He had a military bearing, military formality, even a military haircut. Torie smothered the urge to respond like a bratty teenager and jolt him out of his reserve. Instead, she smiled and offered her hand. "Thank you for taking my case."

His handshake was brief and businesslike. "Glad to be of service, ma'am."

Another "ma'am." Something told her they wouldn't be passing time with small talk. "This is Gigi. The stalker has already threatened her once, and you need to understand that she's family to me. Nothing bad can happen to Gigi."

The bodyguard's gaze flickered down to the dog, then moved impassively back to her. "Very well, ma'am."

Matt rolled his eyes.

Torie pasted on a smile. "Well, then. I have one more appointment; then I'll be ready to go."

"Very good, ma'am."

As she started to turn away, Matt spoke up. "I've hired a private investigator to look into the situation in LA. In the meantime, Reynolds will take you to a safe house in Austin."

She stopped. "Excuse me?"

"It has a darkroom, so you'll be able to work."

"I didn't ask you to hire an investigator," she snapped.

"You agreed you needed one. I'm just helping out."

Torie's emotions were in turmoil. She wanted his help more than anything, but not this way. Since he was sending her away, she needed to *be* away. She needed to put Matt Callahan in the past and take control of her future. This letting her life be dictated by others—be they stalkers or her father or her one-night lover—was for the birds. "It's not your responsibility, Callahan. *I'm* not your responsibility. I'll hire my own private investigator, thank you very much." She whirled on Bill Reynolds. "Do you have a private investigator you can recommend?"

"Yes, ma'am. But—"

"Oh, stop with the *ma'am*s, please. My name is Torie. Who is it? Do you have a phone number? I'll call him right now."

With a glance at Matt, the bodyguard reached into his jacket pocket, and pulled out a half-dozen cards. Shuffling through them, he handed one to Torie, saying, "This guy is the best in the business."

She gave Matt a challenging smile, then glanced down at the card, containing only a name and a phone number. Inwardly, Torie groaned. *Mark Callahan.*

She glanced up at Matt. "Let me guess."

He shrugged. "My brother *is* the best."

"Incoming auto," Reynolds said abruptly, shifting to shield Torie. Matt gave the approaching minivan a hard look. "Who's your next appointment?"

"Sarah Hardeman."

He nodded. "That's a Fain Elementary parking

sticker on the front bumper. This one's okay, Reynolds."

"This is a bullshit way to handle protection," the bodyguard grumbled.

"It's a b.s. way to handle a lot of things," Torie agreed, shooting a fulminating look toward Matt before she turned and walked away.

Torie recognized that she wasn't being completely fair. He'd been up-front with her from the beginning and she'd gone to bed with him last night knowing, and accepting, that last night was all they'd ever have. What she hadn't known going into it was how spectacular the night would be and how depressing she'd find it to be faced with the fact that he could so easily walk away.

She simply wasn't the type for one-night stands.

Not that she was the type for long-term, either. Just ask her father. He'd found it easy enough to send her on her way. She'd learned early on that she wasn't good enough, smart enough, well behaved enough.

Oh, for heaven's sake, Torie. Snap out of it. You're running way too close to pity here.

To cap off her mood, the Hardeman child turned out to be a little monster. That, along with the steady stream of mothers who'd heard about the shoot and wanted their darlings included, which in turn caused Mr. Reynolds to get a peculiar tick in his face, made Torie happy to finish up the sitting, declare her picture taking done, and escape to her room in Cottonwood Cottage. The bed—which she'd never tested—looked inviting and she longed to pull a Goldilocks and lie down.

Instead, she opened her suitcase and began packing. Five minutes later, she tugged the zipper closed, then turned at the sound of a noise from the doorway. Matt Callahan leaned against the doorjamb with his arms crossed.

Torie pasted on a bright, but totally fake, smile. "Well, superspy, I guess this time it's really good-bye."

"Actually, I'm hoping you'll do a favor for me first."

Warily, she asked, "What kind of favor?"

"Would you do one more sitting?"

"Ah, Matt. I've put everything away, and honestly, after that Hardeman boy, I don't think I have it in me to be nice to another kid."

"No kids involved." Appearing pained, he explained further. "It's a dog. Another rat dog. It's . . . oh, hell, Torie."

Torie. Not Victoria. This is interesting.

Matt plowed his fingers through his hair. "Ordinarily, I wouldn't ask, but he's just so . . . goofy . . . about—"

A large, deep voice boomed from downstairs. "Matthew? What's taking so damned long? If you don't hurry up, Paco is gonna roll in the dirt and mess up his outfit before the picture taking."

"—his dog." Matt sighed and hung his head. "It's Branch. Branch Callahan. He's my father."

Torie blinked. "You want me to meet your father? The same father who at the rehab hospital told my sister that if he ever got within arm's length of me, he'd wrap his hands around my throat and choke me dead?"

"Uh . . . yeah. That's him."

"And now he wants me to take a picture of his dog?"

"Well, not exactly."

The expression on Matt's face told Torie to brace herself. "He thinks you're Helen."

Hmm. "And he believes this, why?"

"Well, that's what I told him."

The pang of hurt caught her off guard. "I thought you hated the whole twin-switching-identities thing."

"I do. But he called me a little while ago all but

foaming at the mouth because he'd heard you were in town. He threatened to come over here brandishing a gun. It seemed easier to calm him down by telling him he'd heard wrong, that the Bradshaw who'd come to Brazos Bend was Helen, not you. I just . . . well . . . he walked in on me and Helen one time and ever since . . . well . . . he thinks I have a thing for her."

Everything in Torie went cold. Had her sister lied to her? Had last night been some sort of twin fantasy for Matt? It was bad enough to be a one-night stand, but had she been nothing more than sloppy seconds? "He walked in on you and Helen. Walked in on you doing *what*?"

"It was a kiss. That's all."

That's what Helen had said, but now Torie wasn't so sure. Feeling peeved, the last thing she wanted to do was walk downstairs and pretend to be her sister.

"I've used the name Vicky Bradshaw here. Someone will tell him."

"But you'll be gone by then and I'll have avoided a scene. Look. Do this for me and I'll owe you one. That's a good marker to have in your pocket, Victoria."

He had a point. A girl with a stalker on her tail couldn't exactly turn down markers. "All right, Callahan. It's a deal. Let's just hope that neither one of us regrets it."

The look in her eyes made Matt nervous. But then, he'd been jumpy as a scalded cat all morning long anyway, so this wasn't any different.

Last night hadn't turned out like he'd expected. Going into it, he'd thought he'd have no trouble loving her, then seeing her leave. This morning, his world seemed uncomfortably different, and now his father's presence added one more bump in an already rough road. Wonderful. Just wonderful.

"Don't take anything he says seriously," he warned

her. "Just take the photo as quickly as you can and
stick him on the sitting fee. I recommend you charge
him at least three times the fee you're charging the
others, although if it were me, I'd go for five."

"What's the matter with the dog?" she asked. "Is
he dangerous?"

"He's a . . ." Matt winced. "Pomeranian."

"Ah." Her mouth quirked with a grin. "Another . . .
what's your term? Purse pet?"

"He'll pepper you with questions, probably talk
marriage, but just ignore him. I'll deal with his
nonsense."

"How?"

"Matthew?" bellowed the voice from downstairs.

Matt knew that if it weren't for the state of Branch's
knees, his father would already be upstairs. "I'll wing
it. Don't worry."

When Torie abruptly nodded, then grabbed her
camera bag in one hand, her mutt in the other, he
breathed a sigh of relief. "Thank you."

"I do have one condition," she warned. Depositing
Gigi in his arms, she added, "You have to make
friends."

The damned dog bit him on his right middle finger.
Matt gritted his teeth and said, "Sure."

Torie led the way, and looking over her shoulder,
Matt saw Branch waiting at the foot of the staircase.
At his first glimpse of Torie, a smile started on his
face that grew with every step she took. By the time
she reached the ground floor his father's smile was so
big Matt thought it might split Branch's face in two.

"Helen Bradshaw," Branch said. "Still as pretty as
a Parker County peach. Please tell me you've come
to town to marry my boy."

Torie looked at him, her brow arched. He heard the
echo of her voice in his mind. *Marry my boy?*

Matt's jaw hurt from the pressure he'd put on his
teeth. He consciously unlocked his jaw and said,

"Branch, like I explained before, Helen stopped to say hello as she passed through town."

"Now, that's a bunch of road apples. No one just passes through Brazos Bend. It's on the way to nowhere. She's here to see you, Matthew—admit it. I'll bet y'all have been seeing each other on the sly all this time. You just wanted to surprise me, didn't you, Matthew?"

"No."

"Matt's right. I just stopped to say hello. You actually caught me on my way out of town." Torie smiled politely and held out her hand. "It's nice to see you again, sir."

"Ah, to hell with a handshake." Branch put Paco on the ground, saying, "C'mere, girl. Let an old man give you a proper welcome to the family."

Supporting his weight with the cane in his right hand, Branch pulled Torie into a hug with his left. Seeing Branch teeter, Matt dumped Gigi onto the ground and reached to steady his father.

Gigi and Paco took an immediate and noisy dislike to each other. Matt suspected the stupid miniature cowboy hat Branch had strapped onto the damned dog's head had something to do with it. That'd put any self-respecting male into a pissy mood.

As Paco yapped incessantly, Torie shot Matt a chastising look. She broke the hug and scooped Gigi up into her arms. After making sure Branch wasn't about to lose his balance, Matt retrieved the mutt from his mistress's arms, receiving another finger nip in the process. "Tell me her shots are up-to-date?" he asked Torie.

While she rolled her eyes and nodded, Branch told his Paco to be still. "He's ordinarily a quiet little man. Guess he's trying to show off for the ladies."

Torie's answering smile was strained. "Matt, maybe you should take Gigi upstairs. It's not good for her to get excited before a long car ride."

"Long car ride?" Branch repeated, his brow creasing in concern. "What long car ride? You're not going anywhere, are you? You just got here!"

"Dad, haven't you listened to a word we said?"

Branch broke into a smile. "You called me Dad. Helen, did you hear that? He called me Dad. God bless you, it must be your influence. He's mellowed. I knew the first time I met you that you'd be perfect for him."

Matt closed his eyes and massaged the bridge of his nose. Paco continued to bark. Branch made stupid little clucking sounds that the dog totally ignored. Gigi peered down at Paco and started yipping in that superior manner common to females of all species.

"Take her upstairs and put her in her carrier," Torie instructed Matt. "She'll sleep and we'll have some peace."

Matt gladly escaped back upstairs to her room. He didn't see a pet carrier on her bed, though, just a suitcase and a big purse.

A purse. For the purse pet. *Uh, duh, Callahan.*

By the time he pried the pooch's teeth off his finger, settled it into the cushioned bag, and returned downstairs, Torie had moved his father and the mini-monster-dog outside. He stepped out the door in time to hear his father ask, "So when is the wedding?"

"Mr. Callahan . . ."

"Call me Branch."

"Branch. Your son and I aren't getting married."

His brow furrowed and he frowned. "Well, I won't have you living in sin. Y'all might have gotten away with that in Washington, but not in Brazos Bend."

"Branch, enough," Matt insisted. "Helen doesn't have time to waste. If you want pictures, you need to let her work."

"Oh, I definitely want pictures," Branch replied. "Matthew tells me you're an excellent photographer, Helen."

"Oh, really?" She glanced at Matt.

"I'm sure you're better than that sister of yours, may the good Lord curse the day she was born. I admit that at first I was a little worried about your relationship with Matt, considering That Damned Woman is your twin, but what the hell. Every family has a black sheep."

"At least," she commented, her tone bone-dry.

"I have a hobby, myself," Branch continued. "I've taken an interest in writing. I'm putting together a history of my life for my boys. I enjoy it. I imagine you find photography to be a nice change from scientific research. I can see how one might lend itself to the other. Both disciplines require creativity of a sort, don't they?"

After a moment's silence, Torie offered him a genuine, if reluctant, smile. "That's perceptive of you, sir. I've always felt the two shared a connection, though other people don't see it."

Matt sensed that was a barb directed at him, but it was misplaced. He might not like what she did for a living, but he wouldn't argue with her talent. In the months following the shooting, he'd made it his business to find out everything he could about Torie Bradshaw and that included compiling a portfolio of her pictures. The woman had a gift. It was a shame she wasted it on celebrities. "Your regular work is very good, but I watched you with the children this morning. I'll bet those photographs turn out to be some of the best work you've ever done."

"Just wait until you see Paco through a camera lens," Branch declared. "He'll put those little rug rats to shame."

Torie looked from Branch to Matt, then back to Branch again. Shaking her head, she said, "Let's get to work, then, shall we? Do you want bluebonnet photos for Paco or something else?"

"I definitely want bluebonnets. I want something to

pull out at bingo along with everyone else. Most folks my age have grandchildren to show off. Any chance you and my Matthew will solve that problem for me anytime soon?"

"No," they responded together.

"Well, I can't help but hope. Luke and Maddie sure as hell aren't getting the job done. I thought for sure they'd have made me a granddaddy by now, but I'm still waiting. I'd love to have a whole passel of grandchildren." Branch smiled wistfully, and his voice sounded sad as he added, "Especially a granddaughter. My wife and I weren't blessed with any girls."

He'd sure as hell regretted having sons, hadn't he? Matt buried the bitter thought, then tuned his father out as Branch continued whining about his lack of grandchildren. He'd heard it all before, more times than he could count. He probably should have given Torie a heads-up on that, as well, but it was too late now.

"Speaking of too late," he murmured to himself, glancing at his wristwatch. Mark should have called again by now. He'd landed in LA more than three hours ago, and he'd said he'd call in just as soon as he checked out Torie's apartment. He'd had plenty of time to get the job done.

Matt motioned to Bill Reynolds to take charge of the watch; then he stepped around to the side of the house to block the noise from an overexcited Paco. Pulling out his cell phone, he punched in his brother's number. On the third ring, a woman's voice answered, "Hello?"

Crap. He had a bad feeling about this. "I'm calling for Mark Callahan?"

"May I ask who's calling, please?"

"This is his brother Matt Callahan. Who am I speaking with?"

"Oh, Mr. Callahan. One moment, please."

Matt gripped the phone hard and listened harder.

His stomach did a nervous churn. What was that background noise? Not an outdoor sound. Beeping. What was beeping?

A man's voice asked, "Mr. Callahan?"

"Yes. What the hell is going on? Where's my brother?"

"I'm Captain Frank Hollis of the LAPD."

Matt closed his eyes and braced himself.

"Your brother is one lucky man."

Matt's eyes flew open. "He's okay?"

"He has a concussion, some bruises, and a few cuts from flying glass, and a broken arm, but the doctors say he'll make a full recovery."

"What happened!"

"There was an explosion. Whole place went up. Honestly, I don't know how the man survived. He must be tough as nails."

"What place went up? Please, Captain. A few more details would be appreciated right now."

The police captain obviously didn't care for the implied criticism because his tone went cool and clipped. "Approximately one hour ago, a natural-gas explosion occurred in a fourplex in Santa Monica. From what we've been able to piece together so far, your brother entered one of the apartments and somehow triggered the explosion."

"Was anyone else hurt?"

"As far as we've been able to ascertain at this point, no. Although one occupant is as yet unaccounted for . . ." Sensing the name the man was about to say, Matt shut his eyes. "A woman by the name of Victoria Bradshaw."

Well, hell.

Chapter Ten

Los Angeles

Well, now. That was a disappointment.

From an apartment kitty-corner to Torie Bradshaw's home, the stalker watched the last ambulance pull away from the curb and sighed. An unexpected development, that. An unexpected disappointment.

Two days of waiting, then *kaboom*. Destruction. Chaos. It had thrilled. Empowered. Well worth the wait.

The temptation to join the crowd of gawkers that gathered to watch had been strong, but better sense prevailed. While sirens wailed and women cried, laughter bubbled, ringing out through the apartment.

Then the rescuers had pulled a single injured person from the rubble, an obviously angry male. The sense of power had faded; curiosity surged.

Who was the man and what had he been doing in Torie Bradshaw's apartment? A lover? Perhaps another way to punish Torie Bradshaw?

What a delicious thought.

Must find out about the man.

Torie didn't know what to think of Branch Callahan. He was loud and crusty and demanding . . .

and a marshmallow with his poor Paco. Imagine, dressing the little thing up like a four-legged cowboy. It was one thing to put bows in Gigi's hair—okay, bows that coordinated with Torie's outfit when she cared to dress up—but something else entirely to put clothes and a hat on a handful of dog. Did that make Branch a controlling autocrat or simply an old man with a lot of love to give and too few people to accept it?

Maybe the answer was a combination of both.

But then, it wasn't any of her business, was it? She was on her way out of here. It didn't matter what kind of man Branch Callahan was or why he and Matt seemed to be on guard around each other. *It's not your concern, Bradshaw.*

Yeah, but she sure was curious.

And having fits with poor ol' Paco. "Mr. Callahan, if you want posed pictures, you need to do something to make him sit and stay."

"He's just like my boys. Doesn't mind me worth beans."

"Then let me do candid shots rather than a formal—" Torie broke off abruptly when she spied Matt coming around a corner. He looked grim, all business, hard and focused.

Something was terribly wrong.

Torie recalled what he'd said about Brazos Bend not being the real world. . . . Well, one glance at Matt's face said the real world had come to Brazos Bend. Torie's heart sank to her stomach.

He went straight to Bill Reynolds and the two spoke quietly for almost two minutes. Branch was busy attempting to coax Paco to prop his front paws on an island stump in a sea of bluebonnets, so he didn't notice the development.

Matt and the bodyguard finished their conversation; then Matt shot a quick, hateful look toward Torie. It cut like a knife and she gasped and fell back a step. What in the world . . . ?

"Branch, we're done here. Ms. Bradshaw has a plane to catch at DFW. She needs to get on the road."

"A plane to catch! But . . . what about your romance? What about the wedding!"

"The goddamned wedding is all in your mind, Branch."

"What happened, Matt?"

He ignored her question. The chill in his voice as he spoke to his father could have made ice. "She's leaving Brazos Bend right now."

Torie's mind whirled. He was obviously furious at her. Why? She'd done nothing but take photos of his father's dog! It couldn't be that. "What's going on, Matt?"

"Get in Reynolds's SUV, Victoria."

"Victoria? Victoria Bradshaw? *Torie* Bradshaw?"

Ignoring his father's outraged questions and Torie's own shock, Matt grabbed her arm above the elbow and steered her toward the bodyguard's vehicle.

"But . . . but . . . what about Gigi?" she said. "I'm not leaving Gigi!"

"I'll get the damned dog." Matt all but picked Torie up and tossed her in the passenger seat, then slammed the door. When he returned a few minutes later, he had a snarling Gigi in his left arm. He held his cell phone to his ear with his right. He stood outside the truck for a few minutes, his manner agitated at first, then calming as the call continued. Finally, he opened Torie's door and handed her Gigi. ". . . call in a few favors. Should have some answers by tonight. More tomorrow. Yeah. Yeah. Oh, I plan to. Sure. All right. Give Maddie a kiss for me. Y'all drive careful."

"Matt? What's going on?" Torie asked when he disconnected his call.

"You do what Bill tells you to do. No arguments."

Then he slammed the door and banged his hand against the hood, signaling Bill to go.

The SUV pulled away from Cottonwood Cottage, and Torie sat in stunned stupor. "He didn't even say good-bye." Glancing at her bodyguard, she asked, "Do you know what happened, Mr. Reynolds?"

The bodyguard spared her a quick glance. "Someone rigged a natural-gas explosion in your apartment. His brother triggered it."

Torie froze. "What did you say?"

"Your apartment exploded with Mark Callahan in it."

Oh my God. Fear clutched her heart. She swallowed hard, then asked, "Is he . . . ?"

"Banged up and in the hospital, but alive. Whoever is after you certainly means business."

Relief rushed through her, making her weak. Thank God. "This is terrible. I never intended . . ." She let her voice trail off, not knowing how to complete her thought.

Matt's brother. No wonder he'd given her such a hateful look. Torie knew from her sister that he'd already lost one brother, John. Now she—well, her problems, anyway—had almost cost him another. Shoot, she was lucky he hadn't drawn his gun and drilled her.

Then another thought occurred. "Was anyone else hurt?"

"The couple next door were trapped by debris, but made it out relatively unscathed."

Torie clutched Gigi tight. "Their baby?"

"Baby was fine."

"Thank God."

He didn't say any more and she spent the next few minutes holding back hysteria. An explosion. Someone rigged an explosion in her apartment. Like a bomb. She pictured the big black ball with a sizzling wick like in cartoons. Then Wile E. Coyote with his bundle of dynamite. Nausea rolled in her stomach.

She was scared. She wished she had someone to hold her, to protect her. To tell her everything would be all right. She wished for her lover from last night.

Might as well wish for a Pulitzer prize for paparazzi photography.

She leaned back against the headrest and concentrated on keeping her breakfast down. If her father were here, he'd tell her she shouldn't be surprised by the turn her life had taken. He'd tell her it was all her fault for having attracted a stalker. It was her fault someone wanted to kill her. Her fault Matt's brother had been caught in the cross fire.

She looked at the driver, knowing her eyes must be a little wild. "I need to tell Matt that I'm sorry. I never should have come here. Can I call him? Do you have his number?"

"I'm sure he's busy now. Why don't you wait until tonight and tell him when you see him?"

"When I see him?" She sat up straight. "Where? Aren't you taking me to Austin?"

"No, ma'am. I'm taking you to his lake house. We're to lie low there until he arrives."

Torie sank back against her seat, staring straight ahead, her hands trembling. She felt horrible that others had been hurt in her place. She felt frightened. The pictures, the dog . . . that was bad enough, but to rig an explosion? Who hated her so much and why?

Even as she shivered with bone-chilling fear, a small flicker of warmth burned in her heart.

Matt Callahan hadn't abandoned her, after all.

Matt's phone rang and he checked the number. "Mark?"

"Yeah."

Thank God. Matt briefly closed his eyes. "Am I glad to hear your voice."

"Yeah, well, I wouldn't be so quick to say that if I were you. I talked to Luke."

"Good. So he's filled you in on the plan."

"You know, bro, I'm the one with the concussion, so why do you have a head injury? If you think I'm getting on a plane and coming to the absolute last place in the world I want to be, then you're crazy."

"I very well may be crazy, but I need your help, Mark."

There was a long silence. "Well, shit."

One corner of Matt's mouth lifted. He could always count on Mark's fierce sense of family loyalty—at least where he and Luke were concerned. Branch was another matter entirely. "The plane is fueled and ready whenever you are."

"Fuck me in the heart." Mark sighed, then said, "I'll be there tomorrow."

A dial tone sounded in Matt's ears. He tucked his cell into the pocket of his jeans, thinking, *That's two down and one to go.* He'd saved the hardest nut to crack for last.

Fifteen minutes later, he pulled up in front of the winery. Les was in the vineyard making notes in a spiral-bound book. Matt braced himself for the scolding sure to come and started walking. Les briefly glanced up as Matt approached, then returned to his work. "Shoots are lengthening well."

"I'm sorry I never made it back yesterday."

"I'm not your keeper, Callahan, or your boss. What you do with your time is your own business."

"Still, I said I'd help you with those new barrels and I didn't show. That was wrong of me."

Les peered over the top of his glasses. "I'm not so old a man that I can't appreciate a fellow's choosing to pass time with a lovely lady when the opportunity arises. Ms. Bradshaw is lovelier than most, although I will admit to being surprised you went from bullet holes to bed quite so fast."

"Yeah, well . . ." Matt tried to think of something to say in his own defense, but came up blank. "Radio said there's a chance for thunderstorms tomorrow night."

Les turned a page in his notebook and jotted another note.

"I saw that. We'll keep our fingers crossed they skip us for the next week or so. We need clear skies and gentle winds and maximum sunlight striking the buds and shoots."

"Because it influences the budding process next year, right?" Matt asked, recalling Les's lessons.

"That's right. We'll weave the lengthening shoots through the trellis to maximize sun exposure and protect from wind. If we get a run of warm sunny days, I ought to be able to bring the horticulture kids from the high school out to help with that next week. Think you'll be around?"

Matt rubbed the back of his neck. "Well, I don't know. . . ."

"If I'm allowed to make an observation, in order to figure out whether you want to spend your days working in a vineyard rather than at a desk in Langley, you might be advised to actually spend some time here."

Shoving his hands in his pants pockets, Matt said, "Believe me, I'd much rather be here learning about bud break from you than hunting down the asshole who almost killed my brother earlier today."

"No." Les's head jerked up. "Luke or Mark?"

"Mark."

Les snapped his notebook shut. "Hell, I thought you were fixing to tell me you were taking off with the girl. What's the story?"

Matt briefed him on the events that had occurred since he'd left Four Brothers to have his truck repaired, ending with the plan he'd conceived and put into motion after learning about the explosion. "You're a good tactician, Les. Any changes to suggest?"

Les scratched his whiskered jaw and considered the

question. "Have you contacted the sister? It wouldn't hurt for her to be on her guard."

"Luke is making some arrangements there."

"What about the old bastard? You clueing him in on the arrangements?"

"Hell, no." Matt winced at the thought. "Mark would break my arm. And both my legs. Branch can't know anything about this."

Les smirked at that. There was no love lost between Matt's father and the man who'd in many ways become his dad. "I don't know how else you could handle the problem short of ignoring it."

"Be damned if I ignore it. Mark could have died in that explosion."

"Could have, but didn't. Might be healthier for you to leave it alone."

Because he valued his friend's opinion, Matt gazed out over the vineyard, breathed deeply of the spring-scented air, and considered Les's point. "Healthier for me," he finally replied. "Certainly not for Torie."

"Girl got under your skin," Les observed. Then he gave his head a shake. "I knew it. Moment I heard you fire up your boat last night, I knew she'd lit your wick. Hell, I knew it the minute she pulled the trigger on that stupid pink gun of hers. You just can't stay away from danger, can you, Callahan?"

"Don't be ridiculous." Matt kicked a stone at his feet. "Last night has nothing to do with today."

Les simply looked at him and laughed.

Torie booted up the computer in the lake house's study and said a little prayer that Matt had Internet out here in the boonies. She knew a bone-deep need to contact Helen right away, and her sister rarely answered the phone when she was working.

Torie drummed her fingers against the keyboard as she waited for the little box that indicated Internet connectivity to appear in the monitor's lower right-hand corner. Seeing it, she smiled. When the icon for instant messaging popped up on his desktop, her smile broadened. Excellent, she thought as she logged on under her user name. As always during a workday, Helen was online.

Torie hesitated a moment before typing in a post. She hadn't told Helen about the stalker up until now. She hadn't wanted to worry her and distract her from her work. Her twin had reached a critical point in her research, and if she knew that Torie was in trouble, she'd lose her focus.

But in light of the explosion, on the off chance that whoever was after her might decide to go after those whom she loved, Torie had to let Helen know to be on her guard.

She typed: *You there?*

A moment later, her sister responded: *sorta. distracted. interesting results in lab today.*

I need your attention for a couple minutes. H, someone is after me.

oh, t. what have you done now?

Torie clenched her teeth. Nothing bugged her more than when her sister parroted their father's point of view. Impatience sent her fingers flying.

I'm on the road because I'm being stalked. I don't know who or why, but he's doing scary things. You need to be careful, H. He rigged an explosion in my apartment. I'm hiding and someone is helping me, but I'm afraid he'll come after you when he can't find me.

Almost thirty seconds ticked by without a response before Helen wrote back. *WHERE ARE YOU? CALL ME NOW!!!!!*

Well, at least she had her sister's attention. She eyed the phone and considered using it. But no, she'd avoided the phone up until now because calls were too easily traced. No sense running that risk now. She probably shouldn't even instant message, but she needed some sort of communication with her sister.

Of all available methods, this felt safest. *Can't. I'm safe. Don't worry. Just be careful. Promise?*

Again, another pause, then: *does dad know?*

No. PROMISE, H???????

i'm so scared for u, t.

A lump formed in Torie's throat. She hated upsetting Helen. She just hated it. She was the caretaker in this relationship, not the other way around.

That's why she decided to take one more risk. *Don't be. I'm with Beautiful Buns.*

"Beautiful Buns!" Matt exclaimed from directly behind her.

Torie jumped. Her hands jerked. She hadn't heard him come in.

"Who are you IMing?"

"Matt, I'm so glad to see you." She backspaced the gibberish she'd inadvertently typed off the computer screen and attempted to explain. "It's my sister. I had to warn her."

"Beautiful Buns?" he repeated, his eyes narrowed and hot with temper.

Helen typed: *oooooooohhhhhhh!* ☺ ☺ ☺ *sure you aren't faking the stalker?*

He's here. Gotta go. TTYL.

give him a kiss from me. ttyl

Now it was Torie's turn to scowl. She really didn't like being reminded that Matt Callahan and Helen had locked lips.

"Dammit," he muttered, pacing the room. "I can't believe you—oh, never mind. We don't have time for this."

"How is your brother? I'm so sorry—"

"He'll be all right," Matt snapped, cutting her off short.

"Good. I feel so bad. . . ." Her voice trailed off as she saw him glaring at the computer screen. Her teeth tugged at her bottom lip. "Was this a mistake, Matt?"

"Referring to me as Beautiful Buns? Yeah, I would say so."

"Not that," she said, rolling her eyes. "I meant instant messaging my sister. Is it traceable like a credit card?"

"For me it would be. For the average criminal, no. Here." He tossed a new yellow legal pad onto the desk. "You need to make me a list of every single person in the world who has reason to be pissed off at you. That includes everyone from old lovers to the hairstylist you stiffed at Christmas."

"I don't stiff my hairstylist!"

"There's more paper in the desk if you need it. I'll be back later to get the list." Then he turned on his heel and started to leave.

"Wait a minute!" Torie demanded. Enough was enough. She was *so done* with being treated like dirt. Shoving to her feet, she said, "Look, Callahan, I'm sorry your brother was hurt, but I didn't wire that explosion. I'm not the bad guy here."

"No, you're not the bad guy." His gaze raked her up and down. "But you're still That Damned Woman."

The screen door slammed behind him.

Torie sank back into her seat, scowling after him. She drummed her fingers on the desk for a moment, then opened the drawer to retrieve the package of M&M's she'd spied there earlier. True, these weren't the best of circumstances, but did he have to act like a jerk?

"Having a beautiful ass is no excuse for being one," she muttered, ripping open the package. She poured out a half-dozen M&M's, tossed them one by one into her mouth, then picked up the pen, organized her thoughts, and began to write. He wanted a list?

"By God, I'll give him a list."

*   *   *

The day following the explosion, the Callahan brothers arrived at Four Brothers Vineyard within half an hour of one another. Luke showed up first, his expression grim, his manner curt, just as Matt turned away yet another baked-good-bearing female with the news that Les was ill with something contagious. He asked that she please pass along word that townsfolk should consider Four Brothers under quarantine.

Matt took one look at Luke and knew his brother was as worried and anxious as he, though neither voiced their fears.

"Where's Les?" Luke asked.

"He says he's making a run to Fort Worth for parts for the irrigation system, but I think he has a hot date. Took Angie Rametti with him. He said not to expect him back tonight."

The brothers talked about Luke's wife, Maddie, and his dog, Knucklehead, and the engine trouble he'd had with the *Miss Behavin' II*, the houseboat currently berthed on the Texas Gulf Coast where the couple spent half of the year. Though neither Matt nor Luke had much of an appetite, they told themselves that Mark was bound to be hungry when he arrived, so they fired up the charcoal grill on Les's patio. Upon hearing the sound of wheels on the gravel road, the brothers sauntered around to the front of Les's house.

Wincing, Mark climbed out of his Porsche. Matt's gaze drank in the sight of his brother, and he took his first decent breath since yesterday's phone call. Then in the manner of brothers, they exchanged insults by way of greeting until Mark said, "I need drugs. Now. What do you have?"

Luke glanced at Matt. "What sort of question is that to ask of a DEA agent?"

"Former DEA agent," Mark responded. "You're my partner now, remember? If you ever decide to tear yourself away from your wife long enough to work an investigation, that is."

Matt eyed the abrasion on his brother's face and grimaced. "Didn't you get anything at the hospital?"

"They gave me prescriptions, but I thought I could get by without them. I didn't want to wait around to get them filled."

"Oh, for God's sake. Hand 'em over." Matt tugged out his cell and made a quick call to the local drugstore. The pharmacist was an old friend whose discretion Matt knew he could trust. Minutes later, he ended the call and said, "Relief is on the way, stupid. Next time, get your meds before you travel."

"I'm hoping there won't be a next time," Mark grumbled. "Even so, I needed to keep my wits about me—the few that weren't scrambled by the blast, that is. Didn't want anyone following me here. Can we go inside now? I need to sit down." He swayed, just a little bit, and in a flash one brother stood at each side, offering their support.

Matt and Luke helped Mark to a chair on the back patio. He eyed the rib eyes and smiled with anticipation. "Just wave mine over the flames, would you? I swear I could eat it the way it is."

With that, Matt's appetite came roaring back and he went about preparing the meal with new enthusiasm, while Luke cracked open a beer and asked Mark, "So, you want to give us a rundown on yesterday's events?"

Mark wistfully eyed the beer in his brother's hand as he stretched his legs out in front of him. "I was careless. Hell, I deserved what I got for being so damned stupid. I noticed the smell, but didn't pay enough attention. The photographs hanging on her drying line distracted me."

"Photos of what?" Luke demanded.

"Disturbing stuff. Executions. Mutilations. We need to know where she took those pictures and what the hell for. I mean, damn. The Evil Twin might really be evil."

"*If* she took those pictures," Matt observed. "That doesn't sound like Victoria. They could have been planted by the perp."

"True," Mark agreed.

"I thought she took pictures of starlets," Luke said. "Who the hell did she piss off enough to blow up her apartment?"

"That's what I intend to find out," Matt said grimly. "It's personal now. The bastard could have killed our brother."

"Besides that, his little surprise ruined my favorite pair of sneakers," Mark pointed out. "That's all the motivation I need to continue this investigation."

"You feel up to clueing us in on what you found out before the blast?" Matt asked.

"Won't take long. I don't have much." He gave a brief synopsis of his investigation up to the time of the explosion. The only piece of information Matt found new was that Torie spent two mornings a month rocking sick babies in a hospital nursery. That bit of insight into her character caught him by surprise.

Mark finished up his recitation by asking, "What have you found out on your end?"

Matt grabbed the legal pad he'd retrieved from the lake-house study late last night. She'd filled three sheets with names for him to investigate and another three sheets with complaints and opinions about his character, or lack thereof.

"Victoria made a list of everyone she could think of who might possibly hold a grudge against her."

"That's a good place to start," Mark observed. "Do you think she was thorough?"

"My name is at the top of her list. Yours is at the bottom. Middle includes such likely suspects as the queen of England and her paperboy, who she's repeatedly turned down for dates. He's twelve."

"Twelve is such a difficult age," Luke observed.

Matt rolled his eyes and continued. "After going

over the names, I've picked who I think are the three most likely suspects. First on the list is . . ." He paused, rubbed the back of his neck, and said, "Collin Marlow."

His brothers shared a look. Luke drawled, "Excuse me, but isn't he dead?"

"Well, we can't be quite sure. We never recovered a body."

"He was shot and tossed into a shark-infested lagoon," Luke fired back. "I doubt there was enough left of him to scoop off the sand."

"I still want it looked into."

Mark and Luke shrugged an okay, Mark failing to hide a wince from the effort. Matt continued. "The second name that raises a red flag for me is a guy named Jason Banning. He writes for the tabloids. They worked together. Slept together. She dumped him after"—*she met me*—"the incident on Soledad Island. According to Victoria, his career hasn't been the same since."

"Now, that's a better suspect than a dead guy," Luke observed.

"Maybe. There's a third man I think might be the best prospect of all. Y'all remember the sex scandal last year in Washington?"

"Which sex scandal?" Mark interjected. "There're so many to choose from."

"The one with the senator and his . . . dog?"

"The costume orgy?" Luke asked.

Matt nodded and the Callahan brothers all grimaced at the memory. Matt continued. "Guess who took the infamous shot?"

"No."

" 'Fraid so."

"What the hell was she doing at a sex club?"

"She was following the, uh, dog. The man had landed a role in the next *Pirates of the Caribbean*. The publicity cost him the job."

"So are you counting the senator or the actor as the perp?"

"Could be either one. We'd better look at both of them, but I think the senator is a stretch."

"Not from what I recall about the picture," Mark drily responded. "More like a stub."

Matt and Luke both snorted at that; then Matt turned his attention to the steaks, and the delivery guy from the pharmacy arrived with Mark's painkillers. They took a break from attempted murder over supper. Conversation turned to baseball and rumors of a big pitching trade in the Rangers organization. Despite his plague warning, two women showed up with invitations for Matt during dinner, proving he'd been right to stash Torie elsewhere. Four Brothers was simply too public a spot to make a good hideout.

Once dinner was done, Mark stood and stretched. "I'm sinking fast, guys. Do we have a plan or can we finish this in the morning?"

"The plan is to find the motherfucker who placed that bomb." Matt scraped scraps into the garbage pail and loaded plates in the dishwasher. "You'll sleep here, Mark, but I want you spending your days convalescing at the lake place, while Luke and I track down leads from Victoria's list."

"You want me to babysit Ms. Babelicious?" Mark asked, a slow smile spreading across his face. "I can do that. I'll be happy to do that."

Matt suddenly felt as grim as he had the moment he heard about the explosion. He didn't like his brother giving Torie a nickname. He didn't like thinking about his brother with Torie at all. As irritated as that made him, it paled in comparison with his mood upon realizing that he could put off his news no longer. He had to tell his brothers about the death in Paris.

He cleared his throat. "You're not babysitting. She

has a bodyguard. Bill Reynolds. You, I want on the computer. I have the electronics you'll need at the lake house."

"No problem. I can do both." Mark flexed his shoulders, grimaced, then turned to head upstairs.

"Wait." Matt slammed the dishwasher shut and wiped his hands on a towel. "I have some other news I need to tell you. Something . . . well, fuck."

"Branch?" Luke asked, his green eyes narrowing.

Mark set his jaw. "I'm going to bed. I don't give a good god—"

"Not Branch. Ćurković. The sonofabitch is dead."

His twin brothers met each other's gazes, their identical eyes glowing with delight. "You got him! Hot damn. Way to go, bro," Mark said.

"No. I didn't get him." Matt drew a deep breath, then let it out in a rush. "The asshole had a fucking heart attack in his fucking sleep at a fucking five-star hotel!"

His brothers scowled, echoed Matt's vulgarity, then shrugged. "Now, that's just not right," Luke said. "He should have gone hard."

"But he's gone," Mark said. "That's what matters." Pinning a fierce look on Matt, he added, "That's *all* that matters."

No, it wasn't. But then, Mark and Luke didn't know. Matt had spared his brothers most of the details he knew about John's capture and torture. They didn't know how hard he'd died.

They didn't shoulder the guilt that Matt did. They hadn't been there that god-awful night.

Matt had.

"I'm whipped. Calling calf rope. Where am I sleeping, Matthew?"

"Les's room is up the stairs on the left. Y'all have your pick of the other three. Let's plan on meeting for breakfast around eight at the lake house."

"What about you?" Luke asked. "Branch told Maddie there was some action out on the lake the other night. Where will you be sleeping, bro?"

Matt shot his brother the bird, and walked out into the cool evening air.

Torie watched the sun set from an upstairs guest room at Matt's lake house. Then she took a seat in an antique wooden rocker, tucked her feet beneath her, and clicked on the television set. Three hours later as she blindly stared at a Spanish soap opera, she heard the electric hum of a golf cart arriving, then departing a few minutes later. Next came the mumble of male voices, followed by heavy steps on the stairs.

Matt appeared in the doorway wearing jeans and a T-shirt similar to what he'd worn yesterday when he'd barged in demanding her list. If he'd slept here last night, she didn't know. She'd moved from his bedroom into a guest room. She hadn't heard him come in, and he hadn't been here when she went down for breakfast.

He folded his arms and leaned against the doorjamb, his gaze on the television. "You speak Spanish?"

"And French, Italian, a little German. Army brat." She picked up the slender black remote and switched off the set. "How is your brother?"

"Banged up. Sore. Not bad, considering." He sauntered into the room, took a look around. "You decided to change accommodations?"

Sure, Callahan, throw it on my shoulders. "This is a pleasant room. I love the photos of the old wooden boats. Besides, I don't go where I'm not welcome."

"Really?" he drawled, arching a brow. "Somehow, I doubt Senator Harris would agree with that statement."

She closed her eyes and sighed. "You've studied my list."

"Oh, yeah. C'mon, now, Victoria." He picked up a

decorative stone paperweight from the writing desk and tossed it from hand to hand. "A gay orgy? What the hell were you thinking?"

Her gaze followed the motion of the small rock in his big hands. She smelled the spicy scent of his aftershave and quashed the urge to move closer. "It was Halloween. I thought it was a costume party. I didn't even realize what I was taking pictures of until . . . well . . . later."

"How much money did you make off those photos?"

"I told you earlier that I didn't sell them." Stubborn, thickheaded man. "I turned them over to the police."

"To bring down the senator's career?" He replaced the paperweight on the desk, then lifted her hairbrush off the dresser and began tossing it in a circle by the handle.

"Look, I didn't recognize the senator!" She grabbed her hairbrush away from him. "I didn't recognize anyone but the actor I followed. There were children at that event. I gave the prints to the police because I thought everyone there should be arrested!"

Matt shook his head. "A murder, a political sex scandal, an exploding apartment . . . all in less than two years. You're a trouble magnet, Bradshaw."

She set her hairbrush on the bedside table and visualized pulling her Glock and plugging his good knee. "Do you want something, Callahan, or did you just come up here to give me grief?"

Matt folded his arms and gave her a long, brooding look. The air grew thick with tension, and although she attempted to resist, Torie responded to it. Her breasts swelled; her nipples hardened. Her anger faded, replaced by a need just as basic.

"I'm afraid I do want something," he finally said, his gaze drifting slowly over her body. "But I don't want to want it."

Torie knew exactly what he meant.

This was crazy. Was she so weak that all he need do was give her a heavy-lidded look and she'd fall at his feet? Apparently.

Attempting to distract them both, she again took a seat in the rocking chair, folded her arms, crossed her legs, and lifted her chin. "What's the plan for tomorrow, Callahan? Am I going to sit here alone all day twiddling my thumbs?"

"You're not alone. You have Bill and the rat dog." He was slow to lift his gaze from her legs to her eyes. "I think it's best for you to stay here until we get a location on our suspects. Because we're looking at quite a few people, that may take a few days."

"You don't think he could find me here, do you? In Brazos Bend?"

"I think the chances are really slim. Nevertheless, I want Reynolds to stick around for the time being."

"Whatever you think is best."

He arched one brow. "That's more cooperation than I expected."

"I don't know why. I came to you for help. Why would I fight you when you're giving me what I asked for?"

Again, his gaze made a sweep of her body. "Seems to me like you're asking for a number of different things."

With that, Torie's temper flared anew and she shoved to her feet. "What's that supposed to mean? Are you talking about sex, Callahan? If so, you can go jump in the damned lake. I'm not the one sending mixed signals here."

He shoved his hands in his pockets and looked away. "I'm sorry. I just . . . the other night was . . ." He sighed heavily. "I wish you took bluebonnet photographs all the time."

So he was blaming her job for his withdrawal? What

a crock. "That would be difficult, considering that they have such a short blooming season."

"I hate what you do, Victoria."

"No." She gaped and gently slapped the side of her face. "I never would have guessed."

"Smart-ass." A faint smile played on his lips. "I loved how we were together."

She turned away from him. He made her so angry, so needy, so . . . sad . . . that she couldn't bear to look at him. "We were good."

"We were great. Really great. Great doesn't come along very often, but . . ."

When he didn't complete the sentence, Torie's heart twisted. The man was blind as a bat. He'd liked her too much. She'd gotten too close to him, so he had to find an excuse to push her away. That's what this was.

Well, whatever. She wasn't going to beg him. She still had her pride. Meeting his gaze in the carved oak mirror hung above the dresser, she did the job for him. "We were a one-night stand. You don't have to worry, Callahan. I understand. You want to sleep with me, but you don't respect me."

He swore softly and shoved his fingers through his hair. "That's not—"

"It's been a long day, Matt." Turning, she walked toward the door and maneuvered him outside the room. "Let's call it a night."

"Torie, it's not that simple."

Torie shut the door in his face, firmly and quietly. She stopped herself—just barely—from kicking the closed door with the toe of her favorite sandals.

No man—not 007 or Double-Oh-Yeah—was worth a pair of Manolos.

Chapter Eleven

Following a fitful night's sleep, Torie grabbed a cup of coffee from the thankfully empty kitchen and escorted Gigi out into the glorious morning. Springtime in Texas was hard to beat, she decided. The huge blue sky, perfect weather, and flower-dotted fields soothed her stormy soul.

Torie had grown a thick skin over the years, but Matt's accusations the night before had hurt her. Yes, she'd landed in some unusual, unpleasant situations of late. Yes, she seemed to find more trouble than others of her acquaintance, but the argument she'd given him during their escape from Soledad Island hadn't changed. Her job was vital to the entertainment industry.

Yes, that wasn't nearly as important as having a job vital to the country, but a balanced life needed some fun mixed in with the serious, and different people had different definitions of fun. For some of them, that meant knowing a tidbit about a celebrity's everyday life. Too bad, so sad for Matt Callahan if he couldn't see it.

". . . worried about Matt." A male voice floated on the air.

Always curious, Torie drifted closer. "Because of Ćurković?" another voice asked.

Didn't sound like Bill the bodyguard. Besides, she thought Bill was upstairs sleeping after his overnight guard stint. Torie paused at the corner of the house and peered around cautiously. Two men stood on the back patio, steaming cups of coffee in their hands, staring out at the lake, where Matt was getting in a cold, early swim. Must be the brothers, she thought.

They were both tall and broad with dark hair and really nice tushes. The Callahan men all shared a resemblance in that respect. Torie couldn't see their faces, but she suspected they'd be as fine to look at as Matt.

But their looks weren't nearly as important as what they were saying, so she listened harder. ". . . know he wanted to rip his balls off and make him eat 'em. I wanted the sonofabitch dead as bad as anyone, but Matt . . . he's been intense."

"You know what I think, Luke?" the man—Mark, by process of elimination—said. "I think Matt knows something more he hasn't shared with the class."

"Something like what?"

"Something not good, that's for damn sure. Did you see the look on his face last night when he told us the fucker died in his sleep? Matt's tortured by it."

"I don't know." Luke Callahan sipped his coffee, then said, "The thing you can't forget about Matt is the still-waters-running-deep factor. Maybe it's from being the oldest, but I think he carries responsibility on his shoulders like an anvil. He was bad with us when we were kids, worse after Mom died, and then Branch's shenanigans with the separation, topped with the job he's been doing for years—Matthew needs to lighten up. When he told us he'd bought this place, I had hopes he'd finally begun to chill. Much better to use his downtime growing grapes than his more usual pastimes."

"Like speedboat racing, you mean?" Mark asked. "Hang gliding? Rock climbing? High-altitude skiing? I have to admit, I've never pictured him as a vintner. The man is an adrenaline junkie. Farming isn't in his blood."

"No, but payback is. Remember how he was when we were kids? You'd do something to Matt, you could count on the payback being twice as bad. And he can be subtle about it, too."

"Like buying this land to piss off Branch."

Luke nodded. "It wouldn't surprise me if he hadn't been planning a particularly nasty bit of vengeance that Ćurković up and spoiled by dying on him."

"Yeah, you may be right. But that begs the question. . . . How did we end up here? I know he's pissed about what happened yesterday, but that doesn't explain why he asked me to investigate Torie Bradshaw's problem to begin with. Is it part of some sort of elaborate revenge for her tearing up his leg?"

Torie almost dropped her coffee cup at that.

"Could have started out that way. He's certainly done more diabolical paybacks in the past. I figure that what happened yesterday will supersede any other plan. You could have been killed. Now Matt will go balls to the wall to find out who's responsible."

Mark Callahan rubbed the back of his neck. "He needs to relax. Hell, he needs to retire. Wish he'd find himself a woman like your Maddie and settle down, raise some kids, be a Little League coach."

"Can't argue with that. Matt could use a dose of normal. It's done wonders for me."

"You call your life normal?" Mark asked, snorting with amusement. "You're married to a rock star's daughter and you live on a houseboat with the dumbest dog ever born."

"Knucklehead isn't dumb." Luke gestured with his coffee cup. "That's dumb."

Torie glanced in the direction he indicated, and groaned. Gigi was sniffing at a fire ant pile. "Gigi!" she exclaimed, abandoning her eavesdropping on account of her dog. "Get away from there!"

The dog jumped away whining before Torie took two forward steps. "Gigi, what were you thinking?" Torie scolded. "One of these days your curiosity is going to get you into serious trouble."

"Like mother like daughter," Luke Callahan observed.

Torie glanced at him, at them, and forgot all about Gigi for a moment. Holy cow, Mr. and Mrs. Callahan had bred true. Matt's brothers were gorgeous, and except for Mark's temporary bruises, as identical as she and Helen, right down to the curiosity in their gazes. "You must be Ms. Bradshaw," Luke drawled. "We're—"

"Matt's brothers. Mark and Luke." She pasted on a smile and walked toward them. Addressing Mark, she said, "I'm so sorry you're hurt."

"Thanks." His lips twisted in a wry grin. "That's some welcome mat you had in your apartment."

"Wasn't it, though? I'll have to speak with my decorator about that." Sensing Luke's intense gaze, she met his stare and arched a brow.

Before he responded, Mark said, "Here comes Matt."

He had a towel flung over one shoulder as he climbed the walkway from the dock, and his blue swim trunks clung to his muscular form. "James in *Casino Royale*," Torie murmured. It was all she could do not to purr in appreciation.

"Good. Y'all are early. We have a lot to do today. Faxes came in overnight. I want you to look at them while I'm getting dressed." Glancing at Torie, he nodded. "G'morning."

"Well, hell," Luke muttered. He reached for his

wallet and pulled out a twenty, then handed it to Mark, who pocketed the cash with a grin. Matt opened his mouth, then obviously thought better of it.

Twenty minutes later, the Callahan men ate doughnuts with their coffee and discussed the information Matt had discovered about the former senator's actor friend. "Given his wife and new baby and new job, I doubt he's our boy. But it won't be a problem to stop over in Vegas and talk to him on my way to LA to visit with the boyfriend."

"*Ex*-boyfriend," Torie muttered, seated at the kitchen table playing with a carton of yogurt. The last thing she wanted was for Matt and Jason to meet. "Luke would be a better choice."

The Callahan men continued to ignore her. Any suggestion she made fell on deaf ears. Stubborn deaf ears.

"Idiots."

Matt asked Mark a question that required information from the computer in the study. A few minutes later from his position in front of the window, Luke said, "Great. Got trouble coming, Matthew."

Matt went for his gun.

"Not that kind of trouble. This one rides in a Lexus and uses a cane."

"Branch?" Matt threw a glance in the direction of the study, and muttered, "Well, crap. How did he find out this place is mine? I've kept it quiet." To Torie, he said, "This is gonna be ugly. You probably want to go upstairs."

In the spirit of "Turnabout is fair play," she pretended not to hear him.

"I'd listen to him, sweetheart," Luke told her. "Branch can be a mean sonofagun and he has a grudge against you." Glancing at Matt, he added, "Although she might make a good decoy, giving Mark the chance to make an escape."

"No. I'm tired of running interference between

those two," Matt said. "Torie, quit being stubborn. Go upstairs."

She acquiesced only because she decided she'd probably learn more by eavesdropping. She climbed the staircase, then stopped, out of sight, but well within listening distance. *This is becoming a habit.*

Moments later she heard wheels creaking across the porch. A hand pounded the door. "Matthew? Matthew, let me in."

"Hello, Branch. What are you doing here?"

"Maria's granddaughter dates a boy who works at the drugstore. He said he delivered medicine out to the vineyard. For Mark. And Luke was there, too. I went there, but that old fart wouldn't talk to me, so I came here. Is it true, then? Mark's here? You boys are all here?"

"Fuck no." Mark stood in the doorway of the office. "John's not here, goddamn you."

It went downhill from there.

No one paid a bit of attention to Torie, so she moved out onto the staircase landing, where she had a better view. The elderly man stood just inside the house, a white-knuckle grip on his cane. Matt stood at his right, facing his father, his hands shoved deep into the pockets of his jeans. Luke was positioned at Branch's left, his stance spread, his arms folded, as he frowned at the older man. Mark Callahan stood just outside the semicircle of men, his back straight, shoulders squared, his hands fisted at his side.

"Get him out of here, Matt," he growled, his voice low and hard and ugly.

Torie's eyes widened. Whoa. Lot of hate in one little sentence.

"Mark, they said you'd been hurt." Concern shone in the old man's eyes. "What happened? Are you all right?"

"All right? You have the fucking nerve to ask me that? I haven't been all right since you—" He bit off

the sentence, set his teeth, clenched his fists. Utter
hatred beamed like lasers from his eyes straight at his
father. "Not doing this. Matt, get him out of here
before I—"

Luke stepped toward Mark. "Hey, man, you gotta
calm down."

"Matt?" Mark's soft voice was a warning.

Matt stepped between his father and his younger
brother. "Branch, you don't need to be here."

"But I do." He used his cane to try to shift Matt
aside and, when that didn't work, walked around him
until he could see Mark once again. "Mark, I need to
talk to you, son. There's so much I need to say to
you. So much I want to explain."

"There is nothing you can say that I want to hear.
Nothing that will change anything. Not then, not now,
not ever. But here's something I want to explain to
you, old man. You're dead to me. Get it? Dead."

Wow, that's hard. Torie saw shock register on Matt's
and Luke's faces. The two brothers stood staring
speechless at the third until Mark spoke again. "Matt,
if you don't get him out of here, then I'm leaving."

Mark pivoted on his heel, went into the study, and
slammed the door shut.

"Damned muleheaded boy. My boy." Branch shook
his head and closed his eyes. Torie thought he looked
ten years older than he had the moment he'd shuffled
through the door.

Luke muttered a curse. "Look, Branch. Today isn't
a good day for this. Just . . . give him some more time.
He needs a little more time."

"I thought . . . maybe . . . they said he'd come
home because he was hurt. I thought maybe he'd . . .
changed . . . his mind. You two haven't had any use
for me, but Mark . . . he hates me because . . ." He
stopped and visibly tried to compose himself, looking
pale and old and tired. Looking pitiful, like a man

who'd lost everything. "He's hated me for a long, long time. I guess that's not going to change."

Torie waited for Matt or Luke to contradict their father, but both men remained silent. Wow, and she thought *she* came from a dysfunctional family.

Finally, Matt stepped toward Branch. "C'mon, Dad. You need to get on back home. This isn't doing anyone any good. Mark will be fine—we'll see to it."

Branch's lips silently formed the word "Dad" and some of his tension eased. "Is he all right? What happened to him?"

"He'll be fine. He's just banged up a bit."

"Why *did* he come here? Why are all three of you here? Is Maddie here, Luke? What's going on?"

"Maddie's busy with work, but she'll visit as soon as she can," Luke said. "She'll be by to see you when she gets in."

"But what are you doing?" Branch insisted.

"We're planning our next fishing trip," Matt said, trying to ease his father toward the door. "Gonna take the *Siren Song* down to the Keys again this fall."

"But you're all here, in Brazos Bend. You don't . . . do that. At the service for John y'all swore you'd never . . ."

"Technically, this isn't Brazos Bend, Branch." Luke stepped forward to assist in herding his father back outside. "The oath holds."

As the men moved outside, Torie went back downstairs. She heard a crash of glass in the study and she debated whether or not she should check on Mark. The emotional undercurrents swirling around this place pushed all her curiosity buttons. The expressions on the faces of the four Callahan men had hinted of a story that fired her imagination. She wished she'd had her camera with her on the staircase. Her fingers had actually itched.

Hearing a scratch and a demanding yip at the

kitchen door, she wandered into the kitchen to let Gigi outside, her attention focused inward as she mentally reviewed what she knew about the Callahan family. What all had Helen told her? The sons were estranged from their father because of the youngest brother's death and something else. Torie couldn't remember if she'd ever heard exactly what.

She'd no sooner exited the kitchen with thoughts of checking on Mark than a commotion erupted in the front yard. It sounded like . . . "A dogfight?" she murmured. Looking out the window, she added, "Oh no."

Gigi and Paco stood inches away from each other barking their little heads off. Then the Pomeranian lunged at Gigi and Torie dashed outside, calling, "Oh, Gigi, no. Get away from him. Matt, do something!"

Matt scowled down at the dogs, now a rolling, circling, yipping fur ball. Luke Callahan stood with his hands on his hips laughing, while Branch banged his cane on the stone sidewalk, yelling, "Stop that, Paco. Come to Daddy."

"Gigi. Gigi!"

"Paco. Paco!"

"Oh, for God's sake." Matt grabbed the water hose and turned it on. The spray hit the dogs and they separated, their barks turning to whines.

Paco took a running jump into the backseat of a chauffeur-driven Lexus, while Torie went down on her knees and held out her arms. "Gigi. Come here. What got into you, girl? You know to leave nasty mean dogs alone."

"Nasty mean!" Branch Callahan exclaimed. "I'll have you know that Paco . . . wait. What the hell are you doing here? Matt said you had a plane to catch."

Matt tossed down the water hose and stepped forward. "Dad, let me help you in the car."

"Matthew, why is she here? I demand to know

what's going on. I demand to be told. . . . Oh." Branch Callahan gasped in pain. "Oh . . . oh . . ."

"Dad?" Matt and Luke said simultaneously.

Branch's face went pale. He swayed and his right hand clutched his cane. He brought his left hand up and slapped it against his chest. "Help me, son."

Matt and Luke rushed forward, catching their father seconds before Branch Callahan collapsed to the ground.

"HIPAA laws, schmippa laws," Maddie Callahan railed as she paced the ICU waiting room. "This is Brazos Bend. We have our own way of doing things here. Federal law can go hang. That doctor needs to tell us what's wrong with your father!"

"Calm down, Red." Luke draped an arm around his wife's shoulders and gave her a comforting squeeze. Maddie had rushed to town from Fort Worth, where she'd been lobbying a state senator to support a bill to improve conditions in Texas prisons. "He's new in town. He'll learn in time. The important thing is he said Branch is doing all right."

"Why would he forbid the doctor to give us details?"

"Because he's a crotchety old fart who refuses to give up control of anything."

"I want to see him," she said, in a small voice.

"You know how he is about weakness, honey." Luke pressed a kiss against her hair. "He doesn't like anyone seeing it. That's why he ditches his walker for a cane whenever he goes outside, even though that's when he needs the walker most."

"Mark needs to be here, Luke," she added. "If Branch . . . well . . . Mark should be here!"

"Let Mark be. I think he's wrestling with demons we don't understand." When he'd started on the liquor, his brothers had taken possession of the pain pills. There hadn't been time for questions.

"He'll regret it."

Luke's only response was to hold his wife tighter.

Matt sat slouched in a hard plastic chair, his legs stretched out in front of him and crossed at the ankles. He had his hands folded across his belly and his eyes closed, but he wasn't napping. Far from it. His mind raced a million miles a second.

He was shaken. He didn't need the doctor to tell him what had happened. It was obvious. Branch had a heart attack. He'd gotten worked up emotionally over Mark's situation, then taken a second punch from Torie's presence at the lake house. The stress might not have caused the attack, but it sure as hell hadn't helped.

Matt figured he was the one to blame. He was the one who'd involved Mark in Torie's troubles. He was the one who had taken her into his home. Hell, if Branch knew he'd taken her to bed, he'd have had both a heart attack and a stroke.

Matt let out a sigh. As if his feelings toward his father weren't complicated enough already. He hated the man . . . but he loved him. He was furious with him over his part in John's death, but unlike his brothers, he understood the desperation behind Branch's efforts.

Hadn't Matt been just as desperate?

Against his will, his thoughts returned to that night in Sarajevo, that fateful encounter that no one—not his brothers, nor his father, nor his employers—knew anything about.

He recalled the café, Natalia's ruby lips and smoky voice. John's surprised, "Matt? Is that you? What are you doing in Sarajevo, brother?"

He'd lied. God help him, he'd lied and denied and turned his back on his own brother. And even worse, he'd failed to warn. An hour later, his brother had paid for Matt's failings.

In the hospital waiting room, he lurched to his feet

and shoved the memory away. "I gotta get out of here," he told Luke. "I can't. . . . I just . . . I'll catch up with you later." When he hit the hospital front doors a few minutes later, he was all but running. Maybe Mark had the right idea. Numb the pain. Numb the memories.

No, Matt needed to think. To plan, to plot, to scheme. That's what he did best. He needed to figure out just what to do to bring this whole debacle to an end. He needed to get Torie Bradshaw out of his life and out of the lives of his family before he didn't have any family left.

But the sweet bliss of oblivion called to him. Maybe he would hit a bar in town, buy a bottle, and get stupid on booze. Liquor was a good way to lose yourself for a while.

A woman is better.

Instinct led him to his truck, then back to the lake house. The bodyguard assured him that all had been quiet. The dog was upstairs in Torie's bedroom. He'd find the woman herself down by the water with her camera.

Matt saw her in the boat, lying on her stomach on the sundeck, taking photos of a turtle sunning himself on a big flat rock against the shore. Her ponytail drooped over one shoulder. She wore a blue swimsuit top and short white shorts, her shapely legs bent up behind her, her bare feet crossed at the ankles in the air. Matt couldn't take his gaze off the intriguing curve of her ass. His hands itched to touch her, to trace a lingering, meandering path along her silky skin.

He shouldn't be here. This was wrong on a dozen different levels.

But dammit, she was so . . . alive. Driven by the instincts and urges he couldn't resist, didn't want to resist, he strode down the walkway onto the dock.

"Matt." She rolled to a seated position. "How's your father?"

"Alive." He stepped into the boat.

"Thank God. What happened? Why did he collapse?"

"I don't want to talk about it. I don't want to talk at all." He leaned down and captured her mouth with his, pressing her down onto her back as he came over on top of her.

He kissed her, devoured her mouth with his lips and tongue and teeth. She tasted of mint and chocolate and smelled of sunshine. He wanted to lose himself in the sweetness of her, to move out of the darkness that haunted him and into the blinding light that resulted from joining with a shooting star like Torie. She was hang gliding and skydiving and ice climbing all at once.

He shifted her body sideways until they lay full atop the cushioned deck. His hand smoothed up the bare length of her leg, across the cotton-covered curve of her hip, then again onto the bare skin of her waist. He reached for the button at her shorts when she yanked her mouth from his. "Wait," she panted. "What are you doing?"

Nipping at the pulse in her neck, he murmured, "That's a dumb question."

She pushed hard against his chest, but Matt didn't budge. "All right, then. *Why* are you doing this? I thought we were just a one-night stand."

He didn't like the words, the term. Not in reference to her, to them. She was more than that. He just didn't know what. Didn't know anything, really, except that he needed her to make him whole again.

"I want you, Victoria. Right now." He lifted his head and stared down into her eyes. "I need you."

Her gaze searched his features. She moistened her lips with her tongue. "What's wrong, Matt?"

He ignored her question and pressed his point by dipping his head and licking the valley between her breasts.

"Oh, you don't play fair," she murmured.

"Never." He tugged her swimsuit top with his teeth and bared her rosy nipple. He tongued her to a hard peak and blew a stream of warm breath against the skin he'd made moist. "Say yes, Victoria."

He drew her into his mouth and sucked her, gently at first, then harder. "Oh," she breathed. "I don't . . . ah."

"Say yes." He freed her other breast and closed his hand around her. He rubbed her, kneaded her. He seduced her with his hands, his mouth, his eyes, and ultimately with his words. "Please, Victoria. Let me have you."

She surrendered with a sigh, and Matt smiled in triumph. In deference to the daylight and the exposed location, he dragged her off the sundeck and onto the cushioned bench seat. It was his last conscious thought as he allowed his instincts full rein and plunged into the mindless heat of lovemaking.

When he stripped her naked he forgot about his father. When he slipped his hands between her legs and spread her wide, he didn't think about Mark. When he gazed at her glistening beauty, when he lowered his mouth to taste her, to drink of her sweet nectar, his mind harbored not a single thought of John.

Matt saw nothing but Torie, heard nothing but her needy whimpers, smelled only her musky scent. She filled his mind. She accepted his body. She journeyed with him into the dark, sensual oblivion of basic, primal sex.

When it was over, when he collapsed onto her sated body with a groan, he knew that things had changed.

The plan had changed. He'd changed.

God help them both.

Chapter Twelve

"Enough lollygagging around," Matt said. "We need to go up and get dressed. It's time to go to town."

"Town?" Her heart still racing, her breaths still coming in pants, Torie rose up on her elbows. "Did you say we're going into town?"

"Yeah."

She watched him step into his jeans and tried to focus on his words instead of his very fine behind or the fact that her emotions were in turmoil. She couldn't believe she'd just done what she'd done. Casual sex like this was *so* not like her.

Although she couldn't find much casual about what had just happened.

She dragged her thoughts back to the matter at hand. "I don't understand. Aren't I in hiding?"

"Not anymore. My father outed you, Victoria, and it's necessitated a change in plan."

"What! What did he do?"

"He said it in the ambulance and again at the hospital. He told anyone who'd listen that the woman who shot his son—the infamous Torie Bradshaw—was here in town and that they needed to beware. All that without knowing what you did to my truck."

She thought about that a moment. "Okay, well. So

you think they'll make the connection between Vicky Bradshaw and me?"

"Oh, yeah."

"So I stayed too long. I should have left town like you wanted to begin with."

"No sense worrying about that now." He scooped her clothes up off the bottom of the boat and handed them to her. "Besides, it's not as bad as I made it sound. Your instincts were right, Victoria. Brazos Bend is a good place for you to lie low."

"But you said—"

"I exaggerated. I wanted you to leave town."

"Well. Thank you very much." She yanked on her panties and shorts.

"Oh, don't be snippy. I told you from the first that you got under my skin. I knew we'd end up"—he waved a hand around—"here."

"And is *here* so bad?" She slipped her swimsuit halter over her head, then tied the strings in back. Matt watched the process with obvious regret.

"Not at all. *Here* is pretty much the best I've ever had."

She wrinkled her nose, but his statement did mollify her somewhat. She didn't know exactly what she wanted him to say. Did she want him to tell her that he cared for her, that his heart, not just his penis, was engaged?

Did she want him to confess his undying love?

Yes.

Oh, man. She needed to think about this. She *never* wanted men to confess their undying love. That's when relationships turned awkward and messy and complicated because she never could say it in return. Why would she want to go there with Matt Callahan?

Because maybe this time, you could say it.

She blinked. Gasped a shocked breath.

Face it, Bradshaw. You're falling for him.

"No," she murmured beneath her breath.

Yes. You started falling for him back on the island.

And the chances of Matt Callahan losing his heart to her were about as good as those of the state of Texas deciding to outlaw high school football.

You'd best be careful, Torie Bradshaw. If you don't watch yourself, you'll be headed for a world of hurt.

Holy cow. She scrambled to her feet. "So, why are we going into town? Surely you're not taking me to see your father?"

"Not hardly." Matt's lips twisted in a wry smile. "That'd be the proverbial final nail."

In Branch Callahan's coffin, she silently completed. "So what's the change in plan?"

"I can't leave Brazos Bend now, not with Dad's situation the way it is. I'll call in some markers and get some other guys I know on your case."

"Who? What will they be doing? Where will they go?"

"Look, let's not get into all of that now," he suggested, slipping into his deck shoes. "I'm hungry. Today is all-you-can-eat catfish at P-3. I'd like to take you there for lunch."

Catfish? I don't think so. "That's all right. You have sandwich makings here. That'll be fine."

"Who wants a sandwich when they can have fried catfish?" he asked as he checked the knots in the dock lines. "You're in for a treat. Admittedly, it's not the best catfish I've ever had—you gotta go to Bill's up in Waurika, Oklahoma, for that—but P-3 comes in a close second. I promised myself while climbing a mountain in Pakistan that I'd have myself a P-3 catfish meal at the first opportunity, and this is it."

E-yew. "I've never had catfish."

He flashed her a grin. "You'll love it."

She decided to try another tack. "I've always thought Italian food was very sensual. Much more than seafood."

"Catfish isn't seafood." Matt helped her from the boat onto the dock. "It is fresh, though. P-3's catch comes right out of a farm on this lake."

"So we're having catfish out of Possum Kingdom Lake. How appealing is that?" Her tone made it clear that to Torie, it was anything but appealing.

Matt laughed, but showed no sign of changing his mind. Still, she was glad to hear the laughter. He'd been so serious when he arrived, so on edge. She liked it that she could take the edge off for him. After all, he had saved her life, had he not? She enjoyed making him laugh.

You're doing it again. Don't go there, Bradshaw. You're asking for trouble.

Right. Torie gave her head a shake and started up the walkway. She might like making him laugh, but she wouldn't enjoy catfish. He was wrong about that. Catfish from Possum Kingdom. Ick. "Who would name a lake after semirodent roadkill?"

Walking behind her, Matt replied, "Some fellow from Pennsylvania, the way I remember it. Story goes that back in the early nineteen hundreds some Northerner moved to Mineral Wells to take the waters and got into the fur business. The cedar choppers from this part of the county brought him so many hides he called them the 'boys from Possum Kingdom.' The name stuck when they dammed the Brazos River back in the forties."

"How unfortunate."

"Now, don't be snotty. Go put a shirt on. I need to touch base with Mark and Bill; then I'll meet you at the truck and we'll head into town."

Obviously, there was no changing his mind. Sighing, Torie went up to the house, took a quick shower, and spent a moment in front of the closet debating which of her limited number of outfits was most appropriate for lunch at a place named P-3. He was standing in the living room speaking with Bill Reynolds when she went back downstairs. He checked his watch impatiently and waited for her to join them.

"It's been a pleasure, Torie," Bill said, surprising her.

"You going somewhere?"

Matt said, "He got a call for another job . . . something long-term. Since you'll be staying in Brazos Bend for a while with me, I told him we'll manage without him. I haven't forgotten what you said about . . . what was his name . . . Bruno?"

Torie sensed a need to apply brakes. Things were changing too quickly for her comfort. Neither man appeared willing to listen to her questions or concerns, however, so she gave in, thanked Bill, then attempted to settle her account, only to learn that Matt had taken care of that for her. She brooded about that detail for a moment. It felt a little too much like she was being . . . kept.

Mark Callahan walked out of the study, a manila file in his hand. It was the first time Torie had seen him since he shut himself in the room with a bottle of booze in his hand before the ambulance arrived for his father. "Here's what I have on the boyfriend," he said to Matt, showing no outward sign of inebriation. "He's looking good to me."

Maybe he'd dived into work rather than the bottle, Torie thought.

Matt glanced through the file. "Thanks, I'll see that Luke gets it."

"Hope you know what you're doing, big brother," Mark observed, giving Torie a quick glance.

Matt shrugged, then gestured for Torie to precede him out the door. As she walked to his truck, she asked him about Mark. "He has some issues concerning your father, doesn't he?"

"We all have some issues with Branch."

"But you and Luke went to the hospital. Mark shut himself in the study."

"I'm sure he's had enough of hospitals for a while."

As they climbed into the truck, Torie reflected that the day had certainly taken some unexpected turns. Of course, unexpected was becoming the norm of late. Stalkers, explosions, heart attacks. Boat sex. She'd never had boat sex in her life, and now she had it twice this week.

"We need to make a quick stop at the vineyard," he told her, turning toward the shortcut over the hill. "I need to catch Les up on what's happened today."

Upon their arrival at Four Brothers it quickly became apparent that his partner had already heard the news. "If you've come to give me hell about sending that old man over to the lake house, then you can save your breath. He was determined to find you and your brothers. Knew you were around here somewhere."

"Don't worry about it," Matt said.

"I'm not," Les snapped back, though it was obvious to Torie that he was indeed worried. "As if having that old man show up wasn't enough, starting an hour ago, your harem returned in force. Funeral food," he grumbled. "They're bringing us funeral food now, and the old sonofagun isn't even dead. Three green bean casseroles in the last half hour. I'm not getting a damned bit of work done. You better do something about this, Callahan, or I'm going to tell them they need to take their goodies over to the lake house."

"Don't do that!" Matt hastened to say. "I'll take care of it. I promise. I have a plan."

"I like green bean casserole," Torie piped up.

Matt ignored her. "Les, this thing with Branch has changed the situation."

"Expected it would. Can't see you leaving town with him in the hospital."

"Well, it's even more than that. Mark will be over later to explain."

"That's fine. I just want you to put a stop to all the women showing up."

Hear hear, Torie silently echoed.

Back on the road, Matt played the radio during the drive into town, which effectively discouraged conversation between them. When he pulled into the parking lot of a restaurant with big plate windows and wood shingle siding, he finally turned down the rock and roll and glanced at Torie. "Looks like they have a crowd this afternoon. We're bound to face some questions. Let me do the talking."

"I wouldn't know what to say about Branch."

"They won't just ask about Branch."

"What do you mean?"

"Me showing up with a woman in tow will cause a stir."

Wonderful. "Maybe we should go somewhere else. Like a nice, quiet steak house. Aren't I supposed to lie low?"

"No. This is perfect. Believe me."

Believe him? He was a spy. He lied for a living. Her heart full of trepidation, Torie followed Matt toward the front door of P-3.

The aroma of fried catfish teased Matt's senses as he opened the door. The restaurant was a Brazos Bend fixture, one of several Pioneer restaurants in town that offered home-cooking-style menus. He wouldn't go so far as to call it cuisine. The restaurants did big business at lunch, on Sundays after church, and especially on all-you-can-eat catfish days, when a wait for a table sometimes lasted an hour. Luckily today, they were on the tail end of the rush and the hostess showed them to a table almost immediately.

"Well, this is . . . interesting," Torie said as she slid into the booth's red vinyl seat and stared up at the

Hereford head mounted on the wall above them. "I hope he doesn't drool on my hamburger."

Perusing the selections on the table-side jukebox, Matt replied, "P-3 doesn't serve the regular menu on catfish day. You won't be able to get a burger."

"A salad?"

"The catfish platter comes with coleslaw."

"I don't plan on ordering catfish."

"That's all we're serving this afternoon, honey," came a cheerful feminine voice.

Matt glanced up at the waitress, who set two clear plastic glasses of ice water on the table. Recognizing her as a high school classmate, he gave the woman his friendliest smile. "Hello, Nancy."

"Well, if it isn't Demon Callahan," she said with a grin. "I'd heard a rumor that you were back in town. Welcome home, Matt."

"Thanks. It's good to be back. How are Frank and the kids?"

"They're good." She gave him a brief rundown of her family, then smiled politely at Torie. "I'm sorry. We're being rude. I'm Nancy Snow. I went to high school with Matt."

Torie smiled in return and extended her hand in greeting. "It's nice to meet you, Nancy. I'm"—she glanced at Matt, a question in her eyes—"Vicky. Vicky Bradshaw."

"Oh! You're that photographer who was taking bluebonnet pictures at Cottonwood Cottage. Penny Russell told me about it, but I was too late to get my kids in on the deal."

"Yes, I—"

"*Torie* is a wonderful photographer," Matt said.

Nancy's smile melted like a snow cone in the sun. "Torie? *Torie* Bradshaw? *The* Torie Bradshaw?"

Torie lowered her hand, her brow dipped quizzically. " 'The'? I'm no 'the.' What do you mean, 'the'?"

Wide-eyed, Nancy looked at Matt. "Your father

comes for liver and onions at noon every Wednesday. He was here the day the governor called to tell him you were in surgery at Walter Reed." Glancing back at Torie, she finished, "Branch Callahan had quite a lot to say about you that day. Your name stuck in my head."

"I see."

Matt could tell that Torie was struggling to hold on to her smile. He'd be sure to order peach cobbler for dessert. That should improve her mood.

"So, why are you here with Demon?" Nancy unfortunately continued. "Trying to make amends for ruining his life?"

"I didn't ruin his life!"

"You shot him."

Since Torie's eyes were now firing poison darts, Matt thought it best to intervene. "It's a more complicated story than that, Nancy, and besides, that's all behind us." Ignoring Torie's snort, he added, "Have you heard the news about Branch?"

"What news?"

"We took him to the hospital this morning. Heart attack, it appears."

"Oh, no." The waitress and Matt discussed his family for a few minutes until he mentioned being hungry and she dragged herself back to work by asking, "So, what can I get y'all to drink with your catfish?"

Torie snapped, "I don't—"

"Two teas, Nancy," Matt interrupted. "Thanks."

"—want—"

"To cause a scene," he concluded.

She shot him an irritated frown. "I wouldn't count on that."

Matt couldn't help but grin. "You sparkle like sequins in sunlight when you're in a snit."

"Sequins in sunlight?" She rolled her eyes. "Puhleese. Don't they teach you better lines in spy school?"

"Now, Victoria, no need to—" Matt was interrupted by a shrill, feminine voice cutting across the room.

"Demon! Demon Callahan. You're back!"

And so it began. One after another, the babe parade marched by the table to flirt and fuss and fake welcomes to Torie Bradshaw, whose temper escalated with every introduction. After the third such exchange, she started ignoring them and turned her attention to the booth's individual jukebox. Digging quarters from the bottom of her purse, she selected the single rap song among a playlist filled with country. She repeated her selection each time another woman approached the table.

"Ah, Torie. Please. No more," he protested as she asked a passing waitress for change. "It's not my fault. The thing is, they see me as eligible ever since Luke got married. My brother is the one who deserves your wrath."

"Demon!" came another squeal.

"All right, that's it." Torie tossed down the french fry she'd been nibbling on, reached across the table, grabbed his shirt, and pulled him toward her. She planted a kiss right on his mouth.

Okay. This fits right with my plan. Couldn't be better. Matt was just settling in to enjoy it when she let him go and shoved him away. "He's busy right now," she declared to Miss Brazos Bend 1996.

"Well, I never . . . ," the young woman said.

"That's your problem," Torie fired back.

As the beauty queen marched away in a huff and Matt let out a soft chuckle, she turned on him with a glare. "This is so not working for me, Callahan."

"What do you mean?" he asked, arching a brow. Though, of course, he had a pretty good idea.

She drummed her fingers against the table. "Catfish. Catty women. What are we doing here? I don't understand the plan. First I'm in hiding and then I'm not. You want me out of town, then in your bed and in your boat. I know it's been a difficult couple of days, what with your brother getting hurt and your father collapsing, but it's not been a walk in the park for me, either. I like maps, Callahan. They keep me grounded. I like to know which direction I'm going in all areas of my life—relationships included. I don't like being surprised like I was earlier today when you decided to . . . rock the boat."

"I didn't hear you complaining."

"You caught me off guard. It was after your father's thing and you looked . . . upset."

"I was upset. You helped me." It was one of the few truths he'd spoken for a while.

"Fine. I'm glad." She tucked a stray strand of golden silk behind her ear. "But we go from that to this? This is absolutely not part of my fantasy. The afterglow is definitely doused. When I dreamed about you, you were 007, not Barney Fife."

Now, that surprised him. Matt's fork slipped from his hand and clattered against his stoneware plate. "Excuse me? Did you just call me Barney Fife?"

"Okay, maybe that's too harsh, but come on. On the island you were dark and dangerous and smooth as Sean Connery. Here, you're . . . not."

Affronted, he said, "This is Brazos Bend, Victoria. Not Vienna or Paris or Moscow. A good agent blends in with his surroundings."

She placed her hands flat on the table, leaned forward, and spoke just above an agitated whisper. "A man who has just had broad-daylight sex should listen when a woman wants steak instead of catfish for lunch!"

Okay. Maybe he should have spent a few minutes cuddling before disembarking, so to speak. "But it's really good catfish, honey."

At the same moment he spoke, a trio of women squealed, "Demon!"

Torie curled her lip at him and said, "Then you can have mine."

She dumped her plate in his lap, stood, and marched for the door. Matt frowned down at the coleslaw on his jeans, then followed her path with a narrowed gaze while around him, high-pitched feminine voices blabbered.

Now, he decided. This was the perfect time to take his plan a step further. Taking deadeye aim on his objective, he shoved to his feet, tossed a twenty onto the table, then called after Torie in a loud, clear voice. "Now, darlin', be fair. You're the one who wanted to keep our engagement secret."

The attentive crowd gasped.

Victoria Lynn Bradshaw halted so fast that her sandals squeaked against the linoleum floor. She turned slowly, her expression stunned. "What did you say?"

"Well, hell." Smothering a grin, he grabbed his red cloth napkin off the table and dabbed at the mayonnaise stain on his jeans. "I let it slip, didn't I? Sorry about that, love."

Her mouth worked, but no sound emerged. She finally managed a growl that reminded him of her purse pet; then she whirled around and stormed from the restaurant. P-3 erupted with excited chatter, and as a few bolder souls called out questions to Matt, he winked and waved them off. "Later, boys."

He grabbed a peppermint from the jar beside the cash register, popped it into his mouth, and sauntered out the door. With his secondary objective accomplished, he debated the best route to take in pursuing his primary goal. After considering a handful of possible scenarios, he settled on one that had worked in the past. Catching up with her in the parking lot, he said, "You planning to walk back to the lake house?"

"It's certainly preferable to riding anywhere with you."

He put his hand out to stop her, and she shrugged him off. Chuckling, he clamped his arms around her waist and pulled her struggling form back against him. "What's the matter with you?" she screeched. "I swear, your personality has gone Bond to Bubba in the blink of an eye. Let go of me!"

Bond to Bubba? "Can't let go." He nuzzled her neck. "Gotta make it look good for the audience, since I'm your fiancé and I have to charm my way out of your doghouse."

"Of all the . . . oh, for God's sake. About that engage—"

He twirled her around and launched his best weapon, cutting her off with a kiss.

Whoa. Holy cow. *Mamma mia.*

He was doing it again. Dammit.

Thank God.

Without conscious thought, Torie lifted her arms and draped them around his neck. How was she supposed to take his head off if she melted all over the blacktop? She sank against him, boneless and mindless, but oh, so hot. No wonder they called him Demon. He kissed like the very devil himself.

Her blood raced. Her skin tingled. She ached between her legs. His hands gripped her ass, lifted, and pressed her against his obvious erection.

Holy hell.

Why couldn't she resist this man? Where was her self-control? Her self-respect, for heaven's sake?

He released her mouth and licked her collarbone.

Oh well, who needs self-respect when James Bond is bent on seduction?

Too much. This was way too much. But Torie didn't want it to stop. When finally, he gently nipped his way across her jaw to nibble at her earlobe, she dragged in a breath and said, "You make me totally crazy."

"I know the feeling."

"You can be such a jerk."

"It's a talent of mine."

"So why do you do something so asinine?"

"You mean go from . . . how did you say it?" He licked the whorl of her ear, the curling motion of his tongue creating a tingling sensation on her skin. "From Bond to Bubba?"

"Yes. It totally ruins the mood."

"Does it?" He took her lips again, his kiss long and deep and soulful. Holy Moses. She couldn't think. Could barely breathe.

Then he murmured against her ear. "I want to use you, Victoria."

Yes, please.

No, wait. She had more pride than that. "You already did. Remember? The boat?"

"I'll never forget the boat." He gently bit her neck. She shuddered.

He smiled into her eyes, then spoke matter-of-factly. "By announcing our engagement, I've taken myself off the market. The women will stay away from the vineyard, which will make Les happy. It'll make life around town easier for you because women won't try to compete if they've already thought you've won."

She gaped at him. "Do you know how egotistical you sound?"

"Victoria, you've seen the cupcakes. The brownies. The cookies." He chastised her with a look. "Listen, an engagement explains why we're always together, which we will be, since from here on out I'm your bodyguard, and—"

"But what about your father? Aren't you worried this will kill him?"

"I'll explain the truth to him."

Torie glanced toward the restaurant's windows, where at least half a dozen faces pressed against the plate glass. Buckle bunnies and drooling cow heads and catfish—she should have stayed at his lake house. "I think this is a very bad idea, Callahan."

"I disagree. I think it's a great idea. There's no reason we can't enjoy ourselves until we track down your stalker."

She slapped a hand against his chest. "See? That's an example right there. I agreed to a one-night stand, not an extended affair. Frankly, right now I have absolutely no intention of . . . of . . . going boating with you again. I told you the other night that I don't sleep around. I meant it."

"Sleeping with me isn't sleeping around. Besides, this morning—"

"Was a mistake!"

"It might have been a lot of things, but a mistake isn't one of them."

He was wrong. It *was* a mistake, a huge one. For her, anyway. She was simply too vulnerable to him, her heart was at risk, and he wanted to use her to stave off other women and their muffins. Where was her pride?

She'd left it on the boat. She'd had it when she went down there with her camera, but once he'd walked on board and given her that blue laser look . . . well, he left her pride on the sundeck in melted orgasmic shambles. He'd stolen it right out from under her, and getting it back with him around would be impossible.

This situation was dangerous, very dangerous, because Torie always did like living on the edge. Until she fell. With Matt, she was halfway to the ground already.

She closed her eyes and mentally counted to ten. "C'mon, Callahan. Why are you doing this? Especially now, under these circumstances. Your father had a heart attack this morning. You should be concentrating on him. Why would you create this fake engagement when you should be pacing the waiting room at the hospital?"

"I hate hospitals. Luke and his wife have the waiting room covered. You came to me for help because you trusted me to know what I'm doing, Victoria. You need to let me do it."

"I was thinking of spy sort of things. You know, wiretaps and covert surveillance and gadgets that do neat stuff."

"You've been watching old movies again, haven't you?" he asked drily.

"Maybe I have, but that doesn't change the fact that a fake engagement isn't ordinary espionage procedure."

"You sure about that? I seem to remember a time or two when your hero pretended the B-girl with him was his wife."

"Oh, stop it. Life has gone totally topsy-turvy if you're now the one spouting Bond nonsense."

He grinned wickedly and draped his arm around her shoulders as he guided her toward the truck. "Then let me tell you about a real mission in Vienna when I was 'engaged' to an opera singer whose tongue was as golden as her throat."

"Oh, hush, Callahan." She elbowed him in the stomach. "Fine. I don't like it, but I'll go along with it. I came to you for your expertise, after all. We might as well go buy a box of Cracker Jacks."

"Cracker Jacks?"

"If I'm going to 'marry' a spy, I at least want a secret-decoder engagement ring."

Chapter Thirteen

Los Angeles

Another dead end.

The automatic door whooshed open and the stalker walked out into the Southern California sunshine. All that work to gain access to a hospital computer to no avail. Someone else was here first. Someone else wiped the file. Who? Why? Who was the man in Torie Bradshaw's apartment?

Now how to find the disappearing bitch?

Frustration surged, heightened to rage. Everything was lost because of the bitch. Her and her camera. She'd pay. By God, she'd pay.

Think. Think. Someone was helping her. She wasn't smart enough to cover her tracks so well. The government. The damned government. Had to be. Couldn't forget who her father was.

Fingers drummed against a trouser-clad thigh. Should have moved faster. Green yellow orange had been too much fun. Played with the mouse just a little too long. Should have sprung the trap sooner.

Scared little rodent must have called Daddy. Wouldn't do. Wouldn't do at all.

So, there next? To Washington? To Daddy? No, not Daddy.

Rage calmed. Amusement bloomed along with a malevolent smile. The thought had been right, looking for a loved one. So, the man escaped. He wasn't the only possibility.

The bitch loved her sister.

Following a phone call from Luke telling him that their father had been moved out of intensive care and into a private room, Matt returned to the hospital with Torie in tow, having dismissed all her arguments as to why that was a bad idea. They ran into Luke and Maddie in the parking lot. Maddie's gaze fastened on the proprietary arm Matt had at Torie's waist and her eyes narrowed in speculation.

In turn, Torie studied Maddie with interest. Over the rattles and bangs of construction emanating from the site of a new hospital wing, Matt made the introductions. Torie smiled and said, "Baby Dagger. It's a pleasure to meet you. I've worked with your father on a number of occasions."

"Worked with him . . . or spied *on* him?" the rock star's famous daughter replied, her smile not reaching her eyes.

"Both." Torie said it without a trace of apology. She gave her head a little toss, sending her casual ponytail flying. "I covered the wedding at his country house outside of Derby two years ago. Sneaking onto those grounds was a bitch." She winced with the memory as she added, "I met his dogs. Up close and personal."

Maddie laughed reluctantly. "The Dobermans? George and Ringo?"

Torie nodded. "As a rule, I'm good with dogs, but that pair . . ." She shook her head, letting her voice trail off.

"They took a bite out of your hide?" Luke asked.

Maddie slipped her arm through her husband's. "I expect they knocked her down and all but licked her to death. Am I right?"

"Yep. Strangest pair of guard dogs I'd ever seen. But then, they are your father's dogs."

"He's taught them to play the drums."

"No."

Maddie nodded.

"Now, that would make a great photograph." When Matt snorted derisively, she smiled sweetly and added, "Gee, darling, maybe we can make a stop in Derby on our honeymoon. Since Blade and I will be in-laws of a sort, I'll bet I could even use the front door this time."

"Honeymoon!" Maddie exclaimed while Luke folded his arms and observed, "This should be interesting."

Matt gave them an expurgated version of his plan. His brother knew him well enough to understand that he'd left out some pertinent points. Matt suspected Maddie did, too, but she'd been a Callahan long enough to know to keep her mouth shut. When he'd finished his recitation, Luke delivered a sharp look to Matt before leaning over and kissing Torie's cheek. "Welcome to fam-damn-ly."

Maddie clicked her tongue. "Two Callahan brothers down? Mark might want to rethink his visit to Four Brothers. So, are you two headed up to tell Branch the happy news? For that, I might wait around town."

"You're leaving?" Matt asked.

"I sure am. I have a meeting in the morning with the governor I'd rather not miss, and since your father is too mean to die, I feel safe enough to make the trip to Austin."

Matt's brow arched as he looked at his brother. Maddie adored her father-in-law. For her to sound so acerbic, he must have been in fine form. "Good visit, I assume?"

"He started in on her about babies again." Luke didn't have to say more. He'd confided in Matt that they'd been trying to get pregnant for over six months now, and the lack of success was getting to Maddie. "Anyway, his color is good, but he's weak as a kitten. According to Branch it was a mild heart attack and he'll be able to go home in a day or two."

"What does the doctor say?"

"Stubborn goat still won't let him talk to us. Holding on to his independence, Branch claims. He looks tired and weak, but his voice is strong."

"I convinced him to let me call in one of Home For Now's personnel to sit with him overnight," Maddie said. Lips twitching, she added, "He wanted Sandy McDermott. She was busy, so I called Mabel Perkins."

Matt let it sink in a moment; then he laughed. Last he knew, Mabel owned twelve cats that she never tired talking about. "You're a wicked woman, Maddie Callahan. I love that about you. Why don't you ditch that ugly puss you're married to and run off with me?"

Torie folded her arms and scowled toward Luke. "He's cheating on me already and we haven't been engaged an hour."

"Nah. He just likes to flirt with certain death, which touching my wife would bring. Matt's always been an adrenaline junkie. Likes extreme sports. Dangerous situations." He paused significantly, then added, "Dangerous women."

"Uh-huh," Matt responded in a dry tone. "That's why I own a home and business in Brazos Bend, Texas."

"He likes the thrill of dodging all the women who're trying to kill him with cholesterol," Torie said. "You should see the cake this woman left with Les earlier. Has to have five thousand grams of fat per serving."

Matt shrugged, then arranged a meeting with his brothers later that night. After wishing Maddie a safe trip back to Austin, he ushered a reluctant Torie into the hospital. "I need to tell him before somebody else does."

"I don't see why I need to be there," she muttered as he led her toward the elevator. "Look what happened last time he saw me. Aren't you worried I'll kill him this time?"

"Nah." Matt pushed the UP button and waited. "He might be an ornery old cuss, but there's still some Southern gentleman in him. He won't get as worked up with a lady around."

"That's assuming he considers me a lady." She shrugged. "He hates me, Matt. I think it's a bad idea. I think Maddie thought so, too. Didn't you see the way she looked at me?"

"She wasn't impolite."

"Not with her words or actions, no. Her eyes, though, didn't lie. She didn't like seeing me here."

Okay, he couldn't argue with that, but he didn't like the idea that Torie's feelings were hurt because of it. "Maddie wasn't reacting to you as much as to your job. Remember who she is. The paparazzi have been cruel to her in the past. And Torie, you didn't cause Branch's heart attack. The business with Mark . . . well . . . it was ugly."

The floor indicator dinged and the elevator doors swished open. Torie grimaced as she stepped inside. "I still think it'd be better for me to hide out in the gift shop. Or hang out in front of the nursery windows. I like doing that."

"It'll be fine. Trust me." Matt punched the button for their floor. "I trust you."

She looked at him in surprise. "You do?"

He thought about it a moment, then nodded, almost surprised by the answer himself. Trusting her wasn't necessarily a good development. She turned her gaze to the number panel above the door, and Matt watched her watch the numbers light up as they climbed toward the fifth floor.

Torie dreaded facing his father. She might grumble and complain, but she was game to the tasks Matt put before her. It made his job easier. He liked that quality in a woman. In this woman. Hell, he liked a lot of things about Torie Bradshaw—and they weren't all sexual. Imagine that.

How disturbing was that?

He felt a stir of danger. He'd do well to remember that she was a trouble magnet, a pain in the ass. Part of the paparazzi!

He'd do better to forget that she loved her sister, loved that silly little fur ball of a dog. He shouldn't recall the way he'd watched her put children and parents at ease with her ready laugh and easy smile or how he'd heard her singing in the shower this morning, joyfully and energetically, and with a total lack of concern about being off-key.

Nevertheless, he reached out and took her hand, lacing his fingers with hers. She glanced up at him in surprise. He saw the number 5 on the panel flicker· on. "This is it. It'd probably be best if you waited outside until I've had a chance to explain things. Just stand outside the door, okay?"

"Why don't I wait in the lobby downstairs? Or the parking lot? Oklahoma would be good."

He chastised her with a look, then walked into Branch's room to the smell of roses and the sound of curses aimed at the television hanging on the wall. "Damned Rangers. What is it going to take for that team to get some pitching?"

"Well, I can see you're on your deathbed," Matt drawled, glancing around at the dozens of floral arrangements decorating the room. He hadn't realized his father had that many friends.

Branch collapsed back against his pillow. "If I can't rail against my team, I might as well be dead." He smiled tiredly and said, "You've come to visit me. That's really nice."

The temptation to fire back the usual denial was strong, but Matt resisted. He studied his father, noted the return of color in his complexion, and felt a tenseness inside himself ease. He'd been worried, he realized. Despite Luke's assurances, he'd needed to see for himself that his father really was okay. "What did the doctor say?"

"I don't want to talk about it."

"Then I'll leave."

Branch scowled and yanked at his bedcovers. "I need rest and to watch my diet and to eliminate stress."

"Then why in the world are you watching the Rangers play baseball?" When his father didn't respond, Matt continued. "What about bypass surgery? Angioplasty?"

"Don't need it. Tests all came out okay."

Matt folded his arms and studied his father. Branch told the truth when it suited him. For all Matt knew, the doctor could have given him two days to live. Though he was tempted to steal his father's chart and see what he could make of the information inside, he wouldn't. He could understand the old man's desire for privacy. He'd been that way himself during the rehabilitation of his leg.

He decided to take his father at his word. For now, anyway. "I need to explain what we have going on so you're not surprised when you hear about it from others."

"You mean, you and your brothers? You're bringing me into your plan?" Branch grabbed the bed's safety bars and pulled himself up, his expression eager.

"Hell, Dad. You just had a heart attack. Settle down, would you?"

" 'Dad,' " Branch repeated in a murmur. Smiling, he sat back against his pillow, folded his hands over his chest, and waited expectantly.

Matt gave him a brief recap of what Branch needed to know about events since Torie came to town.

"So that's what happened to Mark?" Branch interrupted when Matt mentioned the explosion. "He got caught in a trap meant for That Damned Woman? Sonofabitch! She's a nightmare! First you, then Mark. You'd better keep her the hell away from Luke! Why the hell is she still here?"

"Calm down, Branch. She's here because I intend to find the person who rigged that explosion. Now it's personal."

Branch pursed his lips and nodded in agreement. "Because of Mark."

And because you took a look at Mark and had a heart attack. And, to be honest, because of Torie.

"So how you gonna find him?"

"Oh, we'll track him down. Between the three of us, we have a lot of resources to tap."

"So you'll all be leaving town." The excitement in his father's face died.

"Actually, no. I'll be running the operation from here. It's safest for Victoria that way."

"So you're protecting her. Her. The woman who shot you. My God, Matthew, you are a good man."

No. Actually, he wasn't. "Just so you know and don't have another heart attack, Branch, we're faking an engagement."

"What sort of engagement?"

"Marriage, Branch." Having noted Torie peeking around the doorjamb, he motioned her into the room. "Earlier today at P-3, I announced that Torie and I were getting married."

Torie smiled hesitantly and wiggled her fingers in a wave hello.

Branch scowled back at her. "Why the hell would you do something that asinine?"

At that, Torie's chin came up and her back snapped

straight. "Asinine!" she repeated, her eyes flashing and her voice bristling with offense. Never mind that she'd used the same word herself about his plan earlier.

Matt watched with rapt fascination as she visibly reined in her temper. "Mr. Callahan," she said in a calm, quiet tone. "I'm glad to see you looking so well. I want you to know that I'm sorry for having brought trouble to your family. I sincerely regret the harm I caused Matt and Mark—"

"Stop it," Matt interrupted. "You're not responsible for that bomb."

She ignored him and continued. "I'll get out of your family's hair as quickly as possible. You have my word."

Branch sneered. "What good is your word? You're a Peeping Tom. You take one picture of our Maddie, one single shot, and . . ." *Cough . . . cough . . . cough.*

Matt took a concerned step forward. Looking hurt, Torie stepped away. "You're obviously ill. I think it's best I wait out in the hall until Matt is finished here."

The look on her face sliced at Matt. "For God's sake, Branch. Do you have to be such a hard-ass?"

"I don't like her."

"Well, I do!"

"That's what I'm afraid of." Branch thumbed the television remote and the set switched off. "You know that I want only what's best for my boys. I admit I had my doubts about growing grapes on a cattle ranch, but I've done some research. You're building something good out there at Four Brothers. Even though you've never said it, I figure you're at an age and experience that you're thinking of trading one kind of fieldwork in for another. The thought of that fills me with such joy."

"Branch . . . ," Matt began.

"Let me finish. With the career you've had, it's

made sense for you to remain single, but if you come home . . . well . . . I know there's a lot of women in the area who'd jump at the chance to have your babies."

"What's with you and babies all of a sudden?"

"A man gets my age, he starts seeing his mistakes. Don't let that Bradshaw woman be one of yours, Matthew. Don't let her get her claws into you. I'm sure she's a gold digger, too."

The banging sound Matt heard coming from the hallway sounded like a door being kicked.

"Look, I have to go. You take care of yourself and do what the doctor tells you."

"Thanks for coming. Really, Matthew, I mean it. Thanks for coming."

"No problem."

He turned to leave, but before he reached the door his father asked one more question. "Matt, can I ask a favor of you? Would you look after Paco? I'm sure he's upset. We haven't been apart for a night since I got him."

Matt let out a long sigh. Paco the barking fur ball. Great. Just great. "Sure."

"He won't eat the kibble unless you mix it with cooked hamburger. With onions. And not Vidalias, they give him gas."

Matt inched toward the door. "Got it."

"And another thing . . . do you think . . . well . . . is there any chance that Mark will come see me?"

"Branch, you had a heart attack today, and you're alive and well enough to throw things at your ball team. You probably shouldn't hold out for more than one miracle a day."

Torie had nothing to say to Matt as they left the hospital. She saved it all up for the relative privacy of his truck as he drove toward the center of town. "That man is just plain rude. If he wasn't sick, I swear

I'd . . ." She huffed. "You could have told him I'm not after your money and that my claws certainly aren't extended in your direction."

"I don't know, Victoria. I think you left some pretty decent scratches down my back the other night."

She shot him a disgusted look. "Those are a different kind of claws, and you know it. I thought my relationship with my father was strange. I think the Callahan family just might have me beat. What's the deal with your brother Mark? Why all the hatred there?"

"Honestly, I think there might be more to it than I know," Matt replied, then acted surprised at what had slipped out.

"What *do* you know?"

Matt shook his head. "It's a long, boring story that I'm not in the mood to repeat. Besides, we have better things to do."

Torie might have argued, but she was distracted by Brazos Bend's charming downtown square. She noted a yarn shop, a barber shop, an honest-to-goodness five-and-dime, and a downtown movie theater. This was what she liked about small towns, she thought as he skillfully whipped the truck into a parking space in front of an ice-cream parlor with the curious name of Princess, Too. "Wow," Torie observed. "I wish I could parallel park like that."

"I've had lots of practice parking."

"I'll bet."

He shut off the engine, then turned to her. "Here's what's going to happen. We're going to walk into the store and act dippy in love. You're going to play along with everything I say. All right?"

"Whatever. I'll never turn down an ice-cream cone." She climbed out of the truck, saying, "I even like ice cream in the winter."

She rattled on about a friend of hers who'd lived in Texas for a while before moving to the Pacific North-

west. "She has Blue Bell ice cream shipped to her.
Costs her, like, sixty-five dollars a gallon. I understand,
though. Good ice cream is . . ."

Torie's voice trailed off as she realized they'd
walked right past the Princess, Too, and stopped in
front of Brazos Bend Jewelers. "What are we doing
here?"

"Gotta get that secret-decoder ring."

"But—"

He shut her up with a kiss—*He's always doing
that!*—then whispered, "Play the game, Torie. It's
important."

He opened the door and led her inside. "Hello, Mr.
Kimbler. We're here to buy your finest diamond solitaire. Show us what you have in engagement rings."

It was a bizarre beginning to an even more bizarre
half hour as Matt Callahan proceeded to subtly spin the
biggest pack of lies she'd ever heard. Considering she
worked with celebrities, that was saying something.

She learned that she'd been hired by *National Geographic* to photograph an expedition in the Polynesian
islands lasting two years. Matt had responsibilities at the
winery to see to and some loose ends at the Treasury
Department in Washington—*the Treasury Department*?—
to tie up, but then he was heading to the South Seas
to be with his bride. The wedding would be on a beach
in Bali in October—a lovely time of year in Bali—and
instead of a white gown, she'd be wearing a red silk
sarong. Matt would wear swim trunks. Both bride and
groom would be barefoot.

The entire time he talked, he touched her. Kissed
her hands, played with her hair, nuzzled her neck. He
stopped spinning his story three times to kiss her
lavishly.

Then he chose a three-carat square-cut solitaire in
a platinum band and asked anxiously if Torie thought
it was big enough.

Torie thought it was gaudy and trendy and nothing

like the classic ring she'd always dreamed of having, but for bling, it worked. Besides, it might be just the style for the other *National Geographic* photographers living in Bali.

"I designed the setting myself," Mr. Kimbler said proudly. "That is a special stone and I thought it deserved something extra."

"You did a wonderful job," she told him.

"We'll take it." Matt bent her over backward for a theatrical, but still toe-tingling, kiss. *The man's lips should be bronzed.*

"I never thought I'd see the day that a Callahan boy came into my shop to buy an engagement ring," the jeweler observed as he wrote up the sale. "Now I've sold two of you. Luke bought his ring for Maddie from me, you know. Why, when word of this gets around, I might have to change the name of my business to Good Luck Jewelers. I'll have women hanging around here in hopes of catching Mark."

"I wouldn't hold your breath for that," Matt observed. "It'll be a cold day in hell before Mark spends so much as a penny in Brazos Bend." He eyed the ticket and pulled a thick roll of cash from his pocket.

I guess spies would tend to deal in cash.

"He's no closer to mending fences with your father?" Kimbler asked, trying to act nonchalant as Matt stacked hundred-dollar bills in front of him.

"None whatsoever."

"Well, now's not the time for sad topics. My heartiest congratulations to you two." He slipped the payment in the cash drawer, then put a ring box and receipt in a bag, which he handed to Torie. "I wish you every happiness."

"Thank you," she said, embarrassed. She surreptitiously peered at the receipt, looking for the store's return policy. She didn't like this sort of playacting, knowing that Mr. Kimbler would celebrate his big sale, then be crushed when Matt returned the ring.

"You ought to make time to flash her ring around at P-3 or the Princess," Kimbler suggested. "Folks are gonna want to see that."

"Not more catfish," Torie murmured.

"I'm always ready to watch Torie eat an ice-cream cone," Matt said, giving Kimbler a wink. "Makes for some mighty fine foreplay."

"Matt!" she protested. Whispering, she added, "That's embarrassing."

"Bet it's true, though."

Matt ushered Torie out the door, still playing the attentive lover with octopus hands. On the street, Torie planted her feet. "What's going on here, Callahan?"

"Put your arms around my neck and just listen." Matt put his hands on her waist and stared down into her face. Onlookers would see lovers, Torie knew. Only she was in a position to see the hard look in his eyes. "I learned a long time ago that details can kill you. A ring is a detail. Now, kiss me like I'm the man you love who just bought you the biggest rock in town."

Torie found that idea insulting. "I may fake an engagement, but I won't fake a kiss. Let's just see if my real stuff is good enough, hmm?"

She gave him a kiss worthy of the silver screen. Worthy of the cover of *Life* magazine. On the town square in Brazos Bend, Texas, Torie kissed Matt Callahan with all the emotion churning inside her. She poured herself into the moment, and his heated response curled her toes, melted her knees, and . . . broke her heart.

She wanted this to be real. She wanted this ring— well, maybe not this exact ring—and this engagement. She wanted this man. And he was using her as muffin repellent. How humiliating was that?

"Hell," he murmured as he broke the kiss. Then he was pushing her away, turning her around. "Let's get that ice cream before I spontaneously combust."

Matt kept his hand at the small of Torie's back as he led her to Kathy Hudson's latest venture, the ice-cream parlor she'd named Princess, Too. It didn't escape his notice that they'd attracted the attention of, not only everyone on the street, but also those peering from the shop windows, and from the courthouse steps in the middle of the square. *Well, that should do it.*

It seemed as if he were working on the ninety-sixth hour of this day, and it wasn't even suppertime yet. But after he took care of this one last detail, he could relax. Go home. Maybe work in the vineyard for a while, then take the boat out and fish. By himself.

Mark could pull guard duty for a few hours. Matt needed some breathing room. He needed some distance—hell, a lot of distance—from Torie.

After he completed this one little task.

Matt pulled open the door to the ice-cream parlor and called out in a loud voice, "Hello, everyone. For those of you who haven't heard yet, I want you to know that I'm a happy man. The beautiful, talented, and sweet-as-a-Parker-County-peach Victoria Bradshaw has agreed to be my wife." Holding up Torie's left hand, he wiggled it so that the rock on her ring finger flashed in the sunlight. "I'm inviting all y'all to come celebrate with us. Double-dip cones for everyone. I'm buying."

As expected, the place went wild with cheers and catcalls and more than a few groans of disappointment. In less than three minutes, the line stretched out the door, down past the jewelry shop, and around the corner. There was nothing the people of Brazos Bend liked better than romance mingled with scandal and discussed over something sweet and free.

At first, Torie kept shooting him glares of exasperation, but after a half-dozen oohs and aahs over the ring, she got into the spirit of the moment.

Matt walked behind the counter, tied on a white apron, washed his hands, and grabbed a scoop to assist Kathy and help move things along.

"Well, aren't you a surprise?" Kathy handed him a sugar cone and pointed toward a tub of Rocky Road. Matt's gaze lingered on the dangling earrings in Kathy's ears. It was the first time he'd seen ice-cream-cone jewelry on a female above the age of eight. "She's a pretty thing, I'll give you that, but isn't she the gal who plugged your leg with a nine-millimeter?"

"I like a girl with spirit."

"Hmm . . ." Kathy handed a cone filled with lime and orange sherbet over to a teenager with a smile, then said, "Maddie stopped by to see me on her way out of town. She didn't mention an engagement in the family."

"That's one thing I love about my sister-in-law. She respects her family's privacy." He smiled widely at a redheaded toddler in his mother's arms and handed over the requested junior-dip vanilla.

Kathy chuckled. "You should know better than to try and put me in my place, Matt Callahan. I don't have a shy bone in my body—comes from being an aging hippie and convicted felon. If you wanted privacy, you wouldn't have come home to Brazos Bend, and you certainly wouldn't have offered to buy everyone in town ice cream at my shop. Thanks for that, by the way."

"No problem. Glad to be of help." Seeing that the crowd around Torie had thinned a bit, he called out. "Sweetheart? What can I scoop up for you?"

"Now, there's a loaded question," she drily observed. "As much as I love ice cream, I think I'll wait. I need to fit into my wedding gown, after all."

"You sure? I bet Kathy has a tub of catfish flavor in the back."

"Cat—" She stopped herself. "Lame, Callahan. Lame."

"That's disgusting is what it is," Kathy commented. She handed Torie a cone of frozen yogurt. "Try this, Ms. Bradshaw. It's low fat and wedding-gown safe. So, when is the big day?"

Torie looked at Matt, who shrugged. He'd completely lost his train of thought when she took a big, long lick of the ice-cream cone. *Hell, this was a mistake.*

"October thirteenth," Torie said with a smile to Kathy.

Kathy gasped with horror at the unlucky date and Torie launched into some silly explanation almost as wild as the tales he'd spun in the jewelry store. Matt tried to tune her out, to drag his gaze back to the next person in line and focus his attention on ice-cream orders. He failed miserably.

Torie licked that ice-cream cone with exaggerated enthusiasm. She played with it on her tongue. She put the whole thing in her mouth and sucked.

She drove him to the very edge of crazy.

The little tease.

When the line finally trickled down to the last customer, Matt was more than ready to escape. He took off the apron and tossed it on the counter behind him. Then, reaching into his wallet, he pulled out the credit card he'd appropriated earlier.

Kathy took the card, checked the name, and lifted her brows in surprise. "You know what you're doing, Matthew?" she asked softly.

"I do," he murmured back. "Run the card, Kathy. I'll make it good. You know that."

She gave him the pen, the two-part receipt, and a disapproving look. Matt signed the cardholder's name, then stuck the receipt and the credit card in his back pocket.

He would return Torie's credit card to the wallet in her purse later.

Chapter Fourteen

She waited until he pulled into the driveway at the lake house. Unfastening her seat belt, she turned to him and said, "Explain why you did that to me."

Had she not been watching him so closely, she'd have missed the slightest of flinches, which betrayed him. "Did what?"

So she'd hit a nerve. Good. "The whole public spectacle. It wasn't necessary, Callahan. I know small towns, too. The catfish caper was enough—you didn't need the whole engagement-ring and ice-cream circus. Was it all some sort of payback? A way to humiliate me? I heard your brothers mention that possibility this morning."

"Don't be ridiculous, Victoria," he replied, amusement lacing his tone as he opened his door and let Paco scramble out.

The amusement did it. Her temper flared and she yanked open the door and climbed down onto the rocky ground. Rather than head for the house, she turned the other way. Right at that moment, she wanted away from Matt Callahan, away from his brother or brothers lurking inside, away from computer printouts and hushed phone calls and all the other paraphernalia of investigation, away from his father's overexcited dog.

Torie wanted her life back.

She took the path leading to the vineyard and walked fast. The pressure of tears built behind her eyes and she clenched her teeth and forced them back. She wouldn't cry. She wasn't a crier. As she swung her arms, the ring caught the sunlight and sparkled. Emotion bubbled up inside her. She wrenched off the ring and threw it down—onto the path where she could find it later, not out into the field. She wasn't that big of a fool.

No, Torie was mad.

Angry.

Furious.

"Victoria, hold up," Matt called from behind her.

She whirled on him as he bent to scoop up the ring. "Don't tell me what to do!"

Then she picked up her pace, broke into a jog, then a run. She ran until she topped the hill; then she stopped to catch her breath. Bent over, her hands on her knees, she waited until the fire in her lungs eased. When she finally straightened, fatigue gripped her. Tears flooded her eyes and a pair spilled down her cheeks.

"C'mere, Shutterbug. This is the best sittin' rock on the ranch. It's a wonderful place to watch the sunset."

Matt patted the space beside him on a flat-topped boulder a few yards to the right of the trail. Torie hadn't heard him come up behind her. "I was going to sit on that rock, anyway," she explained as she took the seat he'd indicated. "I'm not doing it because you told me to."

"Of course you're not." Matt lifted her arm and kissed the back of her hand. "Look, nothing I did today was intended to insult you. I'm not accustomed to explaining myself."

"I'm not accustomed to letting other people run my life. That hasn't happened since I stopped listening to my father when I was a teenager."

His mouth quirked in a lopsided grin. "You are one of no more than three people I can call to mind who are capable of standing up to General Lincoln Bradshaw."

She sniffed with disdain and smelled rain on the air. "I've had a lot of practice."

"When Helen visited me in the hospital, she shared a few stories about the brawls y'all had. I recall one about missing a curfew?"

Torie smiled, her gaze following a hawk soaring on the breeze ahead of the storm clouds building in the east, her mind on events of long ago. "Actually Helen was the one who missed the curfew, but he didn't even notice. He just assumed it was me. I had the dedication of the righteous that night."

"When we were that age, Branch didn't notice if we were at home or on the moon."

"Widowers on opposite ends of the spectrum, then. I've been on my own a long time. I might not have always made the best decisions, but they were always *my* decisions. I hate having that taken away from me."

He rubbed the back of his neck and gave her a sheepish grin she didn't buy for a second. "I guess that means you'd rather get engaged on your own terms, hmm?"

She was tempted . . . oh, so tempted . . . to tell him the truth. How would Matt Callahan react if she said, *I'd rather it was real? I wish you'd meant the kisses and the catfish-house declaration. I wish the ring and ice-cream celebration were real.*

I wish you really loved me.

Maybe he'd pull out his 007 memory-eraser stun gun and blast her back to good sense. Probably, he'd run away from her just as fast as he possibly could.

Her brain must have been scrambled by the stalker. For all her faults, Torie had never been a feeble-minded woman. Falling in love with Matthew Callahan was nothing short of stupid. And that's what she'd done. It'd been fast, but Torie had spent her entire life doing things fast.

No more falling about it. She knew that now. She'd hit ground. Torie Bradshaw was head over heels in love with the man who'd given her an engagement ring two hours ago. As a prop.

A prop. A fake. Torie knew all about fake. She dealt with it daily in her job, and wasn't it fun when her work exposed the lie? Only this time, the tables were turned. The joke was on her. She was in a spotlight she didn't like, didn't want. What made it even worse was that he seemed to enjoy it. The jerk.

What if he'd meant all those things he said and pretended? Like she did. Fool that she was. Imagine if his proposal had been real. Marrying him would be straight out of Cinderella meets James Bond.

Yeah. Right. Like that would ever happen. The Spy Who Loved Me . . . not.

It'd serve him right if she told him how she felt. It might actually needle his conscience just a bit. She knew he had one. Admittedly, it had come as a bit of a surprise, considering the man's occupation, but she'd witnessed it firsthand. What else but a guilty conscience would have made him go by his father's house and retrieve Paco after leaving the ice-cream parlor?

"That's the closest I've ever been to a marriage proposal," she finally said. "Let's just say I had something different in mind for the event."

If he gave her half a lead, she might just do it. Torie tried to be honest and forthright with others. Besides, if she was going to suffer with the knowledge of such a dire predicament, then he should have to suffer, too. It was only fair.

Torie tried to be fair, too.

Besides, what if . . .

No. Don't go there. Absolutely, positively don't go there.

Unaware of her inner turmoil, Matt scooped up a

handful of pebbles off the ground and threw them one by one down the hill. "I admire the way you've kept it together throughout all this, Victoria. If it helps, I don't think it'll last much longer. We'll find the slime who's doing this, and you'll get your life back." Capturing her gaze, he murmured, "I promise."

But will I get my heart back?

They sat quietly for a time, watching the sun sink behind the hilltops, the sky awash with red and gold. As the brilliant colors muted to shades of pink and purple, Matt said, "It's been a helluva day."

"That it has."

"You know, Victoria, I understand what you're feeling."

What? I doubt it.

"My brothers and I did something stupid when I was in my first year of college. In his first act of parenting in years, Branch cut us off financially and sent us away from here and from each other. We didn't know where each other ended up. You know what? A selfish part of me was happy about it. I was the oldest and Branch hadn't been worth shooting since my mother died. Responsibility for my brothers fell on me. I don't know that I recognized it at the time, but I was glad to be off on my own, with no one to answer to but my own conscience. I was glad to finally have the chance to live my life for me, to follow the path I wanted to follow."

"Where did he send you?"

"A ranch in Montana. I hated it. Stayed only long enough to save up enough money to get me where I wanted to go."

"Where was that?"

"A navy recruiter's office."

"Wait a minute. I thought you wanted to make your own decisions, to answer to no one else. So you up and join the navy?"

"You're not seeing the big picture. I've always loved

the water, been fascinated by the ocean. I wanted to travel. I was broke at the time, so the service was my best option to do what I wanted to do. Signing up was my choice, my decision, and I made it independent of expectations by anyone other than myself. I loved the sense of freedom that gave me." His grin was wry. "There's nothing quite like the selfishness of youth."

"Are you telling me I need to grow up?"

He laughed. "No, not at all. If anything, I was reminding myself to tread carefully as I approach another life-changing decision."

"What's that?"

"Physically, I can't do the job anymore. Either I take the desk job they've offered me or I retire and do something else."

"I'm having a hard time seeing James Bond at a desk job."

He groaned. "Would you give up the Bond business, please? I do think I've mentioned it drives me freakin' crazy."

Ignoring that, she asked, "So, what's the problem? Are you having trouble figuring out what you want?"

"Yeah, I am. That's why I came home, although I haven't exactly had much time for it."

"Don't blame me if you can't make up your mind. From my point of view, it's a no-brainer."

"And why would you say that?"

She gestured toward the vineyard. "When did you buy this land?"

"A few years back."

"Before the accident in the helicopter?"

"You mean before you shot me and ruined my leg?"

"Don't be snotty. I'm trying to make a point here. This land represents something."

"Yeah, a way to stick it to my father. I bought it out from under him."

"Maybe that's part of it, but that's not all of it."

"You're going to say that I bought it to give me an excuse to come home. That deep down I want to reconcile with my father and that Four Brothers gives me an excuse to do that. I could come home and grow my grapes and bottle my wine. I could settle down and live the life I'd have lived if my mother hadn't died when she did. I've thought of all that and maybe there's some truth to it, but—"

"You're putting words in my mouth, Callahan." Torie stretched out her legs, crossing them at the ankles. "Here's what I think. I think coming back to Texas and planting roots here would be wrong for you."

He bristled. "What?"

"If you wanted this, you'd have already been here. The gunshot gave you the perfect excuse. You had it all set up so that you could come home and sink your roots. But you didn't do it when you had the chance, so that tells me it's not right and deep down you know it."

He rolled to his feet, shoving his hands in his back pockets, and gazed out at the deepening dusk. "That's certainly a strong opinion from someone who once hung from a helicopter to take Peeping Tom photographs of a celebrity wedding."

She ignored the insult. "It makes sense. You chose the navy. Then at some point, you chose to work for the CIA. You've lived the life of a nomad, an adventurer, and maybe that's what suits you. Maybe you needed to buy the ranch to figure out that isn't what you really want."

"Pretty expensive lesson."

"I understand you have money to burn, so what does that matter? God bless microchips, hmm? Besides, you gave your best friend his dream and that's what really matters to you. People matter to you. Les, your brothers, even your father."

"Hold on a minute." He whirled around and glared

at her. "When did I lose control of this conversation? I'm supposed to be making you feel better, not have you psychoanalyzing me."

"But psychoanalyzing you *does* make me feel better." She grinned like an imp. "It makes me remember that even though I have a crazy creep on my tail, I'm still mentally healthier than most people out there, present company included."

"Oh, yeah?"

"I know what I want, Callahan. Maybe I can't have it, but at least I know what it is."

"So what is it you want?"

Oh, what the heck. Quit being chicken. Roll the dice, Bradshaw. That's what you do. She drew a deep breath, then confessed, "You."

He reared backward. "Me!"

"Pitiful, isn't it?" Now it was her turn to grin wryly. "I'm in love with you, Matt Callahan."

Washington, DC

Perfect.

She exited the building's front door alone, her stubby little skirted legs moving quickly as they carried her into the billowing chill of a stiff spring wind. Silly woman still wore a lab coat. *Wonder if she'll have enough sense to take it off before lunching at the Four Seasons.*

She'd been easy. The woman clueless and flattered by the opportunity to be interviewed by such a prominent and respected magazine. Extracting the information from her would be a breeze.

Coming closer now. *Pull the ball cap lower, hunch down in the rental's front seat. Look at that long blond hair. Clear, healthy complexion.* Grip on the steering wheel tightened.

She looks so much like the bitch.

The bitch.

The bitch.

Blood rushed, pulse pounded. The bitch. The bitch. The bitch.

Foot tapped against the gas pedal.

She ruined everything. Took everything away.

She'll pay . . . pay . . . pay.

Foot stomped, pressed the pedal to the floor. Tires spun.

The bitch the bitch the bitch.

Her face turned. Surprise, then fear. Terror. *Look!*

Cackling laughter rang out inside the rental car. *Wait . . . wait . . . turn the wheel.*

The bitch dived away, fell to the ground, just as the car swerved and roared past.

Laughter peaked, then faded away.

Hmm . . . hope she doesn't cancel lunch.

"She's really good," Mark Callahan said as he flipped through the bluebonnet photographs Torie had developed and printed in the lake house's pantry turned darkroom. "I think she should call the boyfriend."

"*Ex*-boyfriend, and I think that's a dumb-ass idea." Matt prowled the study room, scowling down at the stack of printouts his brother had handed him.

"What's dumb-ass is wasting any more time on someone who I've all but eliminated from our suspect list."

"I still like him for it."

"I can put him in Europe the day of the explosion."

"Last time I checked, they have international flights out of LAX."

"You just want him to be the perp because he used to shack up with your fiancée."

"I'm not his fiancée," Torie said, breezing into the room at the same time Matt snapped, "Shut up."

An uncomfortable silence settled over the room. Matt resisted the urge to rake his fingers through his hair, knowing better than to betray any nervousness under the circumstances. He and Torie had yet to have a private moment to talk since the single most cowardly moment of his life.

He still shuddered to think about his reaction to her punch-in-the-gut declaration. The way he'd lurched to his feet, stammered out a stupid excuse, and fled was damned shameful. Humiliating. It pissed him off to think about it.

And he still didn't know what to say to her.

Torie Bradshaw wasn't the first woman who'd confessed her love to him, but she was the first woman he believed actually meant it. She was the first woman who left him clueless as to a response, even now, a day after the fact.

Oblivious of the undercurrents, Mark offered Torie a sheepish grin. "He doesn't like the idea of you talking to your old boyfriend."

Great. Wonderful. Thanks for the help, brother. "Don't be ridiculous." Matt shot his brother a scowl. "I just don't know what it's going to help."

"I want to do it." Torie folded her arms and faced Matt. Thank God she didn't look wounded or weepy. "I don't see what it can hurt. I never truly did believe that Jason would do these things, and after learning that he was in Rome the day my apartment exploded . . . no. If he'd done something like that, he'd have stayed around to watch the fallout. Jason was always one who fed off the excitement of the moment."

"What would you say to Banning if you did call him?" Matt asked. "You gonna come out and ask him, 'Hey, did you blow up my apartment?' "

Now she got some emotion in her expression. Disdain. Turning to Mark, she said, "I'll have to choose my words carefully. If I were to tell him what's been happening, he'd want to write about it. A stalker-being-stalked story is right up Jason's alley."

Mark's gaze flickered to Matt's. Silently, he asked, *What do you think? Want to go for that exposure?*

Matt indicated no with a barely noticeable shake of his head.

"Jason's birthday is coming up. How about I call and wish him a happy birthday, then wing it from there? I'll feel him out. I'll be able to tell if he's lying to me or not."

"Don't be ridiculous."

"Not everyone possesses your well-practiced talent to lie like a rug, Callahan. Speaking of which, did you happen to read this morning's newspaper?"

"Which one?" Matt subscribed to a number of papers. "The *Times*? *Washington Post*?"

"No, try the *Brazos Bend Standard*. Imagine my surprise to see an article by one Sara-Beth Branson filled with quotes attributed to me. I'm pretty sure I'd remember lying through my teeth to a woman named Sara-Beth."

"You were in the shower when she called, and she was on a tight deadline. I tried to make it easy on everyone."

"I just found it so interesting to learn that the Jays have offered to host our wedding in Bali."

"They love you. They gave you their dog."

"Y'all quit bickering," Mark said. He grabbed one of the prepaid and untraceable cell phones he made a habit of carrying, and tossed it to her. "Call him."

Paco chose that moment to trot into the room and sidle up to Mark. When Mark reached down to pet him, Matt shook his head. The dog had taken a liking to Mark. He followed him around, looked up at him with big, soulful eyes. This from the mutt who wouldn't tolerate anyone other than Branch.

It pissed Mark off at first, but now Matt suspected he liked the attention. He swore he'd seen Mark sneaking table scraps to Paco at lunch yesterday.

He dragged his gaze off the dog to see Torie checking the clock, and Matt could tell she was calculating the time difference between Brazos Bend and Rome. Punching in the numbers, she said, "He won't recognize the number, so he's liable not to answer."

"If he's even in Rome," Matt grumbled. He moved to stand in front of her, his feet braced apart, his arms folded, his mouth schooled into a scowl. "If it's not faked. Put it on speakerphone."

Torie hesitated, then set her phone on the desk and took a seat in front of it. Jason answered on the second ring. *"Pronto?"*

"Hi, Jase."

"Allora, io non sento bene. . . ."

I can't hear very well, Matt translated.

"Jason? It's me."

"Torie? Torie, is that you?"

"Yes."

"Wow. Okay. Hold on a minute." Banning's voice sounded excited, hopeful. "Let me get somewhere I can hear better."

"Sure." Torie chewed at her bottom lip, a spark of guilt in her eyes.

A few moments later, Jason Banning spoke again. "There. That's better. I was in a restaurant and it's noisy."

"Don't let me interrupt your meal."

"No, it's fine. It's just drinks before dinner. I'm in Florence on a story for the *Globe*. It's great to hear from you, Torie. Where are you?"

She shut her eyes. "I'm in the States."

"Oh." Banning's disappointment carried through the phone. "So . . . what's up?"

"I wanted to wish you happy birthday and . . . oh, Jase, that's not it. Things are so mixed-up."

"What's wrong, love?"

"I just . . . I want . . . Jason, I'm sorry about how things turned out with us. I never meant to hurt you."

"I know. I knew it then, too. You have a good

heart, Torie Lynn." He waited a beat, then asked, "Does this mean you're having second thoughts?"

Torie grimaced and rubbed her temples. "No, Jason. It's just that . . . well . . . I've had my heart broken, too, and I know now how it feels. I wish I'd been . . . gentler with you."

Matt gritted his teeth as his stomach took a roll.

"It's okay, Torie," Jason replied. "You were fine. I wouldn't listen. I'm sorry I was such an ass about it. I . . . didn't want to let you go, Torie."

Matt saw a tear spill from Torie's eyes. Jesus. Could he possibly feel like more of a shit?

"You did the right thing, though," Banning continued. "I know it. I knew all along that you weren't as crazy about me as I was about you."

Softly, Torie said, "That's not a pleasant way to live."

"That's why we were both better off ending it when we did." After a moment's silence, he asked, "You okay, Torie?"

"Yes. I'm fine. Really, I am. I wanted you to know that I'm sorry and that there's no hard feelings on my side."

Banning let out a little laugh. "Despite my stalking you?"

Matt, Mark, and Torie all straightened and stared at the phone. "Stalking?" Torie asked.

"I should have taken it like a man. I'm ashamed of the way I kept calling after you moved out. Hope you didn't go over on your minutes."

"No." Torie relaxed, smiled. "No."

"Torie . . . this fellow who broke your heart. Let me tell you something. If he's too big a fool to see what a treasure he had in you, then you're better off without him. You know that, don't you?"

She turned away from Matt. "I do."

"And don't forget it. Hey, did you hear about Giorgio? He took a spill on a scooter in the Piazza Navona and broke both his legs." That signaled a conversational turn to business, and Matt had heard enough. Exiting the study, he motioned for Mark to follow him.

Outside, Mark asked, "What's going on with you and Torie? Tension was so thick in there you could have fried it and served it with syrup."

Matt hesitated. He wasn't accustomed to discussing his personal life with anyone, not even his brothers. Yet, he could use a sounding board right now. "She thinks she's in love with me."

"No shit."

"You knew?"

"After the looks I've seen her sneak your way, I figured as much. So, did you blow her off like all the others?"

"I didn't blow her off." Matt rested both hands on the porch rail and leaned his weight on it. "I didn't . . . well . . . I didn't do anything. I just sort of . . . left."

"You left her hanging."

"Yes, that's pretty much it."

Mark propped his butt on the porch rail and shook his head at Matt. "You asshole."

"I didn't know what to say to her, dammit."

"Why? Did you forget what you usually say?"

It was a legitimate question. How many women had he left over the years when he sensed them growing too close? More than a few. He had a regular routine about it. A good excuse, a compliment, a gift. The kiss-off. "This isn't a usual situation. Victoria isn't like the others."

"Now we're getting somewhere." Mark shoved away from the porch railing and took a seat in the rocking chair. Crossing his right ankle over his left knee, he asked, "Why is Torie different?"

"I don't know!" Now Matt paced the porch. "It's just so damned confusing. She's so damned confusing. She's a paparazzo, for God's sake."

"And this is relevant because . . . ?"

"Because I'm at a crossroads, here. I'm a thirty-six-year-old former field agent with a bad leg and a desk job waiting for me. The days of movie stars and princesses are behind me. What's ahead of me are . . . are . . . schoolteachers."

Mark blinked twice. "You stupid shit."

Caught up in his own misery, Matt barely heard him. "She doesn't think the vineyard is right for me. Thinks if I wanted this life, I'd already be living it. But she doesn't know me. Doesn't know what I want. I've always liked the idea of home and hearth. It just wasn't time. Well, I'm not James goddamned Bond anymore, am I? I don't need a Bond girl riding a Vespa and toting a camera. A vineyard and a casserole queen might be just the right thing for me. I always liked the idea of coaching Little League baseball!"

"You snobby stupid shit," Mark corrected. "So, what, she's not good enough for you? Is that what you're saying?"

"Of course not!"

"That's what it sounds like to me. And I have to tell you, bro, it pisses me off."

Matt stopped, turned around, and faced his brother. "What kind of a comment is that?"

Now Mark shoved to his feet, the words exploding from his mouth like they'd been cooking in his gut for years. "Do you know how lucky you are to have a woman like Torie Bradshaw offer you her heart? Are you so dumb that you'd throw away a chance of happiness just because she doesn't fit your vision of the woman you're supposed to want at this stage in life? And to think I've always looked up to you, respected your intelligence. Shame on me for being such a dumb-ass."

"Now, look."

"No, you look." Mark poked his shoulder with his finger. "I knew more at eighteen than you do today.

I didn't let preconceived notions blind me to possibilities. I didn't let small-town prejudice limit me and as a result, I had the happiest two and a half years of my life. So take this as gospel, bro, and don't attempt to give me advice ever again. I don't listen to fools and fool you are if the reasons you've stated are the reasons you're turning away from Torie Bradshaw."

He turned to leave, but Matt stopped him with a hand on his arm. "What two and a half years, Mark? What are you talking about? *Who* are you talking about?"

His brother blinked. "I can't believe I . . . shit."

"Talk to me, Mark."

Mark looked away, gazed out toward the vineyard, his hands shoved in the back pockets of his jeans. Matt knew his brother well and he identified the signs of an inner struggle. His eyes clouded and he clenched his teeth so hard that a muscle in his jaw twitched. "Mark?"

Mark closed his eyes, swallowed hard, then said, "She reminds me of Carrie. Goddammit, she reminds me so much of Carrie." His voice broke on the repetition of the name.

"Who's Carrie?"

"My wife."

"Wife?" Matt's jaw dropped. His eyes went wide. Holy shit! Mark married? When did this happen? "You never mentioned a wife."

Mark rubbed the base of his ring finger on his left hand, but Matt didn't think he realized it. He gazed blindly ahead. Or into the past. He spoke in a voice rough with emotion. "She was a waitress at a truck stop outside of Atlanta. She hadn't finished high school. Carrie barely made enough money to keep a roof over her head, but she was . . . alive. And she . . . we . . ." He closed his eyes. "I loved her. God, I loved her."

"What happened?"

Mark didn't respond and Matt realized he'd lost his

brother into his past. He didn't know what to say. He wondered if Luke knew about this. Finally, sensing it was time to bring his brother back, he asked, "Where is your Carrie, Mark?"

"She . . . died. Branch—" He broke off abruptly and shook his head. "Look, she's gone. I don't want to get into that. It's over and done with."

"But—"

"Leave it be."

For the first time since John's death, Matt saw tears in Mark's eyes. Beyond stunned, he pushed no further.

"Just don't be stupid where Torie is concerned, Matthew. You'll regret it the rest of your life. Trust me. I know about regret." With that, Mark hopped down from the porch and headed for the hill, taking long, determined strides.

Shocked by the news he'd learned, Matt stood gazing after him, gaping. A wife? A wife he'd never mentioned? *Did* Luke know? And Branch. What role did Branch play in the whole thing? Was that the source of Mark's animosity toward their father? Matt had long suspected there was more to it than the resentment they all held against Branch in relation to John's death.

"A wife." Named Carrie. Torie reminded Mark of his wife, Carrie. "I'll be damned."

"Very possibly." Torie stepped out onto the porch. Oh, crap. "Did you hear?"

"Enough."

"I'm just . . . hell. I don't know what to say. Jesus, why didn't he tell us?"

"I suppose he had his reasons. Whatever they may be, he's still raw."

"Yeah. I just . . . wow." Matt blew out a heavy breath as his brother's words about regret echoed in his mind. "Torie . . ."

"No." She waved her hand, cutting him off. "Back to Jason. Do you now agree that he isn't our stalker?"

"Yeah." Matt pulled his gaze away from Mark's retreating figure and pinned Torie with a look. "Yeah. That man wouldn't hurt you. He's still in love with you."

Torie shrugged. "He's the one who risked his heart. Not my fault, not my responsibility. I believe that, Callahan, all right?"

Matt understood that her comment offered him absolution, and yet . . . "To quote a great philosopher of our age, 'Nothing takes the taste out of peanut butter like unrequited love.'"

She smiled with recognition. "Poor Charlie Brown. He's better off without Lucy, though. I hope someday he realizes it."

Matt watched his brother disappear over a hill. *I hope someday I don't regret it.*

He knocked on her door just before midnight.

Torie was still awake, reading a booklet called *Texas Wine Grape Guide*, published by the state Department of Agriculture, in hopes of boring herself to sleep. So far, it hadn't worked. Her mind continued to spin.

Images clicked through her brain like a toy viewfinder out of control. Jason and her in Paris. Matt and her in the cenote. Her father. Her sister. Matt in the helicopter. Gigi in the bluebonnets.

Rap. Rap. Rap. "Victoria?"

She set aside the booklet. "Come in, Matt."

The door swung open and he stepped inside. He wore khakis and a blue button-down shirt with the Four Brothers Vineyard logo on the pocket. He'd attended a barbecue with Les in town earlier. Something about a planning meeting for the upcoming Texas Wine Trails spring promotion by the Texas Wine and Grape Growers Association. He'd asked her to attend with him, but she'd begged off, using a very real headache as an excuse. Mark had stayed at the lake house until his brother returned. She'd heard Mark leave for Les's place forty-five minutes ago.

"Can I talk to you for a minute?" Matt asked.

"All right."

"How's your headache?"

"Better."

"Good." He shoved his hands in his pockets and rocked back and forth on his heels. "People in town are excited about getting their kid portraits tomorrow. Were you able to get hold of everyone, set up all the appointments?"

"Yes. I should be done by noon."

"Good. Kathy Hudson wants us to come to lunch and I told her we'd be there. No catfish, though. I promise. She mentioned salads. Girl stuff."

"That's fine."

When he made no move to leave, she folded her hands in her lap and practiced being patient. Finally, he said, "I want to apologize. For running off the way I did after you . . . you . . ."

"No need." Really no need. "Let's just forget about it, shall we?"

"I didn't know what to say to you, Victoria. Honestly, I still don't."

"You don't have to say anything, Callahan. I wasn't asking for a reply. I told you what I told you because . . . well . . . it's who I am. I don't keep things inside of me."

"That's a good quality."

"For a photographer, maybe. Probably not for a spy."

"You matter to me, Torie."

An electrocardiogram would have registered a definite spike at that. She mattered. Well, that was nice to know. Nothing to pin her hopes on, though, that's for certain.

"I need you to know that, to believe that. It's one

of the few things I'm certain about right now." As he
spoke, he started pacing. Five steps up, five steps back.
"This isn't normal for me. Ordinarily, I'm a very deci-
sive man. Hell, I can decide to shoot a man easier
than to knock on your door tonight."

"This isn't combat, Callahan."

"I know." He stopped, rubbed the bridge of his
nose, and muttered, "Maybe I should see a shrink."

Okay, that was funny. She could picture him
stretched out on a therapist's couch. He'd have chosen
a female therapist and the transference thing would
happen except it'd go from doctor to patient rather
than vice versa. She'd unpin her hair and shake it out;
then she'd cross her legs and swing her foot, letting
her shoe slide off her heel and hang just by the toe.
. All right. Maybe it wasn't so funny.

"Matt, there's nothing wrong with you. With everything you have going on in your life, it's no wonder
you're confused. You'll figure everything out in good
time. Just be patient with yourself."

"How about you? Will you be patient with me?"

Whoa. Now, that took them to dangerous territory.
Did she dare hope that while he tried to figure it all
out, he might decide he loved her? Could she set herself up for that kind of fall? What about her pride?
Mooning over a man who might never return her
feelings . . . well . . . she might get fat. Peanut butter
had too many calories to keep eating when it didn't
taste good.

She rose, saying, "Arrgh! You still don't get it, do
you?" She fisted her hands and hit his chest. "I don't
need patience because I'm not waiting on anything
from you! I don't expect anything. Well, aside from
having you catch my stalker. I'm not asking for you
to love me back, Callahan. I just want . . ."

Him. She wanted him. Oh, jeez. He was wearing
aftershave. Armani aftershave.

"What *do* you want, Torie? Ask me for something I can give you. Let me do that much."

She had absolutely no pride where Matt Callahan was concerned. He was her weakness. Torie licked her lips. Even knowing heartbreak lay ahead, she simply couldn't resist. His brothers called Matt an adrenaline junkie. Well, she was a Matt addict. She knew the fall might kill her, but for now, she wanted the high. "Okay, Callahan. We can do that. Here's the deal. From now until I leave Brazos Bend, I want us to be a couple."

He grimaced. "Torie . . ."

She stepped toward him, put her hand against his chest. "I want to be with you. I'm tired of fighting it."

"I don't understand. You told your boyfriend that I broke your heart. I want to be fair to you."

"Fair is what they have in October in Texas, I believe. I want adventure, Callahan. I crave it. I crave you. Indulge me."

"It's probably a mistake."

"Maybe so, but it'll be my mistake, and I'm okay with that. I don't want to be afraid to live while I'm busy being afraid to die. Take me to bed, Callahan. Thrill me."

He laughed and swept her up into his arms. "You're a mess."

"You love that about me."

"Yeah, Shutterbug." His voice was a rough, raspy sound. "I do."

Chapter Fifteen

Alexandria, Virginia

The aroma of freshly brewed coffee joined the click of computer keys swirling in the air in the Internet café. Wonderful places, these cozy little computer-and-coffee houses. Perfect spots for snooping. Up until now, unfortunately, a dead end.

A good education had provided computer literacy. Criminal associates had taught the skills utilized today.

The bitch had proved to be surprisingly resourceful, but she couldn't hide forever. Eventually, people always made mistakes.

Like I did. Losing my temper. Wrong. Wrong. Wrong. Should know better. Had been taught better.

The sister failed to show for lunch and was guarded when they met for a rescheduled dinner.

Another way. Find the bitch another way. Hire a professional if necessary.

That could prove sticky, however, when the bitch turned up dead. Better to work alone.

Then, ten minutes later, a possible hit. The right name in a newspaper in a Podunk town in Texas. Excitement rose. The pursuer scented prey.

Then, a church ladies' blog. What fools people were, posting anything and everything for anyone to see.

Finally, a bit of hacking and the clincher confirmed. Credit card use at a restaurant in Brazos Bend, Texas.

Springtime in Texas. What a lovely time of year for a visit. *Wonder if the bluebonnets are still in bloom.*

Matt had already called up the stairs twice urging Torie to get a move on. They'd need to leave in the next five minutes to have time to stop by the hospital before meeting Kathy as planned.

He was tense. The colleagues he'd hit up for surveillance help had been called to Venezuela, forcing him to hire privately. The men came well recommended, but Matt didn't like using someone he'd never worked with for this.

He also second-guessed himself for having sent Luke to Soledad Island. General Bradshaw's men had scoured the island in the days following Torie's escape. What in the world had made Matt think his brother would find proof of Collin Marlow's demise when the general's men had not? He should have kept Luke close.

What if they needed his gun? What if—

"Hell," Matt muttered. "What if I calm down and use my brain?"

He had the situation covered. They weren't going up against Al-Qaeda here. This mission was to stop one man in pursuit of a defined target in a setting Matt knew better than Torie Bradshaw's body, which after last night would be imprinted on his mind for all time.

Having successfully distracted himself from his needless fretting, Matt smiled at the memory just as his cell phone rang.

He checked the number. Langley. "Hello?"

A brisk, businesslike feminine voice spoke without preamble. "I'm sending the report on the former sena-

tor. I don't think he's your man, Callahan, but read it
for yourself and see."

"Tha—" The connection clicked off before he could
get the word out. Stephanie Ross was the best re-
searcher he'd ever worked with, but she was also his
biggest one-night-stand mistake. The woman held a
grudge like nobody's business.

Matt pulled up the report on the computer and
started reading. When Torie finally came downstairs a
few minutes later, he'd seen enough to agree with
Stephanie.

The report supported the information Mark had fer-
reted out, adding a bit more detail. It seemed that in
the wake of the sex scandal, former senator Harris
found religion. Under other circumstances, that would
have increased Matt's suspicions, but the politician
hadn't gone the televangelist route, confessing his sins
in public and rallying the army of forgiveness. The
senator had taken his sins and self to a mission in
Honduras, where he'd dusted off his medical degree
and gone to work at a makeshift hospital. His travel
record, financial record, and communications records
backed up the facts.

So, appeared to be two down and one to go. If Luke
came through with something about Collin Marlow
before Matt's plan played out, then they'd take another look at Torie's list.

"I thought you were in a hurry," Torie said.

"I am. Sorry. Got this . . ." Matt glanced up, then
stared. "You're beautiful."

She smiled and spun around, sending the flirty little
skirt of her pink polka-dot sundress flying. "You like
it? I bought this at a little shop in Arizona. Dresses
aren't usually my thing, but I was really nervous that
particular day. I like to shop when I'm nervous. Spent
too much of my cash stash, though, so I've been working on breaking the habit ever since."

"You sparkle, Torie."

She held up her left hand and wiggled her fingers, smiling ruefully. "It's this."

"No. It's you. Your eyes, your smile. You're just . . . gorgeous."

"I'm a sexually satisfied Callahan girl."

"Callahan girl?"

"A new classification in light of last night. I've been promoted from a Bond girl."

He laughed. He couldn't help it. She was the flame and he was the moth flying wing-singeing close with no thought of escape. He'd thrown in that towel in a blaze of lust last night when he agreed to her terms. She was his until this movie they were living ended, and he was done with attempting to resist her. "Then come on, Callahan girl. Grab your portraits and let's go. We have a full day ahead of us."

They made a quick visit to Branch's room at Brazos Bend General. The old coot was entertaining when they arrived. Two neighbors, the Methodist preacher, and one of his cronies from the barbershop kept him occupied. He looked good, Matt thought. Healthy complexion, ready smile except for when he looked at Torie. Even that grumpiness faded when she presented him with his gift.

"Paco! Well, look at that." Branch held the eight-by-ten framed photograph of his dippy-costumed dog sniffing at the bluebonnets. "If that's not the cutest thing. Doesn't he look like a little imp? Why, you caught his personality perfectly. His spirit shines through."

"I'm glad you like it, sir," Torie replied with a modest smile.

Branch asked one of the neighbors to set the photograph on the windowsill where he could see it. He asked a few questions about Paco's care—which Torie answered—and then Matt made their excuses. "I'll drop by later when your dance card isn't so full."

"He looks good," Torie said as they left the hospital. "When is he due to be discharged?"

"I haven't a clue. Branch still refuses to allow his doctor to tell us what's going on, though I can tell he doesn't like it. It'll be interesting to see who eventually wins that pissing contest."

They drove to Cottonwood Cottage, where Torie had arranged to have her appointments in the dining room. Two mothers and a couple were waiting on her when they arrived. "Sorry I'm late," Torie said as she swept into the room, her arms full of cardboard portfolios.

"We're early," Janice Williams said. "I'm just on pins and needles to see the pictures."

"It's better if we do this one at a time." Torie glanced at Matt, who took the cue and said, "Folks? How about I buy y'all a cup of coffee and a piece of Annie's coffee cake while you wait?"

As he led them to the kitchen, where Annie Jennings always had coffee and sweets at the ready, he heard Mrs. Hill say to Torie, "Oh, you lucky girl. I never thought I'd see the day that Demon Callahan fell in love, but the way he looks at you . . . my, oh my."

My, oh my? What the hell did she see in how he looked at Torie? Come to think of it, he didn't want to know.

Two and a half hours later, Torie said good-bye to the last of her clients. To a person, they'd been thrilled with their photographs. Matt had sucked down enough coffee to keep him wired for two weeks. "If I hear the words 'soooo cute' or 'soooo adorable' one more time, I'll start screaming."

Torie preened as she tallied up her totals. "I'd have done better if I could accept credit cards. Still, the ten percent cash discount I offered sweetened the pot for most of them. Look!" She waved a handful of bills and grinned. "It's not as big as the wad you carry around, but it certainly will help to replenish my dash stash."

"Cash stash" and now "dash stash." Jesus. "So you enjoyed that?"

"Sure." She shrugged. "It was a different experience, Matt. That's why it was fun. That's one of the main attractions to my job. I think I'd wilt if I had to go to the same place and do the same job every day."

He thought of the desk waiting for him at Langley. *Me, too.* The certainty of it washed through him like twenty-year-old scotch. The job itself was bound to be interesting, frustrating at times, fulfilling at others. He'd be good at it, the experience he'd bring to the position invaluable. But sitting on the sidelines? How would he handle that? And he certainly wasn't the only person who could do the job. In the same place, every day. With the same people, every day.

"I don't want that, either." He looked at Torie. "I don't want the desk job."

"Of course you don't." She tucked her money into her purse, and picked up her files. "Did you ever actually think you did? It's no more right for you than staying at Four Brothers would be."

Frustrated by her response, he snapped, "Oh? And you know these things how? And if you say that James Bond wouldn't sit behind a desk, I swear I'll hit you."

"Oh, you'd never hit me, and JB wouldn't sit behind a desk. Matthew, think about it. You wouldn't be so cranky about this whole job thing if the choice you were trying to make was right. I tried to tell you this the other day. You need to start listening to me."

"Careful. You're going to piss me off."

"Fine. I won't say any more." She shrugged and left the dining room, looking for her hostess to thank her and settle up her bill. "I can't thank you enough, Annie. This worked out perfectly."

"It was fun—and good for business. I booked a baby shower and made Starbucks profit on all the coffee Demon consumed."

"Hey. Your coffee can hold its own with any in

Seattle," Matt told her. Having received an all clear from his team, he opened the door and gestured for Torie to precede him.

He waited until they'd safely reached the truck to continue. "So, if you're so clairvoyant, what should I do? If you're so certain what's wrong for me, then you should know what's right."

"I haven't a clue, Callahan. Don't worry so much about it. You'll figure it out and if it takes you a while, it's not like you'll go broke in the meantime."

"It isn't about the money. I need . . ." Hell, what did he need? He didn't know. If a voice buried deep inside himself whispered that what he needed was standing right in front of him, Matt didn't hear it. Or ignored it, anyway. He played too deaf to hear, too blind to see, too stupid to . . . hell.

Matt let that go and thought about what she'd said. He didn't know why her attitude got under his skin the way it did. Hell, he should be feeling good right now. He'd made a major decision about his future. Well, half a decision, anyway. He knew what he wouldn't be doing.

"So what's the scoop on this lunch with Kathy Hudson?" Torie asked as he started the engine. "Is it just old friends getting together or is there more to it?"

"Honestly, I don't know. Kathy is a free spirit and there's no telling what she has in mind. Might be nothing more than what she said—a thank-you for the ice-cream tab. Still, nothing she'd do would surprise me."

He was wrong.

He never expected to accompany Torie to the Dairy Princess and be stopped at the door with shouts of "Surprise!"

"What's going on?" Torie asked him out the side of her mouth.

The paper bells and streamers provided the first clue. When a familiar march started playing on the jukebox, the answer was obvious. "A wedding shower."

Kathy sidled up to Matt and slipped her arm through his. "Not just a wedding shower. A lingerie shower."

"Oh my God," Torie breathed. She clutched Matt's sleeve. "That umbrella is made of thong panties."

Matt's head jerked around to look.

"I like to be original in my decorations," Kathy said, beaming.

Glancing around the restaurant, Matt spied most of the women who'd bought photos from Torie that morning, friends of his from high school—some of whom he'd dated—and some of Maddie's eldercare clients. He noted the table of gifts piled high and winced at the thought of boxes full of sturdy white cotton briefs.

Although come to think of it, recalling some of Maddie's stories about her elder friends, edible panties weren't out of the question. This just might be fun. "Where do you want us to sit?"

Kathy shook her head and clicked her tongue. "No, Matthew. This is a girl thing. You need to leave, but be back here in two hours to pick them up."

"Them?"

"That's my other surprise. We have a special guest!"

With that, Matt's instincts went on high alert. As the crowd parted in front of them, he reached beneath his jacket for his gun.

"Helen!" Torie exclaimed.

"Oh, Torie! I'm so glad to see you." Helen Bradshaw rushed forward, shoving the thing she had in her hand at Matt as the twins fell into each other's arms.

"Demon, dear," Kathy Hudson observed. "Now, that's what I call protection."

Matt glanced down. In his right hand, he held his Glock. In his left, a fishbowl full of condoms.

*   *   *

As Torie hugged her sister tight, she glanced toward Matt, saw what was in his hands, and thought, *Just call me Alice. I've stumbled down the rabbit hole.*

"What are you doing here, Helen?"

"I stopped across the street to buy gas and I asked how to find Matt and they sent me over here. It wasn't twenty minutes ago. I didn't have time to shop anywhere but the Mini Mart."

"*You* bought those rubbers?"

"It's the closest thing to lingerie they sell at a gas station."

"Holy Moses."

Matt found his voice. "Helen, honey? Are you alone?"

She nodded. "Something happened, though. I—"

"Matt?" Kathy touched his shoulder. "Do y'all need a minute?"

"We do."

Kathy raised her voice. "Okay, ladies. I'm gonna switch things around. We'll eat first, then open the gifts. We're gonna give our honoree a minute to catch up with her sister so they can both concentrate on the party. So y'all get in line at the salad bar and load up." She led the way for Matt, Torie, and Helen, threading through the crowd to reach the office in back.

When Kathy left them alone, Torie again hugged her sister hard, then said, "Tell us everything."

"It may be nothing. I could be overreacting, but after your message warning me to be careful, I can't dismiss it as coincidence."

"Dismiss what as coincidence?"

"Someone tried to run me down."

Torie reached instinctively for Matt's hand as he quickly said, "Tell us exactly what happened."

Helen told her story with a scientist's attention to detail. She described the sun's position, the speed of the wind, and the make, model, and color of the vehicle. "I didn't see the driver," she confessed. "It happened so fast and by the time I thought to notice, the car was driving off and I couldn't see through the tinted back window. I didn't get the license plate number because I lost my glasses when I fell. It's possible the driver didn't see me and it truly was an accident, but . . . it scared me."

"Of course it did." Torie studied her sister closely, frowning at the scratches and scrapes visible on her arm. Glancing at Matt, she said, "We have to catch him, Matt."

He nodded grimly. "Did you notice anything unusual at all, honey?"

While Helen considered the question, Torie filed the "honey" away for consideration at a more appropriate time. "No. Not at all. The amount of traffic was normal for lunchtime."

"Do you usually leave the lab that time of day?"

"Most days, yes. I walk a two-mile route for exercise. I might have been a few minutes earlier than usual because I had a lunch date."

"How did you end up here?"

"I bought a ticket to Hawaii with a layover in Dallas. I called a friend who picked me up at the airport, then let me borrow his car." Her teeth tugged her bottom lip. "I watched the road. I don't think I was followed, but I admit I don't have any experience at this sort of thing."

Matt glanced at Torie. "Have you two been in contact I don't know about?"

"One thing I do know is how to research." Helen chastised Matt with a look. "Once I knew she was with you, it was easy."

Torie hugged her sister one more time. "Ah, Helen, I'm so sorry."

"Don't be. I'd have hated missing your bridal

shower. You do know I'm dying to hear all about the engagement. It's so exciting. A wedding! On a beach in Bali, yet. You never cease to surprise me, sister."

"Uh . . . Helen . . ."

"At least promise me you'll choose a flattering sarong for your maid of honor. I want to wear yellow."

"Helen, I need to explain."

"Not here, Shutterbug," Matt interrupted. "Not the right place, not near enough time for explanations. Here comes Kathy."

On cue, a knock sounded on the door. "You girls about ready? The natives are getting restless. We have Edna Wilkins's chocolate cake for dessert and I won't let them cut into it until you've opened your gifts. Believe me, further delay at this point isn't advised."

Torie met her sister's gaze and silently conveyed an apology and a caution. Helen knew her well and she didn't miss the message. She gave Torie's hand a squeeze as they returned to the main part of the restaurant, which Matt refused to leave until Torie gave her solemn promise not to step foot outside the Dairy Princess until he returned.

Following that came one of the most uncomfortable hours of her life. People she didn't know gave her lacy scraps of underwear and filmy gowns and made jokes about her sex life. She heard ribald stories about her lover's youth and listened to three different women— three confessedly happily married women—swoon over Matt Callahan's buns.

As if that weren't bad enough, they started asking her about her job with *National Geographic*. Helen, quick on the uptake and infinitely more experienced than Torie where research trips were concerned, stepped into the breach. Torie was amazed to hear her sister lie so well, and for a few moments, the novelty distracted her.

Edna Wilkins's cake proved as good as promised and offered the opportunity to turn the conversation away from her. While talk centered on speculation about a secret ingredient and Helen participated with unbridled enthusiasm, displaying a surprising depth of knowledge about baking while tidily disassembling the thong umbrella and folding and tucking panties into a gift box, Torie once again experienced the *Alice in Wonderland* rabbit hole moment. What had her sister been doing with her time of late?

Other than dodging wannabe killers behind the wheel, of course?

The chuckle built within her softly, slowly. When it finally spilled from her lips, only someone paying close attention would notice the hysterical note to the sound. Helen noticed. So did Matt the moment he walked back into the restaurant. When he bent down to greet her with a kiss, he whispered in her ear, "What is it?"

"Nothing. Everything. I think you'd better get me out of here, Callahan."

Matt assessed the situation and stepped onto the stage. He made a show of trying to peek into boxes while he made suggestive comments that charmed the guests and elicited some wistful looks from both young and old. He then launched into an effusive thank-you for their generosity that required only a nod, smile, and simple agreement from Torie. Then he ushered her and her sister smoothly out the door.

Had she not already been in love with the man, she'd have fallen then and there.

Matt guided her quickly to his truck, explaining that Mark would drive out to the lake house with Helen. "Are you worried that she was followed?"

He hesitated a moment before saying, "I believe in being careful."

Good. Torie liked that attitude under the circumstances. She shut her eyes and let her head drop back against the headrest. A few minutes later, she commented, "The people of this town are so nice. They don't know me at all and look what they did. I felt awful, knowing it was all a lie."

Matt didn't respond to that, and they rode the rest of the way in silence.

At the lake house, Matt showed Helen to a guest room, then disappeared down onto the dock with his brother. Finally alone, the two sisters reverted to habits of their childhood by sitting cross-legged on the queen-sized bed while Torie launched into her story, thus answering her sister's unspoken questions.

She told Helen about the stalker's tricks, her flight to Texas, and Matt's agreement to help. She neglected to mention the truck-shooting incident or the fact that they'd become lovers.

"That's frightening," her twin said when she was done. "I'll bet you were scared to death. Oh, Torie. Why didn't you contact me? I should have been there for you. You're always there for me."

"At first, I didn't want to worry you. Then I was afraid of putting you in danger." She paused, her teeth tugging at her lower lip. "I guess I did that anyway. I should have called."

"Don't, Tor. This isn't your fault." Helen rolled off the bed and walked over to the window, where she pushed back a pair of nautical-print curtains and gazed out toward the lake. "Isn't this a pretty spot? You did a good job picking a hiding place."

Then she turned around, folded her arms, and said, "But now, tell me about this wedding. Bali? *National Geographic*? What's the scoop, sis?"

It arrived in a flash, seemingly out of nowhere. One second she was fine, the next, an emotional mess. Torie's throat went tight. Pain grabbed hold of her heart and wouldn't let go.

"Oh, Helen. He gave me this ring. He announced it to the world. He made it all up so that the husband-hunting women in town would leave him alone. How sad is that? And I'm putting up with it! That's even worse. I offered myself up like a sacrifice. I'm pathetic."

"No, you're not."

Then her sister was beside her, hugging her, while Torie babbled. "I'm sleeping with him."

"I should hope so."

"I'm in love with him."

"Of course you are."

"You know, I could have hired a private investigator in LA. Even with all the awful stuff, I could have handled it. Until the explosion, anyway. It was an excuse. I wanted to see him again. He's my dream man. My superhero. My fantasy lover."

"Your James Bond," Helen said with gentle understanding.

That's when Torie looked up and met her sister's misty-eyed gaze, and the words poured from her soul. "No. Don't you see? He's not a movie character or a movie star. He's not fake like all the other people in my life, not paparazzi bait. He's not James Bond. He's better than Bond. He's real. The real deal. He's Matt Callahan, and God help me, I love him with all my heart!"

Helen brushed Torie's hair away from her eyes. "I think he loves you, too."

"No. He doesn't love me. We have an agreement. It's over when I leave Brazos Bend. I'm the Callahan girl only until the movie ends."

Helen rolled her tongue around her mouth. "I'm sure that makes sense somehow."

"I'm sorry. I shouldn't be doing this." Torie gripped her head in her hands. "It's just nice to have someone I can count on. Someone who I know is on my side. Someone I can trust."

"Oh, sweetheart, have you told him how you feel?"

"Oh, yeah." Torie summarized that joyous little occasion and how quickly he'd run off.

"He's scared," Helen said with conviction.

"Matt? I don't think so."

"Well, I do and you should trust my opinion. In fact, you need to open your eyes and trust Matt not to hurt you."

"Are you sure you didn't bump your head in your fall?"

Helen simply frowned at her. "I know that trusting a man is the hardest thing for you—Dad made sure of that. I suspect that for you, it's easier to love than to trust."

"I think you're probably right about that." Torie grabbed a tissue from a box beside the bed and blew her nose. "Only that. I think with some of the guys I've been with in the past . . . I always loved them a little. But never enough. I always held something back."

"Not this time, though, hmm? Torie, look into your heart. You love Matt, but you also trust him. Otherwise, you wouldn't have come to him, wouldn't have put up with this nonsense of a fake engagement, wouldn't have subjugated your pride and self-respect, unless deep in your soul, you trust him to do right by you. You trust him, and that's huge for you."

Torie sat for a long few minutes, thinking about what her twin had said. Could Helen possibly be right? Had she made that leap into faith without being aware of it?

"No. It's a nice theory, Helen, but I don't think it holds water. Love him, yes. But trust him? No. He's given me no indication that he wants to continue our love affair after the stalker is caught. I'll go back to my lonely, if adventuresome, life with Gigi and my Hasselblad. He'll eventually figure out what he wants and maybe find a woman who'll give him kids and a white picket fence."

"Why don't you give him that?"

For a moment, the idea sat there like a package under the Christmas tree. Then Torie shook her head.

"I'd screw it up. It's what I do. What I am. Just as the general always said."

"The general needs to pull his head out of the cave in Tora Bora. But then, you need to pull yours out, too. You need to have faith in Matt, but you also need to have faith in yourself. Stop chasing the next big story and make one of your own."

"It's too risky."

"You thrive on risk, Torie. You always have. It's no surprise to me that when it comes to the biggest risk of all—your heart—you go for the biggest prize."

"He is a prize. All the women in town know it."

"And you trust him to see that you're just as big a prize, too."

"Wow. Do you think that's really true? Do you think I made such a life-changing decision without realizing it?"

"I think it's the only way you could make it, Torie. You've acted on instinct, not on what you've learned from being your father's daughter. You trust that Matt Callahan won't betray your faith in him."

Torie thought about it the rest of the day. She thought about it when Matt joined her in bed that night. When he kissed her awake the following morning, it was the first thing that came into her mind.

It was during their shared shower that she finally made peace with the idea. Helen was right. She'd been hiding the truth from herself. She didn't just love Matt; she trusted him.

So she'd be patient, just like he'd asked.

Chapter Sixteen

Matt sat on the back of Les's modified golf cart and scanned the area, keeping close watch on the occupants of the vineyard while he took second-guessing himself to an art form. Tomorrow, the vineyard and winery hosted visitors following the Texas Hill Country Wine and Wildflower Trail. Les expected a crowd. Matt expected the stalker to show up.

At least, that was the plan. He hoped like hell he hadn't made a mistake.

Matt had dangled the unsuspecting bait and given the bastard plenty of time to track the clues, the same sort of operation he'd done dozens of times in all parts of the world. That this time somehow felt different, he did his best to ignore. This weekend's event provided the perfect opportunity for the stalker to get close to his prey, and Matt was confident he'd attempt just that. He wouldn't know that Matt, Mark, and two security guards out of Fort Worth would have Four Brothers under surveillance, ready to act the moment the stalker made a move toward the unwary Victoria.

Unwary. Unsuspecting. That was the part giving him trouble. Was he screwing up by cutting Torie out of the planning?

No, he insisted to himself for perhaps the fiftieth time. Torie couldn't hide her thoughts and feelings worth a damn. She put everything right out front for the world to see—her fear, her happiness. Her love. Even when she tried to hide her thoughts and feelings, he could read her like a book. If she knew what he'd done, she'd be a basket case. She could cost them the element of surprise. He couldn't risk bringing her into the plan. He couldn't trust her not to give it away.

His gaze locked on Torie as she laughed with Les in the vineyard. See, he was doing the right thing. The woman was happy. Why take that away from her? With any luck at all, she'd never need be afraid of the stalker again.

Les certainly appeared content with all creation out there himself, basking in the beauty of the afternoon and the admiration of two gorgeous women. Helen looked happy, too. She giggled like a schoolgirl as she followed Les's instructions on how to weave shoots through the lyrelike trellising system of wires in order to protect them from wind and maximize exposure to the sun. Matt envied their contentment. He wished he could relax enough to enjoy the moment—warm sunshine, a gentle breeze, dazzling women. Instead, he was wound tighter than an eight-day clock.

It didn't help that Luke hadn't called. If something went wrong in Lima, Matt would never forgive himself.

The trip to South America was supposed to be a simple one—an interview with authorities in Peru, where Esteban Romo was in prison for murder unrelated to Collin Marlow's death. Luke's connections in the DEA had led him to believe that Romo might be willing to talk to Luke. The hope was that Luke could either confirm Marlow's death beyond a shadow of a doubt or verify the possibility that he'd left the lagoon alive.

It shouldn't have taken this long. He'd expected the interview to be over an hour ago. What in the world was taking so long?

Finally, a half hour later, his cell phone rang and he found out.

"Romo claims that Marlow is definitely dead," Luke told him without preamble.

Huh. Matt wasn't sure if that made him happy or not. He'd honestly believed Marlow was good for the stalker. "You believe him?"

"I do, Matthew. He claims he has proof."

"Oh? What proof? A body?"

"I don't know. Not yet. He wouldn't say any more without compensation."

"Pay him whatever he wants," Matt growled.

"I wish it were that easy. He's not looking for money, but a deal with the officials down here."

"What sort of deal?" Frustration had Matt pacing the ground in front of the golf cart. "We don't have the pull in Lima to get him out of jail. And I don't know that we even need any more out of Romo. He's given you what we needed—verification of Marlow's death."

"I don't know, Matt. There's something wonky going on. He's only asking for a phone call to his wife. Apparently she and their children have set up housekeeping in the States. I'd like to take a shot at arranging it so I can hear what he has to say. May take me another day, but I think it's worth it as long as you don't need me in Brazos Bend."

A phone call. That shouldn't be impossible for a man with Luke's connections, and if he could learn something of value . . . "Between me and Mark and the two fellows I hired out of Fort Worth, I think we're all right here, but that's not the problem. I promised Maddie you'd be home tonight. I'll be in deep guano with her if you're out another night. You know, when she's mad, she scares me."

Luke laughed. "I'll protect you from my wife. Don't worry. I'll get to work on my end and see what it'll take to pull this together. I'll get back with you when I know something."

After disconnecting the call, Matt returned to his seat on the golf cart and spent a few moments thinking. With the ex-boyfriend, the senator, the actor, and Marlow now eliminated, he needed to reevaluate the list of suspects. Maybe next he should take a look at the invent-a-religion zealots Torie offended last year. He shouldn't discount the actor whose nose she broke, either, or the folks who lost money because of it. Damn fool actor. He should have known that tangling with a woman like Torie brought nothing but trouble.

Hell, solving the case this way could take forever, and they had no guarantee the perp was even on the list. He should consider it one more justification for the actions he'd taken. Luring the stalker to Brazos Bend was by far the best way to bring this matter to an end.

He had no reason to feel so goddamned guilty about it.

"Hey, Callahan!" Torie waved at him from among the vines. "Bring me my camera, would you?"

He grabbed the bag off the seat where she'd left it, and after signaling his watcher on the hill, he made his way into the vineyard. "Thanks, sweetie," Torie said, obviously distracted.

She prepared her camera with practiced movements, and within seconds stalked her prey—a delicate monarch butterfly. Dressed in shorts and a scoop-neck, tight-fitting pink T-shirt, her long blond hair tucked beneath a Brazos Bend High ball cap, her movements fluid and deliberate as she worked, Torie distracted him from his concerns. He thought he could watch her for hours.

"She's amazing, isn't she?" Helen asked.

"She sees the world differently from the rest of us."

"I'm glad you get that, Callahan." Helen linked her arm through his. "For me, the world is mostly black-and-white. It's logic and pattern and formula. Torie's world is a palette of colors and shades that constantly change. She's like that butterfly she's chasing, fluttering from place to place with no defined route—at least that's the way it appears to us. Yet, monarch butterflies somehow make it from Minnesota to Mexico and back every year."

Les looked up from his vine. "Brazos Bend always has lots of monarchs. We're in the flyway."

"Do you know anything about butterflies?" Helen asked Matt.

Without taking his gaze off Torie, Matt responded, "I remember when I was a kid monarchs would be thick on the bushes around the Church of Christ in our neighborhood. So many they'd all but turn 'em orange."

Helen donned her scientist's cap. "Monarchs go through four separate life stages. They begin as eggs before hatching as larvae or caterpillars. The caterpillars feed and grow and molt. After four cycles of molting, they attach themselves to the underside of a leaf and form a delicate, beautiful chrysalis. Inside the chrysalis, the butterfly matures over several weeks until it's time to break loose. The insect pushes its legs downward, splits the chrysalis, and sets itself free. The newly hatched butterfly pumps fluid from its body into its wings. They harden, allowing it to fly."

Matt waited a beat, then asked, "What are you trying to tell me, Dr. Darling?"

"I don't know." Helen laughed self-consciously. "I just want you to see her, Callahan. Open your eyes and see past the paparazzo, see beyond caterpillar stage. She's about to break free and fly. You could fly with her, and she'll take you places you'd never go on your own."

With that, she chased off after her sister, leaving

him speechless. Les sauntered to the end of the row, pulled two bottles of water from the cooler he liked to keep handy, strolled back, and handed one to Matt. "I don't know about you, but I reckon I'll never look at a butterfly quite the same way again."

"Hell, Les. What am I going to do?"

"Don't know. This is new territory for me, too. I've never known you to be indecisive or stupid, Matthew." Les took a long swig of water. "Whatever you decide, just make sure you get me prints of those photos she's taking. I imagine they'll be perfect for next year's Wine and Wildflower brochure."

Small towns were the same all over the world, the stranger observed. Everyone knew everyone else. People pried into one another's business. Gossip was the order of the day.

Let's see if I can't use that fact to my advantage.

"Can I help you?" asked the waitress in the ice-cream shop a few minutes later. She wore an ELVIS LIVES T-shirt, atrocious earrings, and a sympathetic expression. "You look upset about something."

Perfect. "I'm frustrated. I had an important appointment with a Mr. Branch Callahan, but he appears to have forgotten. He wasn't home, nor does he answer his telephone."

"Oh, dear. Well, Branch is in the hospital. He had a heart attack, but word is he's doing well. Don't know when he'll be heading home, though. What was your appointment about?"

A drive past the man's home earlier today had revealed substantial wealth, making the obvious answer, "Investments."

The waitress frowned and rhythmically thumped her stubby pencil against her order pad. "I doubt the doctors would want you in the hospital doing business with a patient. Could one of his sons help? They're in town."

I know. I read it at Blogging the Brazos. The waitress had followed the lead perfectly. "Actually, that might work well. I've papers for a Mr. Matt Callahan to look at."

The waitress waved her hand. "That's easy. He'll be at Four Brothers Winery tomorrow. It's the big weekend for the Wine and Wildflower tour. I will warn you. He's probably awfully busy. They really get a crowd out there at Four Brothers on tour weekends."

"Perfect." It truly was.

Finally things are going my way.

Torie whistled a Jimmy Buffett tune beneath her breath as she brushed the feather duster over the wine-theme ceramics displayed on the baker's rack in the middle of the winery's small store. After spending the afternoon with Les yesterday and learning what to expect during a Wine and Wildflower tour weekend, she could hardly wait for the first visitors to arrive. Les made it sound like today would be half-work, half-party.

With Matt's and Les's blessing, she'd decided to put away her camera for the day and play store clerk. Helen had intended to work with her, but unfortunately, her sister woke up with an upset stomach this morning.

"Oh, this is too cute," Torie said to herself, picking up a hand-painted tile trivet featuring a Four Brothers label nestled in a field of bluebonnets. "I didn't notice this before."

On his way to unlock the winery door, Les said, "Angie brought a box of 'em over last night. She's good with the artsy-fartsy stuff."

Les looked loose-limbed and relaxed. Torie rolled her tongue around her mouth, then innocently observed, "Her cooking is phenomenal. Anything left over from breakfast?"

Les shot her a disapproving frown and she laughed and continued her dusting.

Just as the day's first visitors arrived, Matt joined them in the winery wearing a blue cotton shirt embroidered with the Four Brothers logo. Les stepped behind the tasting bar and Torie watched with frank admiration as a natural salesman went to work.

Twenty minutes later, Matt worked the register to total the two couples' orders.

Torie waited until the door closed behind them before she whirled on Les. "Six hundred dollars? Good grief, Les."

"Just wait until later this afternoon when the tour buses pull up loaded with riders already three sheets to the wind," Matt said. "I predict come five o'clock, we don't have a single bottle of Four Brothers blended red left to sell."

At that point, another group of visitors entered the winery and Torie soon found herself smothered in work. The handcrafted items sold as quickly as the wine, and she was back and forth from the storage room so often that she wished she'd worn sneakers rather than sandals. But just like Les had promised, she was having fun . . . until a pack of local casserole queens arrived to spoil her mood. There were five of them, three brunettes, two blondes, and a redhead.

It started innocently enough, lots of oohs and ohs over her engagement ring, and questions about the Bali wedding. Then one of the brunettes dropped the little tidbit that Matt once had been engaged to be engaged to a local girl, but dropped her like a scalded cat after she wanted to move the wedding date closer.

"Engaged to be engaged?" Torie questioned, keeping the smile planted firmly on her face. "I'm not familiar with the conventions of that idea."

"Well, some folks call it goin' steady," said the blonde. "Here in Brazos Bend, girls ask for more commitment from a fella before . . . well . . . you understand."

Oh, yeah. She understood. These women were looking to cook up trouble. Torie wanted to ask them what year they thought they might finally graduate from high school. Instead, she acted more direct. "Matt told some girl he'd marry her to talk her into bed? How old was he? Sixteen? Fifteen?"

The girls shared a glance that proved her point, so Torie continued. "If girls believe what boys tell them at that age, then shame on them. So, are you here for the wine tasting? Les will be happy to take care of you."

Maybe that would mellow them a bit.

The redhead dawdled behind the rest. She smiled apologetically, but the look in her eyes was hard. Torie figured she must be one of the legion of Matt's old girlfriends. She'd have asked him, but the coward had retreated to the storeroom the minute the women walked through the door. She spied him keeping an eye on things from the doorway, but the local girls never did.

The crowd swelled and visitors exchanged stories with one another, the opening of the new wine bar, market, and bistro down the road in Fredericksburg causing the most stir. Talk about the gourmet takeaway menu had Torie's mouth watering. Why couldn't Matt have taken her for chicken-and-truffle lasagna on a vineyard picnic instead of fried catfish served beneath a stuffed cow head?

"Have you considered adding a gourmet market to the winery?" she asked Les after the local women wandered outside to giggle and gossip.

"It's on the drawing board on down the road," he replied. "That and an art gallery."

Now, that surprised her. "An art gallery? In Brazos Bend?"

"Fine art belongs everywhere," he replied, his tone

just a bit chastising. "You might tuck that into the back of your mind. After seeing those bluebonnet pictures of yours . . . if you decide to give up celebrity chasing, you might consider taking your talent in that direction."

She leaned over and kissed his cheek. "Well, that's the nicest compliment I've had in a long time. Thank you, Les."

"Don't dismiss him," Mark said from behind her, just inside the storeroom, after Les moved back to the tasting bar.

Startled, Torie twisted around, "Mark, I didn't see you."

"That's the idea," he muttered. "About Les, just so you know, when he comments about art, you should listen. Have you heard of Warfield Galleries?"

"In New York?"

"And London and Tokyo. That's his family. His sister is the director."

"You lie," Torie said.

"All the time, but not about this."

"But I thought Les was career navy."

"It's that black sheep thing. It's why he and Matt hit it off so well."

"Matt's not the black sheep of the family," she protested.

"We're all black sheep," Matt said, taking Torie's arm and guiding her away from Mark and over to a display case where a young man wanted a woman's opinion about an Anduze pot he was considering as a gift for his wine-loving future in-laws.

Torie was wrapping up the pot when the casserole queens darted back inside, catching Matt before he could make an escape. The brunettes gushed over his Four Brothers label reds; a blonde waxed on about the port. The redhead hung back a bit, speaking only to ask a question when Matt explained how Les bought grapes from other growers to make the Four

Brothers wines until their vineyards matured and grape production increased. Watching the women and Matt, Torie gained a new understanding of his desire to go to extreme lengths to avoid the babe parade, to use his term. Imagine how bad it would be if he weren't engaged.

The redhead noticed her watching and wandered over. "I understand Mark was hurt in some sort of accident. Is he doing all right?"

"Yes, he's . . ." Torie let her voice trail off. Mark was lying lower even more than Matt. What if this chick wasn't Matt's old girlfriend, but Mark's? He wouldn't want Torie telling her that he was hanging around the back room.

Good Lord, if they knew there were two unmarried Callahans around, the gaggle of women might double in size. Triple. "Mark is fine."

"Is he staying at Matt's lake house?"

Torie glanced over at Matt, but he was busy smiling at the blonde. From what she understood, Matt's ownership of the lake house was still a secret. She decided to play clueless. "What lake house?"

The redhead acted embarrassed. "Oh, I'm sorry. That's just gossip. The girls said a fisherman spied a couple of fancy boats in an isolated boathouse and people are thinking they might be Matt's. I guess the house is a long way from here by water, but rather close by land."

"I wouldn't know." Torie said it flatly, abruptly, in an attempt to shut her up and put her in her place, but the redhead didn't take the hint.

"I know you must think I'm being terribly intrusive, but I worry about Mark. We have a . . . connection."

"What did you say your name was?" Torie asked just as the door opened and a lone man stepped inside. A man Torie recognized.

"Michael?"

Matt's head jerked up as he went on immediate alert.

"I need to talk to you, Torie," Michael Harrison said, moving toward her, his voice fierce and simmering with anger. "Now. Alone. I'm so done with your—*oomph!*"

Matt put him down in an instant.

He stood over the prone man, his boot on the back of Michael's neck, his Glock in his hand.

Oh, wow, Torie thought. He'd never shown her his martial arts moves. How sexy was that?

"Matt, it's all right—," she began as Mark and two other men rushed into the room with guns drawn. The casserole queens started screaming, someone dropped a ceramic cookie jar, and the tasting room emptied in a tipsy stampede.

"Torie!" Michael's muffled voice exclaimed.

She couldn't help it. Mirth bubbled up inside of her and she started laughing.

Les Warfield poured himself a glass of wine.

"Matt, it's okay. I promise. Let him up. I know him. He's Michael Harrison. He's not my stalker."

"How can you be sure?"

Helen sailed into the room. "Because Michael is my husband!"

Summoned by a half-dozen cell phone calls, the Brazos Bend Police Department sent two cruisers and the sheriff's department sent one. They converged on the winery simultaneously. By that time Matt's hired guards, Mark, and Les had cleared the parking lot, sending frightened visitors away with a gift and coupons for a free wine tasting on their next visit.

While Mark dealt with the law in the parking lot, Matt stayed inside and attempted to mediate a marital fight, ignore Torie's requests for a martial arts demonstration, and prevent himself from disappearing into the cellar, tapping a barrel, and drowning his sorrows. The idea had way too much appeal at the moment.

"How long has your sister been married?" he asked Torie.

"Almost six months now."

That took him by surprise. "I had lunch with your father in January and I asked about Helen. He didn't mention marriage. In fact, he tried to set us up."

"The general didn't know she was married in January. In fact, he still doesn't know. They've kept it secret from everyone. Well, everyone but me."

"Why?"

"You'd have to know my father. . . . Oh, wait. You do know my father. You don't know Michael's mother, though, and she makes the general look like a lamb. It's a long story that involves old promises and dreams of dynasties, and well . . . I think there's a patent in the mix, too."

Matt rubbed his temples. A patent?

Across the room, Helen burst into tears and Harrison stormed away from her. He turned a glare on Torie, silently warning her against moving to comfort her sister. He advanced on her, saying, "This is all your fault."

"Now, wait a minute," Matt warned.

"Someone tried to kill her, so what does she do? She turns to you. Not me. Not her husband. Oh, no. Why, she doesn't even pick up the phone and call me. I hear about it in an e-mail. An e-mail!" Harrison fisted his hands at his sides and got in Torie's face. "I'm tired of the worry you cause her. I'm tired of her using you as an excuse not to face the general and be honest about our lives. I'm sick and tired of her always putting you before me!"

"Michael, don't," Helen said, her arms wrapped around herself.

"No, Helen. It's time this was said." He never took

his angry gaze off Torie. "She's dragged you into trouble all your lives."

"That's so not true," Helen insisted. She stepped toward her husband and her sister. "She's pulled me out of trouble all our lives. She has! She's always protected me."

"Was she protecting you when her stalker almost ran you over?" her husband asked snidely. "Hmm?"

Torie let out a whimper.

"Okay, that's enough." Matt stepped between Torie and her brother-in-law. It required all his discipline not to put the bastard on the floor once more. The jerk had hurt Torie's feelings. Oh, she was trying to be stoic, but Matt could tell. Her eyes looked weary. "You'll have time to sort through family issues later."

"Matt is right," Helen said. She wiped the tears from her cheeks with the back of her hand. "What's important now is Torie's safety. Did I make a mistake? Have I put her at risk? How did you find us?"

"Certainly not from your phone calls," Michael snapped, shooting his wife a furious look.

"I had a good reason for not calling, but I'm not talking to you until you calm down," Helen shot back.

Michael folded his arms and stuck out his chin before answering Matt's question. "I hired a private investigator. He found Helen right away."

Looking at his wife, he clarified, "Well, he found Torie, and I knew you'd run to her. You always run to her. I swear I don't know why you married me, Helen. The only thing you need me for is sex, and you honestly don't need me for that, since you're so beautiful and smart that all you'd have to do is snap your fingers and men would line up for the chance to be your lover."

Matt schooled his features into an expressionless mask and hoped Torie had missed the vital piece of information in the midst of the man's pitiable outburst.

"Wait a minute," Torie interjected, dashing his hopes. "Did you say a private investigator found me? How?"

Matt thought fast. This was not how he wanted this to go down, so he interrupted, "Like I said, we'll have time for all this later. It's still Wine and Wildflower weekend, and I imagine Les is about to chew nails for everything to settle back to normal. Helen, why don't you take your husband over to the house and y'all can work on your issues in private. Torie, I need you with me. If I have to face the tourists alone, it just might kill me."

While he spoke, he smoothly separated Torie from the others and led her toward the door. Outside, his hired men had disappeared, he presumed back to their stations. Les picked up trash from the parking lot, while Mark spoke to the occupants of the remaining squad car. Matt recognized the cop as an old friend of Mark's from high school.

"Matt," Torie began. "I'm worried. I thought I'd covered my tracks, but if an investigator found me, the stalker could, too. Was it the instant message, do you think?"

"I think you don't need to worry about it, Victoria. I'll take care of you. You have my word. Let's just—"

He broke off abruptly, thankful for the interruption, when his phone rang. He checked the number. Branch. For once, the old man had good timing. "Hello, Branch."

Except it wasn't Branch on the line, but Branch's doctor. "You need to come to the hospital, Mr. Callahan. Your brothers, too, if you can find them. We have a situation involving your father. An emergency, if you will."

Matt froze. "Another heart attack?"

"No, not that. Please come as soon as possible. It's vitally important."

"Look, Doctor, I have a bit of a situation going on,

myself. I don't know that—" Hearing the dial tone in his ear, Matt stifled the urge to throw the phone.

Torie touched his arm. "What's wrong, Matt?"

"That was Branch's doctor. He said Mark and I need to go to the hospital."

"What happened?"

"I don't know. He said it wasn't a heart attack, but that's all he told me. I swear, I'm putting an end to this privacy bullshit today. Mark?" he called, then waved his brother to come back toward the tasting room. "Got a problem."

Mark nodded, then shook the cop's hand. The policeman continued to talk to Mark as he climbed into his car, and it wasn't until he'd started the engine and pulled in a wide semicircle to exit the parking lot that Mark turned his attention toward Matt.

Meanwhile, Matt's mind raced. He didn't like this. Didn't like it at all. Why would the doctor want the entire family there unless he had bad news to impart?

It must have something to do with the secret that Branch had refused to allow him to share. He hoped it wasn't cancer. After going through that with Mom . . . He couldn't do it again.

Jesus. Why did everything have to happen at once?

"What's up?" Mark asked. "Did you hear from Luke?"

"No, not yet. It was Dad's doctor." Matt recapped the short conversation for his brother.

Mark didn't hesitate. "You go. I'll keep an eye on things here."

"He asked for us both."

"Yeah, well, he might as well ask for snow in July."

"But Mark—"

"Forget it. You need me here. I'll take the women back to the house away from the crowds. Carson and Harwell can maintain surveillance on the tasting room."

"Les can't handle the crowd by himself."

"He's already called his lady friend and she's on the way."

Matt glanced at Torie. "I could take you with me," he suggested, realizing once he'd done so that he'd prefer it that way.

She chewed on her bottom lip, her gaze trailing back toward the winery, where Helen and her hubby waited. "Do you need me to come with you, Matt?"

"No," he answered automatically. He didn't want her out of his sight. It might be nice to have her company when he talked to the doctor, but he didn't *need* her.

He hoped like hell it wasn't cancer.

"Of course not," she murmured. "I'll be fine here. I'd rather not leave Helen until she's had a chance to calm down. You go on, now. You don't want to keep the doctor waiting."

It wasn't until he was halfway to town that Matt's mind stopped spinning long enough to realize what he'd done, what he'd risked. What if Helen's hubby gave the game away?

His fists tightened around the steering wheel. Talk about a dumbshit rookie mistake. "Jesus, Callahan. What the hell were you thinking?"

He hadn't been thinking. He'd been remembering. Mom and that god-awful afternoon when she'd called him into her bedroom and told him she was going to die. When she'd asked him to look out for his brothers. And for Branch. *Sorry, Mom.*

He grabbed his phone, dialed Mark, and started talking the second his brother said hello. "Hey, you gotta keep Victoria away from Helen's husband. He hired private help to find her. He might tell her about the credit card."

When Mark hesitated before responding, Matt's stomach sank. "Uh, you might have mentioned this before, Matthew."

Crap. "They've talked?"

"Yeah. Helen and ol' Mikey got into it again and she ran upstairs and locked him out of her room. He went to Torie for help, and she dragged him into the study. I'll give it the old college try, but judging from the crash I heard a while back, I'm afraid it might be too late."

Matt banged his head against the steering wheel. What would go wrong next?

Chapter Seventeen

Michael Harrison stooped to pick up filing trays from off the floor. "I get clumsy when I'm agitated. I'm agitated today. What's wrong with your sister? Why won't she talk to me?"

Torie folded her arms and tapped her foot. She liked Michael, she truly did, but sometimes he seemed so clueless. "She's angry. You need to give her a little time to calm down. You should know that by now."

"How am I supposed to learn this stuff if we're not living together? I want my wife to live with me, Torie. Is that really too much to ask?"

"If that's the case, then you need to come clean with your mother."

He slumped down into a chair, propped his elbows on his knees, and buried his head in his hands. "I know. I intend to do that right away, first thing when we get home. I decided that on the drive down here."

Finally! Then something good had come from this after all. "Good." She propped a hip on the corner of the desk and asked, "Speaking of the drive down here . . . how did it come about? You said this private investigator found me easily? How?"

"He traced your credit card." He glanced up. "It

was stupid of you to use it if you're trying to hide. You should have known better than that."

"I did know better than that," Torie said, confused. "I do. I haven't used my credit card."

"Somebody did. Racked up quite a bill at an ice-cream shop."

Torie thought she must have heard wrong. "Where?"

"A place called Princess, Too. My guy told me they sold ice cream, but I figure they had to sell more than just that. The bill was almost four hundred dollars."

"Matt," she breathed. Shock hit her like a fist and nausea rolled in the pit of her stomach. No. He wouldn't do that. She couldn't believe it. "Where's my purse? I need my purse."

She ran up the stairs to his bedroom, where it sat on the dresser where she'd left it. As she rifled through its contents to find her wallet, her heart pounded. There. She grabbed the wallet, opened it. Her credit card rested in its usual spot.

She sank onto the edge of the bed and replayed the scene in the ice-cream parlor in her mind. *Matt smiling at Kathy Hudson. Handing over his credit card. Kathy's puzzled look.*

Betrayal rose like bile in her throat.

She thought of the efforts she'd taken to hide her route—like the night in New Mexico she'd spent in her car because the only motel in town wouldn't rent her a room without a credit card. She remembered the long, lonely hours in the car when she'd wanted . . . needed . . . to talk to her sister, but feared a phone call being traced.

I want to use you, Victoria.

"Oh, he used me all right." Icy coldness settled in her bones. *He used me. Used me!* He'd used her in bed and out of it.

Numbness spread through her. Bitterness. She

should have expected it. *That's what spies do, isn't it? Lie to people? Use people?*

How stupid was she to trust a spy? To trust Matt Callahan? That was the absolute worst. She'd *trusted* him.

Oh, he probably had a reason to do what he'd done. To set her up. To use her as bait like the perch he hooked to the trotline in his cove. Maybe he even had a good reason. But to do it without telling her? Without asking her if she was willing? Without allowing her to make the choice when it was her life at risk?

She'd come to him for help. She should have known better. Some white knight. Some hero. To use her as bait . . . all on the sly. What man would do that to a woman he cared about? Only a coldhearted liar. A soulless user.

And I told him I loved him!

Pain struck like an ulcer, bending her over double even as she shuddered with humiliation. She'd put her heart out there, knowing it was risky, knowing he might blithely walk away, but she'd never seen this coming. She'd never expected betrayal.

He'd made a fool of her and, in doing so, revealed his total and complete lack of respect for her.

Staring at her reflection in the dresser's mirror, she said, "Well, they do say that women often fall for men just like their fathers."

As realizations went, it was as humiliating, demoralizing, and hurtful as anything she'd experienced in a very long time.

But Torie wasn't the type to curl up in a fetal position on the bed and cry. Not under these circumstances. Wounded, in pain, she got angry, and it was that emotion that drove her to her feet and carried her down the stairs. Matt wasn't here, but Mark was. He was the next-best thing. He had to have known, to have been in on it. He could darn well attempt to explain to her why his brother had acted without respect for her input, wishes, or willingness.

So full of righteous fury and indignation was she that she almost missed the scene taking place in the great room as she walked through it looking for Mark.

Michael had lifted Helen off the floor and was twirling her around. Her head dropped back and she laughed joyfully. Torie couldn't remember the last time she'd seen her twin look quite so happy. "I take it you two have kissed and made up?"

Michael gently returned Helen to her feet, then looked at Torie with wondrous joy. "She told me, Torie. Isn't it wonderful?"

"Told you what?"

His eyes rounded even more. Then he jerked his gaze back to Helen. "You didn't tell her?"

Love brimmed in Helen's gaze. "No, Michael. I wouldn't do that. You deserved to hear it before anyone else."

"Oh, Helen. I love you."

As the couple kissed, Torie figured it out. "You're pregnant. Helen!" For the moment, excitement chased away her rage at Matt. She stepped toward her sister. "You're pregnant?"

They broke off the kiss, and Helen beamed at her. "I think so, yes."

"Oh, honey. Yes, it is wonderful. You're gonna be a mom. I'm going to be an aunt!" Torie wrapped her arms around her sister and hugged her tight. Then she hugged Michael, which morphed into a group hug.

"Hold on a minute," Helen cautioned. "I'm not one hundred percent positive. I think I am—I have all the symptoms—but I haven't done a test yet."

"What are we waiting for?" Michael asked. "Let's do it."

"I don't have one." Helen gave his mouth a quick kiss. "I just figured it out yesterday, and I haven't been into town to buy one."

"Okay. I'll go get one. I saw the Wal-Mart in town. I'll be back in a flash."

Michael literally ran from the house, jumped off the front porch, then halted abruptly. "His car is at the winery," Helen said.

"My MINI Cooper is in the garage," Torie replied. "He can take it."

"Too late." Helen laughed again. "He's running up the hill."

"What the hell is going on?" Mark said as he walked into the room, Paco trotting along at his heels. "What is Harrison up to?"

When she saw Matt's brother, Torie's ire returned, though it didn't burn quite so hot. She found it difficult to be insanely happy and hotly furious simultaneously.

Difficult, but not impossible. She advanced on Mark with murder in her eyes.

Matt wanted to murder his father. "You want to run that by me again, Doctor?"

"Matthew, just calm down," Branch interjected.

"Calm down? You want me to calm down? The good doctor here just told me that you haven't allowed him to talk to your family, not because you wanted privacy, but because you didn't want us to know that *nothing is wrong with you*! Dammit, Branch!"

"Wait a minute. I do too have something wrong with me."

"Yes, a total and complete lack of conscience. For God's sake. You faked a heart attack!"

"He did experience an episode of angina," the doctor interjected. "Hospitalizing him for tests was justified. Keeping him here another day longer is not, which is the reason for this meeting. Mr. Callahan, physically, your father is in relatively good health for a man his age with his history. However, it is my opinion and that of the psychologist who conferred with me on your father's case that, mentally, he has some issues."

No shit. "You got my father to see a shrink?"

"It delayed his discharge." The doctor and Matt shared a look of understanding; then the doctor let out a long sigh. "We're recommending family counseling. Your father has agreed to participate."

"Family counseling," Matt repeated. Could the day possibly get any crazier? "With my family."

"Yes. He refused to leave the hospital unless I spoke with you about it. Mr. Callahan, the unresolved issues between your father and his sons cause him a great deal of stress that is taking a toll on his body. I understand that a confrontation with your brother Mark contributed to the incident last week. One of the primary reasons he doesn't want to leave the hospital is that he's seen more of you and your brother"—the doctor checked his notes—"Luke since his admittance than he had for quite some time prior to the fact."

Matt shook his head in wonder. To Branch, he said, "I swear, Mark is right. You are the most manipulative, underhanded, scheming SOB I have ever run across and considering my occupation, that's saying something."

"Now, son . . ."

"Stop it." Matt rubbed his temple. He needed to think this through. Counseling. Twenty years ago it might have helped, but now? Luke might agree to it—Maddie would badger him into it. Mark? Not in this century.

And right now, being called down here for this crap in the middle of an operation? Hell. He'd thought the old bastard had cancer! *Family counseling, my ass.*

"It'd be a complete waste of time, Doctor. I know

I'm not in the mood for it, not after this stunt. Besides, I don't have time for it." He had a stalker to catch. And probably, a woman's temper to soothe.

The doctor responded, "You need to be aware I think that resolving these matters is imperative for your father's long-term health. These types of stresses easily could lead to another heart attack."

"Stresses?" Matt snapped. "I could tell you a thing about stresses."

The doctor tucked his pen into the pocket of his white lab coat. "Then perhaps you should make an appointment for a checkup yourself."

"Will you at least consider it?" Branch asked. "Talk to your brothers?"

"Mark won't consider it, Dad."

"Luke, then. You and Luke. That'd be a start, right?"

Matt felt his cell phone vibrate. He pulled it out of his pocket and checked the number. Luke. "I have to take this. Look, Branch, go home. Luke and I will come by in a couple of days and talk about this, okay? No promises, but it'll give you a chance to come clean with him about everything. He's not going to be real happy with you, either."

Branch nodded, his smile shaky, his eyes bright with hope. Matt turned away from him and answered the call. "Hey. Hold on just a minute and let me get somewhere private."

"Sure."

A minute later, he walked out the hospital's front door into the sunshine. "Okay, what do you have?"

"Trouble. I made the deal with Romo work, and after he talked to his wife, he talked to me. It's a good thing I checked, Matthew. The woman in Torie's photographs? The one with Marlow who we identified as Esteban Romo's wife's younger sister? We didn't have the whole story. She's related to Alejandro more closely than a sister-in-law's sister. She's Alejandro's wife. Pilar de Romo."

Matt burst out with a disbelieving laugh. "You're telling me that Collin Marlow had an affair with the wife of the head of a terrorist organization?"

"Yep."

"Good grief, he's lucky he just got shot." He thought about the situation a moment longer. "Which explains why he didn't kill her, too, at the time," Matt said. "I've wondered about that. She must have been a damned fine actress."

"Actually, that's exactly what she was. Esteban and Alejandro saw Marlow escort her onto his boat. Think about the series of pictures and the point at which the Romos arrived. Pilar claimed Marlow forced her, and Alejandro bought it. Esteban says his brother was blind where his wife was concerned. He believed her until he saw proof."

Oh, crap. "Torie's pictures?"

"Yep."

"How the hell did they get hold of them?"

"Romo claims that an American DEA agent used them in a sting operation."

Matt's curses lasted almost a full minute and fear shivered down his back. "Do we have a drug lord after Torie? Is this some sort of Latin-machismo revenge attempt?"

Luke thought for a moment before answering. "I don't know. Esteban said no, but I don't know that I believe him. He makes my skin crawl. Oh, and he also claims his brother will have him out of jail by the end of the week. It wouldn't surprise me at all if he's right. He did give me another lead, though, and I'm on my way to the local insane asylum now to check it out."

"The what?"

"Santa Maria Hospital. Apparently Alejandro decided he couldn't kill the mother of his son for cheating on him, so he shut her away in with the crazies. I have time to try to see her before my flight out. She might be able to give us a different viewpoint."

"That sounds like a plan."

"If you don't hear back from me in an hour, call in the cavalry. I wouldn't want to get lost inside a South American insane asylum."

The brothers discussed a few more details, then ended their call. Matt took a moment to collect himself. He'd lived some tension-filled days in his life with the Company, usually as the hunter, sometimes the hunted. He'd always thrived under stress. He truly loved the adrenaline. Yet, the stress of dealing with his father left him feeling like a man twice his age.

And now he had to face Torie. He let out a grim sigh and headed for his truck. Maybe he'd make a quick run by the florist, first.

The scent of blueberry muffins filled the air. Bought fresh from the oven and piled into a picnic basket, they provided perfect camouflage for the .22 revolver snuggled at the bottom of the basket. "How delicious."

Laughter spilled from smiling lips. Bright eyes gazed around the crowded bakery in search of a decoy. Couples garnered less scrutiny than a single. Hmm . . . so many to choose from.

Ten minutes later, on the road again. How easy this was! Small towns, small minds. Conventional minds.

Although the trap they'd set showed a measure of ingenuity. It might have worked had they faced someone with less experience at deception, less accustomed to dangerous circumstance. What a mistake to reveal themselves under the watchful eyes of their prey, hiding in plain sight.

What a delightful, fatal mistake.

"Matt Callahan doesn't know how big a mistake he's made," Torie muttered as she slammed her bed-

room door. With short, jerky movements she yanked
her shirt over her head. "He thinks drug runners and
Peruvian terrorists and Asian warlords are dangerous?
Wait until he gets a load of me."

Curled in the center of the bed taking a nap, Gigi
lifted her head.

"Right, Gigi?"

Gigi answered with three short yips that Torie took
as affirmative. She stripped off her slacks and underwear, then grabbed her swimsuit from the bureau
drawer. She needed exercise to burn off some of this
anger before she faced him, or she might just go for
her gun again.

Mark had refused to talk to her about what Matt
had or had not done, but the guilty look in his eyes
had given him away. His determined refusal to speak
had revived the temper that had been reduced to a
slow simmer by Helen's news. The jerk. He was just
as bad as his brother.

Dressed in her swimsuit, she slid her feet into flip-
flops, then grabbed a towel from the connecting bath.
"You want to come down to the water with me?" she
asked Gigi, scooping her up into her arms.

As she headed out the door, her gaze snagged on
her Dooney and Bourke handbag with its built-in holster and the pistol stored within. She reached out and
grabbed it. She might need it. After all, wasn't she
just another minnow in the lake?

Bait.

Matt had better beware. Maybe this time she'd plug
one of his boats. Or maybe she'd just sink it.

"What do you think, Mrs. Booth? Roses?"

"You can never go wrong with roses. Just how big
a doghouse are you in?"

He thought about it. "Two stories. And a garage."

"Better get two dozen, then, honey. Long stem.
And red."

"Think I'll buy three."

"You'll need to write a card." The florist handed him a blank card and a pen.

He frowned down at the plain card, then eyed the round display case. "Don't you have one that I can just sign?"

"Yes, but you don't want that, Demon. I've been doing this for over thirty years now and you need to listen to what I say. A two-story doghouse requires a handwritten note. And it must say something more than 'Love, Matt.' Take your time. I'll be a few minutes fixing up your flowers."

Aw, man. Matt picked up the pen and tapped the end against the counter. He never had been good with words.

The parking lot at Four Brothers Vineyard was full once again. Visitors milled conveniently in the vineyard and took pictures in adjacent wildflower-dotted fields. Next year, they could call this the Texas Wine, Wildflower, and Revenge Tour.

It did have a certain ring to it.

How simple to carry a picnic basket and link arms with the decoy. How easy to stroll right past the guards who'd given themselves away by rushing the man in the tasting room, to smile and offer a refreshing bottle of water on the warm afternoon. How effortless to blend, separate, disappear over a hill.

To put the silenced weapon against the back of a head and pull the trigger.

Pilar de Romo gazed down at her first kill impassively, mildly surprised at her lack of emotional response to having taken a life. She'd grown up around violence, had witnessed sudden death for as long as she could recall. Still, she'd expected to feel something. *Oh, well.*

She retraced her steps until she spied the first security man. Adopting an air of panic, she rushed forward. "Help me, sir. Please. There's something wrong with my boyfriend. This way. Follow me this way."

When she judged them safely isolated, she fired again and earned kill number two. A short time later, number three proved just as easy.

Pilar continued her walk. Topping the hill, she stopped and gazed down at her target. "What a pretty house."

Now emotion flowed.

Feel the power.

Feel the hate.

Crave the kill.

"You need to listen to this, brother," Luke Callahan said when Matt answered the phone on his way out of the florist shop. "I have a bad feeling about it. She escaped."

His arms full of roses and his thoughts on his Torie troubles, Matt was slow on the uptake. "Who escaped what?"

"Pilar de Romo. She disappeared from the asylum three months ago, but no one reported it because, frankly, they're afraid of Alejandro."

The wife. Hmm. Timing would work. She would have had to have access to some resources. Matt carefully stored the roses on the floorboard of his truck, then said, "The incidents haven't had a feminine feel to them, but at this point we can't eliminate anyone. I'll make some calls, see what I can find out about her or where she might be. Good job, Luke. Thank you."

"Glad to be of help. So, any sign of trouble around there?"

Matt let out a scornful laugh. Where to start? "From someone other than Branch, you mean? No. We had a little excitement this morning when Helen Bradshaw's secret husband showed up, but that's it so far."

"Sounds like there's a story there, but my plane is about to board. See you tonight."

Matt made a quick call to Mark, asking him to pass word to the men standing guard to be wary of women in addition to men. "They should be doing that already," Mark replied.

"I know." Matt waved to an acquaintance entering the florist's, then added, "Still, every potential suspect we've given them is a man. A reminder to watch everyone won't hurt."

"I'm on it. Anything else?"

"Yeah." Matt started his truck and pulled out onto the road. He heard yapping sounds through the phone. Paco, probably. Little rat dog had taken a real shine to Mark. "How's Torie?"

"You might want to don your body armor before you come into the house," Mark replied.

Matt heard the familiar squeak of the kitchen screen door and made a mental note to shoot it with WD-40 when he got home. "I'm eight minutes away. How about you provide me cover when I get there?"

Rather than answer, his brother made a sound. A pain-filled grunt. The screen door slammed shut like a gunshot. "Mark?" Matt demanded. "Mark!"

Nothing.

Matt stomped on the gas pedal. "Mark!"

He heard a scream. Torie? Helen?

Then a laugh that turned his blood ice-cold.

Chapter Eighteen

Excitement hummed in Pilar's blood as she watched Mark Callahan fall. Though it had taken two shots, it was much more fun than the others because she'd owed him. He was the man who'd triggered the surprise she'd left for Torie Bradshaw in LA.

She walked through the kitchen door he'd opened to let out the dog, who now stood beside the prone body barking noisily. She took aim at the dog, but the scream diverted her attention. Torie Bradshaw screamed and rushed to the man's side, sliding down on her jean-clad knees crying, "Mark."

"Back away from him," Pilar said, using a two-handed grip to keep the gun pointed toward the woman. "Slide the phone over to me. His gun, too. Take it from its holster very carefully."

The blonde hesitated, but when Pilar shifted her finger back onto the trigger, she did as instructed. "Who are you?"

"You don't recognize me?" Pilar stooped, picked up the phone, and flipped it shut. "After all those photographs you took? Why, I'm hurt, Victoria."

"I'm not—" She broke off abruptly. "What do you want?"

Exhilaration filled Pilar and she giggled. "Why, to

make you pay, of course. You cost me everything. So, tell me, did you enjoy my little gifts? I'm quite the photographer myself, don't you agree? Do you know that you snore when you sleep?"

Torie Bradshaw shuddered, and Pilar laughed with delight at the sight. Then the man on the floor moved his hand, and Pilar shifted her gun in order to shoot him again.

"No!" Torie jumped to her feet. "Please. I'll do whatever you want."

"Of course you will. I have the gun. The power. The knowledge. I learned quite a lot at my husband's side. Torture can be an art."

The blonde closed her eyes. "You're the woman who was with Collin."

Rage flushed through Pilar's veins at the memory of that awful day. Needing to vent, she turned her gun toward the plate glass window that overlooked the lake and pulled the trigger three times. Glass shattered and the dog's barks intensified. When Pilar turned to shoot the dog, the Bradshaw woman reached out and smacked it on the rump. It ran away.

"I am Pilar de Romo, and Collin Marlow loved me. He did business with Alejandro and he saw how terribly my husband treated me. He was going to save me, to hide me on that island until it was safe for me to leave. We were going to live in Paris."

The bitch briefly closed her eyes. "I'm sorry Collin is dead, but it's not my fault."

"You took the pictures! He believed me and I was safe and then he saw the pictures!" Pilar's hand trembled. Her fingers itched to pull the trigger, to empty the magazine into the bitch's face. To destroy her.

"No," she murmured, arguing with herself. "That's too quick. After all the trouble I've gone to . . . she has to suffer. Suffer. Until the pain makes her . . . laugh."

Pilar eyed the key rack, noted the logo floats on

two sets of keys. Yes. How perfect. How delicious. She took a step closer to the pair. "Stand up, Ms. Bradshaw. It's time for us to go." She opened the screen door and motioned for her to precede her. "This setting presents the perfect opportunity to bring this matter to an appropriate end."

Torie grabbed hold of the swim ladder and climbed from the water. She couldn't remember the last time she was this chilled, both inside and out. Swimming hard for twenty minutes had burned away the hot rush of temper, and as she reached for the fluffy striped beach towel, she felt raw, weary, and empty. Too empty to think, thank God.

As she dried herself and slipped her feet into her flip-flops, she became aware of her surroundings. Gigi's tags tinkled as she ran up and down the walkway between the dock and land. Her little tail wagged and she was whimpering. "What's the matter, girl?"

Up at the house, Torie heard Paco throwing a fit. "I wonder what that's all about."

In that instant, a cold chill that had nothing to do with water or wind raced over her skin. Helen. Something was wrong with Helen. Her twin was in danger.

"Oh, God." Torie grabbed her gun from her purse and ran for the house. Oh God oh God oh God. The fifty yards felt like five hundred. Her palms were sweaty, her fingers like ice. Her heart all but pounded itself out of her chest.

She heard the sound of shattering glass.

What should she do? Where was Mark? Matt's guards? Paco was on the back porch barking his head off. Maybe she should go in through the front.

What would she find when she arrived? *Who* would she find? *Please, God, let my sister and Matt's brother be okay.*

She reached the house, flattened herself against the stone wall, and tried to catch her breath as she listened hard. Nothing. Cold sweat washed over her in waves. *Helen? Where are you?*

Torie eased around toward the front of the house, stepping quietly onto the front porch and nudging up to the great-room windows. She peered inside. Nothing. On the other side of the house, Paco's barking grew more intense. At her own feet, Gigi arrived and began to whimper. "Shush," Torie whispered.

Yap . . . yap . . . yap.

Torie picked up the dog, dashed past the window, and made her way to the front door. It was locked. *Damn.*

Seconds ticked by and her tension escalated. She eased around the other side of the house and peeked carefully into the dining room, then through to the kitchen. She could see someone's legs. A man. Lying on the floor. Mark? Probably.

Torie's stomach twisted in a knot.

Instincts urged her to hurry. She took two deep breaths, then moved swiftly and as quietly as possible toward the back of the house. Paco stood just outside the kitchen door.

He moved backward as the door began to open.

Matt threw the cell phone down on the seat beside him. Why wasn't anyone answering? Not the guards, not Mark. Not Torie. No one at the house. Hell, he couldn't even get Les to answer the phone. That could be because he was just too busy at the tasting room. Matt hoped that was the reason, anyway.

He had the cops on the way, an ambulance, too. He hoped to hell that it was a false alarm, but his gut told him otherwise.

His speed topped ninety as he flew down the highway, but he slowed as he approached the turn onto his land. This time, rather than a sense of peace and homecoming, he felt utter panic.

He'd screwed up. He'd missed something, his security hadn't held up, and his brother might have paid the price. Hell, it was John all over again. And Torie. He couldn't bear to think about Torie. She had to be all right.

He didn't even slow down as he whipped past the winery, though he did take a quick glance around looking for trouble. Nothing obvious, but he didn't see the security guys. He'd figured on that.

As he started on the last half mile, he faced a choice. Did he go in fast and openly or did he take time to do it so that he wouldn't be seen? Training told him to take his time, but his instincts were screaming that he had no time to waste. Matt decided to trust his instincts.

The truck topped the hill and roared down toward the house. Again, he looked for signs of trouble. Again, he didn't see a goddamned thing.

That scared him as much as anything.

The tires skidded on the gravel drive as he braked to a halt. He threw the truck in park and leaped out, drawing his gun and leaving the engine running. "Torie!" he yelled, running toward the house.

"Here! In the kitchen! Call 911!"

Relief hit him so hard he almost stumbled. Finding the front door locked, he grabbed the hidden key. Seconds later he barged into the kitchen and icy terror brought him to his knees. "Mark."

Blood puddled on the slate-colored tile where Torie knelt beside his still brother. It stained her skin and the white dish towel she pressed against his shoulder with one hand and the side of his head with the other. "I was afraid he'd bleed to death. Tell me you called an ambulance?"

"They're right behind me."

"Good. He made a sound once and his pulse is strong."

Matt moved her hands, checked the wounds. Head was a graze, thank God. Bloody, but not serious.

Chest wound was harder to guess. Looked high, but it could have nicked a lung.

Torie rolled to her feet. "Did you see which way they went? She has Helen."

Matt looked up from his brother to see her reach for that damned pink gun. "What are you doing?"

"I'm going after them. She has my sister. The redhead who was at the tasting room earlier is the stalker and she has my sister and she thinks Helen is me. You didn't pass her on the way in? She took keys off the key ring by the back door. She must intend to take the car in your garage. Unless . . . did you leave the keys in your truck?"

Hell, he'd left it running. "You're not going anywhere, Victoria. I'll—" Matt broke off abruptly as a familiar sound reached his ears. He glanced toward the key rack. Sure enough, the Formula's keys were missing. "That's one of my boats."

"A boat? She's taking a boat? Okay, then." Torie crossed to the key rack and snagged the set with the floating Fountain logo. "These go to the other one, right?"

"Torie, wait," Matt insisted as she headed out the door. "The ambulance should be here any minute. I'll go—"

"No. There's no time. Take care of your brother and I'll save my sister." She walked out of the door, saying, "It's what I do."

But who's going to take care of you? I can't let her go alone. I can't.

Then he looked down at his bleeding brother. Oh, God. Another impossible choice. One eerily similar to the one he'd faced in Sarajevo.

John lies sprawled on a deserted city street while Matt applies pressure to his wounds, trying desperately to stanch the bleeding. He's called for backup; they're on the way. But Cheryl, Matt's MI6 partner on this assignment, is walking into danger. Natalia will kill her with-

out hesitation, just like she tried to kill Matt and succeeded in shooting John once she realized Matt wasn't who he'd claimed to be.

Ćurković's daughter had let the wrong man get too close to the organization.

Torn between love and duty, Matt had chosen duty. He'd left his brother to be saved by someone else. He'd rescued his partner, but he never saw his brother again. By the time backup arrived, John had been taken.

Matt had suffered over his choice every day since.

And now here he was again.

Except today's choice involved one significant difference, Matt realized. This time, he didn't choose between duty and love. This time he had to choose between love for a brother and his love for Victoria Bradshaw.

"God, help me."

Torie was a third of the way between the house and the boat dock when the Formula shot out into the cove, the redhead behind the wheel. Helen sat in the stern, her hands tied to a metal grab bar. Realizing the woman couldn't see her, Torie waved her arm in a wide arc, hoping to catch her sister's attention and reassure her that help was on the way.

Such as it was.

"I'll do my best, sis," she said as she ran onto the walkway and down to the boathouse. She grabbed hold of the radar arch to steady herself as she stepped onto the boat. Moving quickly and efficiently, she slid the key into the ignition and started the engines, allowing them time to warm up as she untied the six lines from the cleats that secured the boat in its berth.

Grateful that she'd had experience driving a boat, she put the Fountain into reverse and, looking over her shoulder, began to ease out of the boathouse. With a boat this big, you had to be careful with maneuvers such as this. The loud engines drowned out all other sound and she didn't take her stare off the back of the boat.

So when the hand reached out to take the wheel, she screamed.

"I've got it," Matt shouted. "Move over."

"What are you doing here!" she yelled back. "What about Mark?"

Matt leaned over and spoke in her ear. "He'd tell me to be here. *Both* my brothers would."

Her eyes widened with alarm. "Is something wrong with Luke, too?"

Matt waited until the boat had cleared the boat-house and it was easier to hear. Then, the whine of an ambulance sounded like music to his ears. "Luke's fine. What's she up to? Why take a boat?"

"I don't know." Torie's gaze scanned the cove for signs of the other boat, but it was gone. "I heard her say the setting presented the perfect opportunity to bring this to an appropriate end, but I don't know what that means. I don't know who that woman is! She was up at the tasting room earlier, but other than a vague sense that I've seen her before, I don't know who she is!"

"Pilar de Romo. She's the woman in the photos with Collin Marlow."

Torie sank down into a seat in shock. "*She's* the stalker? I never considered her."

"Me, either." Matt's expression grew even more grim. "Luke found out she escaped from a nuthouse. I figure it's some sort of revenge. Hell, she could do anything."

"Oh, God. That's it." Torie reached out and clutched Matt's sleeve as icy fingers of terror gripped her heart. "That's what she meant. 'An appropriate end.' She's going to shoot her and dump her over-board, just like that man did to Collin."

"Hell," Matt muttered.

"I should have shot her. I had a chance, before, up at the house. There was a second that I had a shot, but I didn't take it. I froze. Oh, God." She closed her eyes in despair.

"Hold on." Matt pushed the throttle down and the boat surged forward. Cool wind whipped past Torie's face and tears ran horizontally from the corners of her eyes. She was freezing, both inside and out.

They pulled out of the cove and into the main body of the lake. She could see the first boat ahead a hundred yards or more. They were too far away to see Helen with any clarity, although she did remain in the boat. Sitting up. The woman hadn't shot her yet.

Matt set his speed at forty miles an hour, keeping constant distance between the two craft.

"What are we going to do?" Torie asked. "We have to save Helen, Matt. We can't let that crazy woman hurt her."

"I'm thinking."

"Don't you need to go faster? Can you catch her in this boat?"

"Yeah. The other one looks faster, but this has high-performance engines. I'm not sure that's the best way to handle this, though. Don't want to spook her."

"Can you call someone and set up a boat roadblock or something?"

He shook his head. "The lake follows a river channel. It widens and splits in three directions up ahead a little ways. We don't know which way she'll go. Couldn't get something like that put together in time. There's not enough lake patrol boats available and besides, they don't have a boat that'll keep up with mine."

Oh, God. Torie kept her gaze locked on the Formula, on her sister. "Does that woman know we're back here? Do you think she's seen us?"

"Depends on whether she's paying attention or not." Matt bumped up the throttle and their speed increased, gradually closing the distance between the two boats.

"This is stupid," Torie said, raising her voice to be heard over the roar of the engines. She had a lump the size of a bowling ball in her throat. "What does she think she's going to do? Shoot my sister and sail off into the sunset? This is a lake, not an ocean. She can't get away. This is just crazy!"

"Stalkers often are. She's had plenty of time to nurse her hate in the mental hospital, too."

Torie swallowed hard. "What's your plan, Matt? Are we just going to follow her until she stops? That's taking a real risk. What if she . . . she . . . shoots before we get there?"

"We don't have a lot of choices."

She steepled her fingers in front of her mouth. What choices *did* they have? She hadn't a clue. She had experience with car chases. Motorcycle chases. But she'd never been in a boat chase before. "Maybe . . . no . . ."

"What?"

"I guess it's a little too James Bond to think we could catch up and pull alongside and one of us jump into the other boat?"

"We're going fifty miles an hour, Torie. Stunts like that are only done in Hollywood."

Speaking of Hollywood . . . "I don't suppose your boat is outfitted with any special equipment? Like sniper rifles?"

"Nope. Taking the driver out is a possibility, but we'd need to get a lot closer and it'd be a real tricky shot."

"So what are we going to do!"

Half a minute passed before he answered. "She looks like she's handled a boat before. I have an idea that might just work. Torie, put on a ski vest."

"Am I going overboard?" She slipped into a woman's red neoprene vest, then frowned when he shook his head at her offer of a larger one in black.

"Not unless I miscalculate. Sit down and hold on, Shutterbug." He grabbed a pair of sunglasses from the glove box and slipped them on before shoving the throttle all the way down. The boat surged forward.

Oh my God. The spray that hit her stung like ice pellets. She glanced over at the climbing speedometer. Sixty-five, seventy-five. Ninety miles an hour. She had to shout to be heard. "So, are you doing a 007 after all?"

"Think more John Wayne than James Bond," he yelled back. "We want to herd her to the left right up here where the lake branches."

Herd? Like cows?

They'd closed the distance between the two boats. The woman had undoubtedly seen them now because she'd increased her speed, too. He was definitely crowding her, coming up between her and the shore on the right.

"C'mon," Matt muttered as they approached the point where she'd have to choose her path. "C'mon, you crazy bitch."

He pushed the throttle and their speed increased, the bow of their boat now even with the stern of hers. Pilar shot a furious look over her shoulder, then veered left. She kept on going.

Pilar, Torie repeated. What a pretty name for such a wicked woman.

Matt grinned and eased up on the throttle. "This might just work," he yelled.

"Why left?" Torie brushed her flyaway hair away from her face. "What are you trying to do?"

"There's a huge sandbar that's covered by less than a foot of water when the lake is at this level. It stretches well out into the lake and if you don't know it's there, you don't see it. I'll try to run her aground."

"Is that safe for Helen?"

"As long as she's tied securely, she should be okay. She might get banged around a bit, but that's better than being shot."

"She's pregnant, Matt."

He darted a glance toward her. "It's the best I know to do."

Torie nodded. She'd keep her fingers crossed. And her toes. Everything. Oh, God.

A few minutes later, he said, "Here goes," and he bottomed out the throttle once again. The Fountain surged forward and Torie held on tight to a grab bar. Flying across the water this way felt faster than the time she'd driven a lover's sports car almost 130. Were she not scared to death, she'd be . . . not exhilarated. She'd *still* be scared to death.

He was coming up on the other boat again, this time on the left, guiding her closer to the shoreline. Something slammed into the seat beside Torie and her eyes went wide. "She's shooting at us!"

"Get down, baby. We're almost there."

Terror gripped Torie as she watched the redhead wave her gun around with one hand as she steered the bouncing, speeding boat with the other. It appeared that she pulled the trigger again and again, but Torie couldn't tell where the shots went. She kept her gaze locked on the gun, fearing that any second she'd see Pilar point the barrel toward Helen.

Matt's gaze flickered from the lake in front of him to the boat. "Get ready. Ready." He shot a glare toward the other boat. "C'mon, you bitch."

He veered sharply toward the middle of the lake and yanked the throttle back. Torie jerked forward, then sideways as their motion changed and he circled back around. She scrambled to watch the other boat.

It happened in an instant. The outdrives grabbed the wet sand, slowing the boat so that the hull settled into the muck, which brought the Formula to an abrupt stop. Pilar de Romo flew headfirst into the windshield, bouncing off it to go over the bow and into the water off the starboard side.

Oh, God. "Helen. Helen!" Torie scrambled to her feet, clutched the grab bar in front of her as Matt cut the engines. She gazed helplessly toward the other craft for the longest twenty seconds of her life.

She saw her sister's head come up at the same moment she heard the splash as Matt dived in and swam toward the other boat.

"Torie," Helen called, the sweetest sound ever.

"Are you okay? Helen? Are you hurt?"

"No. I'm fine. I'm fine."

Matt climbed into the Formula, pulled a knife from the sheath on his belt, and cut her sister free. Tears of relief fell from Torie's eyes as she watched him give her twin a hug, then settle her gently into a seat.

Then, he walked to the bow, gazed over the side.

Matt gazed across the water toward Torie and called, "It's over, honey. It's over."

Chapter Nineteen

Matt helped Helen over to the Fountain, then returned to the Formula as the lake patrol arrived, having been alerted by residents who'd witnessed the accident. He left Pilar de Romo's body floating out of the women's line of sight.

Matt's first priority was to check on Mark, and upon learning that he was in surgery, he begged a car and the law's indulgence. "I can explain everything," Torie assured the officer escorting them to lake patrol headquarters. "He needs to be with his brother."

Maddie met him in the hospital lobby. "He's going to be fine," she told him. "They pumped some blood into him and sewed him up. He's in post-op now. The nurse said they'll move him to his room in probably half an hour."

Matt relaxed a little at that, but he didn't breathe a full sigh of relief until he heard Mark flirting with the nurse who helped wheel him into his room. At that, he wrapped his arms around Maddie and gave her a hard hug, pretending that his knees hadn't really gone a little weak.

"Really are living dangerously, aren't you, Matthew?" Mark teased. "Be glad it's only me and not Luke."

Maddie laughed, leaned over Mark's bed, and kissed him on the mouth. "There. Now you're in trouble, too." Then her eyes teared and she grabbed hold of Mark's hand. "You worried me, Mark Callahan."

"I'll try not to do that again," he assured her, then looked up at Matt. "What the hell happened?"

Matt explained what he'd been able to piece together about events after speaking briefly with Helen. He finished by saying, "She broke her neck when she hit the windshield."

"Smart thinking on your part to use the sandbar, Matt." Mark shook his head. "At least there was some thinking going on in this debacle. Hell, I deserved to get shot for letting her get close. And where were the security guys?"

"She killed them," Maddie said with a shudder. "And another man she apparently picked up at the bakery in town."

"The fault is mine for leaving," Matt said. "I should have been there."

"What was that about?" Maddie asked. "I heard the doctor's message on our answering machine. Then Branch told me you'd met when he called and asked me to take him home from the hospital. He wouldn't tell me what the meeting was about. He didn't look so good, so I didn't say anything about Mark's being shot. Not until we knew for sure he'd be okay. I was afraid to bring on another heart attack."

"Another? How about the first?" Matt couldn't help but say.

Mark's stare turned knowing. "He faked it."

"Yep. And milked the sympathy for all it was worth." Matt probably should have kept his mouth shut, but considering today's results of his father's interference, he couldn't hold back his frustration. With quick, concise sentences, he explained about the deal Branch had made with the doctor.

Affronted, Maddie said, "He faked it? That old goat

faked his heart attack? And kept faking it? Why of all the nerve! Luke will have a fit when he hears this."

Mark snorted. "Family counseling? Are they serious? Tell me you're not counting on me being part of that nonsense."

"Hell, I'm not going to be part of that nonsense. Not now. That interfering sonofabitch has tried to manipulate this family one too many times. He knew what we were doing out at the lake was important. He knew that lives were at stake. He pulled me away from Torie at the worst possible time. If I'd been there, chances are you wouldn't be here tonight."

Mark allowed his head to drop back against his pillow, his eyes closed. "Matt's turned away from the dark side. Thank God. Now you see him for all he is and always has been. A scheming, controlling bastard."

"Now, guys," Maddie protested. "Yes, what your father did was crappy. Nevertheless, I think the counseling idea has merit. I've tried for as long as I've known Branch to get him to agree to counseling. He needs it and whether you realize it or not, y'all do, too. This might be your chance to—"

"To what, Maddie? Hold hands and sing Christmas carols? Counseling, my shot-up ass. Didn't you hear what Matt said? A lot of what happened today is because Branch lied. As far as I'm concerned, that old bastard can get counseled to death. It can't come too soon for me."

"Mark!" Maddie's eyes rounded in shock. "I know you're angry and I know what he did was awful, but he's still your father."

"My father is dead to me. He has been for a long time."

Matt exchanged a look with Maddie, trying to signal her to let it go. She didn't take the hint.

"But you guys can't keep this up. I've told Luke

the same thing. Nursing this kind of bitterness isn't healthy for any of you."

"No, it isn't. But just maybe, my dear sister-in-law, you need a lesson in the harsh reality of what Branch Callahan really is."

"Mark," Matt warned.

"No. You, too, brother." Mark belligerently met Matt's gaze. "Get my wallet, Maddie. I need to show y'all something."

Maddie shared a curious look with Matt, then started to give Mark the wallet, but his hands shook too much to hold it. "No. I can't."

"I'm sorry. I wasn't thinking about your arm. It's got to hurt to move it."

"That's not it. My arm doesn't compare to the hurt I get from what you're holding in your hand. Flip it open, Maddie. Look behind my driver's license."

Maddie slipped her fingers into the leather compartment and pulled out a worn photograph. A hospital photograph of a newborn with a pink elastic bow around her bald head. Matt put the pieces together in an instant. "Where is she, Mark?"

Maddie just looked puzzled. "Who is this?" she asked.

Mark spoke without opening his eyes. "Margaret Mary Callahan. My wife named her for Mom."

Maddie's jaw gaped.

"Where is she, Mark?" Matt repeated, though in truth, he didn't want to know. Didn't want to hear confirmation of what he suspected. That the baby was gone, too.

"She's dead. They're both dead."

Matt's heart twisted. His brother's loss was even bigger than he'd known. "What did Branch do, Mark?"

"Branch?" Maddie murmured.

"Carrie was seven months pregnant when I deployed to Kuwait for Desert Storm. We were young and stupid, but we were happy together. She made me happy, and feeling the baby kick the day I left her standing on that airport tarmac . . . I can't even describe. That was February 1991. The last time I saw Carrie." He smiled bittersweetly, lost in the past.

Maddie's hands were now over her mouth, her voice muffled as she asked, "What about the baby?"

"The baby was born April tenth. On April twentieth, Carrie received the first letter from Branch. He wanted her to bring Margaret Mary to live with him in Brazos Bend until I came home. Carrie knew how I felt about Branch and she turned him down. He sent two more letters and then a lawyer to the base housing where she lived. She tried to contact me, but you know how things were back then. I didn't get the message until it was too late."

Matt grimaced. He had a bad feeling about where this was headed. He gripped the safety rail on the hospital bed for support.

"The lawyer told Carrie that Branch was going to take her baby away from her. He was going to accuse her of being an unfit mother."

"She believed that?" Maddie asked, aghast.

"She was nineteen years old. Just a kid who was terrified she'd lose her baby. The slimebag lawyer played on every insecurity Carrie ever had."

"That poor girl," Maddie murmured.

"Plus, she didn't have a soul to count on except for me, and I was halfway around the world scratching the sand fleas biting my ass. We had no money to speak of. Branch's lawyer let her know that wasn't the case with the mighty Callahan. He had plenty of money and the courts would see things his way. She was scared. She wrote me a letter, loaded up the baby, and took off in the middle of the night. To this day I don't know where she was headed. All I know is that he'd scared her to death."

"What happened to them, Mark?" Matt asked.

"A drunk driver ran them off the road into a telephone pole. Carrie was killed instantly. My daughter lived for four hours. I learned about it two days later."

"Oh, Mark." Tears poured down Maddie's face. "I'm so sorry. I didn't know. When Branch would dictate letters to you, all he kept saying was that he was sorry. Over and over, he'd say he was sorry. I never knew what for. I asked, but he wouldn't tell me."

"Sorry, is he? Well, that doesn't quite fix it, does it?"

"No, honey." Her smile was full of compassion. "It doesn't."

Matt had to ask. "Why didn't you tell us? Luke and John and me? We'd have been there for you, man."

"You couldn't have done anything. They were gone and besides, I couldn't talk about it. Almost did when John died, but . . ." He broke off, shook his head. He gazed up at Matt with stricken, tear-filled eyes. "At least Johnny's up there now to look out for them, right? Carrie and my little girl?"

"Yeah. Yeah, you know he is." Shit. Matt was about to cry himself. He surreptitiously wiped his eyes. "That's why you haven't mellowed any. You'll never forgive him."

"No, I won't. The drunk driver killed them, but Branch Callahan is just as guilty for setting it all in motion. Had he just left us alone . . ."

Matt didn't think he could forgive this, either. *Damn you, Branch. Damn you once again for your fucking need to control everything.* That poor little baby . . . her mother. Mark. How did he survive such a senseless, stupid loss? All because Branch had to play God.

Mark's eyes were growing heavy. "Now that y'all know, don't bring Branch up to me again."

Ten minutes later, Mark was asleep, and Matt needed to see Torie. As he and Maddie crossed the

lobby toward the parking lot, Branch walked through
the hospital's front doors. Matt muttered a curse, then
said, "Turn around and go home. The nurses have
instructions to throw you out if you so much as show
your face on Mark's floor."

"But Matt . . . Maddie."

Matt walked right past his father. Maddie paused
for just a moment. "Mark told us a story, Branch.
About his wife and daughter." She gave her head a
toss and blinked back tears as she continued. "A baby
girl named Margaret Mary who never got to meet her
daddy because you played the big man and threatened
her teenage mother into running away. You'd best
leave us all alone for a while."

They left the hospital without looking back.

Torie had her car packed and ready to go. A part
of her had wanted to ride off into the sunset and avoid
a final scene with Matt, but she refused to be a coward. Not at this stage of the movie.

She and Gigi sat on the front porch of the lake
house, waiting alone for him to return. A cop had
taken Paco back to Branch, and Helen and Michael
had rented a room at Cottonwood Cottage, where
they were celebrating the color change on the test-kit
stick. Les had attempted to hang around and keep
Torie company, but she'd shooed him away. She'd
needed time alone, to think through the events of the
day. To figure out just where to go from here, and
how to survive the trip. To decide just where exactly
to leave the lie of a ring. She'd left it in the refrigerator like just another cupcake. Somehow, that had just
felt right.

She'd called her father, too, to let him know of Hel-
en's ordeal, omitting the details of her marriage and
pregnancy, but priming the pump by mentioning Michael's presence. To her shock and surprise, the general had actually expressed concern about her. He said

he'd planned a trip back to the States next month and asked if she'd have time to see him. When she mentioned her commitments at Cannes, he hadn't made a single snarky remark.

She'd told him she'd do her best to make it.

The sound of a boat engine distracted her from her thoughts. Matt? She'd expected him to arrive by road, so this mode of transportation caught her by surprise. Walking around to the back of the house, she watched him expertly ease the huge Fountain into its slip. The man and his machine, she thought. Both of them powerful. Both exhilarating. Both, sexy as sin.

"Demon Callahan," she murmured. He'd stolen her heart and her soul, but at least she had taken back her pride.

She hoped.

He took determined strides up the walkway, his gaze finding her, locking on her. She could feel the power of his person across the distance. In defense, she turned away and returned to her seat in the porch rocker. She gathered Gigi into her lap because she needed something warm to hold on to. She was so cold inside.

"Torie," he said as he rounded the corner. "You're a sight for sore eyes. Sorry it took me so long to get back."

"How's Mark?" When Matt's expression turned haunted, her heart caught. "Matt, is Mark okay?"

"Okay? No, he's not. He survived the gunshot wounds, but he's far from okay. He's hurting in a way I can't help him. No one can."

"What are you talking about?"

He waved a hand. "I don't want to rehash it all. It happened years ago. Suffice to say I now understand why Mark hates our father so much. Hell, I'm inclined to hate him, too. But let's not talk about Branch right now."

"All right." She didn't look him in the eyes. She

needed the wall she'd erected to stay up. "How's your other boat? Les said doing what you did can ruin the engines."

"It's a mess, but the local mechanics are good." He stepped up onto the porch and studied her carefully. "I guess we need to talk. You probably want to know why I . . . uh . . ."

"Set me up? Used me as bait? Threw me to the wolves?"

"Dammit, Torie. It wasn't like that."

"Oh, really? Are you trying to tell me you didn't use my credit card on purpose? You didn't intend to get my name mentioned in the newspaper and on the Internet? You didn't intentionally put me out there as bait for that maniac at the same time you were sleeping with me? What would you call it?"

"One had nothing to do with the other," he snapped.

"And of course, I'll believe you because you never lie to me." She gently set Gigi on the ground, then stood. "Did it ever occur to you to explain your plan? To ask for my cooperation? I'd have done it, you know. You didn't have to sleep with me just to keep me distracted from what was going on."

"Stop acting as if our relationship was based on . . ."

He didn't finish, so she did. "Sex and lies?"

"Stop right there." He slammed his hand into the porch post. "You don't believe that. You tell me you don't believe that!"

She didn't want to believe it, but there it was in black-and-white. He'd lied. Over and over, he'd had the opportunity to tell her the truth, but he'd kept his mouth shut. "Why weren't you honest with me?"

"Because that's the way I work. I work alone. You didn't need to know."

"Alone? So you're telling me Mark didn't know the plan? Luke was in the dark? Do you expect me to believe that?"

"They're my brothers!"

He grimaced and she could tell he'd realized what he'd done, but it didn't move her. Not an inch. "And what was I, Callahan? A bed warmer? A way to pass the time?"

"No, goddammit! You're my lover. I love you! Do you hear me? I. Love. You!"

She sucked in a breath. "That's cold, even for you."

She turned to walk away. She needed to get away from him. Right now, before her hard-won scraps of pride evaporated.

Now he was furious. "What? You think I'd lie about that?"

"I think you'd lie about anything and everything. Lying is your profession. It's your first response and your last. It's what you do."

"Well, I'm not lying now."

"I don't believe you. I don't trust you. I thought you were different, Callahan, but you turned out just like all the rest. I came to you for help, and you did the job. My stalker is dead. I'm safe. But in the meantime, you made a fool of me."

"Torie, it wasn't like that."

"It was and it is. It always is. I guess I just needed to be reminded of where I stand. But look, this is unnecessary. I waited to tell you I'm sorry that Mark was hurt on my account once again, and that I'm so glad he's going to recover. I also want to thank you for your help today. If I'd followed that woman by myself, I'm afraid to think how it might have ended."

"Quit talking like that. You're making me crazy. You're talking like it's over."

"I don't think it ever began. Not really."

"How can you say that?"

She couldn't let him see that he'd destroyed her. "We had the boat chase and the villain died and the credits are rolling. Whatever bit of drama we had, it's over. I'm leaving now. Maybe I'll catch you on the red carpet someday."

"You're not leaving. You love me."

Torie called upon every scrap of acting ability she possessed to give a short, careless laugh. "Oh, but I am leaving, Matt. I have a plane to catch and a story to chase. I told you all along that it was temporary. The Callahan-Bond girl loved you, but this movie is over."

"That's bullshit."

"Don't worry, Callahan. There's a new Bond girl in every flick." It was as good an exit line as she was liable to come up with, so Torie whistled for Gigi and headed for her car.

"Stop it. Just stop it," he demanded. "Once and for all, you need to stop this stupid-ass Bond shit. This isn't a damned movie. This is reality. It's our *life*. I love you, Torie Bradshaw. And by God, you love me, too."

A vulnerable place deep inside her heard him, wanted to believe him, but the scar tissue from old wounds and new kept her heart hardened. "All right." She lifted her chin, squared her shoulders, and met his gaze head-on for the first time that evening. "No movies. No make-believe. You want reality? Here it is, then, in hard, cold glory.

"I don't love you, Matt. I let myself get caught up in the romance and adventure of the fantasy I built around you."

"That's a lie, Torie. You love me."

"I thought I did until I realized I was living a part for which I'd been totally miscast. See, that's the world I live in—celebrities and their escapades and their on-and-off-again love lives. It's all fiction. It's easy to get lost in the make-believe when you live it every day, and that's what I did with you. I made you into a larger-than-life hero who would rescue the damsel in distress. You accomplished the job, too, and for that, I'm grateful. But real heroes don't lie, and that part made me realize the truth. The reality. Maybe I knew all along that what we had was just a joyride, and I enjoyed it while it lasted. So did you."

"I can't believe you're doing this. Tearing us apart. It's stupid. I need you, Torie. Can't you see that?"

"What you need is to be free to move on to the next adventure and the next Bond girl. This one has another casting call."

"Once and for all, would you stop with the James Bond bullshit!"

She paused, and in that moment, everything became crystal clear. "You're right, Matt. Of course, you're right. Life isn't a movie and there's no happy ending for us. Just an ending.

"Good-bye, Matt Callahan. Have a happy life."

Chapter Twenty

Côte d'Azur
Three weeks later

"Torie, luv. Thank you so much for coming." Julie Kelley took her hands and kissed her on both cheeks, then flashed her billion-dollar smile. "I know you're exhausted from the insanity of Cannes, but I wanted you to share this night with me and Jack. In fact, you could say this night is all about you. You look gorgeous, by the way. The gown is fabulous. You're divine in red."

"Thank you. I'm thrilled to be here, Julie," Torie replied, trying hard to mean it. "You always throw such awesome parties, and it's certainly no hardship to spend a few days at your guesthouse on the French Riviera."

"I trust Gigi is enjoying her stay?"

"You know she is. Although I still say having a chef prepare fresh food for her is going a little too far."

The actress laughed. "Nothing is too good for Gigi or for you. You have fun tonight, Torie. Do something to chase away those shadows I see in your eyes."

She tried. She pasted on a smile, and flirted and

gambled and danced until dawn. At one particular low point, she considered accepting the French actor's indecent invitation, but better sense prevailed. She wasn't that self-destructive. Not yet, anyway. Now, had he been an Italian, or, better, a Scotsman, she might have had a weaker moment.

Still, she never really enjoyed herself. The glitz, the glamorous crowd with their tanned and toned perfection, didn't appeal like it had done in the past. Also, she never relaxed. Maybe because throughout the entire night, she felt as if she was being watched. It was eerie. Uncomfortable. It reminded her of events she wanted desperately to forget.

Twice during the night, she attempted to leave. Each time her hosts found her and convinced her to stay. Only now, as dawn lightened the sky and the crowd had thinned to mere dozens, did they accept her thanks and allow her to go. "Give the valet your name on the way out. We've a car for you to use while you're our guest. You can drive it down to the guest bungalow."

The bungalow was a smaller version of the Mediterranean mansion the Jays owned, located down and around the hill with its own private beach. Five-star luxurious from top to bottom, it was an isolated fantasy of a place, the perfect spot to do nothing more than sleep and read and heal her broken heart.

As she waited for her car, she yearned for the pampered comfort of the bed. Yet she wouldn't spend the day in bed. Not today. She'd had enough of this vampire lifestyle, awake all night and sleeping the day away. It wasn't healthy. What she'd do was catch a few hours' sleep, then get up, take a swim, jog on the beach, and go to sleep at sundown.

The valet approached. "Miss Bradshaw? Your car is waiting. Would you care to follow me?"

He led her toward . . . of all things . . . a silver

Aston Martin DB9. Against her will and with a pang in her heart, she thought of Matt. "I don't suppose you have a Ford or a Chevy?"

"Pardon me?"

"Never mind."

She tipped the attendant, slid into the seat of the luxury sports car, tossed her evening bag into the passenger seat and made the short drive to the guesthouse. She didn't notice the envelope lying in the next seat until she lifted her evening bag from on top of it. Black ink calligraphy formed "Victoria Bradshaw" on white vellum.

"Hmm . . ." Probably some special instructions about Gigi's menu or something. She opened the envelope and pulled out a note card and a small gold key. *The key unlocks the glove compartment, Victoria. Your first tool is inside.*

"Tool? What do I need a tool for?" She unlocked the compartment and reached inside to discover a long, narrow, black velvet jewelry box. Flipping it open, she found a woman's Omega Seamaster watch and a small, folded note. *Set the correct time to activate the homing-device tracker.*

"Homing-device tracker?" she muttered. What in the world?

Curiosity got the better of her. Torie checked the time on her cell phone, then set the watch. As the minute hand moved, a faint beep sounded. When she moved toward the house, the beeping grew louder. "This is wild."

And a bit unsettling. It hadn't been that long since she'd been stalked.

Then she recalled the live game of Clue that Julie and Jack hosted in Hollywood a few years back. That's what this must be. A game.

If somewhere deep inside she recognized that the Omega Seamaster was the watch that tracked the homing device in the Fabergé egg in *Octopussy*, she tried to ignore it, helped by the memory of Matt's voice echoing in her mind. *Forget the Bond crap, Victoria.*

The Jays had known of her Bond obsession, of course. They had probably set up this game because they thought she'd enjoy it. They didn't know what had happened with Matt. She'd spent the last month pretending her time in Brazos Bend had never happened.

The beeping intensified in frequency and volume as she traced a path to her bedroom. When she spied the cigarette case lying in the middle of her bed, she felt a shudder run down her spine.

She punched off the alarm on the watch and tossed it onto the bed. She held her breath as she picked up the cigarette case. She flipped it open. Four cigarettes, an LCD screen, and another folded note. Her pulse tripped into high gear as she read. *Is it safe to hope that you will recognize the truth?*

"*Moonraker.* The safecracker." She glanced around the bedroom. Sure enough, a landscape hung crookedly on the western wall, the only item in the entire guesthouse out of place. She stared at it for a long moment, almost afraid. "The truth?" she repeated softly. "What truth?"

Did she really want to know?

Torie drew a deep breath, then exhaled in a rush. She crossed to the painting and lifted it down to reveal the wall safe behind it. Then she frowned down at the cigarette case in her hand. How did it work? She examined it closely and spied the small button on the side. On/off? She pressed it. A red light like a laser pointer shone from a small hole on the side of the case.

Chuckling with disbelief, she shone the red beam at the safe. Seconds later, three numbers appeared on the LCD screen. "I'm so not believing this. Has to be a setup."

Nevertheless, she turned the dial on the safe right,

left, right. A metallic click sounded as the lock released. She turned the handle and swung the door open.

Inside atop a flat sheet of paper sat another black velvet box. A ring box. A Tiffany's ring box.

"Okay, Bradshaw. This is just a game Jack and Julie are playing." Still, her hand trembled slightly and her knees felt a little weak as she reached first for the note. *Only you can harness these special features. Use this to shatter or to bond. Your choice.*

"*Die Another Day.* The standard-issue ring that can shatter glass." She lifted the box from the safe and flipped it open. "Oh, wow." It was a classic, classy, round-cut diamond solitaire in a platinum Tiffany setting. Around two carats in size and perfect. Just perfect. "Oh, wow."

Too much a female to resist, she went to slip it on. The moment she lifted the ring from its case, the voice spoke as if from inside the box. "Bring your answer to the beach, Shutterbug."

"Matt." She dropped both the ring and the box. When the box hit the floor, the insert fell out and revealed what she guessed to be a miniature recorder.

The diamond ring lay on the carpet like a . . . like a . . . promise. "Oh, God. Oh my God."

No. Wait. Hold on. She needed to stop. She needed to get ahold of herself. She'd been up all night. She wasn't thinking straight. This couldn't be what she was thinking. She didn't want it to be what she was thinking.

Did she?

Bring your answer to the beach, Shutterbug.

"Okay. All right. I'll bring you my answer." She scooped up the ring and headed for the door, muttering to herself. "You think a few Bond gadgets are going to solve the problems between us? You think I'm that shallow, just because I like a movie series? Because I take photos of celebrities for a living?" She paused on the staircase and called, "Gigi? Gigi? Where are you? Mama needs you?"

She heard a yip, then the rattle of Gigi's tags. The dog met her at the bottom of the stairs, and Torie scooped her up into her arms and headed for the door that led out into the garden. "He thinks I can't see past the game? Can't see past the romance of his following me to Europe and setting up a treasure hunt with stuff he picked up from the Spy Store."

She paused at the gate that opened up onto the beach and added, "And Tiffany's. Okay, that's pretty romantic, but real life is more than romance."

She needed to think a minute, to rationalize it all out. He hated James Bond. Hated the comparisons. Why would he go through all this trouble?

Because he loves me.

She tried to refute the idea, but it was staring at her in platinum and diamonds—perfect platinum and diamonds—right? Only she would want a marriage proposal like this.

And Matt Callahan was the only man who could pull it off.

Because he loved her.

She took a dozen steps out onto the beach, then stopped and kicked off her heels. Then, she looked around for Matt Callahan.

He wasn't here. She saw the cliffs rising behind her, the calm, azure Mediterranean in front of her. An empty beach all around her. Not even footprints in the sand. "Oh. Well." She glanced down at Gigi. "Did I get it wrong?"

Gigi barked and Torie set her down. Her heart sank to her toes. What was the deal here? Hadn't she heard his voice? *Bring your answer to the beach, Shutterbug.*

"Oh, jeez. Did I imagine it? I've been up all night. Am I really asleep and dreaming? Awake and hallucinating?"

Do I miss him that much?

Yes, but reality was in her fist. She held out her hand and opened her palm. Sunlight glinted off the ring's diamond.

"That's real. I feel it. I see it. Oh, wow. Look at it sparkle." She held it up to the sun, up toward the sky, to watch the diamond sparkle in the sunlight, and that's when she saw it.

Saw him.

Matt.

At least, she thought it was Matt. He was still too far away for her to tell for sure. Too high. Up in the air. On a parasail.

"Just like *Live and Let Die.*"

"I'm gonna break my fucking neck."

It had been three years since he'd spent any real time indulging in this sport and he wasn't so much worried about his neck as he was his leg. He'd had his share of bad landings in the past. Having one here would totally screw up his plan. He needed to pull this thing off if he stood a chance with Torie.

The idea was wild and desperate and made him feel like a fool, but that pretty much had been the status quo since about twenty minutes after she'd left him in Brazos Bend. That's how long he'd waited for her to turn around and come back. Dumb-ass that he was, he'd believed she wouldn't walk away, not after he'd just made the biggest declaration of his life. Not after he'd said those three life-altering words. Well, he'd been flat-out wrong. She'd shown him.

He'd been an idiot. He'd screwed the whole thing up. Him. Superspy, Übermeister of Undercover Work, Sultan of Scenarios—and he'd totally sucked at the most important game of his life. Loving her was all well and good, but she didn't believe him and, even worse, didn't trust him, so those three never-before-spoken words hadn't meant a damn thing.

So now he had to put his money where his mouth

was. Now he had to show her. He had to prove to her that he loved her. He had to win back her heart, and more importantly her trust. He'd spent three days trying to decide how best to grovel. He'd attempted to discern the most effective way to gut himself like a fish at her feet so that she'd know without a doubt that he meant what he was saying.

This Bond crap had been the answer. He'd cleaned out the Brazos Bend Blockbuster of 007 classics and spent the next two days watching them one after the other. In some ways, it had been torture. In others . . . well . . . the man did have a certain style. He liked the new Bond the best. He wondered if Torie had noticed that he and Daniel Craig had the same color eyes.

The same color eyes as that asshole Frenchman she'd flirted with at the party. He'd wanted to kill the motherfucker. Only years of on-the-job discipline had kept him out of sight. It had been a hard-won fight to spend the entire night watching the beautiful lady in red without ruining the plan. But he'd pulled it off. Now to nail this landing and grovel at her feet. With any luck, he'd have a James Bond ending to the scene. The man always, *always* got the girl.

Matt had to hope like hell she didn't want to rewrite a classic.

Matt dragged his gaze off the beauty on the beach and focused on his landing target. Moments later, he brought the glider in like a pro about fifty yards up the beach from Torie. His knee held up and he took it as a good sign.

He unfastened the harness and secured the sail. Next, he took off his helmet, took a deep breath, and prepared to make the play of his life. He slipped the pack off his back and removed weapon number one from its snug little carrier. "Wake up, Bruiser, and go be charming."

As he set the sleepy, male Peke-a-tese on the sand,

Gigi let out a yap and bounded toward them. Matt darted a look toward Torie. Her mouth was hanging open. Good.

Then, trying his damnedest to be suave and debonair, he unzipped his flight suit and shrugged it off.

He heard Torie say, "Oh. My. God."

This is it, Callahan. Do it right.

He shot the cuffs of his tux, straightened his black bow tie, and stepped toward her. Then he spoke the words his sister-in-law, Maddie, had assured him would be the most effective way to begin. "Victoria, I was wrong. I'm sorry."

He suffered during the long minute it took her to find her voice. "What in the world are you doing? Have you lost your mind? Parasailing? With a dog and your bad knee?"

He ignored all that. "I shouldn't have put your name out for the stalker to find without getting your okay. I was a fool not to trust you. I was an even bigger fool not to trust myself. I knew I was falling for you and it scared me, so I did what I did the way I did it to put some distance between us."

"You, scared?" she interrupted, obviously shocked by what she was seeing and hearing. He took it as a good sign. "Mr. Superspy?"

"Yellow-striped, panic-struck, like-a-rabbit-in-a-coyote's-mouth scared. It's five thousand four hundred and thirty-four miles between Brazos Bend and here," he continued. "I figure that is still closer than the distance I put between us by betraying you the way I did. I was wrong and I'm sorry and I swear never to do it again if you will give me another chance."

"Oh, Matt." Tears pooled in her eyes before she closed them. "It would be so easy for me to just cave in to the fantasy. But you hurt me."

"I know and I'm sorry. I'm so damned sorry. I love you, Torie. With everything I am, everything I ever could be, I love you. I want to make a life with you. It is *not* a fantasy."

"How can I be sure?"

Then he did something James Bond would never do. Matt Callahan sank to his knees before her. "Because I'm not 007. I won't leave. I refuse to leave. I love you, Torie Bradshaw. Only you. Always you. Forgive me. Love me back. Marry me. I beg you."

For a long moment, she didn't react and Matt felt his heart sink from his throat to his knees.

"Oh my God. Oh my God." She grabbed his arm and tried to pull him up. "Get up. You're going to ruin your tux. It's Armani, isn't it? Oh, my God. I can't believe this."

Her babbling gave Matt a glimmer of hope. If she were totally unreceptive, she'd have let him bleed out on the sand in front of her. She'd have been cold and calm and collected like she was when she left him.

"Why did you do this? Why did you go to all this . . . this . . . I don't even know what to call it? You flew in on a parasail, for heaven's sake. Wearing a tuxedo!"

"It's a hang glider, not a parasail."

"And you brought a dog!"

"I thought bringing her a boyfriend might make Gigi like me."

The laugh that escaped her mouth was the most hopeful sign yet. "Where did you get this stuff? An Omega Seamaster, a cigarette safecracker?"

"You can buy anything on the Internet."

"Even this?" She drew a visible breath, then held out her hand, his ring cradled in her palm. "The glass-shattering ring?"

He smiled and allowed all the love he felt for her to show in his eyes. "That, I bought at Tiffany's in New York."

"So it *is* real." She swallowed hard. "It's not a Bond gadget. It won't shatter glass."

"It's more powerful than that, Torie. Depending on what you do with it, it can shatter my heart . . . or make it whole. Your decision. Your choice." He took the ring and brought up one knee so that he knelt in honor rather than supplication. Offering the ring back to her, he made the gamble of his life. "I love you, Torie Bradshaw. Will you marry me?"

For a long moment—a long, long, too-long moment—she stood frozen and Matt felt his heart start to crumble to dust. But then—*Thank you, Jesus*—she smiled. Her eyes teared and she sank to her knees in front of him. "I love you, Matt. Yes, I'll marry you."

Reverently, he took her left hand and slipped the ring onto her third finger. He turned her hand over and kissed her palm. A promise.

Then he captured her mouth with his and he kissed her with all the love and emotion that dwelled in his heart. A vow.

"Okay," Torie said, a tremor in her voice, when he finally broke the kiss. "This is the most romantic moment ever. Better than *Doctor Zhivago* when Omar Sharif writes Julie Christie a poem at the country estate. Better than *An Affair to Remember* when Cary Grant walks into Deborah Kerr's bedroom and sees that she bought the picture he'd painted. Holy cow, Matt. This is better than when Bogie tells Ingrid Bergman she has to get on the plane!"

Their gazes met and held as he yanked off his tie, stripped off his jacket, and tugged open his shirt. "What about *From Here to Eternity*?"

"The beach scene?" She licked her lips, her gaze following the path of his fingers. "I don't know, Callahan. You'll have to go a ways to improve on Burt Lancaster."

"Oh, I've got that covered." Standing, he pulled her to her feet with one hand even as he lowered her zipper with the other.

"How?" she asked, shuddering as her dress dropped to the ground.

His finger traced a path from her mouth downward, a featherlight caress over the velvet skin of her neck to the lush valley between her bare breasts, across the flat plane of her belly to the tiny strip of lace that remained the only thing she wore. "First, I get you wet."

Epilogue

Soledad Island

If he catches me, I'm dead.

Torie Callahan took one more photograph of her husband—nude, sated, and sleeping on the sand. Irresistible.

This was elemental man. Battle-scarred and beautiful, a perfect male animal in his natural state in a natural setting. Long and lean and powerful, he could have been a cat who'd padded out of the jungle behind him, come to the lagoon to quench his thirst or cool his heated body. *Look at how the sweat glistens on his skin, running in rivulets across the bulge of his biceps.*

She brought her camera to her face once more and adjusted the lens. What a sexy shot.

"If you don't put that camera down, I swear, I'll chuck it into the lagoon. Taking up porn photography now, Victoria?"

She lowered the camera and leered suggestively. "I could make you a star, Callahan."

"I'd rather you make me a ham sandwich. I'm hungry."

Laughing, she grabbed the picnic basket and set it

beside him. "You make your own ham sandwich, Callahan. I have work to do."

He sat up and dug around in the picnic basket, pulling out one of the ham sandwiches left over from yesterday's wedding reception. "What work? You're not supposed to work. We're on our honeymoon."

She held up the needle and thread she'd taken from the small emergency sewing kit she carried in her purse. "I have to mend my wedding gown. You tore it when you ripped it off of me last night."

"Oh. Sorry, but it was necessary. You were taking too long."

"All I needed was thirty seconds. It was a sarong, for goodness' sake."

"That's the problem." He took a bite of sandwich and swallowed it before adding, "Do you have a clue how delicious you looked in it? You tortured me for hours."

"Hey, you have no one to blame but yourself. You're the one who told Brazos Bend my wedding gown was a red sarong."

"Yeah, but you added the sheer details."

As Matt polished off his lunch, Torie smiled and went to work mending the rip in the carefully designed length of silk. When wrapped around her and tied at the breast, it combined enough solid cloth to make it acceptable to her father, who'd actually flown over from Afghanistan to give the bride away, and enough sheer fabric to please the bride, who'd worked very hard to "torture" her groom. "It wasn't very nice of you to make Mark turn around during the ceremony, Matthew. You didn't make Michael or Luke do it."

"Hey, he deserved what he got. I caught him looking at you. Mike and Luke were too busy gawking at their own lush beauties to sneak a peek at mine."

"Did I look lush?" She liked the idea.

"Not as lush as Helen and Maddie, but then you're not seven months pregnant."

"Maddie's only five months."

"Yeah, but she's having twins, so she's got a seven-months lush going on."

Torie laughed and wrapped the mended sarong around herself, covering up the swimsuit she'd put back on following her own nap. "They did look gorgeous, didn't they? Everything was beautiful. It was a perfect day. A perfect wedding. Even Les said so."

"That's 'cause Branch wasn't here."

Torie sighed. "Now, Matt."

"Don't 'now, Matt' me. It was more important to have Mark here than Branch—even if he did goggle my bride."

"I know. I just wish . . . I'm so happy, Matt. I want everyone to be as happy as I am."

He grabbed her hand and kissed it. "Be patient. If I've learned one thing over the past few years, it's that wounds heal at their own pace and you've got to give them time."

"You and Luke have made strides at making peace, but I'm afraid Branch's time will run out before Mark's wound heals."

"If that's the case, then Mark will have to deal with it." Matt rolled to his feet, reached for his swim trunks, and changed the subject. "Sex, sleep, and a sandwich. Life just doesn't get any better. What shall we do next? You want to go back to the boat and maybe pop in a DVD, or stay on the island for a while?"

"You and your DVDs. I swear, I've created a monster." Torie glanced toward the luxurious oceangoing yacht that would be their home for the next two months while she photographed the island's underground caverns for—and she still couldn't believe this one—*National Geographic*. She knew better than to believe Matt's claim of innocence in orchestrating the job offer, but since the idea had appealed to her and

solved the question of where to begin working their
way down her To Do list, she let him get away with it.

He grabbed her hand and pulled her to her feet,
then slapped her butt and flashed her an unrepentant
grin. "Oh, don't be a spoilsport. I told you it's research."

"For your To Do list."

"Yep."

The To Do List had been Torie's solution to Matt's
career debate. Once he'd figured out that the Langley
job wasn't for him, he'd left the CIA, and while he
wasn't ready to give up his involvement with Four
Brothers, neither was he ready to become a full-time
vintner. Mark's offer of a part-time position with his
private-investigation firm had appealed to Matt, but
didn't entirely solve the problem.

The man remained an adrenaline junkie, and Torie
recognized it even if he didn't. That was when she'd
had the idea for them to work on her To Do list.
After all, a good seventy percent of the items involved
a rush of one sort or another. She'd suggested that
they make Four Brothers their base of operations,
with Matt pitching in to help Mark when and where
it suited both brothers. But for two months of every
year, Torie wanted to work on crossing off items on
her To Do list.

Matt had loved the idea—with the caveat that he
be allowed a To Do list of his own. That's when the
DVDs began showing up. What did James Bond movies have to do with what Matt wanted to do before
he died?

"Okay, Callahan, you told me to wait until after the
wedding." She scooped her sunglasses off her beach
towel and slipped them on. "Well, it's after the wedding. Are you finally going to show me your list?"

"Hmm . . ." He dragged his hand across his jaw,
scruffy with a day-old beard. "I guess I probably

should. After all, since we spent the morning fulfilling requirements for your Number Three, it *is* my turn."

Torie couldn't help but smile. She could now mark "To have sex with a man she loved in broad daylight on a secluded tropical beach" off her To Do list with a flourish.

"Let's see it, Callahan. Where's that notebook you've been carrying around with you?"

Now he scratched the back of his neck. "Okay. I hope you're ready for it."

Torie knew what to expect from her adrenaline junkie. Of course. Stunts. Now that he wouldn't have the field agent's constant supply of dangerous situations, Matt would want to turn to fast cars and faster boats. He'd want to take up skeleton as a sport and fling himself down mountains. He'd want to deep-sea dive and jump out of planes. He'd want to ski down an Alp on a broken ski, never mind his bad knee.

And her job would be to grit her teeth and smile. "I guess I knew what I was getting into. I asked for it."

"Yes, you honestly did." He handed her the notebook.

The page was divided into two columns. The word "Places" headed the first column. Torie's gaze skimmed over them. In a lifeboat. On a roof. In a doctor's office? A hotel room in Cuba. A hotel room in Hamburg. A hotel room in Istanbul. A hotel room in Venice.

She began to get the picture.

A hot tub. A speedboat. A train. "A space capsule?"

"That one might take some work."

Her gaze shifted to the second column. It was headed by the words "To Do." She gave him a scolding look over the top of her sunglasses before she began to read. "To Do . . . Honey Ryder, Jill Masterson, Domino, Miss Caruso, Mary Goodnight."

He waggled his brows at the last name. "I think I

can rent Scaramanga's junk. It's built in the traditional Chinese style, fully decked out. Powered by wind or air."

Torie hid her laugh by clearing her throat, then continued. "Patricia Fearing, Kissy Suzuki, Dr. Molly Warmflash."

"A man's gotta have his annual checkup."

"So let me get this straight. Your wish list before you leave this earth is 'To Do' all the Bond girls?"

"Actually, I've left a couple off the list. May Day looks too much like a man and the thing Xenia Onatopp does with her thighs scares me."

Laughter bubbled up inside her. "I truly have created a monster."

He smiled wickedly and grabbed her hands, then held both wrists by one hand as he tugged the knot of red fabric at her breasts. As her sarong slipped to the ground, his index finger traced the swell of her breasts. "So how about it, Mrs. Callahan? You up for a little"—he tightened his grip on her wrists—" 'Bondage'?"

Now her laughter burst free. "I don't know, Mr. Callahan. I'm on board with the hotel rooms, the hot tub, and the ocean scenes. The room at Oxford University gives me pause, but I've always liked the name Inga."

"Inga Bergstrom. Beautiful blonde. He picks up some foreign tongue when she teaches him Danish." He slipped the knot on her swimsuit top and it fell onto the sand. "I knew you'd be game with some role-playing. You're an adventuress at heart, Victoria."

"Up to a point. I'm happy to play Holly Goodhead. . . ." She dropped to her knees before him and reached for his swim trunks. "But never, ever take me to a barn."

It was half an hour later before he could breathe well enough to come back to the question. "Why not a barn?"

"I refuse to play that particular role. I will never, ever be Pussy Galore."

Matt frowned at her. "Torie. C'mon. All this sand is great, but the thought of you . . . like this . . . in a haystack? Remember my Texas roots."

"Hay itches."

Then Matt, the Demon, winked at her and quoted, " 'What would it take for you to see things my way?' "

She wrinkled her nose and tried to keep the smile off her lips. "It's too crass. I'll never—"

As was his habit, Matt shut her up with a kiss, but this time he didn't stop with her lips. Matt kissed his way down her body, tore off her swimsuit bottoms with his teeth, then devoted himself to driving her wild with a magic tongue and mouth. When she cried out her pleasure and collapsed, spent and deliciously sated, he lifted his head, looked at her, and challenged, "Darlin', never say never."

Read on for a sneak peek at
MARK'S STORY,
coming in October 2008.

Lanai, Hawaii

The things we do for family.

Mark Callahan's bloody hands clutched the coarse holds of the blue-black rock face as his right foot searched for the next foothold. A hundred feet below him, ocean swells crashed violently against the rocks. Above him, a three-quarter moon and a sky full of stars cast a silvered light across the land. Soft music and occasional laughter drifted on the gentle breeze from the terraces of the mansion called Hau'oli, still another hundred feet away at the top of the cliff.

From the Zodiac anchored below, his brother Matt's voice sounded in his earpiece. "You doing okay, bro?"

"Nice of you to ask," he drawled, the sarcasm in his voice unmistakable.

"You scared the shit out of me during that slide. I dropped my mike. Took me a couple minutes to find it. What happened?"

"I damn near fell, that's what happened. The wall pancakes from ten feet of solid basalt to ten feet of fractured, crumbly rock. Lost my footing. Sliced my hands to hell."

"Well, be careful. We don't have time for you to climb the cliff twice."

His brother's sympathy overwhelmed him, so Mark responded, "Bite me."

His foot found purchase on a narrow ledge and he ascended another step. Filling his lungs with salt-scented air, he looked up. Twenty minutes more, he figured. Maybe twenty-five. He had plenty of time.

Mark knew what he was doing. He'd climbed more dangerous cliffs in his life under far worse conditions. One instance in the mountains of Afghanistan stuck out particularly vividly in his mind. Wind blowing like a sonofabitch. Gunfire from down below pinging off the rocks all around him. Tonight's climb was a walk along the Brazos compared to that.

Besides, he'd prefer the challenge of a cliff any day or night to what awaited him above. A party. The kind with expensive food and liquor and women—women whose smiles were as plastic as their boobs. Not at all his idea of fun.

He adjusted his night-vision goggles, then spied another foothold. He worked steadily, capably, and quietly until he reached the top of the cliff. "I'm here. Signal Luke."

"Roger."

"No, Luke," he murmured back, repeating an old joke between brothers.

Mark cautiously lifted his head and studied the area in front of him. Solar lamps and spotlights illuminated the area. Beyond a short hedge of flowering bushes, lush green grass stretched toward the house some thirty yards away. To his left he spied a resort-style pool and tropical waterfall and spa. A tennis court lay off to his right. This stretch of land along the cliff was the only section of the estate's perimeter that wasn't fenced, but it was protected by—according to his research—a buried cable perimeter intrusion detection system. Which was, judging by the presence of guests milling on the lawn, disabled for the evening, just as he'd anticipated.

Excellent. His gaze swept the area, then snagged on a woman dressed in red, facing away from him. *Whoa.*

The gown exposed most of her back and clung like a second skin to a world-class ass. She was tall and lean, and she wore her auburn hair piled high on her head. The long slit in the back of her dress revealed shapely legs that stretched on forever. From this angle, anyway, she was one fine example of womanhood. He wished she'd turn around. Wished he was closer so he could see her more clearly. Something about her called to him.

Hold on, Callahan. Remember where you are. What she's liable to be.

He'd outgrown porn queens years ago.

Seconds later, the first explosion sounded, followed quickly by a second, then a third. Luke's distraction successfully alarmed the guests strolling on the lawn and sent them hurrying toward the house—well, except for the woman in red, who took off toward the pool area. A guard rushed past Mark's position, pulling his sidearm as he ran toward the booms. Luke's string of high-explosive, not-legal-in-the-good-old-USA firecrackers were doing their job.

Mark pulled himself up over the crest of the cliff onto level surface. He ducked behind a flowering bush, stripped off his black jumpsuit, and used it to wipe the blood from his hands. After stashing the suit and his climbing shoes in the shrubs, he quickly removed his dress shoes from his pack and slipped them on. A brief glance confirmed that no one looked his way, so he shot the cuffs of his tuxedo, stepped out onto the lawn, and strolled toward the house.

Glass doors led into a sumptuous formal living and dining suite with a wall of floor-to-twelve-foot-ceiling windows that provided a panoramic view of the Pacific. *Bet the daylight view takes your breath away,*

Mark thought as he accepted a glass of champagne from a passing waiter and idly noted the opulence of the furnishings and design of the luxurious estate. The style was classic Louis XV, with magnificent marble and murals, crystal chandeliers, and embroidered silk draperies that framed Technicolor views of the Pacific Ocean.

Obviously, porn paid exceptionally well.

The estate's owner, Harvey P. Selcer, was a second-generation pornographer who had used his father's string of adult bookstores to launch Selcer Films back in the 1980s. A B-school graduate, Harvey introduced a business model that brought modern marketing techniques to the industry, and today Selcer Entertainment Group was sometimes referred to as the Microsoft of the porn world. Now in his fifties, Harvey had billions in the bank, a Hugh Hefner reputation, and Howard Hughes paranoia.

And a porn-queen girlfriend born and raised in Brazos Bend, Texas.

Hence, the Callahans' presence at this party. Sophia Garza had called home for help, claiming that Selcer wouldn't allow her to leave the estate. Her great-aunts, Maria and Juanita Garza, had asked the Callahan brothers to solve the problem. Mark didn't care a flying fig about Sophia—she was a pitiful, pitiable figure, in his opinion—but he loved the Garza sisters. He and his brothers had made this trip for them.

A woman dressed in blue sidled up next to him. Not Sophia—her pretentious habit was to always wear pink. "Hello, handsome. I don't believe we've met before. My name is Eloisa. What's yours?"

Mark arched a brow and gave her a swift once-over. Bleached, Botoxed, lifted, and implanted. He didn't bother to smile as he replied, "Not interested."

She huffed off as Matt spoke into his ear. "Don't be such an ass. Socialize. Remember, you need to blend in."

What he needed was to find Sophia and get the hell out of here. With that objective in mind, he made his way toward one side of the bronze, wrought-iron twin staircase, thinking he could more easily observe the crowd from the upper mezzanine.

Halfway up the staircase, Mark hesitated. The hair on the back of his neck rose. In his peripheral vision, he caught sight of the woman in red. *There is something about her. . . .* But as he turned his head to look at her fully, the sight of another person stopped him in his tracks. "Holy shit," he muttered.

"What is it?" Matt asked.

"Not what. Who. Radovanovic is here."

There was a long pause on the other end of the wire before Matt said, "You're kidding."

"Christ, no." Mark almost, *almost* pulled his nine-millimeter from his shoulder holster and shot the bastard dead. Rad might not be the one who actually kidnapped and murdered Mark's brother John, but he'd damned sure protected the man who had.

In that moment, Radovanovic lifted his head and caught sight of Mark. The shock in the Croatian's eyes quickly morphed into fury.

"You need to get out of there," Matt said.

"No shit. He's seen me." Mark knew he was in a vulnerable position and should move, but he'd be damned if he'd break eye contact first.

Matt let out a long string of curses.

"No sign of Sophia yet, either. Maybe I should just kill him."

Matt hesitated a moment before saying, "No. We don't have the necessary connections in Hawaii. What the hell is Radovanovic doing there? He's on the wrong damned side of the world!"

Finally, ol' Rad caved and shifted his gaze away. Mark continued up the staircase, his mind considering and discarding various scenarios of how to deal with this unexpected complication. What would the Croatian do now? Send his minions after Mark? Maybe he'd run. He wouldn't know that Mark didn't have an army backing him up.

Upon reaching the mezzanine, Mark turned to survey once again the scene below him. Rad stood beside the door leading to the pool area, and there—a flash of pink. Sophia, on Harvey Selcer's arm. Hmm . . . that gave him an idea. Maybe he could pull this off, after all. He'd use Selcer to—

A gun poked into his back, and Mark went still and stiff.

"Of all the ops in all mansions in all the world, he has to walk into mine," said a familiar feminine voice. "Do exactly as I say, Callahan, and you might get out of here alive."

"Annabelle?"

"Hush. Don't turn around, and for once in your stubborn, hardheaded life, listen to me."

Annabelle. It had been Annabelle in that red dress, not a porn queen. Although, had she chosen that particular career path, she would have been a star.

"Give me your Glock."

Mark snorted. "Yeah, right."

"They're watching, Callahan. Don't be an ass." Keeping her gun against his skin, she shifted around to his front, rubbing up against him in such a way that it would appear to casual observers that she was coming on to him. "Shooting you might be one of my favorite dreams, but I'd prefer to do it on my own terms, not Radovanovic's. However . . ."

She poked him hard with her gun. Glancing down, he saw that it wasn't the nine-millimeter Sig she'd always favored, but a red Glock that reminded him of the pistol Matt's wife, Torie, owned. "A girly gun? You're using a girly gun now?"

"It was a gift to match my dress." She slipped her hand into his jacket and lifted his weapon. "From Rad."

Mark went stiff as a fencepost. "For God's sake, Belle. What are you involved in?"

In his ear, Matt's voice said, "Mark? Care to share what's going on? Is a woman holding a gun on you?"

"She's not a woman. She's my wife."

Following a long pause, Matt said, "*Another* secret wife?"

"Yeah." Mark sighed. "Unfortunately, this one is still alive."

Available Now

GIVE HIM THE SLIP

by Geralyn Dawson

Gorgeous, smart and determined to make it on
her own, Maddie Kincaid thought she finally
found the simple life in Brazos Bend—and the
perfect bad boy in Luke "Sin" Callahan. That is
until the killers got on her trail. Now Maddie's
mastered the art of giving them the slip...

"Read Geralyn Dawson and fall in love!"
—*New York Times* bestselling author
Christina Dodd